Dearly Beloved

Books by Wendy Corsi Staub

DEARLY BELOVED

FADE TO BLACK

ALL THE WAY HOME

THE LAST TO KNOW

IN THE BLINK OF AN EYE

SHE LOVES ME NOT

Dearly Beloved

Wendy Corsi Staub

DOUBLEDAY LARGE PRINT HOME LIBRARY EDITION

PINNACLE BOOKS
Kensington Publishing Corp.

This Large Print Edition, prepared especially for Doubleday Large Print Home Library, contains the complete, unabridged text of the original Publisher's Edition.

PINNACLE BOOKS are published by

Kensington Publishing Corp.
850 Third Avenue
New York, NY 10022

ISBN 0-7394-3653-8

Printed in the United States of America

This Large Print Book carries the
Seal of Approval of N.A.V.H.

*For my terrific editor, John Scognamiglio
with love and gratitude*

*And for my own dearly beloved:
My husband Mark
and our newborn son, Morgan James—
(whose unexpected arrival interrupted
the writing of this book . . .
and who often slept on my lap as I finished it!)*

Prologue

Sandy Cavelli glances at her watch as she hurries up the icy steps of the red-brick post office. Four-fifty-nine. She has exactly one minute to retrieve today's mail before the place closes for the day.

She hurries over to the wall that is a grid of rectangular metal doors and eagerly turns her round key in the lock of post office box 129. Jammed, as it always is on Mondays. *Connecticut Singles* magazine comes out on Friday mornings, and Sandy is beginning to believe that every guy in the greater Hartford area who doesn't have a weekend date spends Friday and Saturday flipping through the classifieds in the back of the magazine, answering ads.

She removes the bundle of letters from the box and does a quick mental count. Nine—no, ten. Ten eligible single men have responded to her ad this week. So far. If everything goes according to the pattern that has established itself over the past month, only two or three more letters will trickle in over the next few days. Then, if she chooses to run the ad again—she has to decide by six o'clock Wednesday—there will be a new stack of letters waiting in the box next Monday.

Renting a post office box was definitely a good idea, Sandy reminds herself, even if it has set her back over thirty dollars. This way, she doesn't have to deal with the questions her parents would undoubtedly have if she'd suddenly started getting a blizzard of mail at home every week. They would never go for the idea of their daughter's placing an ad to meet a man through the classifieds. Christ, they still wait up if she stays out past midnight!

Sandy walks slowly toward the double front doors, flipping through the envelopes as she goes. As usual, a few of them don't have return addresses; the ones that do are mostly from Hartford or the immediate area. . . .

But look at this one, from a post office box on Tide Island!

Intrigued, Sandy shoves the other letters into her oversized black shoulder bag, then slides a manicured nail under the flap of the envelope.

"Miss? We're closing," a uniformed postman says. He's jangling a ring of keys and waiting expectantly by the front door.

Sandy looks up. "Oh, sorry."

"No problem." He smiles. His teeth are white and straight, and his eyes crinkle pleasantly. "Pretty cold out there, huh?"

"Yup. It's supposed to snow again overnight."

She doesn't recognize him. He must be new. Almost every face in Greenbury is familiar; she has lived here all her life.

She isn't usually drawn to redheads. Still, he has a nice, strong jawline. And his hair is a burnished-auburn shade, and she likes the way it is cut—short on the sides, up over his ears, and slightly stubbly on top.

"More snow? Where was all this white stuff a few weeks ago, for Christmas?" he asks good-naturedly, reaching out to open the door for her.

"You got me." Sandy shrugs and glances automatically at the fourth finger of his left hand.

Married.

Oh, well.

"Thanks. Have a good night," she says, walking quickly through the door.

She pauses on the slippery top cement step to finish opening the letter she is still clutching.

A brisk wind whips along High Street, sending a chill through Sandy as she slits the envelope open the rest of the way. Her teeth are starting to chatter. It's too cold to read this letter out here, no matter how intrigued she is. She tucks it and the others into her purse and fumbles in her pockets for her gloves. Swiftly she puts them on and clings to the ice-coated metal railing as she picks her way down the four steps to the sidewalk.

Then she gingerly goes, slipping and sliding every few steps in her black-suede flats, along the nearly empty street to her car in the Greenbury municipal lot around the corner. Her footsteps sound lonely and hollow on the brittle frozen pavement.

Just a month ago, in the height of the holiday season, downtown Greenbury was strung with twinkling white lights and festive red bows bedecked the old-fashioned lampposts. Carols were piped into the frosty air from speakers at the red-brick town hall, and High Street bustled well past five o'clock on week nights.

The picturesque, historic village is only fifteen miles outside of Hartford. Even the lifelong residents are aware of the postcard beauty in its white-steepled churches, windowpaned storefronts, and broad common dotted with statues and fountains. And as one of the few small towns in central Connecticut that still has a thriving downtown commerce area, Greenbury performs a feat that's becoming nearly impossible in America. It actually draws shoppers away from the malls and superstores that dot the suburban Hartford area.

But now that Christmas is over, the businesses along High close early and downtown is almost deserted in the frigid January twilight.

Sandy's car is one of few left in the parking lot, which is really just a rutted, grassy area behind the town hall. She hurries toward the Chevy, stepping around patches of snow and absently noting the dirty chunks of ice that cling to the underside of the car just behind each wheel.

She doesn't bother kicking it off. The car is ugly enough anyway, with rust spots all over the body and a sheet of thick plastic covering the triangular opening in the back where a window is missing. She's come to loathe the old clunker; it belonged to her father, and she's long past being grateful to him for handing it down to her without making her buy it.

She's been saving for a new car—a new *used* car, of course—ever since she started working at the Greenbury Gal Boutique last spring. She blew a good chunk of her savings on community college tuition in August, and the spring semester bill will be due next week when she registers for classes. But that will still leave nearly four thousand dollars in her account. She socked away over five hundred dollars in December alone, when her commission checks were considerably higher than usual. Of course, that won't keep up. The store was dead all day today, and her hours have already been cut way back.

Sandy settles into the front seat, her breath puffing out in little white clouds. She whispers "brrr" and turns the key in the ignition. After a few tries, the engine turns over, and she adjusts the heat control to high. A blast of cold wind hits her in the face and she closes the black plastic vents. She'll probably be home before the hissing air actually becomes warm, but she leaves it on high anyway.

Eagerly, she reaches into her purse and retrieves the letter with the Tide Island return address. She takes out the single sheet of paper inside and notices that it's real stationery, creamy and heavy.

That's a first, she thinks, pulling off her right glove with her teeth and leaving it clamped in her mouth.

Most of the men who have responded to her ad so far have written on either yellow legal paper or their company letterhead.

The interior light of her car burned out long ago. Sandy tilts the paper so she can see better in the filtered glow from the streetlamp a few feet away.

Dear Sandra:

I saw your ad in Connecticut Singles *and was struck by how similar our interests are. You sound like the kind of woman I've been waiting for my whole life. Like you, I never thought I'd resort to personal ads to meet someone; but since I'm a medical doctor with a thriv-*

ing practice, my hectic lifestyle makes it hard to meet anyone the traditional way. I've enclosed a photograph of my-self. . . .

Photograph? Sandy frowns and checks the envelope. Yes, she missed it. There's a picture tucked inside. She grabs it and holds it up in the light.

He's gorgeous! is her immediate reaction.

He has rugged, outdoorsy good looks— and what a bod! He's shirtless in the photo-graph, which was taken on a sailboat as he hauled the sheet in, or whatever people do on sailboats. Even in the shadows, Sandy can make out his bronzed, hairless chest and bulging arm muscles. He's grinning into the camera, revealing a face that she in-stantly decides is honest, intelligent, and friendly.

She anxiously turns back to the letter.

. . . so that you'll recognize me when we meet—which, I'm hoping, will be soon. However, I'm on call at the hospi-tal every weekend until mid-February. I've taken the liberty of assuming you'll agree to spend a romantic weekend

with me on Tide Island, where I have a weekend house. Since I realize you may be hesitant about staying with a stranger, I've arranged accommodations for you at the Bramble Rose Inn. Your expenses will, of course, be paid entirely by me. I'm a romantic at heart, and hope you'll agree that prolonging our meeting until Valentine's Day weekend will add to the enchantment of what may become a lasting relationship. The innkeeper of the Bramble Rose, Jasper Hammel, has agreed to act as our liaison. You can call him at (508) 555-1493, to accept this invitation. I'll look forward to our meeting, Sandra.

> *Fondly,*
> *Ethan Thoreau*

Ethan Thoreau?

Sandy shakes her head and tosses the letter onto the passenger's seat beside her.

This has to be a fake . . . some nut who gets his jollies by answering ads and propositioning strange women.

Grimly, she puts on her seat belt and shifts the car into Drive. As she pulls out onto the street and turns toward home, she mentally runs through his letter again.

He sounds too good to be true, a gorgeous MD with a name like Ethan Thoreau. Like a character in one of those category romance novels Sandy likes to read.

A romantic Valentine's Day weekend on an island.

Yeah, right.

Bramble Rose Inn—the place probably doesn't even exist.

Call the innkeeper.

Sure. And find out that this whole thing is a stupid trick.

Well, she should have known that sooner or later, some nut case was going to answer her ad. Her friend Theresa, a veteran of the singles classifieds, warned her that would happen.

Still, what if there's a chance that this guy is for real? After all, he did send a picture. . . .

A doctor.

A gorgeous, muscular doctor.

A gorgeous, muscular doctor with a thriving practice and a weekend house on Tide Island.

Sandy chews her lower lip thoughtfully as

she rounds the corner from High onto Webster Street.

Well, what if he is for real?

Things like this happen, don't they? Sure they do. She recalls reading, a few years back, about some lonely bachelor who had rented a billboard, advertised for a wife, and proposed to one of the women who responded before they ever met in person.

This guy—this Ethan Thoreau—didn't propose. All he'd done was invite Sandy to meet him. He doesn't even expect her to stay with him.

The Bramble Rose Inn. Jasper Hammel.

Hmm.

Sandy slows the car as she approaches the two-story raised cape where she lives with her parents. The house is pale green, the color of iceberg lettuce, and it desperately needs a paint job.

A grime-covered, white panel truck bearing the name *Cavelli & Sons, Plumbing and Heating Contractors* sits in the short driveway. Sandy parks the Chevy behind it, inwardly groaning. Now that she's on break from college, she likes to beat her father home at night so that she doesn't have to get up early to move her car out of the way when he leaves in the mornings.

She grabs her purse from the seat beside her. Then she thoughtfully picks up Ethan Thoreau's letter and photograph.

"So what's the deal?" she asks, and sighs, her breath coming out in a milky puff of frost. "Are you real, or not?"

Sighing, she puts the letter into her purse with the rest of them. Then she steps out onto the slippery driveway and makes her way along the frozen walk to the house.

In the kitchen, Angie Cavelli is stirring a pot of sauce on the stove. The front of her yellow sweatshirt is splashed with greasy tomato-colored dots.

"Hi, Ma," Sandy says, closing the door behind her and stamping her feet on the faded welcome mat by the door.

"You're late," her mother observes, then takes a taste from the spoon. "I thought you got off at four-thirty."

"I did. I had to run an errand afterward." Sandy shrugs out of her coat and walks across the worn linoleum.

"Your father's already at the table. He wants to eat."

Sandy fights back the urge to say, *then let him eat.*

After twenty-five years of living in this house, she should know better than to consider questioning her father's rule. If you're living in his house, when it's five o'clock, you sit down at the dining room table and you eat. Everyone. Together.

Sandy walks toward the hallway off the kitchen, carrying her purse.

"Ah-ah-ah—where are you going?" her mother calls.

"I just want to change my clothes. I'll be right back down for supper, Ma. Two minutes."

"Two minutes," her mother echoes in a warning voice. She's already at the sink, dumping a steaming kettle of cooked pasta into the battered stainless steel strainer.

In her room, Sandy kicks off her shoes and takes the letter out of her purse again.

She stares at it.

If she doesn't call this Bramble Rose Inn place, she'll probably always wonder whether she passed up the chance to meet a handsome, wealthy doctor.

If she calls, she might find out that he actually has made paid reservations for her. That he really does exist.

Sandy pauses for another minute, thinking it over.

Then she takes the letter across the hall to her parents' room. Unlike the rest of the house—including her own room—which holds an accumulation of several decades of clutter, Angie and Tony's bedroom is spare. The walls are empty except for the crucifix hanging over the bed, and the only other furniture is a dresser and the wobbly bedside table. On that sits the upstairs telephone extension.

Sandy perches carefully on the edge of the old white chenille spread, lifts the receiver, and starts dialing.

Liza Danning hates Monday nights.

Especially rainy, slushy Monday nights in early January, when you can't get a cab and the only way of getting from the office on West Fortieth Street to your apartment on the Upper East Side is the subway. That, or a bus . . . and the glass shelters at the stops are so jammed that waiting for a bus that isn't overcrowded to finally roll by would mean standing in the rain. Which wouldn't be so bad if she had an umbrella.

And she doesn't.

She'd left for work this morning from Alex's place, where she'd spent the night. And since the sun had been shining brightly when they rolled out of bed, borrowing an umbrella from him, just in case, hadn't occurred to her. Besides, she'd been too busy dodging his efforts to pin her down for next weekend.

"I don't know, Alex," she'd said, avoiding his searching gaze as she slipped into her navy Burberry trench—a gift from Lawrence, an old lover—and tied the belt snugly around her waist. She'd checked her reflection in the floor-to-ceiling mirror in his foyer and tucked a few stray strands of silky blond hair back into the chignon at the back of her neck. "I think I have plans."

"What plans?"

She'd shrugged. "I'm not sure."

"You think you have plans, but you're not sure what they are," he'd said flatly.

So she'd told him. She'd had no choice. "Look—" She bent to pick up her burgundy Coach briefcase. "I like you. Last night was great. So was Saturday. And Friday. But I'm not ready for an every-weekend thing, okay?"

He'd stared at her, the blue eyes she'd found so captivating on Friday night now icy and hard. "Fine," he'd said, picking up his own Coach briefcase—black leather— and Burberry trench, also black.

Then they'd walked to the elevator, ridden the fifty-three stories down to the lobby in silence, and stepped out into the brisk Manhattan morning. Alex had asked the doorman to hail them separate cabs, even though his law office was just two blocks from the publishing house where she was an editor.

The doorman had blown his whistle and immediately flagged a passing cab. Alex stuffed some bills into his hand, then leaned over to again narrow that ice-blue gaze at Liza as she settled into the back seat.

"West Fortieth at Sixth," she'd said to the driver. Then, to Alex, "Call me."

"Right," he'd replied, and she knew he wouldn't.

She'd shrugged as the cab pulled away from the curb. So he'd expected more out of their little tryst than she had. He'd get over it.

She hesitates on the street in front of her office building, trying to talk herself into taking the subway. But it will mean walking the two and a half blocks to the station near the library on Forty-second Street. Then she'll have to take the Seven train one stop to Grand Central and wait for the uptown local. That will take forever.

She shakes her head decisively and checks the Movado on her left wrist. Six-fifteen. If she goes back upstairs and works until seven-thirty, she can take a company car home. The publishing house pays her peanuts and doesn't offer many perks besides free car service for employees who work late. But it's the least they can do. After all, most of the editors are females, and Manhattan's streets are increasingly dangerous after dark.

Liza walks briskly back into the lobby.

Carmine, the night guard, looks her over appreciatively, as he always does. At least this time, he doesn't tell her how much she resembles Sharon Stone, or ask her if she's ever considered becoming an actress.

"Forget something?" he asks, his eyes on her breasts even though she is bundled into her trench coat.

"Yes," she replies shortly, walking past him toward the elevator bank, conscious of the hollow, tapping noise her heels make on the tile floor.

An elevator is just arriving, and she steps aside to let the full load of passengers step off.

"Liza, what's up? I thought you'd left," says a petite brunette, emerging from the crowd.

Liza vaguely recognizes her as one of the new editorial assistants who started right before Christmas. The girl is one of those bubbly, fresh-from-the-ivy-league types. The kind who can afford to take an entry level job in publishing because her rich daddy pays the rent on her Upper East Side studio.

"I have to go back up. I forgot something," Liza tells her briefly.

"Oh, well, have a good night. See you tomorrow," the girl says cheerfully, fastening the top button of her soft wool coat.

Liza recognizes the expensive lines, rich coral color, and ornate gold buttons. She'd reached for that coat in Saks a few months ago. The price tag was over a thousand dollars.

She'd put it back.

"See you," she echoes, and strides onto the elevator. She rides alone up to the sixth floor and steps into the deserted reception area of Xavier House, Ltd.

She fishes in her pocket for her card key and flashes it in front of the electronic panel beside the double glass doors behind the receptionist's desk. There is a click, and she pushes the door open.

Liza walks swiftly down the dimly lit hall, past a janitor's cart parked in front of one of the offices. She can hear a cleaning lady running a vacuum in another part of the floor. She turns a corner and heads down the short corridor toward her own office. The other editors who share this area are either long gone or behind closed doors, probably catching up on manuscript reading after taking the holidays off.

Liza unlocks the door marked LIZA DANNING and steps inside. She slips her coat over the hanger waiting on a hook behind the door, then smooths her cashmere sweater and sighs. She isn't in the mood for reading, although she *should* try to make a dent in the pile of manuscripts that sit waiting on her credenza.

You could open the mail, she tells herself,

glancing at the stack in her IN box. She hadn't gotten to it today. Or Friday either, for that matter.

She sits at her desk and reaches for the first manila envelope, slitting the flap with the jewel-handled letter opener that had been a gift from Douglas. Or was it Reed? She can't remember anymore. And it doesn't matter, anyway. He's long gone, whoever he was. Like the others.

She removes a sheaf of papers from the envelope and scans the top sheet. It's a painstaking cover letter, composed on an ancient typewriter whose vowels are filled in with smudges. Some anxious would-be writer, a midwestern housewife, describes the enclosed first chapter and outline of a historical romance novel about a pirate hero and an Indian princess heroine. The woman has spelled desire *d-e-z-i-r-e.*

Liza tosses the letter into the wastepaper basket and reaches into her top drawer for the packet of pre-printed rejections letters she keeps there. She removes one and slips it under the paper clip holding the partial manuscript together. She tucks the whole stack into the self-addressed, stamped envelope the woman has included, seals it, and tosses it into her OUT basket. Then she reaches for the next envelope.

Fifteen minutes later, the stack in her IN box has dwindled and her OUT basket is overflowing. She has worked her way through all the large packages and is now starting on the letters in their white legal-sized envelopes.

She glances idly at the return address on this first one.

What she sees makes her sit up and do a double take.

D.M. Yates, P.O. Box 57, Tide Island MA.

P.M. Yates—David Mitchell Yates, reclusive best-selling author? She recalls that the man has a home on some New England coastal island.

Liza grabs the letter opener and hurriedly slits the envelope open. She unfolds the single sheet of creamy white stationery and notices that a train ticket is attached to the top with a paper clip. Amtrak. Penn Station to Westwood, Rhode Island. First Class.

Intrigued, she skips past the formal heading to the body of the letter.

Dear Ms. Danning:
As you may or may not be aware, I

am the author of several best-selling spy novels released by Best & Rawson, a New York City publishing house, over the past ten years. Since my editor, Henry Malcolm, retired last month, I have been searching for a new home for my novels. Would you be interested in meeting with me to discuss the possibilities of a deal with Xavier House, Ltd.? I have enclosed a round-trip train ticket to Westwood, Rhode Island, for the second weekend in February. You will be met by a limousine that will transport you to the dock in Crosswinds Bay, where you will board the ferry to Tide Island. I have arranged for you to stay at the Bramble Rose Inn. I will, of course, pay all expenses for your journey. I will be traveling abroad for the next several weeks. To confirm, please contact the innkeeper, Jasper Hammel, at (508) 555-1493. It is imperative that you keep this meeting confidential. I'll look forward to meeting with you.

Sincerely,
David Michael Yates

Liza is electrified.

David Michael Yates.

The man is gold.

He's also an eccentric recluse whose face has reportedly never been seen by the world at large. The jackets of his books bear no photograph; not even a biography. Over the years, it has been rumored that David Michael Yates is actually a pseudonym for a high-ranking government official; that he's really a woman; that he had his face blown off in Vietnam.

Just last week, the cover story in *Publisher's Weekly* chronicled the retirement of Yates's longtime editor and the bitter contract battle that resulted in the severed deal between the author and Best & Rawson. According to the article, Yates was about to depart for Europe to research his newest novel and hadn't yet decided upon a publisher, although several of the most prestigious houses were courting him.

How on earth did he decide to approach me, of all people? Liza wonders.

True, she's been getting some PW press herself lately. She recently put together a well-publicized nonfiction deal with an elusive, scandal-ridden senator for a tell-all book. Of course, the powers-that-be at Xavier aren't aware of just how Liza had managed to persuade the man.

And she'll never tell.

Eagerly, she reaches for the phone and begins to dial the number for the Bramble Rose Inn.

Jennie Towne hears blasting music—an old Springsteen song—the moment she steps into the first-floor vestibule of the restored Back Bay town house. She rolls her eyes and hurries toward the closed white-painted door ahead, which bears a nailed-on, dark green *1.*

She transfers the stack of mail from her right hand to her left, then fits her key into the lock and turns it. It sticks a little, as always, and she tugs.

Finally the door opens, and she steps into the apartment. She stomps her snowy boots on the rug and deposits the mail on the small piecrust table that once sat beside her grandparents' front door in the old house in Quincy.

"Laura?" she calls, walking straight to the stereo on the wall unit across the living room. She lowers the volume to practically nothing and promptly hears a disgruntled "Hey!" from the other room.

"It was too loud," she tells her sister, who appears in the doorway within seconds.

"Oh, please." Laura tosses her head. Her ultra-short cap of glossy black hair doesn't even stir.

"Come on, Laura, do you want Mrs. Willensky down here again, threatening to call the landlord?"

Laura shrugs. She says, "Keegan called."

"What did he want?" Jennie looks up from tugging off her boots.

"What do you think? To talk to you. He said he'd tried you at the shop but you'd already left. He wants you to call him. He's on the overnight shift and he's leaving for the precinct at six-thirty."

Jennie just nods.

"You going to call him back?"

"No."

"Oh, come on, Jen, cut the guy a break. He sounded so pathetic. I mean, he didn't *say* anything specific, but I could tell the guy's going crazy without you."

She tries to ignore the pang that jabs into her at the thought of Keegan hurting.

"Laura, I can't. I have to make a clean break. Otherwise we'll keep going back and forth forever."

"I see what you mean," her sister says dryly, folding her arms and fixing Jennie with a steady look. "You love him; he loves you; you both love kids and dogs and the Red Sox and antiques and the ocean. . . . It'll never work."

"Laura—"

"I mean, Jen, I know what your problem is, and you have to get over it. It's been three years since—"

"I don't want to talk about that," Jennie effectively cuts her off, fixing her with a resolute stare.

Laura sighs and transfers her gaze to the stack of mail Jennie dumped on the table by the door. "Anything good come for me?" she asks hopefully. "Like an airmail letter?"

Her new boyfriend, Shawn, is spending a month in Japan on business. She's been moping ever since he left right after New Year's.

Jennie shrugs. "I didn't look."

She unbuttons her winter coat and hangs it in the closet while Laura flips through the stack of mail.

Bill, bill, bill, b—hey, what's this?" she hears her sister say.

She glances up. Laura's holding an oblong white envelope.

"A letter from Shawn?" Jennie asks, running a hand over her own shiny black hair, exactly the same shade and texture as Laura's, except that hers hangs well past her shoulders. And right now, it's full of static, annoying her.

I should just get it chopped off, like Laura did, she tells herself, even as she hears Keegan's voice echoing inside her head. *I love your hair long, Jen. Don't ever cut it.*

"No, this isn't from Shawn. The return address is a post office box on Tide Island," Laura is saying with a frown. "I don't know anyone there."

"Well, open it."

"I'm afraid to."

Jennie knows what she's thinking. Laura's ex-husband, Brian, pursued her relentlessly after their marriage ended last spring. Her sister had finally been forced to get a restraining order against him. He'd dropped out of sight right after that, presumably returning to Cape Cod, where his parents still live.

Jennie's aware that her sister is still afraid he'll resurface and start bothering her again. Brian is a deceptively mild-mannered guy; but when he's drunk, he's a monster. Jennie witnessed his violent, alcohol-induced temper on more than one occasion and had suspected he was abusing Laura long before her sister ever admitted it.

"Don't worry," she tells Laura now, watching her carefully. "It's probably just some travel brochure, or a charity asking for money. And if it's not—if it *is* from Brian—you can take it straight to the police."

"I know." Laura, her face taut, opens the envelope carefully and withdraws a sheet of white paper.

Jennie watches her sister's features, identical to her own except for a small scar by her left eye—courtesy of her ex-husband—gradually relax over the next few seconds.

"What? What is it?" she asks, hurrying across the room and peering over Laura's shoulder at the letter.

"I can't believe it. I mean, I never win anything," Laura says, handing her the letter. "Read this."

Jennie takes it, noticing that the stationery is heavy and expensive. There is a delicate pen-and-ink drawing of a charming house on the top. The imprint on the stationery reads *Bramble Rose Inn, Box 57, Tide Island MA.* Jennie scans the bold type.

Dear Ms. Towne:

It is our pleasure to inform you that you have won the grand prize in the annual New England Children's Leukemia Society fund-raising sweepstakes. You are hereby entitled to an all-expenses-paid solo visit to Tide Island on the second weekend in February. The prize includes three-nights, four-days deluxe accommodations at the Bramble Rose Inn, all meals, and round-trip transportation on the Crosswinds Bay ferry. Please confirm with me at (508) 555-1493, upon receipt of this letter.

Sincerely,
Jasper Hammel
Innkeeper

Jennie lowers the letter and looks at Laura. "This sounds pretty good," she says cautiously.

"It *would* be, if it were any other weekend. Shawn's coming home that Saturday in time for Valentine's Day. I already arranged my hours at work so that I could take off and be with him. I can't go."

"Maybe you can switch to another weekend," Jennie suggests. "Then you and Shawn can both go."

Laura shakes her head. "See that small print on the bottom? It says this offer is only good for that particular weekend. And I remember buying the sweepstakes ticket right before Christmas. The man who sold it to me said the prize was for *one* person, no guests. Sort of a pamper-yourself, getaway-from-it-all thing."

"I never heard of the New England Children's Leukemia Society," Jennie comments, scanning the small print.

"Neither did I. But he told me it's been around for a while. Actually, I think I've seen him before—he looked familiar. He's probably been collecting for charity before, and I'll bet I ducked him. If I hadn't just gotten paid and been feeling rich that day, I probably wouldn't even have bought the ticket from him. Although, I may have if I knew what it was for," she adds soberly.

Of course Laura would never refuse to

contribute to that particular charity. Jennie wouldn't either. Their younger sister, Melanie, had died of leukemia fifteen years ago.

Jennie glances again at the letter. "Where'd you buy the sweepstakes ticket, Laura?"

"In the parking lot at Stop and Shop. Don't worry, Jen. It was legit."

"I didn't say it wasn't," Jenny says.

"But you're thinking that Brian might have something to do with this, aren't you? That it's some sort of set-up to lure me to this island so that he could convince me to give him another chance. Right?"

Jennie meets her sister's lilac-colored eyes guiltily. "The thought did cross my mind."

"Trust me. Brian's not this clever. Can you see him going through all the effort of making up a fake charity, hiring some stranger to persuade me to buy a ticket, and then somehow getting his hands on the stationery for this Bramble Rose place and forging a letter from an innkeeper?"

Jennie grins. "You're right. He couldn't do that in a million years." She glances down at the drawing of the inn again. "Too bad you can't go. It looks really cozy."

"Why don't *you* go instead, Jen?" Laura asks suddenly.

"Didn't you read the rest of the small print? It says the prize can't be transferred."

"So? We're identical twins. When was the last time we switched places?" Laura asks with a grin.

Jennie smiles. "I thought we agreed never to do that again after that time in high school."

Her sister's boyfriend hadn't been very appreciative to discover that Laura had sent Jennie on a date with him while she went out with someone else. Of course, he probably wouldn't have figured it out if Jennie hadn't done such an unconvincing job of faking a sudden stomachache so she wouldn't have to have sex with him.

Laura had neglected to mention to her sister that they'd been sleeping together for over a year and he might expect it.

"Jen," Laura says, "this isn't high school. Take my driver's license as ID and go to the island. You can spend some time drawing and painting, or whatever. The place is really artsy. You know, that's why they call it Tie-Dye Land."

"Huh?"

"Tide Island—Tie-Dye Land. That's what everyone calls the place. Didn't you ever hear that before?"

"Nope."

"Figures. Sometimes, Jen, you're in a total fog," Laura says, shaking her head. "Anyway, a lot of artists hang out there in the summers. You know—long-haired types who wear grungy tie-dye outfits and sit around painting the scenery all day."

Hmm. The idea of bringing her art supplies to a picturesque island is tempting to Jennie. She's been too busy lately to spend any time on her hobby. Still . . .

"You have short hair in the picture on your license. Mine's long," she points out to Laura.

"So? I got it renewed over a year ago. I could have grown my hair out. Go ahead, Jen. You need to get away after all this craziness with Keegan."

Keegan. She winces.

Oh, God. Will she ever be able to hear his name and not react this way?

Jennie glances again at the drawing of the inn. It shows an old-fashioned, scallop-shingled house complete with plenty of gables and a picket fence with a kitten perched demurely on the gatepost. It appears to be a dreamy, quaint little place where you can curl up with a sketch pad and a mug of tea and forget about the painful end of a relationship.

"Maybe you're right," she tells Laura slowly.

"I *am* right." Her sister bounces the few short steps to the telephone on a nearby table. She picks up the receiver and dangles it from her fingers, looking expectantly at Jennie. "Read off the phone number on the letter. I'll dial. And don't forget—you're Laura."

Jennie sighs. "Right. I'm Laura." She looks down at the letter and starts reading the number aloud.

One

The ferry isn't yet a far-off speck on the dusky horizon, but he knows it's there, cutting toward Tide Island through the choppy gray waters off the New England coast. Complete darkness will fall well before it docks at the landing down the road to release its load of weekend passengers.

In summer, the Friday-night ferry is always crowded with commuting husbands and vacationing families, college students who work as weekend waiters or lifeguards, couples in love, sticky-faced children.

But now, in the shortest month of the year, when winter is at its bleakest and the island offers nothing but silent, chilly isolation, there won't be many people on board. Just the few hardy nature-loving souls willing to brave the elements; perhaps some island-dwellers returning with groceries from the mainland; maybe a handful of summer house owners coming out to inspect the damage December's Nor'easter inflicted upon their property.

That's about it.

Except for *them.*

He knows they're on board—all three of them. Still strangers to each other, but not to him.

He has been watching them for so long now.

Waiting.

A quiver of anticipation passes over him and he cautions himself to relax. He has to maintain control at all times. He can't afford to take any risks at this point, just when it's all coming together at last.

After all these years . . .

Soon enough, he assures himself. *It won't be long now.*

He casts his gaze back out over the water, giddy with excitement. He'd heard on the radio a little while ago that there's a growing likelihood this weekend might be stormy.

Wouldn't that be perfect?

Even at this moment, they're probably enjoying the brisk twilight ride. He pictures them scattered in different corners of the deck or cabin, lost in their own thoughts, thinking about the weekend ahead, filled with excited expectations.

They aren't the only ones who are looking forward to it.

His features twist with mirth, and he stifles a giggle.

Very, very soon.

He lets the filmy lace curtain drop back into place and turns away from the window.

He still has a lot to do before they arrive.

As the ferry leaves Crosswinds Bay and heads out into the open Atlantic, Jennie turns her face into the cold, salty wind and smiles.

What a relief to be leaving everything behind, if only for a few days. Already, she can feel the chronic tension starting to loosen its grip on her body. She takes a deep breath of the sea air and lets it out on a satisfying sigh.

By the time she reached the ferry terminal twenty minutes ago, her jaw ached from clenching and her neck and back muscles had been a jumble of stress knots.

Knowing Friday night traffic out of Boston was always bad, she'd left at three o'clock to beat it. Unfortunately, a jackknifed trac-tor-trailer had rammed into a car on I-95 and brought her to a standstill by three-fif-teen. And she'd lost an hour by the time she'd managed to creep by the accident scene, ducking her head after a fleeting glimpse of the emergency vehicles with their flashing red lights.

Spinning domed lights—and sirens—al-ways bring her back to that awful day three years ago.

So does the sight of blood, no matter how scant. Just two days ago, she'd cut her finger on a paring knife and found her-self still trembling uncontrollably a half hour later.

Today, she had struggled to shake the disturbing memories from her mind and concentrate on the road. She really had to step on it to make the five o'clock ferry from Crosswinds Bay on Rhode Island's south-western coast.

As a rule, she hardly ever went more than five miles above the speed limit, but she didn't really have a choice if she wanted to get away for the weekend. And she was de-termined to do that.

The cozy Bramble Rose Inn seemed to

beckon silently from miles away, promising refuge. She couldn't miss the ferry—it was the last one tonight. She was willing to risk a speeding ticket to catch it.

Besides, everyone else on the road seemed to be flying by at eighty miles an hour anyway. Jennie had slid her small red Hyundai out into the passing lane and let the speedometer climb to seventy.

Just past Providence, she was stopped by a humorless trooper who promptly slapped her with a speeding ticket.

Now, shaking her head at the thought of having to part with a precious fifty dollars to pay the fine, she pulls her black leather gloves out of the bag at her feet and slips them over her winter-chapped hands. It's freezing on the deck, but she doesn't want to go inside yet.

There's something cleansing about standing out here with the fresh, fishy air whipping through her hair and stinging her cheeks so that they feel swollen. A bell clangs on the bridge somewhere above her, bidding a hollow farewell to the shore they are rapidly leaving behind.

"Excuse me, do you know what time it is?"

Jennie turns toward the voice. A young woman stands behind her, clutching the railing with one hand to keep her balance as the boat rolls over the waves. She's so bundled in a parka and scarf that all that's visible is a pair of pretty brown eyes and a snub nose that looks bright red from the frosty air.

Jennie pushes her glove up her wrist and peeks at her watch. "It's almost a quarter after six." She practically has to shout to be heard over the wind and crashing waves.

"Thanks. Do you know when the ferry is supposed to get in?"

"I think at around seven-thirty. At least, that's what the schedule said."

"Good. I'm starving."

"Me, too." Jennie remembers that she hasn't eaten since the half a blueberry muffin from Dunkin' Donuts that she'd gulped down this morning in the car on the way to work. She'd been too busy trying to wrap things up and make an early getaway to even think about lunch.

The other woman reaches into her pocket and produces a fat-free granola bar in one fuzzy-mittened hand. "Want half? It'll tide you over."

Jennie hesitates. "Oh, that's all right, you don't have to—"

Abruptly, the woman snaps the bar in two and hands one piece to Jennie with a grin. "Here. I'd feel guilty gobbling the whole thing down myself. Besides, I'm on a diet."

"Thanks," Jenny says.

"Don't look so grateful. It's fat free and it tastes like cardboard, so I'm not being as generous as you think."

Jennie smiles back at her and clumsily pushes the bar up through the torn wrapper with gloved fingers before taking a bite.

For a moment, they stand side by side, crunching and staring out at the water.

Then the other woman says brightly, "I'm Sandy Cavelli."

"Nice to meet you. I'm . . . Laura. Laura Towne." Might as well get into the habit now so she won't be as likely to slip and say Jennie when she gets to the inn.

For another long moment, they both lean on the railing and stare out at the darkening sky and sea, munching the granola.

"Have you ever been to Tide Island before?" Sandy asks, popping the last bite into her mouth. She crumples the empty wrapper and shoves it into her pocket.

"No. Have you?"

"Once when I was younger, with my parents and brothers. I don't remember much about it, except that we came across some people skinny dipping one day when we were trying to have a picnic on the beach. My parents freaked out."

Jennie smiles. "I bet."

"They didn't like the island much, anyway. They thought it was overrun with hippies. That's what my father kept saying."

"Tie-Dye Land," Jennie says, remembering. "That's what people call the island, according to my sister."

"Exactly."

"Well, the place is beautiful, from what I've heard."

"Yeah, and deserted at this time of year." Sandy shakes her head. "I wasn't even going to tell my parents where I was going for the weekend, but my mother overheard me talking about it on the phone with my best friend. And she asked me about it, and then she told my father, and he blew up, as usual. But they can't stop me, you know? Even though I live under their roof, I'm an adult." She lifts her double chin stubbornly. "You know what I mean?"

Jennie nods, thinking she doesn't seem so sure of that as she wants to be. She looks and sounds almost like a rebellious teenager.

Abruptly, Sandy changes the subject. "So how come you're coming here, and not jetting off to St. Thomas or something? I mean, isn't that what people do when they go on vacation in the dead of winter?"

Jennie shrugs. "I don't know. The Caribbean is probably so crowded when it's winter in the northeast."

Probably. Why'd you say that? You know it is.

But she doesn't want to remember her November trip to Jamaica with Keegan.

"True." Sandy grins. "But I'll bet it's crowded with lots of eligible guys."

"You're single?"

"Unfortunately, yes. I was engaged once, but it didn't work out. How about you?"

Jennie nods. She's on the verge of saying, "I just broke up with someone," but catches herself. It isn't at all like her to spill the details of her life to a complete stranger. And of course, she would never tell this Sandy Cavelli her *whole* painful, horrible story. The people she works with don't even know about that.

"It's so hard to meet anyone halfway decent. I haven't even had a date in two months," Sandy says wistfully. "How about you?"

Something about this woman is making Jennie uncharacteristically tempted to confide in her, but again she holds back. "Not really," she says simply.

"I'm meeting someone on the island," Sandy informs her.

Jennie assumes she just means that she's determined to find a nice guy this weekend until Sandy goes on, "It's kind of a blind date."

"That's nice."

"Yeah. This was his idea. He has a house out here. He's a doctor."

"A doctor—wow," Jennie comments because she knows Sandy expects it.

"Wow is right."

"Where does he practice? On the island?"

"No, this is just where his weekend house is," Sandy says a bit smugly. Then her expression grows a little embarrassed. "I, uh, I'm not sure where his practice is. Like I said, this is a blind date. I don't know much about him."

"Huh," Jennie says, nodding. "Sounds romantic."

"You're telling me. And it doesn't matter where he works, because wherever it is, I'd move out there in a minute if we hit it off. It would be a pleasure never to set foot in Hartford again . . . unless he happens to live there, too."

"That's where you're from?"

"Yeah. Actually, not Hartford. Near it, though . . . a little town called Greenbury." At Jennie's blank look, she nods. "Never heard of it, huh? I'm not surprised. How about you?"

"I live in Boston."

"What do you do?"

"I'm an antique dealer," Jennie says, before she remembers that she's supposed to be Laura, and Laura is a sales-clerk at the Gap. Well, it's too late to take it back now.

Her expression must have revealed something, because Sandy says, "Not all it's cracked up to be, huh?"

"No, it's not that, it's just . . ."

It's just that every damn thing in my life reminds me of Keegan, that's what.

"What don't you like about it?"

"Oh, I like it." Jennie tilts her face upward. "Did you just feel a drop?"

"No, but I'm so bundled up a baseball-sized hailstone wouldn't make me flinch. Is it raining?"

"Maybe it was just spray. But I think I'm going to go inside anyway. My feet are starting to get numb."

"Okay. I'll stick around out here for a while longer. Maybe I'll get windburn on my face. I look a lot better when I have some color."

"Thanks for the granola."

"Anytime."

"See you later." Jennie lets go of the railing and moves toward the door on unsteady feet.

A blast of warm air rushes at her as she steps into the cabin. The silence there is pronounced after the roar of the wind outside. Jennie loosens the top button of her coat and heads toward a vacant spot on the bench against the wall.

As she sits down, she notices that the striking blond woman beside her is clutching her stomach, looking wan. Still feeling the effects of Sandy's outgoing friendliness,

Jennie reaches into her pocket for the Tums she put there earlier, just in case.

"Excuse me, but would you like one of these?" she asks the stranger, holding out the roll.

The woman barely shakes her head, then closes her green eyes abruptly, effectively shutting Jennie out.

I guess I wouldn't be very friendly if I felt seasick, either, Jennie tells herself, slipping the Tums back into her pocket and reaching into her bag for a magazine.

She settles back to read as the last streaks of pink fade from the sky and the ferry chugs swiftly through the darkness toward Tide Island.

Liza steps from the gangplank onto the old wooden pier and looks around. There's nothing to see. Blackness is everywhere—the water, the sky, the buildings a few hundred feet away. The only light is on the boat deck behind her, and even that casts a murky glow that only makes the place seem eerier.

She doesn't know what she'd expected. She'd known the island wouldn't be hopping in the off-season, that there wouldn't be many shops or restaurants open.

But this . . . this is like a ghost town.

Across from the landing, through the wisps of fog that hang in the air, she can make out the main street. She recognizes it from a brochure she'd picked up at a travel agency in her neighborhood. She'd been enchanted by the street in the photograph, with its row of grand Victorian hotels and quaint shops.

Now their mansard roofs and gables loom in spooky silhouettes against the night sky. They're obviously deserted, the windows boarded with plywood against winter's harsh weather.

Liza hesitates as other passengers disembark and scurry toward a nearby parking lot. She can hear a few shouted greetings; apparently some people are being met at the landing by friends or relatives.

She glances around, wondering what happened to the woman on the boat who had offered her the Tums. Apparently, she'd thought Liza was seasick. She wasn't.

She had been thinking about Robert, a man she'd been dating lately. He'd left at least twenty-five messages on her home answering machine this week. Couldn't he take a hint?

When the other woman had approached her on the boat, Liza hadn't been in the mood for company. But those friendly lilac-colored eyes would be beyond welcome right about now.

There's no sign of her.

Feeling suddenly alone, Liza reaches for her gloves again. She sets her Vuitton bag on the rough planks at her feet, slips her hands into the cozy cashmere lining, and feels instantly better.

She tries to figure out which direction she has to walk in to find the inn.

When she'd made her reservation, Jasper Hammel had said to bear right along Main Street and it would be a quarter-mile up the road. "You can't miss it," he'd assured her.

Somehow, Liza can't seem to force herself to move away from the landing and into the deserted street. She can hear car engines starting in the parking lot. Several pairs of sweeping headlights swing in the opposite direction, turning down the deserted main street and fading away.

Behind her, a few passengers are still trickling off the ferry. In another moment, they—and the boat itself—will be gone. She'll be completely abandoned in this desolate place.

Liza takes a deep breath, picks up her bag, and heads for the street.

She makes her way along the empty boardwalk, her boot heels making a hollow, lonely sound that triggers her heart to beat faster. There are no streetlights, no passing cars—nothing.

The wind whistles mournfully as it blows in off the water. Over it, Liza hears the grinding of the ferry engines as the boat turns around in the harbor.

She peers ahead through the darkness. Never before has she been in such a desolate place. Never before has she experienced such utter and complete darkness. There's no moon to illuminate her path. No reassuring neon signs, or even lamplit homes, to tell her that there are people nearby.

Fighting back a growing sense of panic, she steps down off the boardwalk at the end of the row of buildings and into the wide, sandy road. It curves away from the water now, heading slightly uphill.

Liza hesitates, uncertain whether or not

to keep following it. She can always turn back, and—

Above her head, a shutter bangs suddenly.

Liza jumps and cries out before she realizes what it was.

Clutching her trembling hands in fists against her mouth, she acknowledges that her nerves are shattered.

This is ludicrous. What is she doing out here, fumbling in the dark all alone? In New York, she never walks down a deserted street by herself at night. Any idiot knows better than that. A woman alone, in the dark—it's just asking for trouble.

She has to go back.

Forget D.M. Yates.

All she wants to do is be back in familiar Manhattan.

The ferry bell clangs just then, telling her that the boat is heading back out toward the mainland.

Wait, she wants to scream. *Take me with you! Don't leave me here alone!*

But it's too late. She'll never catch the boat, even if she runs all the way back to the landing.

So she hurries on, clutching her bag so

tightly her nails dig into her palms even through the gloves.

The fog seems to grow more dense by the minute, rolling in off the water, carried by the ever-present wind.

There are a few low buildings at the side of the road here; but they, like everything else, look deserted. Their signs—bearing cheery names like "Sun 'n Fun Surf Shop" and "Buddy's Beachfront Bike Rentals"— seem ridiculously out of place in this somber setting.

Gradually, Liza becomes aware of a pebble working its way down into her boot. After trying to walk several steps on it, she finally stops to get it out. She sets her bag down and balances on one foot while she removes her boot and dumps the little stone out onto the frozen concrete.

As she laces her boot again, she wonders how far she's come. Surely it's been a quarter of a mile by now.

Suddenly, the skin just above the hairline on the back of her neck begins to prickle and an unmistakable feeling steals over her.

The feeling that she's being watched.

Leaving her boot half-unlaced, Liza grabs her bag and begins walking again.

The eerie awareness mounts.

She doesn't know who's peering at her through the night, or even where they're hiding; she's only acutely conscious of invisible eyes boring into her from somewhere nearby.

She quickens her pace.

Then she hears it, even over the incessant howling and the crashing sea.

Footsteps.

They're coming from somewhere behind her. Not *right* behind her, but they're there.

Someone is following her.

She doesn't take the time to turn her head and find out who it is.

She doesn't care.

Breaking into a run, she heads up the dark, sloping road. Her eyes frantically scan the brush lining the sides.

On a low rise overlooking the water ahead, she thinks she glimpses a light.

Please, God . . .

There! That has to be the inn. As she rounds a bend, she sees that it is, indeed, a house. And a weathered sign by the foot of the steep drive bears the name Bramble Rose Inn.

Liza's heart thumps painfully, threatening

to shatter her rib cage as she quickly makes her way up the winding path. Glancing up at the house, she half-expects to see someone in a window, looking out into the night.

But there's no one, and she tells herself to stop being ridiculous.

He steps back from the window.

Had she seen him?

She'd looked up just before the evergreen branches below enveloped her, screening her from his sight. But he'd glimpsed enough of her to see which one she is.

Liza Danning.

She's still startlingly pretty, with enormous seafoam-green eyes.

Wary eyes.

And she still doesn't even know what lies in store for her.

He waits, tapping a pen against his palm impatiently. The antique mantel clock ticks a steady rhythm behind him.

Within moments, the shrill ring of the old-fashioned door buzzer shatters the silent house.

Realizing he'd been holding his breath,

he exhales now. Carefully, he puts the pen into the holder on his desk and walks out of the room toward the stairs.

The first guest has arrived.

The others will soon follow.

And soon it will begin.

Jennie is just about to ring the bell a second time when the heavy wooden door is flung open before her.

"Well, hello! I was beginning to wonder if you had gotten lost." The man who stands there is of medium height, with a somewhat stocky build. He has a neatly trimmed mustache that is the same auburn shade of his hair. His friendly smile is like a beacon, reaching out into the chilly night air and enveloping Jennie.

"Hi," she says breathlessly. "I was beginning to think I *was* lost. It's really dark out there."

"It is, isn't it? Cold, too. Come on in." He steps back and motions her through a short entry hall and into the brightly lit foyer, then closes the door behind her, shutting out the incessant wind at last.

Jennie sets her bag on the wide-planked

wooden floor and breathes an audible sigh. She's made it. What a relief.

The foyer is cozy and pleasant, with lots of plants in wicker baskets, a few wing-backed chairs, and globed lamps on low antique tables. Beyond the tall reception desk, a narrow wooden staircase leads to a landing, then turns sharply. The cinnamon-berry scent of potpourri wafts invitingly in the air, and classical music plays softly in the background.

Her host has walked briskly around to the back of the desk and is scanning a registry book. "Let's see now. Ms. Danning has already checked in, so you must be . . ."

"I'm Laura Towne." Jennie assumes the blonde she'd followed over from the boat was Ms. Danning.

She might have tried harder to catch up to her if the woman had been friendlier on the boat . . . and if she hadn't been walking so fast. Jennie had thought she looked spooked. Actually, she doesn't blame her. The place *is* pretty creepy in the dark, although it'll probably be perfectly delightful tomorrow morning.

"Ah, yes, Laura Towne," the man behind the desk is saying.

"That's me." She feels a twinge of guilt at the lie.

"You're our sweepstakes winner. We spoke on the phone a few weeks back, didn't we? I have you down right here. You're staying for three nights."

Jennie notices that there's something effeminate about his movements, and his voice is slightly high-pitched.

"That's right." She runs a hand through her long, dark hair, trying to tame the flyaways.

"Well, then, you're all set." He looks up and smiles again. "Have you ever been to Tide Island before?"

"No."

"Well, let me be the first to welcome you. I'm Jasper Hammel, and I'm here to make your stay as pleasant as possible. If you have any questions, or if there's any way I can—"

The doorbell cuts him off. He holds up a finger, motioning to Jennie that he'll be right back. Then he hurries toward the entry hall.

Jennie sees a copy of *Country Living* magazine in a basket on the desk and starts flipping idly through it.

Cold air blows into the room as soon as

the door opens behind her, and the blustery howl drowns out Jasper Hammel's voice as he greets someone there.

It isn't until he's closed the door again and is leading the new guest into the foyer that Jennie recognizes a voice.

Spinning, she sees Sandy from the ferry.

"Hey, long time no see" is the first thing she says when she sees Jennie. With a grunt, she deposits her oversized suitcase unceremoniously on the floor in front of the desk.

"You're staying here, too?" Jennie asks.

She doesn't know if she's pleased or disappointed. It might be nice to have some pleasant company over the weekend. But on the other hand, she isn't really in the mood for this woman's brand of cheerful chitchat. She's counting on some solitary time to draw and paint . . . and sort things out.

Still, Sandy did mention that she's meeting some man here. She'll probably be busy with him.

"I see that you two have met already?" Jasper asks, returning to stand behind the desk.

"Uh huh. We ran into each other on the

ferry," Sandy says distractedly. "Um, listen, I'm meeting someone here—Ethan? Ethan Thoreau? I thought he'd be waiting for me down at the landing, but he wasn't."

Must be her blind date, Jennie thinks, noting the breathless way she says his name. Her round face is flushed, probably from excitement as much as from the cold.

"That's right, you're Mr. Thoreau's guest this weekend," Jasper says, smiling and nodding. "He called an hour ago. He said to tell you that he was still at the hospital—some sort of surgical emergency—but he'll be here as soon as possible."

Sandy's face falls. "But I thought we just took the last ferry in tonight."

"That was the last ferry, but the airport is still open, of course."

"He's flying in?" Sandy asks.

"I didn't think the airlines served this island," Jennie comments. She'd checked, wanting to avoid the long ferry ride if at all possible.

"They don't," Jasper says. "Mr. Thoreau will be arriving on his private plane."

Sandy perks right up at that news. "Private plane," she murmurs, turning to Jennie. "Figures. I mean, a rich doctor—surgeon?"

she adds, glancing at Jasper Hammel for confirmation. At his nod, she goes on, "Of course a rich surgeon would have his own plane."

"Of course," Jennie agrees, wondering how someone like Sandy had managed to hook up with this guy in the first place. Oh, she's nice and friendly, and even pretty despite her chubbiness. But she doesn't seem like the type who would appeal to a wealthy surgeon.

For Sandy's sake, Jennie hopes the guy didn't suddenly draw the same conclusion and stand her up.

Jasper Hammel clears his throat. "I'll just get the two of you settled into your rooms now. I'm sure you're anxious to relax and warm up."

A floorboard creaks above, and Jennie looks expectantly at the stairs behind the desk, waiting to hear footsteps descending.

But there's no other sound. It's as if someone is poised there, listening to what's going on below.

Jasper, busy writing in the registry, doesn't appear to have noticed it. But Sandy catches Jennie's eye, knitting her brow slightly. Apparently she heard the sound, too.

Jennie remembers the figure she'd seen at the window upstairs, at the very top of the house, as she'd approached the inn. She decides that the silhouette couldn't have belonged to Jasper. The outline of the man in the window had been longer, narrower, than the innkeeper's short, round frame.

Someone else had been watching her from the window.

So? Jennie tells herself. *Big deal. Probably a bored guest.*

But is that same person now standing someplace above, eavesdropping?

And if so . . . why?

As soon as Jasper Hammel's footsteps retreat down the hall, Sandy turns the latch on her door, locking it.

Then she surveys the room.

Raspberry-colored floral wallpaper. White-painted woodwork. Lace curtains. Rose-sprigged bedspread with flounces that reveal a matching dust ruffle. Framed pastel watercolors. Dried rosebuds in a white wicker basket on the table by the bed.

She peers into a delicate pink-and-white china bowl on the mantel and discovers the source of the lavender scent that fills the air: potpourri.

This room must be reserved for female guests, she decides. No way would a man be comfortable here.

She turns and opens her suitcase, which Jasper Hammel deposited on the stand near the door. The first thing she removes is the new outfit she bought for her date with Ethan Thoreau. She bought it at Greenbury Gal, and it was outrageously expensive even with her employee discount. But it was worth it.

Her friend Theresa had assured her that the long, navy-blue knit skirt concealed her saddlebag thighs and that the cream-colored angora sweater accentuated what Theresa kindly called her "hourglass figure."

Sandy would gladly sacrifice her forty-double-D boobs if she could get rid of her forty-six-inch hips as well. But nature—and a weakness for junk food—has padded her generously, and she's resigned to the fact that she's never going to be thin.

Not like Laura, whom Jasper showed to a room at the other end of the hall before depositing Sandy in here. Laura has one of those cute, petite shapes that Sandy has always envied. Sandy hadn't missed the way several men on the ferry had checked Laura out, even though she was bundled into a winter coat.

Well, not all men like stick figures, she reminds herself. *Some men like women who have some meat on their bones.*

Oh, God. Now you sound like Ma.

Angie Cavelli, roly-poly in her own right, is always telling Sandy that there's no reason she shouldn't be able to find a husband. Besides, she always adds, at twenty-five, Sandy has no time to waste. After all, as Angie likes to point out, by the time she herself was twenty-five, Tony Junior was in kindergarten, Frankie was potty trained, Danny was on solids, and she was pregnant with Sandy.

Good for you, Ma, Sandy always wants to add.

But she doesn't. She was taught to respect her parents. No matter what they say or how they make her feel.

So she doesn't say anything to her

mother, and she doesn't say anything to her father, either, when he tells her—only when her mother's out of earshot, of course—that if Sandy would just lose some weight, she could find a husband. After all, "no man wants a fat wife."

She knows that her father is thinking of Joe, assuming that he broke the engagement because of her being overweight. She knows neither of her parents believe that *she's* the one who called it off and that they both think the best she could ever get out of life is to become Mrs. Joseph Marconi with a houseful of kids.

Sighing, Sandy carefully hangs her new outfit in the tiny closet, which is empty except for several wire coat hangers bearing paper sleeves that read "Sampson Bros.— 42 Years as Tide Island's Premier Dry Cleaners."

As she turns away from the closet, she hears a floorboard creak overhead.

Nothing unusual about that. The inn has three floors. She noticed the narrower staircase that leads upstairs when Jasper Hammel led her and Jennie along the hallway on the way to their rooms.

But Sandy thinks of how the floorboard

had creaked on the second floor when she and Jennie were checking in awhile ago and how she had almost felt as though someone might be lurking there, eavesdropping.

Why anyone would want to do such a thing is beyond her, but the notion that they might definitely gave her the creeps then and does again now.

You're just not used to big old houses, she tells herself, shaking her head. *Besides, you're afraid of your own shadow.*

If she weren't such a baby, she would have moved out of her parents' house years ago. But she can't stand the thought of living alone.

Not that she'd admit that to anyone, not even Theresa. She tells her friends that she doesn't move out because she can't afford to. Luckily, her parents don't think a woman should leave home until she gets married, so they don't charge her rent.

Going back over to her suitcase, she removes the rest of her clothes—a few oversized sweaters, turtlenecks, and pairs of leggings—and stacks them neatly in the drawers of an antique bureau. She catches sight of herself in the mirror above it and leans closer to examine her reflection.

You have such a pretty face. . . . How many times has she heard that?

She knows it's true—her eyes are big and brown and fringed with thick lashes, and her lips are full and red, and she has dimples in her cheeks when she smiles.

Will Ethan Thoreau think she has a pretty face, too?

She takes her quilted pink makeup bag out of her suitcase and unzips it. She opens a compact and begins meticulously applying blusher, tracing the contours of her cheekbones the way the girl at the Clinique counter showed her.

She wonders what time Ethan will arrive on his private plane and whether she should change into her new skirt and sweater just in case he decides to pop in at the inn without calling her first.

She decides against it. Why waste her best clothes on a chance? She looks fine in the chocolate-colored stretch pants and matching oversized tunic she has on. Not only does the outfit camouflage her bulges pretty well, but it exactly matches the shade of her eyes. At least, that's what Danny told her when she wore it on Christmas.

Sandy smiles when she thinks of him. She can always count on her favorite brother to compliment her.

She can't seem to help feeling a little wistful ever since he married Cheryl, his college sweetheart, and moved out of the house last summer. Of course, they only live a few blocks away and Danny still goes out of his way to be nice to Sandy, but things aren't the same between them.

Not that Sandy resents Cheryl.

It's just that she wishes she had someone, too.

Maybe things will work out with Ethan.

Maybe he and Sandy can buy the cute little split level down the street from her parents. She's always loved that house, and just the other day, she noticed a For Sale sign on the snowy lawn. It would be a perfect starter home, and it already has a swing set and sand box in the backyard.

Sandy reaches for her eyeliner and smiles as she imagines the children that she will have with Ethan Thoreau.

And when the floorboard creaks above again, she doesn't even notice.

Two

Liza is starving.

If it weren't for that—and the irresistible savory aroma wafting up to the second floor—she wouldn't be on her way down to the dining room for dinner. She certainly isn't in the mood to mingle with the other guests—small talk isn't her forte, and there's no point in wasting an effort on people she'll never see again, anyway.

But she can't ignore her rumbling stomach.

And anyway, it's not as though she has anything else to do tonight.

D.M. Yates isn't going to contact her until tomorrow. The innkeeper, Jasper Hammel, had handed her a pink telephone message slip when she checked in. All it said was that Yates had called and would be in touch again in the morning.

When Liza questioned Jasper Hammel about the message, he'd shrugged and told

her he wasn't the one who had taken it—
must have been the hired girl, but she had
already left for the weekend.

And when Liza asked Jasper Hammel
what he knew about the famous author,
he'd shrugged again. Yes, Yates had a
house on the island. No, Hammel had never
met him. Didn't Liza know he was a recluse?

"Of course I know that," Liza had
snapped, biting her tongue to leave off the
you idiot that would have followed naturally.

Jasper Hammel hadn't seemed fazed by
her tone. He'd regarded her calmly from behind his wire-framed glasses, then said,
"You will be joining us for dinner in the dining room, won't you? Eight-thirty sharp."

"No, thanks," Liza had muttered.

And now here she is, hurrying down the
stairs to the main floor, lured by the rich,
mouth-watering scent that fills the air.

She hesitates in the entryway for only a
moment before following her nose through
the archway to her left, passing through a
cozy parlor and into the dining room.

Though she hasn't seen or heard any of
the other guests until now, for some reason,

she's expecting to find a crowd gathered for dinner.

Instead, only two other people are seated at the enormous, polished wooden table, tucked away at the far end, across from each other. Classical music plays softly in the background, and it's especially fitting in a room like this, with its old-fashioned furnishings and decor.

Candles glow on the ornately carved sideboard and in the center of the table. Heavy burgundy-colored drapes are drawn over the two windows, and the elaborate crystal chandelier gives off only a dim glow.

It takes a moment for Liza's eyes to adjust to the lighting. When they do, she's startled to recognize the woman from the ferry—the one with the kind, lilac-colored eyes and the straight dark hair. The other person seated at the table is a pudgy, round-faced woman who's wearing too much makeup and yammering away to the brunette, who's obviously trying to seem interested.

At first, neither of them sees Liza.

Then the chatterbox turns around and spots her.

"Hi!" she says brightly, waving.

Liza clears her throat and wishes she'd stayed upstairs. But it's not too late to go back. She mumbles a reluctant "hello," but before she can take a step backward, Jasper Hammel sweeps into the room carrying a huge platter. On it is an elaborate presentation of lobsters and shellfish and what looks like heaps of wild rice and vegetables.

"Oh, good, Liza, you've decided to join us," he says, spotting her in the doorway. "I was counting on you."

He motions to the head of the table, where a third place setting waits.

Liza moves toward it and slips into the chair, aware that both of the other women are regarding her curiously. She focuses on the table, taking in the hunter-green brocade place mat, the delicate china with its ivory background and gold trim, and the silver that's obviously been lovingly polished. An etched crystal goblet sits in front of her place, and it's already filled with amber liquid.

"The wine is great," Sandy says, and Liza looks up to see that she's watching her with wide, friendly brown eyes. "Not too dry. I hate dry wine."

"Really? I like dry wine." Liza reaches for the glass, taking a sip. Not as fine as the bottle of chardonnay she'd shared last night on her first date with Albert, a stockbroker, at Le Cirque on the Upper East Side. But not bad, either.

"Liza Danning, this is Sandy Cavelli," Jasper says, sweeping a hand to indicate the chubby woman, then motioning toward the brunette, "and Laura Towne. I'll be right back." He disappears into the kitchen again.

"Nice to meet you," Sandy says cheerfully, turning back to Liza.

"You, too." Liza glances at Laura, including her.

The woman seems subdued, merely nodding over her own wineglass.

Liza recalls the way she snubbed her on the ferry. Well, how was she to know she'd be sitting at a dinner table with her later?

Nothing like an awkward beginning, though.

"So you're staying here alone, too, huh?" Sandy asks Liza, breaking the strained silence.

"Yes." Liza frowns slightly, realizing that no other places are set at the table. The other guests must have gone out to eat—even though it's raining steadily outside now. And where could they have gone? She hadn't noticed a single open restaurant, or even a sign of life, on the boardwalk.

Come to think of it, she hasn't seen any signs of other guests, either. . . .

"What a coincidence," Sandy comments.

Liza catches her hungrily eyeing the platter full of food on the table.

"What's a coincidence?" Laura speaks for the first time, putting down her glass.

"You know, that three girls would all come to a place like this, alone."

Liza arches a brow at Sandy's reference to them as *girls.* She's about to open her mouth, but Laura says, "I don't usually travel alone. My—I won this trip, and it was only for one person."

"You won it? How? I never win anything," Sandy tells her wistfully.

"It was one of those charity sweepstakes things."

"What charity?"

"I can't remember," Laura says simply and reaches for her wineglass again. She doesn't sip it, just spins the stem in her fingers, and Liza decides she's looking for something to do with her hands. For some reason, she looks uneasy.

"How about you, Liza? What are you doing here alone?"

Doesn't she ever mind her own business? Liza wonders, studying Sandy's eager, curious expression.

"I'm here on business," she informs her tersely, and waits for the inevitable.

Sure enough . . .

"What kind of business?"

"Publishing."

"Wow. Are you an editor?"

Liza nods.

"Where?"

"New York."

"What publisher?"

"Xavier House."

"Wow."

Liza can't tell if Sandy's ever heard of them or if she simply says *wow* to everything.

Sandy clears her throat and says, "I don't usually travel alone, either."

Liza nods. She can tell Sandy wants her to ask what she's doing on the island this weekend. But she doesn't really care. And she isn't in the mood to be polite.

After a pause, Sandy looks at the platter of shellfish and rice and licks her lips.

Liza glances at Laura again and sees that she's staring off into space, still fiddling with her glass.

After a few more moments of silence, during which the strains of classical music and the pattering of raindrops against the windows seem to grow steadily louder, the door leading to the kitchen suddenly swings open.

Jasper Hammel breezes back into the room, carrying a cloth-covered basket that gives off the unmistakable yeasty aroma of hot bread.

"Here we are," he says, setting it on the table and reaching for a silver serving spoon near the platter of hot food. "I'll serve. Sandy, why don't you lift your plate for me?"

"Sure. Um, what is it?"

"Steamed fresh shellfish on a bed of wild rice with grilled spring vegetables. I prepared it myself, and I'm sure you'll find it tasty."

"Steamed and grilled . . . that's great. Low fat." Sandy lowers her heaping plate and smiles at Liza and Laura. "I'm on a diet."

They nod.

As Jasper fills Laura's plate next, Sandy goes on, "I'm meeting a guy here this weekend. A surgeon. He's totally great-looking. And he's flying in on his private plane."

Liza arches a brow. Either Sandy's lying or the great-looking surgeon is pretty hard up. Why else would he date such a dumpy, unsophisticated chatterbox?

She finds herself asking, despite her vow not to make conversation, "Where did you meet him?"

"Oh, we haven't met yet. It's a blind date." She hesitates. "He . . . uh, he answered an ad I placed in the personals."

That explains it.

Liza lifts her plate for Jasper, who dumps a heaping serving of rice on it, then scoops up some oysters and mussels.

The food is delicious, which isn't surprising. Liza would expect to find excellent shellfish on Tide Island, and Jasper Hammel strikes her as the kind of man who would enjoy cooking.

As they eat, he hovers, pouring wine and urging them to have more rice, another piece of bread. He makes conversation about the island as he bustles about, telling them that it's a lovely place, particularly in the winter, when there aren't many tourists around "to spoil it."

"We're tourists," Liza can't resist pointing out.

The man actually blushes, and his mouth quivers nervously beneath his trimmed brown mustache. "Oh, but I didn't mean *you*," he says quickly. "I meant all the people who have no regard for the wild, natural beauty of the place. They litter and they stomp all over the dunes and they make a dreadful racket with their blasting radios and screaming children." He shudders. "It's not pleasant."

"How long have you been running the inn?" Sandy asks.

"Not long. Oh, I almost forgot—the dessert! It's in the oven, and I can't let it burn. If you'll excuse me . . ." He darts into the kitchen again.

Sandy looks at Liza and Laura, then whispers, "He's kind of strange, isn't he? Do you think he's gay?"

Laura's lilac eyes widen.

Amused, Liza asks, "What makes you say that?"

"My father said there are a lot of homosexuals on this island. That's part of the reason he doesn't like it. He's not very—you know, liberal."

And you are? Liza wants to ask, but she doesn't. She just spears a chunk of eggplant with her fork and pops it into her mouth.

"So what do you think?" Sandy asks again.

"I have no idea," Laura says. "Does it matter?"

"Of course not. I was just wondering."

Sandy turns her attention back to wrestling with the lobster claw on her plate.

By the time Jasper Hammel reappears five minutes later, they've all finished eating and Sandy has initiated a new conversation, mostly one-sided, about whether a person should count calories or just fat grams when trying to lose weight.

"Why don't we have coffee and dessert in the parlor?" he suggests, starting to clear the table.

"I'll pass," Liza says, rising and tossing her green-brocade napkin onto the table.

"Oh, but you can't!"

Startled, she looks at the man, who offers a nervous little smile. "It's a tradition here at the Bramble Rose for *all* of our guests to adjourn to the parlor for dessert."

"Well, what about the other guests?" Liza asks.

"They'll join us. . . . Won't you?" Jasper asks Laura and Sandy.

Laura offers a reluctant nod, and Sandy says cheerfully, "Sure we will. I can never pass up dessert. What is it?"

"Chocolate raspberry torte with real whipped cream," Jasper tells her. "And we have wonderful fresh berries to serve over—"

"Not these two guests," Liza interrupts him. "I'm talking about everyone else who's staying here at the inn."

"There's no one else staying here, besides me," Jasper informs her. "You three are the only guests."

There's no one else staying here.

Jennie can't get Jasper Hammel's words out of her mind—nor can she shake the memory of that floorboard creaking above when she and Sandy were checking in earlier.

If there's no one else here at the inn, then it must have been Liza lurking on the floor above. But why?

Jennie isn't crazy about the sleek, snobby blond. But she certainly doesn't seem like . . .

Well, like she's up to something.

And ever since she's arrived at the inn, Jennie's been feeling uneasy. As though things aren't what they seem. As though something odd is going on.

If Liza wasn't the one who was eavesdropping at the top of the stairs, then Jasper Hammel is lying about there not being anyone else at the inn.

That wouldn't be hard to believe. The man seems distinctly nervous. It could just be his personality type, but Jennie can't help wondering whether there's more to it than that.

On the other hand, why would there be something sinister going on at a quaint island inn?

You must be imagining things Jennie tells herself again. And it wouldn't be the first time she's done that since that horrible day three years ago.

Sometimes, she would be standing in line at Stop and Shop with a cartful of groceries and manage to convince herself that the person behind her had a gun.

And once, when she had been driving on the Mass Pike, she'd been so certain that she was being followed that she'd had to pull off at the rest area, so shaky that it was over an hour before she could calm down enough to keep driving.

Lately, those episodes were fewer and farther between. But she knows she still isn't entirely okay—that sometimes, her mind plays tricks on her, sending her into near-panic over imaginary threats.

And that's all it is this time, Jennie assures herself as she settles into a Victorian rosewood parlor chair and looks around.

This is a cozy room, cast in a warm glow from a fringe-shaded Victorian floor lamp and the small blaze that crackles in the hearth. The lace curtains and floral-patterned wallpaper are similar to the decor in Jennie's room upstairs; and the parlor, too, is filled with antiques.

Jennie's skilled eye notes that all of the

furniture and bric-a-brac appear to be authentic period pieces—and expensive. She bought a nineteenth century coatrack like the one in the corner at an auction in Marblehead just last week and paid a fortune for it.

She glances at Liza, who is perched on the edge of the matching parlor chair on the other side of the fireplace. The woman runs a manicured hand over her smooth blond hair, looking bored.

Sandy flops her heavy body onto the sofa beneath the only window. "Hey, did you notice there's no TV?" she asks, looking around. "There's not one in my room, either. Do you guys have them in yours?"

Liza ignores her, concentrating instead on adjusting the belt buckle on her trim black slacks.

Feeling sorry for Sandy, who's obviously trying hard to make conversation, Jennie says, "A lot of inns don't have television sets in the rooms, and some don't have them in the public areas, either."

"Why not?"

Jennie shrugs. "Probably to maintain authenticity, in this case. After all, television didn't exist a hundred and twenty years ago, and that's probably when this place was built."

"Oh, yeah, that's right—you're an antique dealer, aren't you?" Sandy asks. "You must love this place. Everything looks really old."

"It is." Jennie runs her fingertips over the curved arm of her chair, noting the worn spot in the nubby raspberry-colored fabric.

"My room looks like it popped out of a Laura Ashley catalogue," Sandy tells her. "I love it. But I don't think my brothers would be crazy about it. I guess not all the rooms are so frilly."

"Probably not," Jennie agrees, though her room has lilac-sprigged wallpaper and a lace-covered canopy bed.

Liza, who hadn't even appeared to be listening, comments, "I don't know about that. My room looks like it was decorated for a ten-year-old girl. The wallpaper's covered in pink roses, and the bedspread has eyelet trim. Definitely not up my alley."

"Well, I think my room's beautiful," Sandy says, almost defiantly. "How about you, Laura?"

Jennie nods.

"I'll bet you have all kinds of antiques in

your house in Boston, too," Sandy says. "What kind of place do you live in?"

"It's an apartment, actually." Jennie shifts on her chair.

"Do you live alone?"

"No." Then, because she knows Sandy is waiting for her to elaborate, she adds, "I live with my sister."

"What does she do?"

"She works at the Gap. Liza," Jennie said, turning away from Sandy in an effort to change the subject, "what part of New York do you live in?"

"Manhattan. The Upper East Side."

Jennie nods, because there isn't much to say to that. Suddenly, she wants nothing more than to be up in her room, alone, where no one is prying into her personal life and where she doesn't have to make forced conversation with strangers.

Or, better yet, she wishes she were back in her familiar town house in Boston, even with Laura blasting Pearl Jam from the stereo and spilling something or other on the carpet or upholstery. And it's a Friday night, so right about now, Keegan would probably be on his way over with a pizza. . . .

No, she corrects mentally. *He wouldn't be. Not anymore.*

It's so hard to believe she'll never spend another night with Keegan—cuddled on the couch under the antique wedding-ring quilt she'd bought at her first auction, watching a video and eating pizza and wearing matching thick gray cotton socks with red-banded tops, the kind that are toasty warm but tend to unravel in the laundry, leaving red threads all over everything.

Jennie thinks about how Keegan always likes to have his feet sticking out of the bottom of the quilt—he can't sleep with them covered, either. He has huge feet, and so does she—he always teased her that when they had kids, they would have to order special custom-made giant baby shoes.

When they had kids—not *if.*

Keegan was always so certain of their relationship, right from the start. But then, he's like that about almost everything—casually confident, breezing through life with an easygoing, happy-go-lucky assurance that things will go his way.

Jennie pictures the stark pain that took over his handsome features when she told him it was over. Pain, and surprise, as though he couldn't believe she would do this to him—that she would abandon him.

She feels a stab of sorrow in the vicinity of her heart—a distinct physical sensation that nearly takes her breath away.

This must be what people mean when they talk about heartache, she realizes.

"Laura?" Sandy says loudly.

Jennie blinks. "Yeah?"

"You're on another planet, aren't you? I was talking to you and you were looking right through me."

"Oh, I, uh—I'm sorry." Jennie is about to stand up and excuse herself when Jasper Hammel suddenly shows up carrying a cherrywood tray. He has a way of doing that—appearing with no warning.

"All right, ladies, here we are. Coffee and a rich dessert—just the thing for a blustery February night."

"I think I'll pass," Liza says, rising. "I'm pretty exhausted."

But her sharp green eyes don't look sleepy. She seems edgy—as edgy as Jennie feels.

"Oh, come on, now. . . . You have to taste

my torte," Jasper informs Liza firmly, putting a porcelain pedestal mug into her hand and motioning for her to sit down again.

She does; and once again, her eyes collide with Jennie's. Her expression is wary. Jennie instinctively realizes that Liza, too, is uneasy about this place and this man.

Sandy, on the other hand, seems oblivious. She happily accepts a mug and a plate and tells Jasper that the torte looks "yummy."

Liza catches Jennie's gaze again when Sandy says it, and this time, she rolls her eyes.

Jennie quickly looks away. Sandy might be a little on the immature side, but she's a nice person.

Liza, on the other hand, is something of a bitch, and Jennie isn't particularly eager to align herself with her.

Again, she wishes she were back at home in Boston. She would give anything to have Keegan's arms around her right now.

Because Keegan has always made her feel safe.

And right now, for some reason she can't

pinpoint, even as she sits in this quaint, quiet parlor, she feels vaguely threatened.

By what, she doesn't know.

But it's *real;* something dark and terrible—as dark and terrible as the nightmare that changed her life forever on that bloody day three years ago.

Two floors above the parlor, on the top floor of the inn, in an ancient, upholstered rocking chair, he sits and rocks and waits.

At one time, the attic room must have been servants' quarters for the inn's summer help. A deep, stained white porcelain sink and an ancient gas stove are tucked into an alcove. In another corner, behind a warped wooden door, there's a tiny bathroom with a steep, sloping ceiling. There's no shower, only a chipped clawfoot bathtub. And the toilet no longer flushes on its own; he has to lift the tank, reach into the clammy water, and pull the chain.

He thinks of the enormous master bedroom suite back at his estate on Long Island's north shore. It has a king-sized bed, a fireplace, and an adjoining Jacuzzi in a glass solarium with a sweeping view of the sound. It also has his-and-hers dressing rooms, each with its own private attached bathroom.

His dressing room and bathroom are cluttered with his belongings.

The other one—the one he'd intended for his bride—is empty.

It always has been.

Sighing, he flips to the first page of the photo album in his lap. It's a special album, one that only has room for a single eight-by-ten picture on each page.

A wedding album, actually—bound in white leather, its cover stamped in gold with the words, "Our Wedding Memories."

This first page belongs to Sandy. There's an empty slot, waiting for the photograph he'll place there.

He has already labeled the oval opening with an ivory place card that has a raised rectangular border, the kind of card you find on the tables at a wedding reception.

On it, he has meticulously lettered her name in calligraphy, using a special pen.

He remembers the day he went to the art supply store to buy that pen.

The clerk, a pretty blond in her teens, had smiled pleasantly at him and said, "Will that be all, sir? You don't need a bottle of ink to go with it?"

He'd smiled back and said, "No, thank you. I have plenty of ink at home."

It was a lie, of course.

He wasn't planning on using ink at all.

Instead, he'd used his own blood.

It's really quite lovely, he decides, studying the lettering on the card below the empty photo slot. Over the past few months, the blood has faded to a soft, brownish-maroon color that complements the rich ivory surface of the place card. Very elegant.

But this card isn't permanent, of course.

He'll replace it, very soon, with an exact replica.

Except that this time, the blood he'll use to letter Sandy Cavelli's name will be her own.

"Sandy?" Jasper Hammel asks. "Would you like another slice of the torte?"

"I really shouldn't," she says. After all, both Liza and Laura refused, and neither of them has even finished their first servings.

But she can't help glancing at the rich

chocolate concoction that's still left on the doily-covered plate Jasper is offering.

"Oh, go ahead," the man says, stepping closer to her and practically holding the torte under her nose. "Just a sliver?"

"All right," she relents, because she's never been able to resist anything chocolate.

I'll do fifty sit-ups before bed tonight, she promises herself as she holds up her dish to let Jasper serve her.

He spoons on the fresh raspberries and a generous dollop of whipped cream.

A hundred sit-ups, Sandy amends, then stifles a yawn behind her hand. *If I can stay awake long enough.*

Suddenly, she can't wait to crawl into bed. Must be all this fresh sea air.

As Jasper discreetly heads back toward the kitchen with the torte, Sandy picks up her fork again and tries to return her attention to the conversation she and Laura had been having. Actually, she had been doing most of the talking, but she suddenly can't remember what about.

Oh, yes. She had been telling Laura about her brothers.

"Anyway," she says, cutting off a piece of

the torte and raising it to her lips, "Danny is my youngest brother. He's the only one who's not in the plumbing and heating business with my dad. He's a gym teacher at St. Agnes High."

Laura nods.

Sandy swallows the bite of torte, then yawns again. "Oh, gosh, excuse me," she says. "I'm really tired."

"So am I." Liza stands and places her mug and the delicate plate containing her half-eaten cake on a polished table beside her chair. "I'm going up to bed. Good night."

"Night," Laura murmurs.

"Good night. See you tomorrow," Sandy calls after Liza, who doesn't even turn around.

"She's not very nice, is she?" Sandy whispers to Laura when she's sure Liza is out of earshot.

Laura shrugs and looks uncomfortable.

"I mean, it's not that I don't like her," Sandy lies. "It's just that she doesn't seem very friendly. But then, maybe she's just shy," she adds hastily. After all, it isn't right to talk about someone behind her back—especially when the person you're talking about, and the person you're talking to, are both virtual strangers.

"Maybe she is shy," Laura agrees. She stretches and glances at the watch on her wrist. "I should get to bed, too. It's getting late."

"How late is it?"

"Almost ten-thirty."

"Uh-oh." Sandy remembers something.

"What's the matter?"

"I forgot to call my parents. They would have gotten home at a quarter to ten—they work bingo at the church hall every Friday night—and I promised I'd call and let them know I'd arrived safely. Jasper?" she calls, hearing the man's footsteps approaching from the kitchen again.

"Yes?" He appears in the doorway.

"Is there a telephone I can use?" When he seems to hesitate, she adds, "I'll call collect."

"Of course," he says. "There's a phone in the hall, behind the check-in desk."

Sandy gulps down the rest of her dessert in a single bite and stands up, brushing the crumbs off her lap. "Thanks. I'll just—"

"I'll show you where it is," Jasper says, moving toward the hall. "Right this way."

Both Sandy and Laura follow him out of the parlor.

In the front hall, Laura yawns and says, "I'm going up to bed. Good night."

"Good night," Sandy and Jasper answer in unison.

Sandy makes a move toward the desk and the telephone, but suddenly Jasper is standing over it, lifting the receiver and asking her what the number is.

"I can dial it," she says. "I'll call collect."

"That's fine." He makes no move to hand her the phone or step aside so that she can walk behind the desk.

Sandy shrugs and recites her parents' telephone number, wondering if it's her imagination or if Jasper suddenly seems even more nervous than usual.

He must think I'm not really going to call collect, she decides. Maybe other guests at the inn have used the phone and rung up major long distance phone bills.

"All set, here you are." Jasper hands the receiver to Sandy.

As she speaks to the operator, he steps away, but remains behind the desk, straightening an already neatly stacked pile of papers.

He hovers there the entire minute or so that she talks to her mother, making her feel self-conscious. Actually, it seems somewhat rude, the way the man doesn't allow her to have a private conversation.

Maybe he just doesn't know any better.

"Make sure that you're careful, Sandy," her mother says, before they hang up.

"Careful of what?"

"Everything. After all, you never know."

Sandy sighs. "I'm always careful, Ma. You worry too much," she adds, watching Jasper Hammel carefully flick a nonexistent speck of dust off the polished surface of the desk.

He doesn't venture out of the attic room until well after midnight, when the house is silent.

Outside, the wind has picked up, blowing in off the water to rattle the windows. The rain has turned to sleet, and he wonders, as he creeps down the stairs, whether the storm will become a full-blown nor'easter.

That would be perfect.

Tide Island is practically deserted at this time of year anyway, but nasty weather would virtually guarantee that no one will disturb him as he carries out his plans.

He stops at the bottom of the stairs. Behind this first door, he knows, is Laura Towne. She will have locked herself in from the other side, no doubt feeling secure.

He licks his lips.

All he has to do is use his master key to slip into the room.

He pictures her the way he last saw her and wonders whether time has altered her beauty.

Is she asleep now, on the other side of this wall?

Of course she is, he reminds himself. Thanks to the sedative she'd unknowingly ingested, masked by the strong flavors of chocolate and raspberries.

He wants desperately to open the door and see her. It's been so very long, and there have been many nights when he has ached for her. The knowledge that she's here, that she's once again under his roof, fills him with tantalizing urges.

But this time, he's the one in control.

Of himself.

And, though she doesn't know it, in control of Laura.

And the others, as well.

Liza Danning.

Sandy Cavelli.

He sighs. Then he reaches into his pocket, removing a single key. Carefully, he slips it into the top lock, the one that only works from the outside.

He turns it and listens for the click that means Laura Towne is locked into the beautiful room with the lilac-sprigged wallpaper that exactly matches the shade of her eyes.

I'll be back, he promises her silently. *But not tonight.*

The next stop along the hallway is Liza Danning's room, where he swiftly but stealthily locks her door, too, from the outside, then moves on.

Anticipation is building within him now.

In front of the last door, he again brandishes the key. But instead of putting it into the top lock, he inserts it into the bottom one—the one that works from both sides.

And instead of locking Sandy Cavelli into her room, he ever so quietly turns the key, opens the door, and slips over the threshold.

He pauses just inside the shadowy room

until he hears the slow, rhythmic sound of her breathing.

Closing the door quietly behind him, he tucks the key back into his pocket and moves cautiously across the wooden floor until he's standing over the bed.

She's lying on her side, her brown hair tousled on the white linen pillowcase. Her mouth is slightly open, and he fights the urge to run a gentle finger over those full lips. She should be sound asleep, thanks to the torte, but he doesn't want to take any chances.

So he simply looks at her.

And as he looks, his fingers slip down his belly to the top button of his trousers. He unfastens it, then slowly begins to edge the zipper down.

Her face, he notes, is much rounder than it used to be. And though she's wearing a long-sleeved flannel nightgown, he can tell that the arm that's thrown over her head is chubby.

It doesn't matter to him.

Struggling to remain in control, he gingerly extends his left hand and tentatively pulls the bedspread and sheet away from Sandy's body. He lowers them to her waist, then pauses to make sure she isn't stirring. When he's satisfied that she's still deeply asleep, he continues pulling the bedding down until her legs, too, are exposed.

The nightgown is bunched around her hips, revealing white thighs that are full and dimpled. Holding his breath, he moves his left hand to grasp the flannel hem and raise it, past her high-waisted white cotton underwear and the soft rolls of her belly to her heavy, bare breasts that sag almost to her navel.

Still, she doesn't move, and he desperately longs to touch her.

But he can't.

Not yet.

Not tonight.

His left hand curls into a tight fist and he forces it to fall at his side.

The fingers of his right hand probe past his open fly and fumble in the layers of his Brooks Brothers boxer shorts until they close over his own hot, hard flesh.

Staring at Sandy Cavelli's near-naked body in the bed, he strokes himself, lightly at first so that his skin tingles all over.

His movements become more rapid,

more urgent as he nears release, and he bites his lower lip to keep from moaning.

He closes his eyes.

Images flash in his mind.

Past, present, future . . .

Sandy as she had looked at thirteen, when he had known her—all sweet and awkward and willing to please . . .

Sandy as she is now, sleeping before him, blissfully unaware of his presence . . .

And Sandy as she will be tomorrow—her big brown eyes wide with terror, her full lips quivering as she begs him to let her go, her plump body clad in the pure white wedding dress he's had custom-made for her . . .

The dress that, after tomorrow, will be stained with her blood.

Three

Overcome by stark, black terror, Jennie runs for her life.

Someone is chasing her through the Colonial Mall in Boston—someone she can't see or hear, yet she knows he's there, closing in behind her. The wide corridors are eerily dark and deserted, silent except for the echo of her pounding footsteps and desperate panting.

She's looking for someplace to hide, for an open shop where she can duck behind the clothing racks or underneath the cashier's counter. But every store she passes is closed, the security gates lowered and padlocked.

Panicked, Jennie pushes on, dogged by the knowledge that her time is running out.

He's going to get me, she tells herself frantically. *There's no escape.*

Suddenly, just as she feels him looming behind her, just as clammy fingers grab her throat, the air is pierced by a shrill ringing sound.

Jennie sits straight up in bed, gasping and looking around. She instinctively reaches for her travel alarm clock on the nightstand and pushes the button on top to still the jangling bell.

Where am I?

She blinks and gazes from the lilac-sprigged wallpaper to the red-brick fireplace to the lace-curtained window that reveals only rain-splattered glass and a patch of gray sky.

Tide Island. The inn.

She takes a deep breath and releases it, then runs a hand through her tangled hair. Groggily, she struggles to clear the fog in her brain and take hold of her senses.

I'm safe. It was only a dream.

Not a dream, she amends—*a nightmare.*

And this isn't the first time she's had it. For three years, the same familiar, terrible images have haunted her sleep.

Never, in the past, has her invisible predator caught her.

This time, though, is different. This time, she felt his evil touch.

She shivers at the memory of his cold

skin against hers, even as she reminds herself that it wasn't real.

He can't get you. He's dead.

Always before, that awareness has com-
forted her.

This time, even though she knows it was
just a nightmare and she knows the person
who triggered it can no longer harm her,
Jennie finds herself feeling distinctly uneasy . . .

And uncertain.

This time, she can't help but wonder
about the person who was chasing her
through the Colonial Mall.

You know who it was. It's always him.

Or is it?

In her whole life, with all its hardship, only
one person has ever put her in mortal danger. Only one person, in a few chilling, mercifully fleeting moments, ever held the
power to shatter her world—and did.

But he's gone. She saw him take his own
life in a blast from the same gun that had
demolished everything Jennie held dear.
She saw his crumpled, lifeless body with
her own eyes.

So why can't Jennie shake the feeling
that she's suddenly in danger again? And

that this time, the threat is more ominous, more deadly, than before?

Shuddering, Jennie abruptly throws the covers back and swings her bare feet to the cold wooden floor. As she stands, she finds herself swaying unsteadily, almost sinking back down to the mattress.

What's with you? she asks herself, frowning and clinging to the headboard for support. She feels woozy and a little queasy, almost as though she's got a hangover. But of course, that's impossible. She only had that one glass of wine last night.

Maybe it was the rich chocolate dessert. Jennie isn't usually much of a sweet-eater. It's Laura who loves stuff like that. And Keegan.

Unbidden, an image enters her brain— Keegan sitting at the kitchen table in her apartment, eating gooey brownies she's just taken out of the oven. She can hear his voice telling her how delicious they are, can taste the warm chocolate on his lips as he kisses her. . . .

She cringes and shuts out the memory.

She grabs her robe from the bedpost and wraps it around herself, then crosses on slightly wobbly legs to the window.

Last night when she checked in, it was too dark to see the view.

This morning, although the weather is gloomy, she can make out the sloping terrain below—the rocks and sand and long brown grass that cover the landscape, and beyond that, the sea. The water, foaming with whitecaps, is the same murky color as the sky so that there's no distinguishing line at the horizon.

Suddenly, Jennie longs to be down there on the narrow strip of beach, with the roar of the water and wind in her ears and cold salt air filling her lungs.

That's what I need. A walk by the ocean would wake me up and maybe even snap me out of this weird, paranoid mood.

She grabs the small blue case that contains her toiletry items and walks across the room, hoping that no one is already using the shared bathroom across the hall. She flips the latch that unlocks the door, then turns the knob and pulls.

Nothing happens.

Overtaken by an intense, sudden stab of claustrophobia, Jennie tugs the door again. This time, it budges. Relieved, she quickly steps out into the empty hallway.

It probably just sticks in damp weather, she tells herself. That happens a lot in old houses like this.

You really need to calm down, Jen. . . . You're completely on edge and there's absolutely no reason. Relax.

A half hour later, freshly showered, her hair still damp and caught back in a black headband, Jennie is feeling much better, though not totally relaxed.

For some reason, she can't seem to let go of a nagging sense that something isn't quite right.

A walk on the beach will probably help clear her mind, though.

She pulls on her heavy down jacket as she walks down the stairs. She's dressed for the damp, chilly New England morning: her oldest, softest, most faded jeans; rubber L.L. Bean boots; a thick navy cable knit sweater.

"Good morning, Laura," a voice says as she rounds the landing.

Startled, Jennie glances down to see Jasper Hammel standing in the front hall. He's holding a feather duster, which looks out of sync with his clothing: an expensive-looking black turtleneck and pleated dark-gray corduroy slacks.

"Oh . . . good morning." Jennie walks down the last few steps, fumbling with the zipper on her jacket.

"There's a continental breakfast set up on the sideboard in the dining room," Jasper informs her, flicking the duster over the carved newel post at the bottom of the stairs. "Nothing elaborate . . . just coffee and danishes. Feel free to help yourself."

"Um, no thank you." Jennie hesitates. "I was just going to go for a walk on the beach."

"I'm afraid it's not a very nice day for that," he says, glancing toward the window. "According to this morning's radio forecast, there might be a storm on the way. Quite a nasty one, for that matter . . . but don't be alarmed," he adds quickly, catching sight of her expression. "The weather on Tide Island is always unpredictable. For all we know, the nor'easter will pass us by and blow right out to sea."

"I hope so," Jennie murmurs, tugging the zipper on her jacket up to her chin.

"Just the same, I wouldn't advise you to wander too far, Laura. The island may seem small and easy to maneuver, but there are some remote patches, and you wouldn't want to get lost."

"I won't," Jennie assures him, and heads for the door.

As she steps out into the windy, rainy morning, she tries to ignore the little voice inside her head . . .

The one that's warning her to leave the island—before the storm rolls in and strands her here.

Before it's too late, the voice adds.

And though she tries not to acknowledge it, telling herself it's just paranoia again, Jennie can't help wondering . . .

Too late for what?

"Damn, damn, damn."

Liza jerks the black silk stocking back down her leg and tosses it across the room, scowling.

How can she have been careless enough to give herself a run when she only brought one pair with her?

Just to be sure, she gets up and walks over to the bureau drawer where she put her clothes when she unpacked last night.

She digs through the neatly folded stacks carelessly. Nothing but two pairs of black knee-highs and one pair of tan pantyhose.

Now what's she going to do?

Feeling frazzled, she stands in the middle of the room and contemplates the situation.

It's no wonder she ran her stocking, after the way things have been going this morning.

She's been feeling out of sorts ever since she forced herself to get out of bed an hour ago. Her head is pounding and she can't seem to wake up. She got out of the shower and was drying off when she remembered that she'd forgotten to shampoo her hair, which meant she had to get back in and wait again for the ancient plumbing to groan into action. And she'd dropped her favorite compact on the floor of her room, cracking the mirror and breaking the pressed powder into crumbly chunks.

I hope this isn't an omen for how my meeting with D.M. Yates is going to go.

Liza glances at her reflection in the full-length mirror on the back of the door. She smooths the soft cashmere fabric of her well-cut black suit, with its three gold buttons on the jacket and the skirt that's just long enough to be professional, but short enough to show off her long, firm legs.

Legs that, right now, are mismatched—one clad in the un-run black stocking she'd put on first, the other bare and winter-white.

Rolling her eyes, Liza unhooks the good stocking from the garter hooks and unrolls it, then tosses it onto the still-rumpled bed.

She takes off her suit, careful not to muss her hair. It took her fifteen minutes longer than usual to get it into a perfect French twist at the back of her head. The first few tries, it either came out too severe or too tumble-down sexy.

Now her hair is just right—swept back to reveal her high cheekbones and expertly made-up eyes, with a few soft tendrils escaping around her ears.

This is the same suit and same hairstyle that she'd worn last fall when she'd met Senator Albert Norwood that first time for dinner at the Japanese restaurant in the Waldorf-Astoria. She remembers how he'd commented, over sushi, about how silky and "touchable" her hair looked and how his fat fingers had slowly climbed up her silk-covered leg beneath the table and how shocked he'd looked when he'd discovered that beneath her proper suit she was wearing a garter belt . . . and nothing else.

She has imagined treating D.M. Yates to a similar experience, and it simply won't work if she has to wear pantyhose.

Sighing, Liza buttons a plain black cardigan over her champagne-colored Christian Dior lace chemise and yanks on a pair of slim-fitting black leggings. She pulls on her warmest wool socks and flat black lace-up boots that probably aren't practical for the miserable weather outside, but who cares?

If the fine Italian leather gets ruined, she can always have Albie buy her another pair.

Liza grabs her down-filled Nautica ski jacket, which she hasn't worn since her Christmas trip to Aspen, and leaves her room.

Hopefully, D.M. Yates won't call her until she gets back. But just in case, she'll let that scrawny fruitcake Jasper Hammel know where she is.

Conveniently, he's right at the bottom of the stairs when she gets to the first floor. He looks up from watering the large parlor palm with a bright-yellow enamel watering can that looks like something out of a nursery rhyme.

"Good morning, Liza," he chirps.

"Morning." She finds herself irritated at his cheery tone and broad smile beneath that squirrely mustache of his. "If Mr. Yates calls—"

"Mr. Yates *already* called you . . . bright and early."

She blinks. "He *what*?"

"He called you, bright—"

"Why didn't you let me know he was on the phone?"

"No need," he says simply, reaching up to tip the long-necked spout into a hanging pot of ivy beside the front door.

"What do you mean, 'no need'?" Liza asks evenly, glaring at him.

"He merely called to tell you that he's been detained by unexpected business and won't be able to meet with you until tomorrow."

"*Tomorrow?*" Liza stares at Jasper Hammel in disbelief. "He's putting me off until tomorrow . . . and you didn't even have the decency to let me speak with the man?"

Jasper shrugs and says, in his clipped, formal manner, "I didn't want to wake you at such an early hour after your long trip on the ferry last night. But," he adds quickly, "apparently, I made the wrong decision. I'm sorry I didn't alert you to the call."

"So am I," Liza snaps.

Suddenly, she longs for Manhattan, where people are sharp and mind their own business, not taking it upon themselves to make important decisions for total strangers.

Liza strides toward the door.

"There's a continental breakfast set up in the dining room," Jasper tells her, stepping out of her way and looking unruffled by the black look she sends him.

"All I need," she says in a clipped tone, "is directions to a store that can sell me a pair of good stockings."

"I'm fairly certain that Hartigan's General Store on the boardwalk carries pantyhose."

"Not pantyhose. Stockings."

Jasper eyes her levelly. "I'm afraid you'd probably need a women's clothing store for that. And they're all closed off-season."

"It figures."

Liza opens the front door, steps out into the raw February morning, and lets the door bang shut behind her. Then she starts trudging down the steep driveway toward the deserted road, cursing Jasper Hammel,

D.M. Yates, and this whole stupid godforsaken island.

The first thing Sandy sees when she arrives on the first floor of the inn is Jasper Hammel. The little man is polishing a carved wooden table near the front door, a thick yellow rag in one hand and a can of Pledge in the other.

The second thing Sandy sees is the enormous vase of red roses sitting on the front desk by the telephone she used last night.

"Good morning, Sandy," Jasper says with a smile. "Did you sleep well?"

"Like a rock, actually." She yawns. "I thought maybe the sound of the ocean would keep me awake since I'm not used to it, but I was out cold. What beautiful flowers on the desk, there."

"I'm glad you like them, because they're yours."

Sandy gasps. "You don't have to . . ."

"I'm not. They were delivered here for you from the Island Breeze Florist Shop this morning."

"I can't believe it." Sandy hurries over and plucks the small rectangular card off the tall plastic fork that's nestled among the buds. She knows, even before she opens the envelope, who sent the flowers.

Sure enough . . .

Sandra,
I'm sorry I didn't make it in last night. I stayed on the mainland, but will be there tonight. Dinner at eight? We'll dine at my home. I'll pick you up at the inn.

Yours,
Ethan

She closes her eyes and leans over the vase, breathing the fresh, sweet floral scent deeply into her lungs.

"Mmmm," she murmurs, opening her eyes and glancing at Jasper. "I love roses."

"And they're certainly appropriate—aren't they?—for a guest at this inn . . . the Bramble Rose."

"You know, I hadn't even thought of that." Sandy does a quick count and realizes that there are two dozen buds in the vase. This must have cost Ethan Thoreau a fortune.

But then, he's rich. He probably sends women flowers all the time.

Sandy has never received flowers in her life, unless you counted the corsage from her prom date, Frankie DeRusso, her senior year, and the daisies her brother Danny picked and brought her when she had her tonsils out as a kid.

What would it be like to date—no, to *marry*—a man who would send roses for every occasion, and sometimes, maybe, for no occasion at all?

Joe had never even remembered to send her a card on Valentine's Day or her birthday, Sandy thinks wistfully. And when they got engaged, he used a ring he'd bought at a pawn shop, one that had someone else's initials engraved in the band. "You can have that buffed off," he'd told her.

She'd never bothered, knowing, even as she first slipped that ring over the fourth finger of her left hand, that she wasn't going to marry him. She'd stayed engaged to him for three months, long enough to work up her nerve to tell him that she didn't want to get married.

Who would have guessed that he would have reacted the way he had? Sobbing hysterically—a man, crying!—begging her not to leave him, telling her that she was the only woman he'd ever loved. He hadn't taken no for an answer. Even now, after almost a year, he still drove by her house every now and then, and he always called Sandy when he drank, incoherently asking for another chance. . . .

"Are you hungry?" Jasper Hammel is asking her, snapping her out of her reverie.

"Starving . . . as usual," she admits ruefully.

"There's coffee and danish in the dining room, on the sideboard. Please help yourself."

"Thank you." Sandy glances toward her roses again.

"You can leave those here until after breakfast, if you'd like," Jasper tells her. "I'll keep an eye on them."

"Oh . . . okay. Thanks."

Hating to turn her back on the beautiful blooms even for a short time, Sandy heads toward the dining room.

Then she pauses and thinks of something. "Jasper?" she asks over her shoulder.

"Yes?"

"Do you know where Ethan Thoreau's house is? I thought I might go for a walk, and . . . you know." She feels her cheeks growing warm, wondering what he thinks of a woman who would pull a junior high stunt like checking out someone's house.

"You know, I haven't been here on the island very long," he tells her, not looking fazed by her question. "I don't really know where Mr. Thoreau lives . . . somewhere on the other side of the island, I would imagine. That's where all the wealthier people have their private homes."

"Okay. Thanks."

Still feeling embarrassed, Sandy walks into the dining room.

She seats herself at the long, empty table with a cup of coffee and a plate containing two cheese danishes, wondering where Laura and Liza are. Maybe one of them will want to do something this afternoon.

On the other hand, Sandy doubts that. Liza doesn't seem to have any intention of being friendly, which is just as well, since Sandy knows she probably has nothing in common with the woman anyway.

And Laura, though she's a lot nicer and warmer, seems lost in her own little world.

Besides, neither of them is around, anyway.

It looks like Sandy's on her own.

As she shoves the last bite of the second danish into her mouth, she decides she might as well do some exploring since there's really nothing else to occupy her until tonight.

And she might as well start with the other side of the island.

Hartigan's General Store is a two-story wooden building in the center of the boardwalk, nestled in a row of other businesses, all of them boarded up for the winter. There's a huge orange "Open" sign hanging in the glass front door of the store.

Jennie sees it from the beach and heads toward it, hurrying across the wet sand. Though it's stopped raining for the moment, the icy wind is picking up again, and suddenly, she can't stop shivering. Hopefully, the store will have hot coffee, and maybe something she can gobble down for breakfast.

Jennie opens the door and finds herself wrestling with it as a sudden gust kicks up, struggling to keep it from blowing backward and slamming into the side of the building.

Finally, she pulls it closed, shutting out the roaring cold.

"Gettin' pretty nasty out there, isn't it?"

Jennie glances around and sees an elderly man standing behind a cash register to her right. He has a shock of thick white hair, a ruddy complexion, and eyes that twinkle from his handsome face.

"It's freezing out," Jennie tells him, stomping her numb feet on the mat in front of the door.

The store is surprisingly roomy, with several aisles of groceries near the back and what looks like a soda fountain and a few booths off to the side in an alcove. Jennie sees that only a handful of people are here, a few browsing for food and a few others seated in the alcove.

"We're in for a bad one, this time," the man says, gesturing toward an old-fashioned radio on the shelf behind him. Jennie can faintly hear the staticky sound of big band music coming from the speaker. "Been listening all morning, and the announcer keeps saying that it's looking like a full-blown nor'easter's on the way. Rain, cold, high winds—supposedly worse than what hit the Cape a few years ago on Halloween. We get these storms every once in awhile," the man tells her. "You're not from here, are ya?"

"Nope."

"Where you staying?"

"The Bramble Rose."

The man nods, then asks, in a friendly but somewhat nosy way, "Where you from?"

"I live in Boston," Jennie says, "so I know all about nor'easters, actually."

She knows enough to realize that she's not going anywhere for a few days—not if this storm is worse than the Halloween nor'easter. She and Laura had been visiting a friend of theirs out in Chatham that week, and Jennie remembered how the furious, foaming waves had attacked the coast and carried away houses and cars and trees.

"You're from Boston? What part?"

"Back Bay."

"Nice there, isn't it? I grew up in Quincy."

So did I, Jennie almost tells him, but she stops herself. No reason to get into a conversation with a stranger, nice and friendly as he seems.

She casts a glance at the soda fountain. "Do you serve coffee there?"

"Are you kidding? Of course. Go on over

and Shirley will fix you up. She's my wife, and anyone can tell you that she brews the best coffee on the island."

Probably the only coffee on the island, Jennie thought, heading toward the alcove. This place wasn't exactly hopping.

The beach had been deserted the whole time she'd spent walking—well over an hour. First she'd gone north, away from the inn, where the strip of sand gradually became wider and the landscape along the coast rougher and more desolate. A few houses dotted the shore here and there, but all of them were deserted.

It was hard to imagine what those places must be like in summer, when the windows and doors would be open and flowers would be blooming in windowboxes and people would be sitting around on decks.

It was hard to imagine the beach itself in another season, too—when children would be building sandcastles, teenagers listening to radios and gossiping, and people jogging and swimming and tossing frisbees.

Now, in winter, the shore was a gray, wild, lonely place—so like the coast in England. Jennie unexpectedly found herself with memories of the semester she'd spent there. With Harry.

Harry of the wide grin and twinkling eyes and surprisingly gentle touch . . .

She'd walked and thought about him until the beach gave way to a rocky cliff that loomed ahead, rising straight up and jutting out into the water. On top of the cliff was an enormous, sprawling house with turrets and peaks and porches, looking like something out of a gothic novel.

With a shiver—mostly cold, but partly a response to the creepy-looking house— Jennie had turned away and headed back toward the inn. She'd planned on going in, but when she reached it, she realized she wasn't ready. She wanted to be alone awhile longer, with the ocean and her memories of Harry.

"Hi, sweetie. What can I get you?" asks the angular, gray-haired woman behind the counter in the alcove.

"Just a cup of coffee, please—with milk, instead of cream, if you have it," Jennie tells her, then spots a glass bakery case. "And a croissant, too," she adds, and suddenly her mouth is watering and her stomach feels completely empty.

"Coming right up, sweetie. You can go ahead and have a seat."

Jennie nods and turns toward the booths. Out of five, only two are occupied. In one, an artsy-looking couple—he with long dreadlocks, she with a crew cut and an earring in her nose—sits having an animated conversation.

In the other booth, Jennie sees, is a blond woman who looks an awful lot like . . .

"Hello—Laura, isn't it?"

Reluctantly, Jennie nods and approaches the booth where Liza Danning is waving to her. She doesn't look particularly friendly, but her tone is civil enough.

"Mind if I join you?" Jennie asks, because it would be awkward not to.

"No, go ahead." Liza gestures at the empty seat across from her, and Jennie can't tell whether or not she's pleased to have company. Her expression is cool and her manner detached.

Maybe that's just her way, Jennie thinks. It's what Gran would have said. She always wanted to give people the benefit of the doubt, and she'd taught her granddaughters to do the same.

Laura is so like Gran—optimistic and trusting, even with strangers. Unlike Jennie.

But I'm trying, Jennie silently tells her grandmother and her sister. *See?*

She puts on a smile and asks Liza Danning how she is.

"Lousy," the woman says, taking a sip of her black coffee, then shaking her head. "I've had the worst day already, and it's barely even started."

"What's wrong?" Jennie knows she'll be sorry she asked, but what else can she do?

"I ran my only pair of stockings when I was getting dressed, for starters. I have an important business meeting here and now I don't know what I'm going to wear."

"Doesn't this store sell pantyhose?" Jennie looks over her shoulder, thinking that even though the place is small, its crowded shelves look like they must hold a pretty good variety of items.

"Sure, they sell *pantyhose,* but I need silk stockings," Liza says, a pout curling her pink lips.

Jennie frowns. She doesn't know anyone who wears real silk stockings, the kind you attach to a garter belt—although Laura did buy some when she was shopping for honeymoon lingerie a few years back. She'd gleefully reported that Brian had actually ripped them off of her on their wedding night. Back then, Jennie had thought that sounded passionate. But that was before Brian had shown his true colors.

"Well, what are you going to do?" Jennie asks Liza.

"I have no idea. Probably buy pantyhose. But of course, this rinky-dink place doesn't have any black ones."

She says it loudly, and Jennie realizes it's so that Shirley, the waitress, will hear. She's walking toward them with Jennie's coffee and croissant, and her expression doesn't look nearly as friendly as it did before. Obviously, Liza has already registered a complaint or two.

"Here you go," Shirley says brusquely, plunking Jennie's order down in front of her and walking away.

Great, Jennie thinks. *I'm making enemies by association.*

Hanging around with Liza obviously isn't a good idea, especially on such a small island. Jennie decides to steer clear of the blonde after this.

"And on top of this whole wardrobe fiasco," Liza goes on, as though there has been no interruption, "that twit at the inn, Jasper Hammel, didn't call me to the phone when the person I'm meeting tried to get in touch with me."

Jennie murmurs, "That's too bad," and stirs her coffee.

"Oh, well," Liza says with a sigh. "Too late to do anything about it now. So how's your day? Better, I hope."

"So far, it's fine." Jennie marvels at the way Liza can seem like a self-absorbed bitch one moment and turn on the charm the next. Maybe she's an actress in her spare time.

"You didn't opt to have breakfast at the inn either, I see," Liza comments, motioning at Jennie's coffee and croissant.

"Uh, no, I—"

"Couldn't wait to get out of there?" Liza supplies. "It's creepy, don't you think?"

Jennie isn't sure what to say. "I guess it is a little. . . . I don't know. . . ."

"Creepy. Like I said. Not my kind of place at all," Liza tells her. "But business is business, and it's not like I *chose* to come here."

Jennie recalls what Liza had told Sandy

last night. "You said you were in publishing?"

Liza nods. "I'm an editor."

"Must be exciting."

"It is. What do you do?"

Jennie's pretty sure the woman was around when Sandy was asking about her job last night, but obviously Liza hadn't cared enough to remember. She probably doesn't care now, either, but Jennie tells her, "I'm an antique dealer."

"Really? I'm not crazy about antiques."

"Oh . . ." Jennie has no idea what to say to that.

"I like modern things. Although someone once gave me an exquisite antique gold locket that I really loved."

"That's nice."

"Yeah, it was. I sold it for a lot of money."

Again, Jennie's at a loss for words, so she just repeats, "That's nice."

Liza decides she likes Laura Towne. She's nice to talk to, and she doesn't ask too many questions—not like that chubby chatterbox back at the inn. Personally, she herself isn't much of a conversationalist when it comes to talking to strangers, but she finds herself curious about the woman sitting across from her. There's a haunted look in her lilac eyes that's been there since last night, and Liza wonders what she's hiding.

She takes another sip of her coffee, which by this time has grown cold. She looks around, considering asking that old lady behind the counter for a refill. But then again, it's not even that good. Liza usually drinks only gourmet latte from Starbucks.

She sets down her cup and looks at Laura. "Where are you from?" she asks directly.

Laura looks a little taken aback, but says, "Boston."

Figures. She looks like the preppy New England type. "Perfect place for an antique dealer." Liza wrinkles her nose. "After all, Boston's full of old buildings and churches and museums and that sort of thing, right?"

"Right. Just like New York."

Liza grins. She knows Laura's making a point, and she decides she respects her. In Liza's opinion, there's nothing worse than someone who shrinks from her sharp tongue.

"Yeah, I guess New York's just as historic as Boston," she concedes. "And some of those older landmarks in Manhattan are actually halfway decent."

Laura raises an eyebrow.

"Although personally," Liza goes on, just to bust her chops, "if I had the choice of an apartment in the Dakota or in Trump Tower, I'd go for the Trump. You can't beat being right upstairs from Tiffany's."

"I don't know," Laura says, "I'd rather be in the Dakota, with Central Park across the street."

"You know New York?"

"Yeah." Laura looks down and stiffly stirs her coffee.

"How? Did you go to school in the city or something?"

There's a pause.

"I had a . . . friend who liked to spend time there," Laura says softly.

Liza watches her. Then she says, *"Had?"*

Laura looks up and meets her gaze. "Yeah. He died."

"Oh. Sorry."

"It's okay. It was awhile ago."

There's an awkward moment of silence, and Liza wants to ask the details, but somehow, she can't bring herself to do it. Instead, finally, she asks, "Do you have family in Boston?"

"Just my sister."

"Older or younger?"

Again, Laura hesitates, then says, "Actually, she's my twin."

"Interesting."

"Yeah."

"Is that your only family, then?"

"Uh huh." Laura bites her lip, then adds, "I had a younger sister, too—Melanie—but she died when I was seventeen. And my dad died when Melanie was just a baby. He was a cop, and he was killed in a robbery. My mom was devastated. We moved in with her parents after it happened, because Mom couldn't cope alone. She missed him so much that I heard her crying in her room every night for years. I did a lot of crying, myself."

"That's rough." Liza thinks of her own father, who raised her single-handedly. It would have been much better, she decides, if Chet Danning had been a hero and died when she was little, instead of being a hopeless alcoholic and still living in the same shabby Brooklyn apartment after all these years.

"How about you?" Laura asks. "Where are you from?"

"New York."

"Manhattan?"

Liza never tells anyone the truth, and she isn't about to start now, so she nods.

"What about your family?" Laura nibbles her croissant.

"What about them?" She's sorry as soon as the sharp retort leaves her mouth and tries to make up for it by saying, "I don't have much family. Just my dad. I lost my mother when I was young."

"I'm sorry. I know how it is."

Liza nods.

She doesn't tell Laura that she didn't lose her mother to a tragic accident or illness, but instead to a rich Arab businessman who carried her off to Kuwait to live happily ever after—without her husband and daughter.

During the Gulf War, Liza had wondered often about her mother, whether she was still alive and whether she was sorry about leaving. But she never heard from Diane Danning again. And now that the war is a dim memory, now that Liza has escaped that miserable Flatbush apartment, she no longer cares.

"Are you close to your father?" Laura asks.

"Not really. Are you close to your mother?"

"No . . ." Laura looks like she wants to say more, and Liza waits. Finally, Laura says, "My mother died, too. After we lost Melanie, she kind of fell apart. It was like it was too much for her, after losing my dad and everything, and she slowly faded away. They said it was cancer; but I know that if my dad and my sister were still here, she would be, too."

Liza nods. No wonder Laura Towne's beautiful eyes always seem so sad. She's been through a lot. Liza wonders who the "friend" was—the one who died, too—but she can't bring herself to ask.

She looks toward the plate-glass window up at the front of the store. It's raining again—pouring, actually. She wiggles her damp toes inside her thin, leaky leather boots.

"It's going to be fun walking back to the inn, huh?"

Liza looks up at Laura and sees that she, too, is staring out the window.

"I don't suppose they have taxis on Tide Island," she says wistfully.

"I doubt it." Laura sighs and slides her empty plate and cup away. "Guess we'll have to make a run for it."

"Or," Liza says impulsively, "we can just order more coffee—even though it does taste like mud—and stay here until it lets up."

Laura looks surprised, then smiles and says, "That's fine with me."

And Liza realizes, as she smiles back, that she doesn't have any real friends anymore—that maybe she never has.

Not that she wants or needs them.

She's better off living a solitary existence. She has plenty of work—and plenty of men—to keep her company when she needs it.

But, Liza decides, if she *did* ever decide to make a new friend, Laura Towne is the kind of person she would choose.

He slips silently into the room with the lilac-sprigged wallpaper, knowing that Laura's safely out of the house, but still somehow feeling the need to be cautious.

He locks the door behind him, of course, just in case.

Then he hurries over to the suitcase that's lying open on the luggage stand beneath the lace-curtained window.

His breath comes more quickly in anticipation as he reaches in and carefully pushes aside the neatly folded stack of jeans and tee-shirts and sweaters. Beneath them, he finds what he's looking for.

Lovingly, he takes out a pair of panties and a bra.

Then he frowns.

These simple white cotton garments aren't at all what he was expecting . . . what he remembers.

No, Laura always went for the daring lingerie—wisps of black lace, sheer teddies, push-up bras . . .

He checks the suitcase again to see if she's hidden the good stuff, but there are only a few more pairs of plain white underwear.

And something else isn't right . . .

He leans forward, burying his face in the

sweater on top of the pile of clothing in the suitcase.

That scent that clings to the cotton knit . . . it's not right either.

Too light and . . . floral.

Laura always wore a heavier, musky fragrance. He remembers how it used to drive him crazy, how he would burrow into the soft skin at her throat and breathe her essence until he felt intoxicated with the mere scent of her.

He remembers what it was like to slide his hands beneath her clothes to stroke her warm skin, what it was like to undress her, sometimes gently, other times roughly in his impatience to consume and possess her . . .

How she used to throw her head back and moan his name and pull him to her with the same urgency he felt . . .

That was before she started pushing him away whenever he came near her.

Before she cast him aside carelessly, telling him she no longer needed him, that she never really wanted him in the first place . . .

He squeezes his eyes shut against a stab

of pain that's as sudden and fresh as if he's just lost her all over again.

And when it subsides, he reminds himself that it was a long time ago. That Laura Towne will never hurt him again.

No one will ever hurt him again.

Not Laura.

Not Liza.

Not Sandy.

And not Lorraine.

The thought of Lorraine, and what he'd finally done to her, makes him giddy with excitement.

Soon, he promises himself, he'll have that delicious sensation again . . . power and control . . .

He hears a tearing sound and, startled, looks down to see a pair of Laura's panties, ripped in his hands.

For a moment, he feels panic rising in his throat, threatening to gag him . . .

What have I done? She'll know I've been here. She'll figure out what's going on, and she'll escape before I can carry out my plan . . .

Then he gets hold of his senses.

Calmly, he tucks the torn panties into his

back pocket and replaces everything else in the suitcase, just as it was when he found it.

She'll never know. Even if she notices the panties are missing and gets suspicious, she would never, ever suspect that you're here.

And even if, somehow, she happens to catch sight of you before it's time, she still won't know.

As he walks toward the door he glimpses his reflection in the mirror nailed to the back and he pauses to examine himself, pleased with what he sees.

Hair that's permed so that it looks wavy, and that's dyed a natural-looking shade of brown.

Eyes whose true shade is hidden behind light-blue-colored contact lenses—cornflower blue, the lady in the optical shop had called them.

And a chiseled, handsome face—the face that he picked out of a catalogue in his plastic surgeon's office three years ago.

Sandy huddles under the overhang of rock that juts over the beach like an awning. Here, her body flattened up against the steep, rocky incline that rises from the sand toward the road above, she's partly sheltered from the driving cold rain and the wind that roars in off the water.

And from here, she can see most of the magnificent houses that sit atop the crescent-shaped, windswept shoreline. One of them, she's certain, belongs to Ethan Thoreau. She's half in love with him already.

As she waits for the rain to let up, she dreams about tonight . . . about what it will be like with Ethan. And the goosebumps that cover her flesh have nothing to do with the chill wind or her drenched clothes.

Sandy knows that she'll make love with Ethan tonight. There's no question of waiting, like she had with Frankie, and with Joe. There's no need, this time.

After all, with Frankie, her high school boyfriend, it was different because she was a virgin. They both were, actually, and though Frankie had pressured her for the first year they dated, she had suspected that he was secretly just as terrified as she was. And when they finally made love, rather than being a wonderful experience that was worth waiting for, Sandy couldn't believe what a letdown it was.

She'd continued to date Frankie anyway, until graduation, when he'd enlisted in the navy. He was married now and stationed in Washington State, the last she'd heard. His wife was someone he'd met in Florida during training. Theresa had met her when Frankie brought her home to Greenbury one Christmas. She had told Sandy that Mrs. Frankie, as they called her, was cute and petite even though she was seven months pregnant and that she had a thick southern drawl.

When Sandy had told Theresa she was happy for Frankie, Theresa had just patted her arm, as if to say, *Sure you are.* Sandy knew Theresa was thinking that she was jealous of Mrs. Frankie. The truth was, Sandy had never wanted to marry him. She just missed sleeping with him . . . not because the sex was terrific, but because she missed having sex, period.

She'd been celibate for two years after he left for the navy, until she'd started dating Joe. She still remembered how attracted she'd been to him, that first time she'd seen him at the Knights of Columbus Mardi Gras Night. He'd been wearing a v-necked sweater and tight jeans that emphasized his beefy build, and she'd thought the tattoo on his forearm was sexy.

She'd poked Theresa and pointed him out. Theresa, of course, had zipped over to some guys she knew and found out that the stranger was Joe Marconi, a twenty-five-year-old beer-truck driver from Hartford, and that he was single.

When Sandy met him a few minutes later, she'd seen that Joe wasn't quite as perfect up close. He had a beer belly that wasn't quite camouflaged by the dark sweater, and his teeth were stained yellow, probably from the cigarettes he chain-smoked. But still, there was something about him that drew Sandy; and when he'd asked her out, she'd eagerly said yes.

And when, after their first date—dinner at Pizza Hut and a Jim Carrey movie that had Joe laughing uproariously, to Sandy's embarrassment—he had taken her back to his apartment, she'd eagerly slept with him.

If sex with Frankie had been disappointing, sex with Joe was even less satisfying. He was purely selfish in bed, and he insisted on the missionary position, lights out, every time. Sandy, who was ashamed of her lumpy body anyway, didn't mind the dark, but she did mind the routine love-making and the fact that Joe never even bothered to kiss her anymore, or hold her afterward. It was a wonder that he'd been so traumatized when she'd broken the engagement— he'd never acted as though he were in love with her, especially when they had sex.

I bet Ethan Thoreau is fantastic in bed, she thinks now, gazing up at the huge houses overlooking the beach. And as she stares dreamily into space, thinking about her date tonight, it gradually dawns on her that the rain has stopped. The sky still looks ominous, though, as if it could open up again any second.

Sandy scrambles out from beneath the overhang and picks her way up the craggy slope from the beach to the winding road that follows the shore. The wind is in her face and she keeps her head bent as she heads back toward the inn.

She doesn't see the middle-aged woman who's walking a black Lab along the side of the road until she nearly bumps into them.

"Hi," the woman, who's wearing a yellow rain slicker and matching hat, greets Sandy with a smile as her dog lifts its leg and urinates on a bush.

"Hi." Sandy points to the dog. "He's beautiful. What's his name?"

"He's a she, actually. Lady."

"I used to have a yellow Lab." Now that the dog is finished with her business, Sandy bends over to pat her sleek head. "Hello, there, Lady. Hi, girl. You're just beautiful. Yes, you are. Yes, you are."

"You're not from the island, are you?" the woman asks, winding another length of leash around her hand.

"No, I'm not. . . . How'd you guess?"

"You don't look the type. Most of the young people who come to Tide Island are hippie types. They call it Tie-Dye Land."

"I've heard that." Sandy straightens and asks, "Do you live here year round?"

The woman nods and points to a large house with weathered gray shingles that's set back from the road. "My great-grandfather built that over a hundred years ago. I grew up here. Now my husband and I are about to move to Boca Raton, and my son and his wife are going to move out here. They're both investment bankers in New York, and they're taking an early retirement."

"That's nice." Sandy smiles politely. The

woman seems to be the chatty type, so she adds cautiously, "Um, I was looking for a friend of mine who lives around here someplace. Maybe you know him . . ."

"If he lives around here, I'm sure I do."

"His name is Thoreau . . . Ethan Thoreau?"

At the woman's blank look, Sandy says, "He's a surgeon in Connecticut, so he wouldn't be a year-round resident, but . . ."

"I've never heard of him," the woman informs her decisively. She glances down at her dog, who's nosing along the weeds at the edge of the road. "You must have the name wrong."

"I don't think so . . ."

"Then he doesn't live around here. Maybe on the other side of the island, where there are some newer, smaller houses. A lot of those are rentals, and—"

"I doubt he'd live in a small rental," Sandy cuts in. "He has a private plane and he's very wealthy." She wishes she could take the last few words back. They make her sound so . . . pathetic.

The woman purses her lips and yanks the dog's leash. "Come on, Lady, get out of there." To Sandy, she says, "If your friend lives in this area, then I'm afraid I somehow haven't met him."

"Maybe he's new to the island."

"Most of these homes stay within families for generations, like mine. If one had been sold recently, I'd know about it."

Sandy shrugs and watches as the woman tugs Lady onto the concrete and starts back toward the huge gray house.

"Thanks anyway," Sandy calls, and the woman dismisses her with a brief wave.

These island people sure are strange, Sandy decides.

She glances back at the majestic row of waterfront homes, again wondering which one belongs to Ethan.

Then, as she feels icy raindrops on her face, she turns and hurries in the opposite direction, toward the inn.

Four

Liza sweeps into the foyer of the inn on a gust of wind and rain and slams the door shut behind her with a curse.

Thanks to this lousy weather, she's drenched and chilled to the bone. She and Laura had waited as long as they could in the general store for the rain to let up, but finally, Liza's patience wore thin and she decided to make a run for it.

Laura had stayed back at the store, saying she wanted to browse around a bit.

"In *here*?" Liza had asked incredulously, looking around at the meager inventory.

"I need some art supplies, and there's a whole section of them over there," Laura had pointed out.

"It figures. No stockings, but this place sells all the paintbrushes and canvases anyone could want."

"A lot of artists come to Tide Island," Laura said quietly.

"And you're one of them, obviously."

"Not professional. I just like to paint."

"Well, knock yourself out," Liza had said, heading for the door.

Even as she'd walked out onto the stormy boardwalk, she'd regretted being so snippy with Laura. Why did she always find herself doing that . . . jeopardizing the few potential friendships that ever came along by displaying a generous dose of attitude problem?

It wasn't that she had disdain for Laura's painting hobby, or even for the outdated excuse for a store. It was just that Liza couldn't help herself sometimes. The hurt little girl she'd once been seemed to surface when she least expected it, lashing out at anyone who happened to be around.

Like poor Laura Towne, who, to her credit, hadn't seemed all that thrown by Liza's bitchiness.

I'll make it up to her later, Liza thinks, squishing across the foyer floor in her ruined Italian leather boots.

There's no sign of Jasper Hammel.

She reaches for the small silver bell on the counter and rings it impatiently. She wants to ask Hammel whether D.M. Yates has called for her again, but there's no response to the bell.

Frowning, Liza rings it again. When there's still no response, she walks toward the back of the first floor, checking first the parlor, then the dining room and a small library off the hall. They're all deserted and the whole house seems eerily silent except for the ticking grandfather clock in the hallway.

Liza pokes her head into the kitchen. It's a large room with an old-fashioned black cookstove and double white porcelain sink. Built-in glass-paned cupboards display several different sets of dishes and glassware. A cozy nook off to one side holds a small table covered in a blue-and-white-checked cloth and surrounded by four chairs.

It occurs to Liza that this is the kind of kitchen that belongs in a quaint country farmhouse inhabited by a happy, messy family—not in this remote New England inn. It's almost too perfect—every dish and glass in perfect order, the counter-tops and stove sparkling, the dishtowel hanging over the sink folded just so. It doesn't look *lived* in—and neither does the rest of the inn.

No, it's hard to believe that, even in season, the Bramble Rose is ever overrun by tourists with the accompanying noise and disorder a houseful of people would bring.

Liza's brows knit thoughtfully as she steps back out of the kitchen and returns to the front of the house. There's still no sign of Jasper Hammel. After a moment, she starts up the stairs.

She pauses in front of the door to her room, struck by a sudden impulse to keep snooping around.

What do you think you're going to find? asks a little voice inside her head.

Nothing in particular . . . I'm just curious.

Well, maybe more than curious. Maybe a little suspicious, she admits to herself. There's just something strange about this inn, something she can't put her finger on.

The other doors on the second floor are closed, with the exception of the one to the bathroom. Liza quickly and gingerly uses the ancient facilities, wrinkling her nose as she reaches out to pull the old-fashioned chain on the toilet. The pipes creak as she turns on the faucet in the sink, and she's reminded of the uncomfortable shower she took in the battered clawfoot tub this morning. The water kept going cold and waning to a trickle, and she had shivered her way through, cursing D.M. Yates the whole time.

Now she hurries out of the bathroom and hesitates in the hallway, staring at the steps leading to the third floor.

There's no reason why I shouldn't just go up and have a look around, she tells herself. *After all, what else is there to do?*

On the third floor, she finds herself in a long hallway identical to the one below. There are several closed doors in roughly the same locations as on the second floor.

Liza tries the one that corresponds with the room she's in, and is surprised to find that it swings open.

The room is the identical shape and size as hers, with a similar fireplace and windows in the same spots. But the decor here is drastically different: the furniture is merely functional, the bedspread and tightly drawn curtains an austere white cotton. The floors are wooden and lack the high polish and pretty area rugs of the room below, and the walls are painted a pale yellow that, Liza concedes, might glow warmly on a sunny summer afternoon, but looks drab in the gray cast of winter.

It's clear that no one is occupying this room at the moment. The open closet door reveals empty hangers, and a musty smell permeates the air, as though it's been a long time since the curtains were opened and the windows raised.

Liza makes her way down the hall, peeking into the other rooms, and sees that they're similarly devoid of embellishment and are obviously deserted. In the third-floor bathroom, the small sink is dry and the white towel on the rack is precisely folded in thirds and lacks even the slightest wrinkle or smudge.

At the end of the hall, Liza reaches for the knob on the last door, assuming that it must lead to the top floor and cupola, which she'd noticed from outside the house.

Funny . . . the door won't budge.

And it can't be locked, because there's no keyhole . . . Unless it's bolted from the other side.

And if that's the case, Liza realizes, then someone must be up there, someone who has locked himself in.

She leans forward and presses her ear against the cool wooden door. Sure enough, she hears the faint sound of classical music coming from above.

Rattling the knob, Liza calls, "Jasper?"

"What are you doing?"

Gasping, she turns to see that the little man is standing behind her in the third-floor hallway.

His voice is calm, but his eyes are narrowed and his mustache twitches nervously.

"I . . . uh, I was just looking for you," Liza tells him, stepping back from the door and dropping her hand to her side. "I thought you might be up there."

"I'm right here."

"Obviously." Liza quickly regains her composure. "Who's upstairs?"

"Nobody. It's used for storage."

"I heard music coming from there," she informs him. "And the door's locked from the other side."

Is it her imagination or does Jasper Hammel look panicky for a moment before a look of cool detachment settles over his features once again?

"Nonsense," he says, stepping closer to

the door and cocking his head. "I don't hear anything."

"But I just . . ." Liza presses up close to the door and frowns. Nothing but silence. "Well, I heard it," she tells Jasper. "And the door's locked."

"It can't be. There's no keyhole, as you can see."

"It's locked from the other side."

"That's impossible. But I can explain why you couldn't open it. In damp weather, some of the doors in this place stick. Very common in old houses."

"But—"

"Anyway, I'm glad I found you, Ms. Danning, although I'm afraid it's too late. David Yates just stopped by the inn a few minutes ago, looking for you."

"He *what*?"

"He was sorry he missed you."

"Why didn't you—"

"I went up to your room, hoping you'd returned from town, but there was no reply to my knock."

Flabbergasted, Liza simply stares at him.

"I told him you'd gone into town," Jasper Hammel continues, "and that I wasn't sure when you'd be back."

"Where did he go?" Liza demands, hurrying toward the stairs. "I'll catch up to him."

"I have no idea. He was quite perturbed at your absence and said he's a busy man and doesn't have time to waste. But he did say he'll contact you later this afternoon."

"I don't believe this," Liza mutters, striding down the stairs to the second floor, Jasper Hammel dogging her heels like a nervous puppy. "At this rate, I'm never going to hook up with D.M. Yates. It's like fate's playing a cruel joke on me."

"Yes, it almost does seem that way, doesn't it?" Jasper agrees as Liza heads off to her room in a huff.

The man listening on the other side of the bolted attic door loosens his hold on the knife handle as he hears both sets of footsteps retreat.

He'd grabbed the knife and crept down the attic stairs when he'd heard the doorknob rattling. When he'd recognized Liza Danning's voice calling for Jasper, he'd formulated an instant plan.

She'd been scheduled to die second, after Sandy Cavelli, but it had occurred to him that there was no reason he couldn't switch the order on a whim. After all, *he* was the one in charge, here . . .

This time.

Yes, everything was up to him, and a feeling of power had surged through him as he clenched his sweaty fingers around the handle of the knife.

He was just about to open the attic door and clamp his hand over Liza Danning's startled mouth when he'd heard Jasper's voice in the hallway.

Oh, well.

Liza's turn would come soon enough anyway.

Stealing back up the stairs, he sighs and decides to stick with the original plan.

Sandy first.

Liza second.

Laura last.

When he'd first come up with his plan, he'd considered luring them out here to the island one by one to prolong his pleasure. But then he'd thought better of it. Prolonging the pleasure would also prolong his chances of being caught.

He'd decided he'd better take care of all of them in a single weekend.

And what could be more fitting than the one before Valentine's Day?

Come Monday, it will all be over.

Sandy, Liza, and Laura will have joined Lorraine in a place where no one will ever find them.

And *he'll* be on the way to a place where no one will ever find him. . . .

Jennie slips out of the inn with the blue canvas bag containing her art supplies tucked under her arm.

There . . . I made it, she thinks as she heads around to the path leading down to the beach. She'd successfully avoided an encounter back at the inn; no one had seen her come back from town.

As she hurried down the stairs just now, she had heard Jasper's voice humming along to classical music somewhere toward the back of the house. But he hadn't come out to talk to her. She's grateful for that. The little man is pleasant enough, but something about him makes her distinctly uncomfortable.

And it's not just him. It's this whole place. She knows Tide Island is beautiful and idyllic and quaint—and so is the Bramble Rose Inn—but Jennie doesn't want to be here.

Maybe it would be different, she tells herself, if she weren't here by herself. And if it were summer.

But even being here in winter wouldn't be so bad, she thought, if she had some company. Maybe if she and Keegan had come here together . . .

No! Stop it! Keegan's out of your life.

With a sigh she picks her way around a tangle of wet sea grass and vines, continuing toward the water.

The weather can't seem to make up its mind. One minute it's windy and raining furiously; the next—like right now—it's curiously calm, though the air is still misty and the sky remains threatening.

As Jennie scoots down the last few feet of the sloped path behind the inn to reach the beach, she scans the horizon and sees that it looks dark. There's no doubt that a storm is on the way—she can sense it.

She wonders, not for the first time since this morning, whether she should just leave—pack her things and hurry to catch the ferry to the mainland while she still can.

She's tempted, so tempted that her legs

feel jittery and she has to fight the urge to run back to the inn. She can't get past the feeling that she's in danger here, that something evil is lurking nearby.

But you know why you feel that way; and after three years, it's time to get over it. You can't spend the rest of your life being terrified of everything . . . of nothing.

Besides, if you leave, what are you going to tell Laura? She'll want to know what you're doing back home two days early. And she'll talk you into going back to that psychiatrist.

Dr. Bonner.

Jennie scowls at the mere thought of the man, remembering his thoughtful, bearded face and piercing black eyes. She'd seen him several times in the months after the . . . incident. One of the social workers she'd met during the police investigation had referred her to his office, telling her he specialized in post traumatic stress disorder.

Unfortunately, Laura had been right there with her when the social worker said it, and Jennie had agreed to see Dr. Bonner at her sister's insistence.

She'd disliked him instantly, but had returned to his office a few times because it was easier than arguing with Laura. She knew her sister was just worried about her and wanted to help; but Laura couldn't know that it was pure torture for Jennie to talk about what had happened, that she relived the horror every second of every day in her mind, and that nothing anyone said was going to help her.

Not that Dr. Bonner had said much, anyway. Just fixed her with his level stare and told her to tell him what she was feeling.

What the hell did he think she was feeling after what she'd been through?

No, Jennie can't bear the thought of going back to his office again, or of facing Laura's well-meaning concern. There's nothing to do but stay on this island for the weekend, the way she's supposed to, and try to ignore the irrational feelings of panic that keep creeping over her.

Jennie sets her jaw resolutely, and, for the second time today, makes her way across the wet sand. She finds the wide, flat rock she'd noticed this morning and climbs onto it, carefully pulling her coat down in back to sit on it so that her jeans won't get soaked.

There. This isn't so bad, she decides, looking out over the churning water again and taking a deep breath, drinking in the cold, salty air.

She reaches for her blue bag and removes her sketch pad and pencils. It's too damp to paint, but she's not in the mood anyway. She feels like working with charcoal, has an urge to fill page after page of creamy paper with bold, dark strokes.

Her hand poised over the sketchbook, she looks up and sees a lone gull swooping over the water. To her left, for about a mile, the beach curves out toward the horizon in a crescent shape, and through the gray mist, she can barely make out a scattering of enormous houses sitting above the rocky shoreline.

It looks just like England, she realizes, remembering the remote seaside homes along the shore on the other side of the Atlantic. She gazes out over the ocean and thinks how strange it is that it's still out there, hundreds of miles away—that isolated patch of beach where she had sat, sketching and feeling homesick, the day she'd met Harry.

She still remembers how startled she'd

been to hear a voice behind her—a voice with an American accent, no less.

"If it's any good, I'll buy it," he'd said, and she'd looked up to see a lanky, sandy-haired guy standing there grinning at her.

"Excuse me?" was all she could say in response, and he'd gestured at the sketch pad in her lap.

"Your drawing. Can I see it? If it's good, I'll buy it and frame it and hang it on the wall of my room. I love this spot. It reminds me of the beach back home. In fact," and he'd held up the camera in his hand, "I was just about to take a picture of it so I can keep it with me forever."

She'd known what he meant. There was something special about this lonely stretch of shore where the waves foamed over jutting rocks to crash against the crescent of sand. The tiny beach was only about a half-a-mile wide, separated from the rest of the coast by rocky cliffs that jutted out into the water, topped by magnificent homes.

Jennie had discovered the spot soon after arriving the month before to spend the semester at nearby Hillshire University, and she went there often to be alone with her thoughts.

Her mother had already been dead for two years at that point, while Gran was growing weak from the heart disease that had always plagued her and Gramps was terribly concerned over her. Jennie had felt guilty leaving Laura alone with their failing grandparents in Quincy while she went off to England, but Laura had insisted that she go.

"After all, one of us has to go to college and see the world, and it's not going to be me," her twin had pointed out cheerfully. Laura had only lasted a semester at a community college in southern Massachusetts before dropping out to become a bartender in Cambridge, much to their grandparents' dismay.

It was while Jennie was overseas, in fact, that Laura had started dating Brian. Jennie has always thought that if she had been around, her sister never would have fallen for him. She would have glimpsed his dark side and could have talked Laura out of it. By the time she'd returned to the states, Laura was engaged and it was too late for Jennie to do much but paste on a smile and tell her sister she was happy for her.

But even though her absence had, in her

opinion, resulted in a disastrous relationship for her twin, Jennie wouldn't have traded England for anything. If she hadn't gone, she would never have met Harry.

Then again, she thinks wistfully now, *if you hadn't met Harry, he would still probably be alive . . .*

Jennie had found England quaint but so foreign that she couldn't seem to shake her homesickness during those early days. Maybe that was why she had latched so eagerly onto Harry from the start. It wasn't like her to flirt with a stranger; but when he'd told her that he thought her sketch was terrific, she'd ripped it out of her pad and handed it to him.

"Hey, thanks! How much do I owe you?"

She'd shrugged. "How about just a cup of coffee?"

That easy grin had spread over his handsome face and he'd said, "Sure. Come on. Only it'll probably have to be tea. You know . . . when in Rome."

It turned out that Harry was also spending the semester at Hillshire. He was from a small town on the Oregon coast, and he, too, was homesick. Even that first day, as he'd enthusiastically told Jennie about his hometown, and how he couldn't wait to go back, she'd found herself feeling oddly regretful.

After all, Oregon was on the opposite side of the country from Boston. Jennie had no intention of leaving the northeast, not with Gran and Gramps doing so poorly. And the way he was talking about his friends and family back home, Harry didn't seem like the type who'd relocate, either.

Looking back, Jennie never ceases to be amazed that even in those first moments she'd spent with Harry, she'd had hopes of a permanent relationship.

They'd been inseparable during that semester in England. And when it was over, they'd prolonged their time together, spending the summer traveling through Europe together. Too soon, it was August and time to head back to the States. Harry had spent several days with Jennie in Boston before flying back to the west coast to finish his senior year.

She hadn't seen him until Christmas break, when she'd flown out to visit him. There, she had seen how truly connected Harry was to the scenic Oregon town and to his large, warm family that included five brothers and sisters. And there, Jennie had realized that she was deeply in love with him and couldn't bear to be without him.

Harry had proposed to her on Christmas Eve, and she had fiercely wanted to accept. But she thought of Laura, who was planning a spring wedding to Brian—they had already moved into an apartment on the Cape together. And she thought of her grandparents, both of them old and feeble and Gran so sick. They couldn't be left alone. And Jennie had already had her taste of freedom. It was Laura's turn, now.

So she'd told Harry she couldn't marry him. She couldn't leave Boston, and she didn't expect him to leave his home, either.

The rest of her visit was subdued. There wasn't much for them to say to each other. Jennie had managed to fight back the tears until she boarded the plane back to Boston. Then, knowing she would probably never see Harry again, she had spent the entire five-hour flight sobbing miserably.

When she'd walked heavily into the familiar old house in Quincy, though, her grandfather had said, "Harry called and he wants you to call him the moment you get in."

Reluctantly Jennie had dialed the familiar

number, not wanting to hear his voice, unable to bear the thought that it was over between them.

"Jen?" he'd said breathlessly when he'd answered the phone. "I need you to do me a huge favor."

"What is it?" she'd asked dully.

"Find me an apartment for June first. One that's cheap and close to your grandparents' house."

"You want to spend the summer here?" she'd asked slowly. She forced herself to get past the tingle of excitement at the thought of seeing him again, to be realistic. Prolonging the inevitable would only be more painful in the end. "But Harry, I don't think that's a good idea. We both know you'd just have to leave again in the fall, to go back to law school in Oregon."

"What, there aren't any law schools in Massachusetts?"

Her heart had instantly jump-started as she realized what he was saying. "Harry, you can't mean you're moving to Boston," she'd protested weakly.

"I can't? Why not? Don't you want to marry me?"

The lump that rose in her throat was so

enormous she couldn't speak for a moment. Then, in a strangled voice, she'd said, "I want to marry you more than I've ever wanted anything in my life. But I can't—"

"What? You can't marry me?"

"I can't leave Gran and Gramps," she'd said in a whisper, casting a glance over her shoulder toward the living room, where her grandparents were watching "Wheel of Fortune." "I already told you. They took care of us when we had no one else. Now it's my turn to be there for them."

"Well, I'll be there for them, too. Okay?"

She'd paused, letting it sink in. Then she'd said, in disbelief, "You'd actually leave your family and friends and your hometown for me?"

"I love you, Jen. And yes, I can leave my family and friends and my hometown. It's you I can't leave."

"Do you promise?" she'd asked, her voice choked with tears. All her life, she'd been abandoned by the people she loved. First her father. Then Melanie. Then her mother. Now even Laura had left, caught up in a new life.

"I promise, Jen," Harry had said. "I'll never leave you. Never."

Now, as she stares out over the gray Atlantic, his words echoing in her mind, she feels something wet on her cheeks.

Raindrops . . .

And tears.

Lying flat on her stomach, Laura reaches under the couch to retrieve the can of furniture polish that had rolled when she'd dropped it.

Her fingers find something small and round, and she pulls out a dust-covered silver hoop earring she'd lost awhile back. She'd accused Jennie of borrowing it without asking, actually . . . not that she can imagine her twin wearing jewelry this flashy, come to think of it.

No, Jennie only wears the small gold-and-diamond studs that Harry had once given her, when she bothers to wear earrings at all.

Laura sets the silver hoop on the coffee table, which is half-coated in a white film of lemon-scented polish, and reaches under the couch again.

The doorbell rings just as her hand closes around the can of Pledge.

Frowning, Laura pulls it out, scrambles to her feet, and heads for the door, wondering who can be dropping by in the middle of a rainy Saturday afternoon.

"Hi, Laura."

"Keegan!" she says, surprised to see him standing in the hall. "What's up?"

He shrugs. "I just wondered—"

"Jennie's not here," she tells him, wondering how her sister can possibly resist him. His shoulders are incredibly broad beneath that worn jean jacket and gray sweatshirt he's wearing, and his face is so handsome, with a generous mouth and sculpted bone structure that might look *too* pretty on someone else but that's masculine on Keegan.

"She's not here? Where is she?" He doesn't look like he believes her, and Laura can't blame him. After all, every time he's called lately—which has been often—Jennie has made her lie and say she's out.

"She's away for the weekend."

"Oh, yeah? Where'd she go?" Keegan's sharp eyes are looking over Laura's shoulder, as if he's searching for clues that Jennie really is here.

"I'm telling the truth, Keegan," Laura says. "She really is away."

Disappointment settles over his features. "Oh. Where'd she go?" he repeats.

"To Tide Island."

"Tide Island? What's she doing out there?"

"I won a free weekend at some inn there, but I can't go because Shawn—he's the guy I'm seeing—is coming home from Japan this weekend. In fact," she checks her watch, "I have to leave for the airport in about twenty minutes to pick him up and I need to finish cleaning the apartment first, so . . ."

"*You're* cleaning?" He looks suspiciously at her. "Are you sure you're not Jennie?"

She rolls her eyes. "Very funny."

"No offense, Laura, but you're not exactly the world's best housekeeper."

"Well, Shawn's pretty whipped on me, and I don't want to scare him away, you know?" She brandishes her can of Pledge. "Now, if you'll excuse me . . ."

"Wait. What about this free trip to Tide Island?"

"What about it?"

"How'd you win it?"

"I bought a sweepstakes ticket at Stop and Shop. It was for a good cause. The New England Children's Leukemia Society."

"Never heard of it." Keegan frowns. "You wouldn't still have that ticket around, would you?"

"Are you kidding? I'm lucky if I manage to hang onto my purse. You know me—hey, wait, you know what? I do have the ticket!"

"You do?"

"Yeah . . . I wrote Shawn's flight number on the back of it. I remember because the day he called to tell me he was coming home was the same day I found out I won the sweepstakes and I had to pull out the ticket to confirm the number. It's stuck to the fridge with a magnet so I wouldn't lose it." She's halfway to the kitchen, followed by Keegan, before she turns to look back at him, puzzled. "Why do you want it?"

"Because I've never heard of the New England Children's Leukemia Society, that's why. And a friend of mine at work—do you remember Buddy?" At her nod, he continues, "Well, he's working on a task force to uncover a ring of bogus charity collectors that's operating in the area."

"What, you think the sweepstakes was a scam?"

"I didn't say that."

"Well, it's definitely real because they awarded the prize." Laura continues to the kitchen, plucks the ticket from beneath a "Cheers" magnet on the refrigerator door, and hands it to Keegan.

"That doesn't mean the sweepstakes was legitimate, Laura. They probably collected thousands of dollars selling tickets. A free weekend at an inn—particularly on Tide Island in the middle of winter—only costs a few hundred at most. How do you know the rest of the money really went to charity?"

"I don't." She shrugs, then says, "Hey, what are you doing with that?" as Keegan starts to tuck the ticket into his jacket pocket.

"I'm giving it to Buddy. He'll probably want to check it out."

"Well, at least let me copy Shawn's flight information off the back." She grabs a pen from the table and writes the information on a napkin, then hands the ticket back to Keegan. "Here, it's all yours now."

"Thanks. So, how's Jennie doing?"

"She's all right. You know . . ."

"No, I don't. I haven't talked to her in weeks."

"Well, she thinks it's better that way."

"Oh, really? And why is that?"

"Because if she talks to you, she might not be able to stay away from you."

His face clouds over. "Well, what I want to know is why she thinks she has to stay away in the first place."

"Come on, Keegan," Laura says, even though she's wondering the same thing. "You guys are broken up. Forget about her."

"I can't," he says, and she's startled by the raw pain in his voice. "I keep trying, but . . . I don't know, maybe if I could understand why . . ."

Laura hesitates. She wants, more than anything, to tell Keegan what had happened to Jennie three years ago. In her opinion, her sister should have at least explained it to him—that because of her ordeal, she doesn't want to love a cop. That she's afraid of losing him to violent death. Just like she'd lost her father . . .

And just like she'd lost Harry . . .

But Laura clamps her mouth shut. It's not

up to her to tell Keegan why Jennie left him. She'd promised her sister that she wouldn't . . .

And besides, she realizes, glancing at her watch—there's no time to get into it now.

She wants to be there when Shawn walks off the plane, and Saturday traffic is always heavy around Logan.

So she just shrugs and tells him, "Look, Keegan, I'm very sorry about you and Jen, but that's really between the two of you. I don't like to get involved in her personal life."

He gives her a look that says *since when?* But he simply nods and starts back toward the front door.

He pauses, his hand on the knob, and turns back to Laura.

"Just for the record," he says quietly, "I really love her. And I'm not going to give up. Will you tell her that for me?"

Laura nods.

But even as the door closes behind him, she fights the urge to run after him, to tell him the truth about Jennie.

And if she weren't running so late, she would do it.

But I will, she promises herself. *Next time*

I get the opportunity, I'll tell him, no matter what Jennie says. It's for her own good.

She tucks the napkin containing Shawn's flight information into the back pocket of her jeans and thinks again about that sweepstakes ticket.

Now that Keegan has planted the idea that the charity might have been a fraud, she finds herself going back over what happened that afternoon in the Stop and Shop parking lot.

She remembers being frazzled as she rushed toward the double glass doors of the store. It was a blustery December day and she had lost her gloves, as usual—as well as the grocery list Jennie had jotted for her. She'd been trying to recall what her sister needed for the gingerbread cookies she wanted to bake when a voice had interrupted her thoughts.

"Hey, miss . . . want to take a chance in a sweepstakes? You might win a free vacation, and it's for a good cause."

She'd turned to see a man standing there with a roll of tickets. He was wearing a button that said New England Children's Leukemia Society. Instantly, she'd thought of Melanie and had smiled and said sure.

He'd waited patiently while she dug a dollar out of the bottom of her purse—she'd lost her wallet before Thanksgiving and hadn't gotten around to replacing it yet.

Frowning, Laura searches her memory and pictures the man. He'd been bundled up against the cold, with a bulky down coat, a ski hat, and a thick scarf wrapped around the lower half of his face. His voice had been muffled, and he hadn't spoken much except to thank her after he'd handed her the ticket.

But now, as she thinks back over the incident, she recalls vaguely thinking, at the time, that he sounded familiar. But she didn't recognize him.

No, she'd decided then that he was a stranger.

And she's still positive of that now.

After all, scatterbrained as she sometimes is, Laura never forgets a face.

Especially someone whose eyes are the same striking, light shade of blue as those colored contact lenses Shawn wears.

Cornflower blue.

Five

Sandy wraps her robe more tightly around her wet body and hurries across the deserted second-floor hallway back to her room.

She'd planned on taking a leisurely bubble bath to get into a romantic frame of mind for her date with Ethan. But after only a minute or so of running the water into the ancient clawfoot tub in the inn bathroom, it had gone from lukewarm to chilly. And even if it had been steaming, it was only a trickle when the faucet was on full blast, so it would have taken hours to fill the tub.

Sandy had settled for taking a shower that was icy enough to set her teeth chattering and body shivering.

Back in her room, she locks the door and goes over to the window.

Dusk falls early during New England winters. It's only late afternoon, but already the stormy sky is rapidly darkening. The wind has picked up again, rattling the window-panes and moaning around the drafty old house, and raindrops splatter furiously against the glass.

Sandy imagines how romantic it will be to snuggle before a roaring fire with Ethan Thoreau as the weather rages outside. Maybe, if this actually turns into a full-blown nor'easter as threatened, she'll be stranded here on the island with him for a few days.

And a lot can happen in a few days, Sandy tells herself, turning away from the window and flicking on the floor lamp near the bed.

Who knows? Maybe I'll go back home engaged. And it won't be like it was with Joe. This time, I'll definitely go through with the wedding.

Dreamily, she closes her eyes and imagines what her wedding day will be like.

A long, frilly white gown, definitely. Sandy has always dreamed of being an old-fashioned bride. She can just picture the dress . . .

Of course, she has quite a few pounds to lose between now and the day she gets married.

Her eyes snap open and she strips off the

robe. Standing naked in front of the full-length mirror, she examines herself from head to toe.

Hair . . . fine, once you've used some mousse and blown it dry.

Face . . . not bad at all, once you get some makeup on.

Boobs . . . well, they certainly are big. Too big—considering that your nipples sag to your bellybutton—although maybe Ethan Thoreau won't think so. Maybe he likes women with giant breasts. Most men do, don't they?

Stomach . . . definitely flabby. Look at those rolls. Yuck.

Hips . . . much too wide, and so is your butt.

Thighs . . . well, at least the new skirt will hide your saddlebags.

Legs . . . not bad—but uh-oh! They're bleeding in a few spots from where you nicked them shaving over goosebumps in that freezing cold shower.

Sandy grabs some Kleenex from the packet in her cosmetics bag and cleans the blood off her legs, making a face when she sees the red smears on the clean white tissues.

She's always been squeamish at the sight of blood.

Liza restlessly tosses aside the manuscript page she's been trying to read for the last five minutes and glances at her watch.

It's after four. Why hasn't D.M. Yates called back?

Is he trying to punish her for not being here earlier?

Or . . .

Liza stands and paces across the room, not wanting to even think that this whole thing might be an elaborate hoax.

But how can she help but be suspicious? After all, it's not as though she were born yesterday. It's not as though she actually believes that famous, elusive writers routinely go around giving breaks to relatively unknown female editors.

The more time she spends on Tide Island, stewing and waiting for D.M. Yates to show up, the more she wonders whether she's been had. Only . . .

Who would go to the trouble to play such a nasty trick on her?

Albie.

His name is the first to enter her mind. Only, would a high-powered man like Senator Albert Norwood actually have the time and energy to pull something like this off?

He might, Liza realizes. He might, if he were angry enough at her.

And there's no question that he's not exactly thrilled with her these days.

After all, he hasn't taken kindly to being blackmailed.

But it's his own fault, Liza tells herself. *Married men who have a lot to lose politically shouldn't go around sleeping with women like me.*

It certainly hadn't been very hard to seduce Albie.

She cringes slightly at the memory of his naked body—a white, quivering mass of Jello—hovering over hers and of his hot, garlicky breath in her face as he'd pounced on her, forcing himself into her with no foreplay other than roughly squeezing her bare breasts once or twice.

It certainly hadn't been difficult to hide the video camera in her bedroom, either. Albie was always so hot for her that he probably wouldn't have noticed if a film crew had stood at the foot of the bed.

Once Liza had the incriminating evidence on tape, all she'd had to do was send him a copy and threaten to give the original to Cathy, his wife of thirty-seven years. Albie had been furious, at first. Then he'd tried acting like the whole thing was just a big joke.

But when he'd realized that Liza meant business, his demeanor had changed and he'd become desperate to do whatever she asked. "Just don't show Cathy the tape," he kept begging.

And Liza hadn't . . .

Yet.

At first, she'd used it to get Albie to write his autobiography for Xavier House. Every publisher in New York had been after him for years, trying to make a deal, thanks to his famous, scandal-ridden background.

His father was Tyson Norwood, the oldest son in a family that had been America's premier political force before the Kennedys arrived on the scene. And his mother was Lexie Jones, who had been one of the most famous Hollywood starlets of the thirties. Albie was their only child—the lone heir to the Norwood legacy since Ty's brother Miles was unable to have children and his brother Wendell had been killed in the D-Day invasion without ever marrying.

Ty, a charismatic congressman, was a notorious ladies' man who was rumored, at one point, to be sleeping with the First Lady right under the President's nose. As a result of his philandering, Lexie had killed herself when Albie was a teenager, jumping off the Empire State Building at high noon on their twenty-fifth wedding anniversary. Ty had promptly made headlines by turning around and marrying a beautiful, recently divorced English duchess only a few months later. During the mid-sixties, the two of them were gunned down on the sidewalk in front of their Manhattan brownstone by someone who had never been caught. There were rumors that the murder was connected to Ty's gambling debts or that he had been caught sleeping with a famous Brooklyn mobster's wife, but no one was ever arrested for the crime.

Despite his family's high-profile activities, Albie had managed to lead a fairly quiet life. But that didn't stop the press from hounding him everywhere he went, or from speculating about his family's colorful past.

Now, thanks to Liza, the world was going

to learn the darkest secrets of the Norwood family, via Albie's soon-to-be-published autobiography.

And thanks to that book, Liza had earned a fat bonus at work, not to mention a promotion and that write-up in *Publisher's Weekly.*

The last time she had seen Albie, for dinner a few weeks ago, he had seemed resigned to the fact that she had a degree of power over him. He hadn't seemed bent on revenge . . .

But then, if his idea of revenge is sending Liza on this wild-goose chase to a rattletrap inn on an out-of-the-way island in the dead of winter; she should probably be relieved.

After all, she isn't exactly a stranger to using men to get what she wants.

In fact, it's a wonder no one has tried to get even with her before now.

If this D.M. Yates thing turns out to be a hoax, she'll be pissed as hell. But, she supposes, there are worse things someone could do to her . . .

The rain beating on the roof above the attic drowns out the sound of the classical music coming from the small portable CD player, so he shuts it off.

It's almost time to go, anyway.

He notes a tremor of anticipation in the pit of his stomach and wonders if Sandy's feeling the same way. Is she jittery with excitement over the prospect of a date with Ethan Thoreau? Is she primping for him, right this very moment, behind the door to her room two floors below?

He pictures her round face and thinks about how different she looked back when he first met her.

Of course, she'd been much younger then.

She wasn't quite thirteen, her body already curvy and womanly, but not yet overweight.

And he, at fifteen, had been a poor little rich kid: acne-ridden, clumsy, painfully shy—and that wasn't all. He had a hideous, horribly ugly face. His features were elongated and thrust forward, as though a giant suction cup had forced them out. The doctors had told his parents that something must have happened to his face as he passed through the birth canal, and that it would probably look better as he grew older. But it hadn't.

Once, when he was about seven, he'd overheard his mother telling one of her friends that it was as though God had played a horrible trick on her and his father. After all, they were both beautiful people.

He closes his eyes and thinks back to that long-ago, hot June day. After spending the morning aimlessly wandering along the water behind his parents' summer home on the Connecticut shore, he'd walked in the back door, and there she was. Sandy Cavelli. Sitting at the kitchen table, looking bored, while a fat, dark-haired woman spoke with his mother.

He'd quickly realized that the woman, Angie, was interviewing for a part-time maid's position. The house already had a staff of four—a full-time housekeeper, a cook, a gardener, and a handyman who doubled as a chauffeur. But lately, his mother had been complaining that the housekeeper, Tess, couldn't keep up with all the entertaining they did on weekends. His father, barely looking up from his *New York Times,* had told her to go ahead and hire part-time help then.

"And what about your daughter?" his mother had asked Angie, casting a glance of displeasure in Sandy's direction.

"She'll have to come with me when I work," Mrs. Cavelli had said. "Her father and brothers are busy working on weekends. My husband's a plumbing and heating contractor, and my sons are all involved in the business."

He still remembers the look of pride on the woman's face as she said it, and the look of disdain on his mother's.

"Well, if you have to bring her, she'll have to help," she'd said in her clipped tone.

"That's fine. Sandy's always a big help."

And she was. She regularly dusted and vacuumed and made up the guest rooms, which were always occupied on weekends by his parents' friends from the city. And she often helped the cook in the kitchen, making wonderful canapes for his parents' Friday and Saturday night cocktail parties.

It took him several days to work up the courage to say hello to Sandy. Until he did, he spent a lot of time watching her—peeking through the doorways of guest rooms as she bent over to make up the beds or watching her through the kitchen window as she worked over the stove, pausing every now and then to wipe trickles of sweat off her neck before it could drip down between her breasts.

As far as he knew, she never realized he was there.

When he'd finally been brave enough to talk to her, she'd responded with a broad, cheerful grin and a bright, "Hi! It must be great living in a house like this, huh?"

How could he tell her that most of the time, it was a nightmare? That his father was never there emotionally, even on the rare times that he was there physically. And that his mother . . . well, he couldn't tell anyone about his mother. About what she did to him. About what she made him do.

He'd never told another soul about that.

So, in response to Sandy's question, he'd smiled and shrugged and said, "Sure, it's great."

And from that day on, they'd been friends.

Though to him, it was always more than that. He'd thought it was more to her, too. He'd been wrong.

But how was I to know? he wonders fiercely, clenching his grown-up fists in his attic room. *She acted like she cared about me . . . like she loved me. She was the first person who ever treated me as though my looks didn't matter.*

But obviously, they had mattered.

Because in the end, she'd abandoned him.

Just like the others would, in years to come.

With a sigh, he opens his eyes and his gaze falls on the portable stereo.

Oh, yes. He mustn't forget to bring the music.

He hurries over to remove the round silver CD he'd been playing, presses it into the plastic case, and puts it away in alphabetical order.

Then he reaches for a cassette tape from the stack on the table. It took him several days of combing record stores to find all the right songs to record on this tape.

He checks the neat lettering on the inside sleeve of the plastic cassette case to make sure he has the right one.

Yes, this is it.

The one that begins with "One Hand, One Heart" and ends with Mendelssohn's wedding march.

* * *

"I'm telling you, it isn't right," Tony Cavelli repeats, this time thumping the table with his fist so hard that the ladle topples out of the bowl of sauce, sending tomato-colored splatters all over the plastic tablecloth.

Danny and his wife Cheryl, who is seated to his right, exchange a glance.

Cheryl raises her eyebrows slightly, as if to say, *Aren't you going to stick up for your sister?*

Danny sighs inwardly. Cheryl's right. But he hates to get into this whole thing about Sandy and some weekend trip she's apparently taken.

He and his father don't get along very well as it is. Never have. Pop doesn't understand why he'd insisted on going to college or why he hadn't gone into the family business. Or why he'd married a girl who wasn't Italian when he could have settled down with Donna Aglieri, his high school sweetheart.

It isn't that Tony Cavelli doesn't like Cheryl. Who can help but like her? She's sweet and kind and pretty with dark blond hair and big blue eyes and the kind of smile that lights up her whole face.

No, Pop is crazy about Cheryl. But that doesn't mean he doesn't think Danny should have stuck with his own kind and married Donna.

After all, both Tony Junior and Frankie managed to find Italian wives. You wouldn't find a happier family man than Tony Junior, as Pop points out every chance he gets. Maryanne is pregnant again—with their fourth child; they're trying for a son—Tony the third, of course—to add to their brood of daughters, all of them under seven.

Meanwhile, Frankie and Sue have been separated more than a year now, but Pop refuses to acknowledge that one of his sons might end up divorced—or that it might be Frankie's fault. Everyone in Greenbury knows about Frankie and Char, the new beautician down at Hair and Now. Of course, no one in the Cavelli family ever brings it up. No one ever asks Frankie about Sue, either.

Danny clears his throat. "You know, Pop, a lot of women travel on their own these days. It's not like when you were young. It doesn't mean Sandy's a . . . well, you know."

A *putana* is what his father had called her.

Italian for whore. Well, Pop hadn't exactly said his sister is one, just that when single girls go away alone, people talk. People, according to Tony Cavelli, would say that Sandy is out looking for men.

And even though Danny suspects people would be right, he isn't about to tell his father that. What his sister does is her own business. Still, these days, you can't be too careful.

"I know it's not like when I was young," Tony says, wiping an orange smear of sauce from his mustache before spearing another gnocchi on his fork. "You don't have to tell me. I just expect my daughter, my own flesh and blood, to behave like a young lady. Not like a—"

"Frankie, what's the matter with you?" Angie interrupts, jabbing her middle son in the arm. "Don't tell me that's all you're gonna eat."

"Ma, I had a huge plateful." Frankie pushes back his chair and stifles a burp.

"Where are you going?" Tony Junior asks, resting an elbow on the back of Maryanne's empty chair. She's in the kitchen, making sure the kids are eating.

"What do you mean where am I going? It's Saturday night. Bowling, where else?"

"Well, before you go, you have to come over and help me move that dresser out of the baby's room. You said you would."

"Oh, geez, I forgot. Come on, Tony, I'm late already," Frankie says, checking his watch. "I'll help you do it tomorrow."

"Can't. We have Maryanne's mother's birthday party right after church."

"Danny will help you," Angie says, looking at him. "Right?"

This time, Danny sighs out loud. "I'll help you," he tells his oldest brother. "But we have to make it fast. Cheryl and I are going to the movies at eight-thirty."

Maryanne, just coming back into the dining room, says, "The movies! God, Tony, remember when we used to go to the movies on Saturday nights?"

"We still go to the movies sometimes."

"Yeah, Disney matinees." Maryanne looks at Cheryl. "Enjoy it while you can. As soon as you have kids, you two will never get away by yourselves again."

Cheryl catches Danny's eye.

He knows what she's thinking. *If only we had kids.* They've been trying since their wedding night, with no luck. For a while, Cheryl had been pestering him to let her see a specialist, a doctor who's had a pretty good success rate with patients who have difficulty conceiving. Danny has resisted, not wanting to get into that.

A friend of his at work has been through the whole gamut. Tests. Fertility drugs. *In vitro* fertilization. He and his wife drained their bank accounts, took out a second mortgage on their house, endured years of stress and prayers, and nothing worked. Now they're trying to borrow money to adopt.

Danny supposes that as a last resort, he and Cheryl can go that route, but he can't help wanting to hold out longer, to see what happens. And Cheryl seems to have started to see things his way lately. At least, she hasn't pestered him about that doctor for the last month or so.

There's a sudden sound of breaking glass in the kitchen, followed instantly by the sound of one of Danny's little nieces wailing and another one saying, "I told you not to touch that."

"Ashley? What happened?" Maryanne is in there like a shot.

Angie jumps up and follows her, saying, "Eye-yi-yi, I hope that wasn't my new water pitcher."

A moment later, the crying has escalated, and Danny's oldest niece, Caitlin, appears in the doorway, her dark eyes solemn. "Daddy? Ashley cut herself on some glass and she's bleeding."

Tony Junior gets up. "Where?"

"Over by the stove."

"No, I mean, where on her body? Never mind, I'll come." He, too, disappears into the kitchen.

Frankie pulls on his leather jacket, says a quick "later," and heads out the side door.

"Crazy," Tony Cavelli says, throwing his hands up in the air, then picking up his fork again.

"What's crazy, Pop?"

"This family, what else?" He shovels some gnocchi into his mouth, then says around it, "Three girls. Your brother better hope this new baby isn't another one. He has his hands full already. Raising a daughter isn't easy."

"Oh, come on, Pop, Sandy never gave you any trouble growing up."

"Then, no. Now . . ." He shakes his head.

"What's she done now?"

"She won't lose weight. She won't get married. She's off alone on some crazy island. . . ."

"What island?" Cheryl asks brightly.

"That's the worst part. Tide Island. I took you kids there when you were little, remember?" Tony asks Danny, who nods. "Crazy place. All kinds of hippies there. Not the kind of place where a young lady should go alone."

Danny pushes his chair back abruptly. "Come on, Cheryl. Let's go make sure Ashley's okay."

As they head into the kitchen, leaving his father alone at the table, Danny wonders if the day is ever going to come when he can stop coming to Sandy's rescue.

Sandy's heart has been pounding for the last half hour or so as the time for her big date drew near.

Now, when she peeks through the glass in the front door of the inn and sees the shiny black sedan outside, her heart starts pumping so violently that it almost hurts.

Relax, she tells herself as she reaches for

the knob. *Act as though you've seen it all before . . . done it all before . . .*

"Ah, Sandy, your date must be here."

She jumps and turns to see Jasper Hammel behind her. "I guess that's him."

"May I help you with your coat?"

"Oh . . ." She has it slung over her arm.

She'd pictured Ethan Thoreau coming up to the door to greet her, had imagined how his hands would brush against the bare skin at her neck as he gallantly helped her into her coat.

Now, it's Jasper Hammel who takes it from her and holds it open so she can slip her arms into the sleeves. Disappointed, she glances out the window again with a frown.

"Um, are you sure that's Ethan?" she asks Jasper.

"Ethan? Oh, no, that's not Mr. Thoreau. It's his driver, of course."

"Of course." Though startled, Sandy can't help but feel relieved. Her mother had taught her, back when she was in high school, that if a date didn't come up to the door, she shouldn't go out with him again.

But chauffeurs don't count, Sandy thinks gleefully now as Jasper holds the door open for her and she walks out into the rainy night.

The driver's side door opens and a tall, dark figure puts up an umbrella in one quick movement. He comes to the bottom of the steps and tips his hat at Sandy. "Good evening, Miss Cavelli."

"Good evening," she says coolly, practicing for later. She wants Ethan Thoreau to think that she's sophisticated.

Like Liza.

An image of the woman flits into Sandy's brain, and she frowns. She has nothing in common with Liza Danning. But it probably wouldn't hurt to imitate her haughty attitude, under the circumstances.

The chauffeur holds the umbrella over her head as they walk back to the car. He opens the door and helps her into the back seat, grasping her arm firmly with a black leather glove. He's wearing tinted aviator-framed glasses and a long, dark wool overcoat.

As they pull away from the Bramble Rose, Sandy settles back against the leather upholstery and takes a deep breath, then exhales slowly.

This is it, she thinks. *I'm off to meet the man of my dreams.*

Then she feels a sudden prickle of panic.

What is it? What's wrong with you?

She knits her brows, confused.

There's something. . . .

Something triggered a completely negative sensation inside her just now. She has no idea what it was, but it was there, as real as anything she's ever felt in her life.

In the dark back seat of the car, she starts to chew her lower lip, then stops when she realizes that she'll ruin her lipstick, which she applied so carefully for Ethan's benefit.

What's bothering her? She stares vacantly at the back of the chauffeur's head, trying to put her finger on whatever it was that made her uneasy.

Was, because she no longer feels an acute sense of something unpleasant. Still, though the anxiety is fading, she can't shake it entirely.

In the depths of her consciousness, something has stirred.

Something disturbing.

She blinks and looks over the front seat, through the rain-splattered windshield. The road ahead, the one she walked along earlier this afternoon, is rain-slicked and deserted. The headlights cast a murky glow in the rain. Outside, the steadily howling wind mingles with the rhythmic crashing of the ocean and the squeaking of the windshield wipers.

"Is the house far from here?" Sandy's voice is strained even to her own ears.

"No," the chauffeur says simply, not turning his head.

She looks at his black-gloved hands, notes the way they clench the steering wheel. His posture is stiff and he focuses intently on the road.

He must be nervous about driving in such nasty weather, Sandy tells herself. It certainly is getting worse. The rain is streaming over the windshield despite the furiously moving wipers, and she can feel the car being buffeted by the gale.

Is that why I'm so edgy? she asks herself. *It must be the storm.*

That makes sense. After all, who would want to be out in weather like this, in a strange, out-of-the-way place? Anyone might feel a little nervous about it. Anyone might confuse that feeling for something else.

Déjà vu.

That's what Sandy thought she was feeling a moment ago. It was as though she'd done this before, somehow. But . . .

A romantic weekend on a beautiful island, a chauffeur, a date with a wealthy, gorgeous man . . .

Nope, you've never done anything like this before, she tells herself wryly. *But if you're lucky, maybe this is only the beginning. . . .*

Liza lies on her bed, trying to read the manuscript she'd started this afternoon. Normally, her experienced editor's eye can whiz through three-hundred-and-fifty pages in a matter of hours. But it's taken her ten minutes to read two paragraphs, and she finally shoves the white pages aside again in frustration.

D.M. Yates still hasn't called back again, and Liza is more and more certain that she's been had.

The only thing that's keeping her from being entirely sure is Jasper Hammel.

If he'd merely spoken to Yates on the telephone, it would be one thing. Someone could have called the inn pretending to be the reclusive writer.

But Jasper said Yates was actually here, in the inn, looking for her.

Would Albie—or whoever is behind this scam—actually come all the way out to this island and pose as Yates? Or, even more farfetched, would he go to the trouble of hiring an impostor?

Somehow, Liza can't picture it. After all, Albie—he's the only one she really suspects—is an incredibly busy man. If she's not mistaken, he's in Washington until the end of the month anyway.

So what's going on here, then?

If it's not a wild-goose chase, there's only one other solution. D.M. Yates actually did summon Liza to this island, and he really did come looking for her.

And if that's the case, then sooner or later, he's going to show up again.

When—*if*—he does, Liza plans to be ready for him.

The way she was ready for Albie, and all the others before him.

Men.

If there's one thing Liza knows how to handle, it's a man.

She learned young. As a teenager, she realized she could wrap her father around her little finger. All she had to do was make him feel special. The disgusting, slobbering drunk actually believed her when she told him she loved him, that she thought he was the best daddy in the world.

She wonders what he thinks now. . . .

Now that she hasn't seen him in over ten years.

She walked out of that Brooklyn apartment on the morning after her high school graduation, and she never looked back. Never made an effort to contact him, to let him know where she was or why she had left. Never bothered to find out, in all these years, whether he was dead or alive.

She doesn't care.

At least, that's what she tells herself.

Leaving wasn't something she'd planned to do. Not until she'd marched into the auditorium in her cap and gown and looked toward the spot where her father should have been sitting. It was empty.

And he'd promised. He'd *promised* he'd be there for her, that afterward, he'd take her to White Castle and let her have as many greasy little hamburgers as she could eat.

She had known where he was instead that day, where he always was when she needed him. At the run-down bar a few blocks from their building.

How many times had Liza, as a child, gone in there looking for him?

How many times had she found him, with bloodshot eyes and reeking of liquor, slumped on a stool in the corner of the bar? How many times had he already been passed out when she arrived so that the bartender would have to round up two volunteers to carry him home as little Liza led the way through the seedy neighborhood to their dilapidated building?

Well, she was through. She wasn't going to show up at the bar in her cap and gown, demanding to know why he hadn't shown up to watch her receive her diploma, why he'd allowed her to be the only person in her class who had no one in the audience. Who had no one, period.

Even now, ten years later, Liza feels tears welling up at the memory of that horrible day.

But the next day—the day she left—well,

that was the best day of her life. Because that was the first time she'd realized she didn't need that lousy excuse for a father.

That was the day she'd marched into realtor George Vlapos's office clutching the classified section of the *Times* in one hand and her imitation Chanel purse in the other. Inside the purse was the several hundred dollars she'd just received from a pawnbroker. She'd sold him her mother's wedding and engagement rings.

She'd always known where her father kept them—in the small wooden box on his dresser, along with a lock of his own dead mother's hair and a faded photo of his former wife holding newborn Liza.

Through all the bad times, all the times when there was no food on the table and no heat in the tiny apartment, all the times when her father was desperate for a drink but couldn't even afford cheap wine, those rings had been in that wooden box. Liza had often wondered why he didn't just take them out and sell them.

Deep down, though, she really knew why.

Maybe she felt the same—that as long as the rings were there, a part of her mother remained. A part of the family they had once been.

The pawnbroker was a shifty-eyed slob who had terrible b.o. and leered at Liza over the counter of his shop. He'd snatched the rings in his grubby hand and held them up to the light, then offered a fraction of what Liza knew they were worth. But she didn't care. She needed money, and she needed it fast. Money, and an apartment.

But George Vlapos didn't want to let her rent one of his apartments without references and a security deposit of a month's rent. Unless . . .

Unless what? eighteen-year-old Liza had asked eagerly, sensing a loophole.

There was a loophole, all right. All she had to do was go out to dinner with the swarthy, leering realtor. And, over dinner, she understood the rest of it.

All she had to do was sleep with George Vlapos, and she'd have her apartment.

It was surprisingly easy.

She hadn't let herself think of it as losing her virginity. She hadn't let herself think about it at all, once it was over. Once she had her own apartment—a shabby studio in

Hell's Kitchen, but it was *hers*—she hadn't ever looked back.

And she hadn't dealt with George Vlapos again . . . at least, not until he tried to raise the rent. When he did, she slept with him again, and her rent remained the same.

Men, Liza thinks now, stretching and getting off the bed. *They're all the same. And I know exactly how to handle them.*

D.M. Yates will be no different.

If D.M. Yates is really the one who had summoned her here.

And if not . . .

If Albie, or one of the others, thinks he can get back at her this way . . .

Well, Liza will show him that he can't get the best of her.

Just as she had shown her father.

The shiny black sedan pulls to a stop in front of the last house on the seaside road—a massive Victorian that sits at the tip of the rocky ledge that juts into the ocean.

Sandy stares up at it through the rain-spattered window as the driver turns off the engine and gets out. The house has a classic scallop-shingled mansard roof crowned by an iron-railed widow's walk. Its shuttered double windows are tall and narrow with curved tops. The lamplit ones on the third floor are dormered and the shades are partly lowered, giving the eerie appearance, Sandy thinks, of lidded eyes glowing from beneath a dark hood.

There's a somber air about the place, and Sandy shudders inwardly as she stares up at its silhouette against the stormy night sky.

This isn't what she pictured when she imagined Ethan Thoreau's home. A mansion, yes—this creepy gothic monstrosity, no.

The chauffeur puts up his black umbrella, opens the back door, and offers a gloved hand to help her out.

Sandy wavers for only an instant before placing her fingers in his leather grip.

He holds the umbrella over her head as they hurry through the driving rain up the wooden steps of the porch that runs the length of the house. He turns the knob on one of the double doors and pushes it open. Sandy steps inside, vaguely wondering why it isn't locked, then realizing that there probably isn't much crime on the island. And what burglar would want to come out in this weather?

The door closes behind her, abruptly shutting out the roar of the storm. She turns and sees that maybe she was wrong about crime on the island. Looking out of place on the old-fashioned door panel is a shiny silver deadbolt, the kind that, once it's locked from the inside, requires a key to open it again.

Her father wanted to put one of those locks on their front door back in Greenbury after someone broke into one of their neighbors' homes.

But Angie had talked him out of it, saying it would be a fire hazard.

"What are you talking about?" Tony had asked. "We'll just leave the key in the lock all the time so that if there's a fire, we can get out."

"If the key's in the lock, the burglar can just break the window, reach in, and unlock it anyway," Angie had argued.

They'd settled for a sturdy chain instead.

But in Ethan Thoreau's house, Sandy notices, the double doors don't have windows and the key is sitting in the inside lock.

She wipes her feet on the mat beneath

her feet and looks around. She's standing in a dimly lit entrance hall that rises two stories with a sweeping wooden staircase that leads to a second-floor hallway lined with closed doors. The decor is formal and old-fashioned with dark, heavy drapes over the windows and a tapestry-style carpet on the floor. The dark woodwork is elaborately carved, and the wallpaper is a deep maroon brocade that's illuminated in patches where gaslight sconces dot the walls.

"Wait in there," the chauffeur says, and Sandy turns to see him pointing at a room that's through an archway to the right.

She nods and heads in that direction, again feeling an elusive pin prick of *déjà vu.*

Frowning, she steps into the room and sees that it's a parlor filled with heavy, old-fashioned furniture along with more dark brocade wallpaper, more sconces, more dark woodwork.

She spots a gilt-framed painting hanging over the fireplace and is moving closer to inspect it when she hears a telltale *click* from the foyer.

She knows what it is even before she peeks over her shoulder and sees the chauffeur moving away from the double front doors.

The key that had been in the shiny silver lock is gone.

And Sandy realizes, with a pounding heart, that she's locked in.

Six

Jennie looks up from the magazine she's been trying to read, startled by a knock on the door of her room.

Must be Jasper Hammel.

She'd told the man, when she'd returned from the beach, that she wasn't interested in coming down for dinner.

Oh, but you must, he'd said, his mustache twitching. *I'm making my special rock cornish game hens.*

She'd insisted that she had a stomachache and wasn't hungry, but he'd just smiled and said she'd probably feel better later. *I'll see you in the dining room at eight-thirty,* he'd said.

It's eight-twenty now, according to the travel alarm on the nightstand.

Sighing, Jennie rises from the wingback chair by the fireplace and goes to answer the door, prepared to be rude if she has to be. After all, the whole point of this week-

end was to relax, not to be bullied into joining strangers for dinner and conversation.

Throwing the door open, Jennie opens
her mouth to speak, then clamps it shut
again when she sees who's standing there.

"Hi, Laura." Liza Danning tosses her
blond hair over her shoulder. She's taken it
out of the French twist, and it falls past her
shoulders in straight, silky strands.

"Hi." Jennie wonders what she could
possibly want.

"What are you doing?" Liza peers over
Jennie's shoulder into the room.

"Reading."

"What?"

"I'm reading." Jennie idly notices that
Liza's black sweater is cashmere with velvet
trim and part of an expensive fall designer
collection. Laura has one just like it, and
she splurged more than a week's pay to buy
it. Of course, then she couldn't come up
with her half of the rent and Jennie had to
cover her, as usual. And though that was a
few months ago, Laura still hasn't paid her
back—as usual.

"No—I meant, what are you reading?"
Liza asks.

"Oh . . . just a magazine. *Country Living.*"

"Oh." Liza wrinkles her nose. "I'm not really big on this country stuff. In fact, I'm going nuts out here. There's absolutely nothing to do."

"What about your business meeting?"

"Oh. That."

"What's wrong?"

Liza shrugs. "I just haven't heard from the guy I'm supposed to meet yet, that's all."

"Well, the weather isn't that great." Jennie glances toward the window, which is rattling from the fury of wind and rain outside. "Maybe he couldn't get here."

"You mean to the island? He lives here . . . supposedly."

Jennie frowns. "What? You don't think he really does?"

"I'm not sure. Who knows?" Liza throws her hands up and shakes her head. "But anyway, I wondered if you wanted to come down to dinner with me."

"I wasn't going to—"

"I know, I wasn't either." Liza lowers her voice. "He's a little too weird for me."

Jennie doesn't ask whom she's talking about. Obviously, she isn't the only one who's put off by Jasper Hammel.

"But," Liza continues, "I'm starving. And I

refuse to go down there alone. I bumped into that other person who's staying here, Sandy something-or-other, going into the bathroom a few hours ago, and she was getting ready to go out for the night."

"Well, as I said, I—"

"You've got to eat. And you have to admit, whatever he's making smells pretty good. Come on."

Jennie hesitates. On the one hand, she isn't crazy about Liza's tone, which isn't so much cajoling as it is commanding. On the other, she isn't thrilled by the thought of spending the entire evening alone with her magazine—and her memories.

"Okay, I'll come down with you," she tells Liza, who promptly looks relieved and flashes a smile that actually seems genuine.

"Thanks, Laura. I appreciate it."

"No problem." Jennie gestures at the room behind her. "I'll just comb my hair and meet you—"

"That's okay. I'll wait here for you."

Liza's already past her, walking into the room and glancing around. "It's so frilly," she says with a look of distaste. "Like the one they stuck me in. Only mine's done in pink, not purple."

"Uh huh," Jennie says, watching Liza pick up a gold-rimmed porcelain bud vase, examine it briefly, and plunk it back down on the piecrust table by the bed.

"You know," Liza gestures at the lilac-printed wallpaper, "this light color purple is the exact same shade as your eyes."

"I guess."

"That's kind of a coincidence, don't you think?"

"I guess," Jennie says again.

Liza turns to meet her gaze directly, her own eyes sharp and narrowed. "Does this place give you the creeps?"

"You asked me that before, when we were in town."

"I know. I'm asking you again. Because it seems even creepier now that it's dark out and the storm is going full force."

"It doesn't bother me," Jennie lies.

"Well, it bothers me. I can't wait to get off this island and back to civilization."

Not knowing what, if anything, to say to that, Jennie goes to the dresser and runs a brush through her hair, conscious of Liza watching her. She sets the brush down and picks up a cherry-flavored Chapstick, running it over her dry lips.

"Don't you wear makeup?" Liza asks.

"Not really."

"Mmm."

Jennie knows what she's thinking. It's what Laura always says to her, too—*you'd be so much prettier, Jen, if you'd just take some time to fix yourself up. Wear makeup. Change your hairstyle . . .*

There was a time when Jennie used to take the time to make herself attractive. Back when she and Harry were together . . .

But once Harry was gone, she hadn't bothered. It seemed so unimportant, so frivolous, somehow, after what had happened.

Laura had told her, after she lost Harry, that she should get right back out there and make an effort to find someone new. As if they were in eighth grade again and a boyfriend of the week had dumped her.

At least put on some mascara and use some gel in your hair. You'll never find a man if you don't at least try and look sexy, Jen.

But she'd proved Laura wrong without intending to.

It was almost a year ago that Keegan had materialized in her antique shop one Saturday afternoon in early May, wanting to look through the Haviland china she had on hand. It was for a Mother's Day gift, he'd told Jennie, looking a little sheepish—his mom collected the stuff.

It wasn't until their third date that he'd told Jennie the truth—*he* was the one who collected antiques, including china. Most women, Keegan had added, thought that was a strange hobby for a man to have. *But you seem different, Jennie. . . . You're special. I don't know you that well, but I want to. And I want you to know me, too.*

Jennie fell in love with him on the spot.

But, she reminds herself now, Keegan—like Harry—is history.

Jennie puts down the Chapstick, looks in the mirror again, and sees a reflection of Liza, behind her, zeroing in on the sketch-pad she'd carelessly left open on the bed. She's standing over it before Jennie can divert her.

"Is this what you drew today?" she asks, picking the pad up and looking at the sketch.

"Yeah." Feeling invaded, Jennie turns away from the bureau and is about to tell Liza she's changed her mind about dinner.

But Liza's expression has softened. She smiles at Jennie and says, "This is good, Laura. *Really* good. I mean, I'm not usually crazy about drawings of scenery—I usually like modern art, abstract stuff, better—but I think this is wonderful."

"It's the beach behind the inn."

"Yeah, I recognize it. It's got such a lonely aura. Sad. Not the place itself, but . . . your drawing. Is it your interpretation of what you see out there?"

"I guess it is." Jennie thinks that she obviously revealed too much in her sketch. She doesn't want Liza prying into her private world, asking questions about her past, so she changes the subject. "Why don't we go down to eat? I'm ready."

"Good." Liza takes another look at the sketch, then puts it carefully back on the bed, exactly the way she found it.

Jennie picks up her room key from the dresser and tucks it into the pocket of her jeans. It's probably not necessary to lock the door, but she can't help feeling that she should.

Just in case . . .

In case what? she asks herself, and realizes she doesn't know the answer.

Somehow, she just can't shake the feeling that this inn might not be as idyllic and charming as it seems. That her belongings aren't safe unless the door is locked securely . . .

And that maybe *she* isn't, either.

He hums to himself as he buttons his pristine-white pleated shirt, standing in front of a full-length mirror in the large master bedroom that overlooks the dark, storm-churned sea.

So far, it's been so easy . . . so wonderfully easy that he can't help but worry that something might go wrong.

Relax. . . . What can go wrong now? Everything is in order. Sandy Cavelli is downstairs waiting for you.

He wonders what she's doing right this moment, what she's thinking, whether she's frightened. Probably not. Not yet.

But it won't be long before she's terrified.

Before she's suffering, just as she made him suffer all those years ago.

Just as Lorraine suffered.

He smiles at the thought of her . . .

Lorraine LaCroix.

He will never forget the first moment he laid eyes on her, in the lobby of the American Embassy in France. She was the most beautiful woman he'd ever seen, with that milky skin and deep red hair and eyes the color of emeralds. Her clothes were so impeccable, so stylish that he'd thought she had to be French. No, considering her last name, she'd apparently had French ancestors, she'd told him, but she was an American, working at the embassy as a translator.

He will never forget how sophisticated she was, how she treated him with cool detachment until she found out who he was—rather, who his family was.

Then, those emerald eyes had twinkled at him and her voice had warmed to him. She'd allowed him to take her out to dinner at the finest restaurant in Paris and to make love to her that night in his suite in the finest hotel in all of France.

As dawn filtered through the plate-glass windows on that morning, he'd whispered that he loved her. She hadn't looked horrified or shrunk away from his touch. She had simply smiled the mysterious, close-lipped smile that he would grow to know so well, and she had slipped down beneath the sheets to do incredible things to him. Things no one had ever done to him, not Sandy . . . not Liza . . . not Laura . . .

No one but his mother.

And he wouldn't allow himself to think about that—not then, and he won't now.

He reaches for the bow tie that waits on the dresser and slips it around his neck, tucking it beneath the pointed collar on his shirt. With fluid, expert movements, he ties it, still humming to himself, watching his reflection in the mirror and remembering the last time he wore this tuxedo.

That morning, his hands had been trembling, and he certainly hadn't been humming.

But then, as now, he was fantasizing about the woman who waited for him, and hoping that nothing would go wrong.

Now, the woman is Sandy Cavelli.

Then, it was Lorraine LaCroix—his bride.

It had been her idea to plan a large wedding and to have it in his Manhattan brownstone. She said she wanted everyone they knew to bear witness when she became his wife. She said she wanted the most perfect wedding anyone could imagine, the kind of wedding she had only dreamed of when she was growing up in a bona-fide orphan-age where she had been forced to live an austere, loveless existence.

He remembered the intricate details that had gone into planning the affair, the details Lorraine had embraced with her usual fer-vor.

Nothing but the finest for his fiancée. Wa-terford crystal toasting glasses for all of the guests and imported champagne and caviar. A silk wedding gown created espe-cially for her by the most famous designer in Paris. A guest list that included not only their friends and her family, but New York's social elite, as well as European royalty. Two tickets for a honeymoon trip that would take them around the globe, with reserva-tions for the most exclusive hotels and re-sorts on every continent.

And, of course, red roses. Hundreds of dozens of them. Roses for the brownstone, for her hair, for her bouquet, for his lapel. They were her favorite flower, and their fra-grant aroma would forever remind him of her.

He had sent one-hundred-and-two red roses—one for every day they'd been to-gether—to her suite at the Waldorf-Astoria on the morning of the wedding, along with a carefully composed note that told her how happy he was that she was going to marry him . . .

And how sorry he was for what had happened the night before.

After the rehearsal dinner, he had gone up to her suite with her, assuming he would spend a few hours there, if not the entire night.

Lorraine had told him she didn't want him to come in, that she didn't want to make love to him that night. She had gone on to tell him something about how she wanted their next time to be after they were married.

He hadn't been able to focus on what she was saying.

Stung, he had only stared at her, seeing only rejection on her face, hearing it in her voice . . .

Once again, seeing and hearing Sandy Cavelli . . .

Liza Danning . . .

Laura Towne . . .

And now Lorraine, too.

Suddenly, he had gone into a frenzy, grabbing his startled fiancée and throwing her down on the bed. As she protested, then screamed, and finally cried hysterically, he had forced himself on her, violently invading her body with his mouth and fingers and ultimately with his penis, mercilessly thrusting into her over and over again until he at last was able to release several years worth of pent-up fury.

Only when he had rolled off of her and seen her tear-stained, scratched and bleeding face, her torn dress, her terror-filled eyes, had he realized what he'd done.

Too stunned to react, he had simply gotten dressed and left the suite, leaving Lorraine still whimpering and huddled on the bed.

He hadn't slept that night.

He had lain in his own king-sized bed in the brownstone, listening to the traffic going down Fifth Avenue and wondering how he could have lost control that way.

He was sorry, truly sorry.

And Lorraine, he knew, would forgive him.

Because Lorraine loved him. She wanted to marry him. She wanted to spend every moment, the rest of her life, with him.

Lorraine was his, would always be his.

At exactly noon, dressed in his tuxedo with a white rosebud carefully pinned on his lapel, he had taken his place in the drawing room on the first floor of his brownstone. There—in front of the twenty rows of rented white folding chairs, in front of the two hundred people who at first smiled and chattered quietly, then began to shift uncomfortably on their seats and check their watches—he waited.

And waited . . .

And waited . . .

Sandy sits on the edge of an uncomfortable antique sofa, her clammy hands clasped tightly in her lap so that they won't tremble so much. Beneath her long navy skirt, the one she chose so carefully for her date tonight, her right leg is bouncing rapidly up and down from nerves.

But not the kind of nerves she'd expected to have now as she is about to meet the man who summoned her here.

She's not breathless with romantic anticipation.

No, she's breathless with fright.

For the last twenty minutes, as she's sat

here in the parlor waiting for Ethan Thoreau to appear, she's repeatedly told herself that she needs to calm down. That there's absolutely no reason to feel panicky. That she's certainly not in any kind of danger.

Even though this house looks like something out of a gothic horror movie.

Even though the chauffeur locked her inside, then vanished up the stairs.

If she were a different kind of person, Sandy thinks for the umpteenth time, she would get off this sofa and leave this room and look around the house, making sure there's another way out.

Just in case.

But, being spineless Sandy Cavelli, she just sits here in the parlor, looking helplessly back at the archway leading out into the hall and at the French doors on an interior wall at the other end of the room, their glass windows made opaque by heavy draperies on the other side.

And she grows more and more agitated, wondering. And listening . . .

For something. Anything.

Outside, the wind grows more and more ferocious, sweeping in from the sea to batter the house.

Inside, the minutes tick by on the old grandfather clock in the corner of the parlor.

The parlor is lit only by the fire on the hearth and the white votive candles that glow from tables and shelves around the room. The effect might be cozy or even romantic somewhere else, Sandy thinks; but here, the flickering light only seems eerie.

Finally, she hears a creaking from the hall; someone is descending the stairs.

One step at a time.

No longer caring about her lipstick, Sandy bites down, hard, on her bottom lip and clenches her hands even more tightly, holding her breath and listening.

Finally, the footsteps reach the bottom.

Sandy braces herself for whatever is going to happen. She turns and looks expectantly toward the archway leading to the hall.

But instead of coming into the parlor, whoever is out there—can it really be Ethan?—passes by, still moving in that same methodic manner, fleetingly casting a tall shadow on the wall opposite the sofa where Sandy waits.

This is too strange. . . .

There's something wrong. . . .

I have to get out of here. . . .

Sandy's eyes dart wildly around the room. She looks at the two sets of narrow double windows which stretch almost from floor to ceiling. Can she open one and climb out?

No. Instinctively, she knows that they, too, will be locked. And they're paned, so she can't break one and escape that way, either.

Escape.

Are you crazy? You've been waiting for weeks to meet Ethan Thoreau. And now you want to break a window and escape from him? What are you thinking? What will this man think if he hears shattering glass and sees you fleeing into the night? You've definitely lost it. You have to—

Suddenly, she hears a faint sound coming from behind the French doors.

Music.

Wide-eyed, she turns in that direction and strains to listen. She knows this melody. . . .

It's from *West Side Story,* she realizes abruptly. She's seen the movie countless times. This is the song Maria and Tony sing when they pretend to get married.

"One Hand, One Heart."

The lyrics become audible as the song

grows louder in the next room, as though someone has turned up the volume. The familiar tune is reassuring, and Sandy feels her body relax slightly.

He's setting the mood for seduction, she tells herself. *This is classic. Soft music, candlelight . . .*

Everything is going to be all right.

For a long time, she sits there, listening to the song and waiting for something to happen.

"One Hand, One Heart" ends and a new song begins.

Sandy recognizes this one, too. "Color My World." Her cousin Maria sang it at Danny and Cheryl's wedding.

She hears the footsteps again, this time approaching the French doors. There's a click; and then, as she watches, the knobs turn and both doors swing slowly open.

A man is standing there, his face lost in the shadows, but his tall, broad-shouldered frame clearly silhouetted in the doorway.

"Sandra Cavelli . . . you're here with me at last." His voice is low and soft, so soft that she has to strain to hear him above the music.

She clears her throat and stands, subconsciously wiping her sweaty palms on her skirt. "Hello . . . Ethan?"

He doesn't respond, just stands there. She can't see his eyes in the dim light, but she can feel him watching her. She fights the urge to squirm under his gaze.

When he doesn't move or say anything else, she takes a few tentative steps toward him. As she draws closer, she sees that he's wearing a tuxedo.

A tuxedo! For a date in his own house!

She takes a deep breath and notices that the air suddenly seems filled with a heady floral scent, like potpourri or perfume . . .

"You look lovely, Sandra," he says quietly.

This time, something strikes her about his voice. She's heard it someplace before . . .

The chauffeur!

An involuntary shiver shoots through Sandy. She nearly gasps out loud as she realizes that the man standing in the doorway is the chauffeur who drove her from the inn.

But why? Why would he do it—pretend to be someone else?

She struggles to maintain her composure, telling herself that he's probably just eccentric; lots of rich people are that way, aren't they?

Hysteria mounts inside her; yet outwardly, she forces a smile and says, "It's so nice to meet you at last, Mr. Thoreau."

She expects him to say *call me Ethan.*

But he doesn't. He says, "Oh, we've met before, Sandra."

Should she admit that she realizes what he's done?

"Do you recognize me?"

He steps closer to her, and she peers at him through the flickering light. "Actually, I do recognize you," she says, deciding to play his game and thrusting lightness into her voice. "You're the chauffeur who picked me up at the inn, aren't you?"

He laughs, a surprisingly robust sound that catches Sandy off-guard . . .

A sound that again triggers that feeling of *déjà vu* she experienced in the car.

I know him, she realizes uneasily. *Not just because he drove me here earlier. I know him . . . from a long time ago.*

But who is he?

"Who am I, Sandra?" he asks as though he's invaded her thoughts. "I *am* the chauffeur, but who am I, really?" There's a smirk in his voice.

A prickle of panic shoots through her

again. Her mind races, searching for the answer.

Who is he?

Who *is* he?

It becomes a refrain that screams inside her brain as she stares at him, trying to remember.

"You don't know, do you?" he asks, the smirk fading into a sinister chill. "Damn you. I knew I didn't matter to you. But I didn't think you cared so little that you'd forget me entirely. Admit it, Sandy. Admit it!"

"Admit what?" she asks in a small, strangled-sounding voice.

"Admit that you don't even know me!" He takes another step closer to her. Suddenly, his face is illuminated in the path of a candle on the grand piano.

Sandy freezes, then claps a hand over her mouth.

"Say it, Sandy. Say it, damn it!" His voice is hoarse with vehemence. "Say you don't know who I am!"

But she can't.

Because suddenly, she does know exactly who he is.

And she's paralyzed by stark terror.

* * *

Rain is pouring from the black night sky as Danny Cavelli slams the car door and walks up the driveway to the back door of the house he and Cheryl bought right before they were married. He notices, as he stomps heavily up the back steps, that another piece of wood has crumbled away from the edge of the tiny back porch.

He turns to Cheryl, who's hurrying through the rain a few steps behind him, and gestures at the splintered floor. "Look at that. This whole place is falling apart. But I'll never get around to fixing it because I spend all my time helping my family fix things around their houses."

They climb onto the porch, where the leaky roof keeps some of the rain out.

Cheryl sighs. "Danny—"

"I mean, Tony says he needs help moving a freakin' piece of furniture, and I get over there, and what does he have me doing? Cleaning the gutters on his house. In the pouring rain. In the dark."

"Danny," Cheryl says again as he jabs the key into the lock, "you know he didn't plan on having you do it. He just noticed that tree branch had fallen into the gutter, and he can't climb because of his knee, and he—"

"Yeah, the knee he hurt running away the day he and Frankie left me alone in the woods when I was six years old, Cheryl. Nice guy, huh?"

Muttering to himself, Danny opens the door and steps into the kitchen. He flips on a light and tosses his keys on the counter.

"Danny, come on, don't ruin our night," Cheryl says, following him in and locking the door behind her.

"*I'm* not the one who's ruining it," Danny tells her. "My brother ruined it. Thanks to him, we missed the movie."

"I told you that if we hurried, we could have gotten there only a few minutes late."

"Who wants to miss the first few minutes? You really have to pay attention in those John Grisham movies. We wouldn't know what was going on."

"They never start them on time at the Cineplex anyway," Cheryl points out. "They have coming attractions."

"Yeah, well, whatever." Danny goes over to the refrigerator and pulls out a can of beer. "You want one, babe?"

Cheryl shrugs. "Why not? I'll make some popcorn and we'll watch TV."

"Nothing good on—not on a Saturday night."

"Well, then we'll think of something else to do," Cheryl says, shooting a meaningful smile in her husband's direction.

"Yeah," Danny says, meeting her gaze as he pops open one beer, then the other. "Maybe we will. Hey, maybe Tony didn't ruin my night after all, huh?"

"Laura! I'm so glad you decided to join us after all!" Jasper Hammel looks up from the tapered candles he's lighting in the middle of the dining-room table.

"Oh, um, yes . . . I'm feeling better." Jennie smiles faintly and glances back at Liza, who's two steps behind her.

"Did you hear from D.M. Yates again?" Liza asks Jasper abruptly in a no-nonsense voice.

"No, of course I didn't," he replies in his unruffled way. "If he had called or come by again, I would have come up to get you."

"Are you sure about that?" Liza scowls and plunks herself into a seat at the table.

Jasper seems to be ignoring her as he bustles over to the sideboard and uncorks a bottle of wine with a flourish.

Only two places are set at the long oval table tonight.

"Where's Sandy?" Jennie asks, settling into the chair across from Liza's.

"I'm afraid she had a change of plans."

"What do you mean?"

Jasper sniffs the open wine bottle, his eyes closed. "Mmm, an exquisite bouquet. Yes, well, Sandy decided, earlier, to go back to the mainland."

Liza, who had been fiddling with her silverware, looks up sharply.

Jennie frowns and glances toward the window. "In this weather?"

"I'm afraid so."

"But what about her hot date?" Liza asks. "I thought she was meeting some guy here tonight."

"Apparently, she changed her mind. She was driven to the ferry dock a little while ago."

"But I thought the last ferry of the day left this afternoon," Jennie says.

Jasper looks up from the wine decanter

he's tilting over her glass. He clears his throat, and his mustache twitches. "Oh, it normally does leave early. But not today. Because of the, er, holiday weekend, there are extra ferries scheduled for today. Sandy caught the last one."

"Oh." Jennie toys with the blue cloth napkin she was about to spread in her lap.

"I'll be right back with some rolls," Jasper says and hurries through the door into the kitchen.

As soon as he's gone, Liza leans toward Jennie. "Did you hear that?" she asks in a low voice.

"Hear what?"

"What he said about Sandy and the ferry?"

"What about it?"

"He was lying."

Jennie tries to ignore the jittery feeling in the pit of her stomach. "Why would he lie?"

"Who knows? I told you he was strange. But trust me, Sandy wouldn't change her mind about going out with that guy."

"How do you know? You barely know her."

Liza rolls her eyes. "Oh, come on, Laura. I

know enough to be sure that a chub like her wouldn't turn down a chance to date some good-looking guy who has a lot of bucks."

Turned off by Liza's attitude, Jennie just shrugs and says, "Whatever." But inwardly, her heart is pounding. It didn't take Liza to tell her that Jasper Hammel wasn't telling the truth. She sensed it herself.

"Laura, I'm telling you," Liza whispers loudly, "something's up." Her green eyes are wide.

Looking at her, Jennie senses that Liza has a vulnerable side.

And that perhaps her own nerves about this place aren't merely due to her post-traumatic stress disorder after all.

But if Jasper Hammel really is lying . . .

Why?

And if Sandy didn't really leave the island . . .

Where is she?

"What's wrong, Laura?" Shawn asks, leaning across the small table in the crowded Newbury Street restaurant.

"Nothing," she says brightly, snapping out of her reverie and stabbing a large piece of shrimp tempura with her fork. She pops it into her mouth.

"You look preoccupied."

"I was just thinking about how glad I am that you're back. . . . I really missed you." That last part is the truth, although it wasn't what she'd been thinking about.

"I missed you, too." Shawn smiles at her and reaches across the table to pat her hand before picking up his chopsticks again.

Laura looks at him, wondering how long it'll be before she screws up this relationship, as she has all the others. Somehow, she can never keep a man. Well, not any man she'd want, anyway.

The only ones who ever get hooked on her for the long term are the losers. And her ex-husband, Brian, was the biggest loser of all.

A dangerous loser at that.

Laura still has the scar on her cheek, just beneath her left eye, where he burned her with his cigarette the night he accused her of sleeping around on him. She'd hysterically tried to explain that she hadn't come home because she'd been at the emergency room with her grandfather, waiting for the prognosis on her grandmother, who'd had another heart attack.

But Brian, crazed with jealousy and booze, had only reached out to burn her again. That time, at least, the red tip of his cigarette had missed her face, instead landing on the couch cushion after she'd ducked. She'd let him keep the couch when she left; had let him keep everything, in fact, except the few mementos she had of her parents and the antique set of china that Jennie had given them as a shower gift.

She still has the china, in a box under her bed in the town house. Since she and Brian never actually used it, she figures she won't mind keeping it for when she's married again. *If* she's married again . . ."

She sighs inwardly and looks at Shawn, whose dark, boyish good looks have attracted quite a few appreciative glances from the other women in the restaurant.

"Don't you like your tempura?" he asks.

"Sure, it's good." She eats another piece of shrimp. "I can't believe you wanted Japanese food after spending a month in Tokyo."

"I got used to it." Shawn shrugs and grips

a glistening red slab of raw tuna with his chopsticks.

Laura wrinkles her nose, watching as he dunks it into the small porcelain bowl that contains a mixture of soy sauce and some disgusting green goop—wasabi, he calls it.

"You know, Shawn," she says as he reaches for another slimy piece of fish, "sushi isn't good for you. It's full of worms—you know, parasites."

"Oh well."

"Jennie doesn't care, either. She loves that stuff," Laura says, shaking her head and having another bite of her shrimp with its light, deep-fried breading.

"How *is* your sister?"

"She's okay. I guess."

"What's wrong?"

Laura looks at him. "I don't know. I mean, I keep thinking about her tonight. It's like I'm worried about her, or something. Not that there's any reason to be. But Keegan—"

"He's her boyfriend, right? The cop."

"*Ex*-boyfriend now. He stopped over right before I left to pick you up at the airport, and I guess he started me thinking about my sister. She's out on Tide Island for the weekend, staying at some inn."

"Alone?"

Laura nods and quickly fills him in about the charity sweepstakes and how she'd won and given the trip to Jennie, who is posing as her.

Shawn rolls his eyes. "I thought you said you guys never pull that twin stuff anymore."

"I said I would never switch places with Jennie to fool you," Laura says with a grin.

"Don't worry. . . . You couldn't fool me. Even if your hair was long like Jennie's, I'd know you from your sister the second we got into bed."

"Shawn!"

"Laura!" He grins at her, and his corn-flower-blue eyes look her up and down. "You're about a hundred thousand times more uninhibited than Jennie."

"Oh? And how do you know?"

"Be serious. Your sister's a little . . . strait-laced."

"And what am I?"

He bobs his eyebrows suggestively. "I'll tell you later."

Laura smiles, puts her fork down, and wipes her mouth with her napkin. "Why wait until later? Leave the rest of that stuff you're eating here—it'll probably swim away on its own—and let's get out of here. Unless you're still hungry."

"You know, I'm suddenly feeling full." Shawn puts down his chopsticks and motions for the check. Then he turns back to Laura. "Forgive the cliché, but—your place or mine?"

"You're joking, right? You have three roommates. My sister's away for the weekend."

"Right. But I do have to stop home first."

She groans.

"Come on, Laura, I haven't been there in a month. I just want to check my mail and messages and find something unrumpled to wear. It'll take two minutes."

"Shawn, with you, two minutes is usually two hours."

"I'll be fast. I promise."

"Fine." She pushes her chair back as the waiter drops the check on the table. "But then we go straight back to my place."

"Definitely." He lowers his voice and leans forward. "Believe me, Laura, I want you as much as you want me. It's been a helluva long time to go without it."

She murmurs her agreement.

But she can't help thinking that eagerness to be alone with Shawn isn't the only reason she wants to get back to the town house she shares with her sister.

For some reason, she feels compelled to make sure Jennie's all right, that she hasn't called from the island, or perhaps come back early.

Of course she's all right, Laura tells herself as she follows Shawn out onto the street. *What could be wrong?*

Nothing.

Jennie is probably having a wonderful time.

But Laura can't seem to shake her concern for her twin. And the last time she felt this way—the *only* other time she was ever plagued by this nagging anxiety about her sister's well-being—was the fateful day three years ago when disaster struck and shattered Jennie's life.

"Stephen? Stephen Gilbrooke?" Sandy finally manages to utter his name and sees him stiffen at the sound of it.

"You remember."

"I . . . yes." Sandy clamps her mouth shut and stares at him through frightened eyes.

"How did you recognize me? I had the best plastic surgeon in Europe make me into a new person. I don't look anything like my old self."

Sandy isn't sure what to say. A moment ago, he was disturbed that she didn't know who he was. Now, he seems disturbed that she does.

He's waiting for an answer, standing absolutely still and watching her.

"It's your eyes, actually," she tells him. "They look familiar."

"But I'm wearing colored contacts. Blue. My eyes are usually brown, like yours."

"I know," Sandy says around the lump of fear in her throat. She can't tell him that it isn't the eyes themselves that triggered the memory. . . . It's the expression in them.

An expression that fills her with dread now, just as it did so long ago.

Though she hasn't thought of it in years, that day has suddenly come back to her with crystal clarity.

The day she told Stephen Gilbrooke to get lost.

It was early September, the last Friday

before Labor Day weekend. Sandy had spent so many days that summer at Stephen's parents' estate on the Long Island Sound. . . .

It was the year her father had twisted his back crawling out from under a sink and couldn't work for several months. Her mother had been forced to take a part-time job as a maid for Andrew Gilbrooke, who owned a thriving import-export business, and his wife, Aurelia.

Their only child was Stephen, who was about thirteen that summer. Sandy had felt sorry for him from the moment she first saw him hovering outside the kitchen door, shyly kicking the manicured grass with the toes of his immaculate white sneakers.

He was ugly . . . pitifully ugly.

His hair was black and kinky and stuck out awkwardly around his teacup-handle ears. Acne covered his face, and his features were misshapen. "Funnel Face," the other summer kids called him. At least, that was what he'd told Sandy.

She'd been kind to him, because her mother had told her to be and because she felt sorry for him. She knew how cruel other kids could be. The boys at school had taken to calling her Thunder Thighs that spring.

Sandy had accompanied her mother to the Gilbrookes' estate many times that summer, and she and Stephen had become friends. Sandy had taught him how to fish, just as Danny had taught her a few years earlier. He'd shown her where wild raspberries grew in the woods, and the two of them had eaten the sun-warmed berries until their fingertips and tongues were stained red.

Toward the end of the summer, Sandy had started feeling uneasy when she was with Stephen. There was something unnerving about the way he looked at her and the way he spoke to her.

Almost as though he worshipped her, or something.

No one—especially no *boy*—had ever treated Sandy that way. She'd always thought it would be wonderful if someone would.

Maybe if it were someone else . . .

But something about Stephen made her want to squirm. It wasn't his homely looks that bothered her, or his painful shyness.

It was more the quiet intensity that radiated from him, the sense that though he said little, a lot was happening in his mind. Things Sandy might rather not know . . . particularly when it pertained to the kids who called him Funnel Face.

Or to his mother.

She had seen Stephen's back stiffen and his jaw clench at the sound of his mother's voice, and she had seen something dark glinting in his eyes whenever he mentioned her.

Stephen frightened her.

It seemed that the more uncomfortable she grew around him, the more attached he became to her.

Angie Cavelli wouldn't let Sandy stay home alone while she was working and her father and brothers were all busy with the business, so she had no choice but to go to the Gilbrookes' estate with her mother through the end of the season.

It was about a week before Labor Day that Stephen tried to kiss her.

They'd been walking up the lane from the pond where they fished, and Sandy had been lost in thoughts of school's starting in a few days. With no warning, Stephen had suddenly grabbed her and planted his lips over hers.

Astonished, Sandy had shoved him away and shrieked, "What are you doing?"

He'd looked even more startled than she was. "I'm . . . I'm so sorry. I mean . . . God, I'm sorry." He'd blushed so quickly and completely that Sandy found herself feeling sorry for him.

"It's okay," she'd said, even though it wasn't. "We'll forget it happened."

Thank God, she was thinking, that there were only a few more days left of seeing him.

He had been more subdued than usual for the remainder of that week. Then, on that Friday, the last day Sandy would be at the estate, he had grabbed her and tried to kiss her again.

That time, she had reacted by slapping his pock-marked face, hard.

His jaw had dropped in shock, and she had seen fury in his eyes before he grabbed her and forced his lips over hers again. This time, he held her head firmly beneath his, his fingertips digging painfully into her scalp as he ground his wet, open mouth against hers.

Only when she'd let out a strangled sob did he release her.

"What do you think you're doing?" she'd screamed, her voice echoing through the quiet woods around the pond.

"Kissing you," he'd said calmly.

"Well, I don't want to kiss you." She'd wiped her mouth furiously with the back of her hand. "I don't even like you."

"What do you mean, you don't like me? You've been hanging around with me all summer."

"I wouldn't be here if it weren't for my mother's job," Sandy had heard herself saying. "She makes me be nice to you because she wants to suck up to your mother. Thank God today's the last day I'll have to hang around with an ugly freak like you. Because I can't stand you."

For a moment, he'd just looked at her, and the pain in his expression was raw enough to cut to Sandy's heart.

But before she could take her cruel words back, he changed. As though something had snapped inside of him, his eyes had hardened and his mouth was set grimly.

"Get away from me," he'd said in an ominously quiet voice.

"But Stephen, I—"

"Get the hell away from me. And don't

ever come back here again. Because if you do, I'll . . . I'll kill you."

How many times had her two oldest brothers told her exactly that?

I'm going to kill you, Tony Junior or Frankie would say when she'd threatened to tell their parents about something or other or when she'd teased about a girl from school or when she was simply being a bratty little sister.

I'm going to kill you.

She'd heard it so many times before.

But never in her life had the words struck her with such icy force as when Stephen Gilbrooke uttered them on that long ago, sunny summer day. Though she'd been shaken at first, she'd eventually forgotten all about that, had forgotten him, too, until now.

And now, as Sandy looks into those same hard, cold eyes, the threat echoes back at her over the years.

I'm going to kill you.

Seven

Liza sets her dessert plate on the low table in front of the sofa and glances at Laura, who's still picking at the pastry on her plate.

"Don't you like strudel?" she asks lightly, reaching for her teacup, which is nearly empty.

"What?" Laura looks up at her, then shakes her head. "It's not that. I'm just . . . I guess I'm not very hungry."

"Are you okay?"

"I'm fine."

Liza shrugs and drains her cup. Laura Towne isn't fine. For the last fifteen minutes, as they've sat here in the parlor in silence, the woman has worn a haunted, faraway look in her lilac-colored eyes. She hasn't touched her tea, and she's barely eaten the pastry Jasper Hammel painstakingly arranged on her plate.

At least, Liza thinks, he hasn't been buzzing around them as much tonight. Earlier, she heard the sound of water running and pots clattering in the kitchen, which meant he must be doing the dishes. And now there's only silence at the back of the house.

Liza is about to reach for the porcelain teapot on the serving table beside her when she hears a faint knocking.

Laura, too, looks up sharply at the sound.

"What was that?" Liza asks.

Laura shrugs.

They both sit absolutely still, listening.

At first, there's only the ever-present wind and the staccato spattering of raindrops against the windows.

Then the knocking sound again.

"That's coming from the front of the house," Laura says, and Liza nods.

"I think someone's at the door," she tells Laura.

"But why would someone knock? Isn't the door kept unlocked at this hour?"

"Who knows?" Liza hears the knocking again, this time more persistent. "Maybe that fruitcake in the kitchen can't hear it."

"I'll get him." Laura stands and goes over

to the door, poking her head into the hall-way. "Mr. Hammel?"

Liza watches as she moved down the hall and opens the kitchen door, repeating, "Mr. Hammel?"

After a moment, Laura returns and says, "He's not around."

"He's not? Where could he be?"

"I have no idea. There's a back stairway in there—maybe he's upstairs."

"Well, we'd better answer the door." Liza is already halfway there.

In the foyer, she sees a tall figure standing on the other side of the glass door. Sure enough, the bolt is turned, and Liza hurries to open it.

Maybe this is D.M. Yates at last, she thinks, as a tall man steps inside, his face obscured by the hood of a bulky black storm coat.

He shakes the water off like a wet dog, then lowers the hood and pulls the door closed behind him.

Liza stares. He's a large man, not hand-some exactly, though his red-hair, freckled complexion, and wide, easy grin are ap-pealing.

"Hi," he says cheerfully, wiping the rain

off his ruddy cheeks. "How are you ladies tonight?"

Ladies? Liza turns and sees Laura standing behind her beside the front desk.

"I'm Pat Gerkin," the guy continues. "You two must be staying here at the inn."

"We are," Liza tells him.

"Is the manager around?"

"He's here someplace, but we're not sure where. Why?"

"I wanted to let him know that if this storm gets any worse, the homes along the coast are going to be evacuated. You can all take shelter at the Congregational church. It's pretty much in the center of the island."

"Do you think that'll happen?" Laura asks, sounding concerned.

"What? The storm getting worse? Maybe. It's a nor'easter, and right now, it's blowing right for us. Hurricane-force winds, and maybe even some snow, too. Of course, it might still veer off and miss the island; but as of the last weather report, we're in for trouble."

"You seem pretty happy about it," Liza observes, noting the guy's perpetually twinkling blue eyes.

He shrugs. "I've been through a lot of these storms. I'm a fisherman on the island year-round. And in the summer, I work part time on the local police force. These things are rough while they last; but eventually, they blow by and we clean up the damage. Hopefully, this one won't be too bad."

"How do we know if we should evacuate?" Laura asks.

"Someone will come around and let you know. Have some things packed to take with you, just in case." Pat looks around. "The manager didn't go out in this weather and leave you here, did he?"

"Who knows?" Liza shrugs. "Do you know him well?"

"Who?"

"Jasper Hammel."

"Oh, that's his name? The little guy with the mustache, right?"

She nods.

"Yeah, I've seen him around here and there, but we've never met. He's not the friendly type. And he's new on the island."

Liza frowns. "How new?"

"Only been here a few weeks. And this is the first weekend the inn's in operation again since it was sold to the new owner at the end of last summer."

Liza and Laura exchange a glance.

"Who's the new owner?" Laura asks.

Pat Gerkin shrugs. "I have no idea. Some businessman from the mainland. He hasn't been out here since he bought it, but he's kept the people who live here pretty busy with renovation work."

"Let me ask you something," Liza says, frowning. "Have you ever heard of D.M. Yates?"

"The writer?"

"You know him?" she asks, relieved at the expression of recognition that crosses the guy's features.

"Sure."

"Then he does live out here, after all," Liza says. "Thank God. I was really starting to think this was just a wild-goose—"

"Who lives out here?" Pat interrupts. "Yates?"

"Doesn't he?"

"Live on Tide Island? Nope."

"What do you mean? I thought you said you knew him."

"I know his work. Just finished *Before a Fall* last week, as a matter of fact." Pat leans against the wall and folds his arms across his chest. "It was hard to get through those first few chapters; but once you got into it, it was a good story."

"When you said you knew him, I thought . . ."

"You thought the man himself, not his books. No, I read a lot. Hey, don't look so surprised. I may be a fisherman now, but I was an English major in college. Used to write poetry and everything."

"I'm not surprised about that," Liza murmurs, glancing over her shoulder at Laura, who looks a little paler than usual. "It's just that I was supposed to meet Yates out here, and I've been waiting for him to show."

"Well, I guarantee you that he doesn't live here. I'm on this island year-round and have been all my life. I know everyone here, except for the tourists. And even if Yates is on his way out here to meet you, you're going to have a long wait. The ferry schedule has been suspended until the storm passes by. Water's too rough."

"You mean we can't leave?" Laura asks, her voice sounding slightly high-pitched. "The last ferry tonight was the last one, period?"

"There was no ferry tonight," Pat Gerkin says, looking puzzled. "There never is on Saturday nights."

"Not even on holiday weekends?" Liza asks, her heart flip-flopping erratically in her chest.

"Nope," Pat Gerkin says. "The last Saturday ferry left this afternoon."

Slowly, Liza turns to look at Laura again. She knows what Laura's thinking. It's the same thing that Liza is thinking.

That Jasper Hammel really did lie about Sandy.

That she didn't leave the island on the late ferry, because there was no late ferry.

That somewhere on this island, right this very moment, Sandy Cavelli might be in serious trouble.

Keegan McCullough is sitting in front of the television on the verge of biting into the enormous ham-and-cheese sandwich he just bought at Subway, when the phone rings.

He reaches for it with his left hand, still holding the sandwich with his right.

"Hello?" he says, then bites into the sandwich.

"Hey, Keegan, it's me."

"Buddy?" he asks around a mouthful. He hurriedly chews and swallows.

"Yeah. What are you doing?"

"Watching the tail end of 'Cops' and eating dinner. Why? What's up?"

"You know that sweepstakes ticket you gave me?"

Keegan lowers the sandwich. "What about it?"

"That charity is bogus."

"No way." The food he just swallowed churns in Keegan's stomach. "Are you sure?"

"Yup. I'm telling you, these crooks are all over the city."

"Bud, Jennie's out on Tide Island for the weekend, courtesy of that bogus charity."

"Yeah, you told me that before. At least whoever put this scam together awarded the prize. They usually don't."

"Why would they?" Keegan asks, trying to ignore the chill that's creeping through him.

"I don't know—probably to keep people from being suspicious. You know, they probably figure that whoever wins will tell people about it, which means those people will be more likely to buy tickets for that same so-called charity the next time around."

"I guess . . ."

"Listen, Keegan, do you know the name of the place where Jennie's staying on the island? I'm going to call the management there and see what they can tell me about whoever made the arrangements."

"I don't know the name of the inn, but I'll find out for you. Her sister Laura will know."

"Good. Give me a call back when you get it."

"I will." Keegan puts the sandwich aside, rewrapping it, then shoving it back into the Subway bag. He no longer has an appetite. "Hopefully, Laura will be home now. If not, I'll keep trying tonight until I get her."

"No big rush."

Maybe not for you, Keegan thinks, saying goodbye to Buddy and hanging up. But he can't help feeling a sense of urgency. The sooner he tracks Jennie down, the better.

With swift but fumbling fingers, he begins dialing the familiar number of the Back Bay town house.

* * *

Trembling from head to toe, Sandy tears her eyes away from Stephen Gilbrooke's strangely expressionless face.

For the first time, she looks into the room behind him, the one beyond the French doors. What she sees there is puzzling, so puzzling that she glances at him again, wondering if this is some kind of joke.

"What do you think, Sandy?" he asks in a low, crooning voice. "Isn't it lovely?"

She stammers that it is, then takes an involuntary step backward when he reaches for her arm.

"What's the matter?" he barks. "You don't want me to touch you? You don't want me near you? Just like before?"

"I'm sorry," she says helplessly, forcing herself to remain still as his fingers close over her wrist.

"Come with me, Sandy."

He propels her through the doors, then stops and sweeps a hand through the air. "This is for you. I did all of this for you."

She nods, afraid that if she tries to speak, she'll sob.

The room is enormous, with a delicate

crystal chandelier hanging in the center. It must have been a ballroom once, Sandy thinks vaguely as she takes in the scene before her.

The music wafting from the portable stereo on a table—"Sunrise, Sunset" from *Fiddler on the Roof.*

The rows of white folding chairs.

The white runner stretched along the center aisle.

The vases of red roses that are everywhere, filling the air with a floral scent so overpowering that Sandy feels dizzy.

Stephen lets go of Sandy's arm, and she glances wildly about, looking for a place to run.

But then he's grabbing onto her again with one hand and waving something at her with the other.

Puzzled, she can only gape.

It's a hanger . . .

On it is a white dress . . .

A wedding dress.

"I had this made for you," Stephen is saying.

His words aren't sinking in.

Sandy stares at the dress, her mind racing.

He's crazy. I have to get out of here.

"I *said,* put it on," Stephen shouts, pinching her arm painfully.

"I'm sorry. . . . I didn't hear you." Sandy winces as he thrusts the dress at her with a rustle of silk. Her fingers automatically close around the fabric.

"Good. Now wear it."

"But—"

"Now." Stephen steps back and folds his arms, watching her. "It should fit perfectly."

"But how . . ."

"I had it made just for you. It wasn't hard to do. All I had to do was find out your size, and that was easy. Your co-worker at Greenbury Gal was very cooperative."

Greenbury Gal. The store where Sandy bought the outfit she has on right now, the special outfit for her date with Ethan Thoreau . . . who doesn't even exist.

"Andrea told you what size I wear?" Sandy asks incredulously, staring at Stephen Gilbrooke's smirking face. "Why would she do that?"

"Why does anyone do anything? Money. And I've got plenty of it. But then, Sandy, you already know that, don't you?"

"What do you mean?"

"Just put the dress on. And the veil."

Sandy glances down and sees the layer of illusion netting that's fastened to a headpiece looped around the top of the hanger.

Then she looks up at Stephen again.

"I don't want to wear this," she says resolutely, hoping he'll back down. He always was a wimp.

For a long moment, he just stares back at her and she fights not to let herself break the eye contact.

Then he reaches into the inside pocket of his black tuxedo coat and pulls something out.

It's a butcher knife.

"If I were you, Sandy," he says in a quiet, lethal tone, "I'd put on the wedding gown."

Laura sits on Shawn's rumpled twin bed, bouncing impatiently as he unpacks his luggage, tossing nearly everything into the blue plastic laundry basket on the floor.

"I can't believe you went away for over a month and didn't make your bed before you left," she says, leaning back against the pillow.

"Well, not everyone is as good a housekeeper as you are." Shawn holds a folded T-shirt up to his nose, sniffs the sleeve, makes a face, and tosses it into the basket.

"I just like to keep things in order," Laura lies, toying with the frayed edge of his beige comforter.

What would Shawn say if he knew she's a bigger slob than he is? So far, she's managed to fool him, cleaning her room every time she knows he's coming over. The rest of the place always looks fine . . . as long as Jennie's around.

At the thought of her sister, Laura sits up again and checks her watch.

"In a rush to get someplace?" Shawn asks, glancing up at her.

She pins on a sexy smile and purrs, "Yeah. Home. With you."

"In that case . . ." He crosses over to the bed and leans down to give her a long, lingering kiss. "Why bother going back to your place?"

"For one thing, I have a double bed."

"The smaller the cozier," Shawn says, patting the mattress.

"And you have three roommates. Not to mention paper-thin walls."

"So? Eddie's over at Lisa's apartment, and Craig and J.C. never hang around at home on Saturday nights. They're probably getting ready to go out as we speak."

"In this weather?" She looks toward the rain-spattered window. "It's crappy out there."

"Right. All the more reason for you and me to stay here."

"But—"

Shawn silences her with another kiss. This time, his expert hands slide down over her shoulders and up under her shirt. The moment his warm fingers encounter her bare skin, Laura moans and leans back helplessly.

"I kinda thought you'd change your mind," Shawn murmurs, trailing hot kisses along her neck.

Jennie looks around the rose-papered room and tells Liza, "It's nice."

"Get serious. It looks like it was decorated for someone's Sweet Sixteen."

Jennie sighs. "Some people, including me, like antiques and floral prints."

"And some people, including me, like

grown-up stuff. . . . Oh, God, Laura, I'm sorry."

Jennie raises an eyebrow at Liza, who sinks onto the edge of the bed and rakes her manicured nails through her hair. She looks exhausted all of a sudden.

"I'm just stressed," Liza says, "and when I'm stressed, I get bitchy."

Jennie nods, thinking that Liza's pretty bitchy all the time. But right now, she's all Jennie has, and sitting here with Liza is better than sitting in her own room, alone.

She suddenly hears a creaking sound above and looks at the ceiling, wondering if Jasper Hammel is on the third floor. There has been no sign of him since dinner.

Liza, too, glances up, then at Jennie. "We probably should have just gotten out of here—gone with that guy."

"Who?"

"Patrick Gerkin—who else?"

Jennie shrugs. "It's too late now." The man had left after telling them again where the Congregational church was and that, if they were evacuated, they should bring blankets and pillows with them.

"He seemed normal, at least. Although

anyone who lives on Tide Island year-round can't be all that normal."

"Some people say the same thing about people who live on *Manhattan* Island," Jennie quietly points out.

"True," Liza says, and to Jennie's surprise, she grins. "You know, Laura, I'm really glad you're here. I'd hate to be stuck alone . . . or with Sandy. She'd drive me nuts with all her chattering."

Just when I thought she was being nice, Jennie thinks.

"I wonder where she is?" Liza asks then, sobering. "You think she's in some kind of trouble?"

"I have no idea."

"If she is in trouble, Jasper Hammel must have something to do with it."

"Unless Sandy lied to him about leaving," Jennie points out.

"Why would she do that? And anyway, we know *he* lied. About the ferry schedule."

"Maybe he was just telling us what Sandy told him." Jennie wants desperately to believe that.

Liza shakes her head. "Wouldn't you think he'd know there's no late Saturday ferry? After all, he's been on this island for a while."

"Not that long. Maybe he doesn't know."

"You want to believe that he's not up to anything."

Jennie hesitates, then nods. "I guess I do."

"Well, so do I. But, Laura . . ." She pauses to yawn, then continues, "I'm positive something's going on. And, to tell you the truth, I'm a little rattled. I thought it just had something to do with me, but—"

"What do you mean?"

Liza pauses, then exhales heavily and says, "When I kept missing Yates, I started to think someone got me out here to this crazy place as some kind of practical joke."

"Who would do that?"

"I have no idea," Liza says quickly. Too quickly. "But anyway, now that something's up with Sandy, I wonder if maybe . . ."

She trails off, and after a few moments of silence, Jennie says, "You wonder if what's going on with Sandy—if anything is going on—has anything to do with you?"

"Something like that."

"But she's a total stranger, isn't she?"

"Of course she is."

"Well then . . ."

Liza throws up her hands. "I don't know. I don't know. I just have a bad feeling. . . ."

You're not the only one, Jennie thinks.

"Laura, what should we do?" Liza asks, looking frightened and vulnerable—not Liza-like at all.

"What *can* we do?" She shrugs. "I mean, there's no way to leave the island now—and anyway," she adds, catching herself, "why *would* we? Nothing has really happened."

Maybe if I keep saying that, I'll start believing that there's nothing strange about this place. That it's just my own stupid paranoia getting the best of me . . . again.

"You're right," Liza says abruptly, standing and stifling another yawn. "I'm really tired . . ."

There's nothing for Jennie to do but stand and say, "Me, too. I'm going back to my room."

Even though she isn't tired.

Even though she knows she won't sleep a wink tonight.

"Okay. G'night," Liza says, stretching. Her eyelids already seem droopy.

"Night." Jennie pauses with her hand on the doorknob. "If you . . . you know, want to talk or anything, you can knock on my door."

"Thanks. You, too."

Jennie nods and slips out into the hall, then freezes when she hears another creak from above. She glances at the stairway that leads to the third floor, wondering what's up there. For a moment, she contemplates finding out.

The wind suddenly picks up outside, slamming into the house with a high-pitched howl, and Jennie shivers.

No, there's no way she's going to go sneaking around this place, taking a chance of bumping into Jasper Hammel ... or someone else.

Instead, she hurries down the hall to her room.

She locks the door firmly behind her.

There. You're perfectly safe now.

But somehow, she can't quite convince herself of that.

"It fits perfectly, doesn't it?" Stephen croons, staring at Sandy as though he's mesmerized.

She's trembling uncontrollably as she

stands before him in the white wedding dress, the veil perched precariously on her head so that a layer of illusion falls over her face.

She hopes that he can't see how frightened she is, can't see the tears that keep rolling down her cheeks to land on the white silk gown.

"It's not too tight in the waist, is it, Sandy?"

She shakes her head mutely.

"Is it?" he bites out, and she cringes.

"No," she says in a small voice, trying to keep her teeth from chattering.

"Good. Because you're fat, and I'd hate to have that pot belly of yours bursting through the dress. I paid a lot of money to have it made just for you."

"Th-thank you."

"I have shoes for you, too. Here you go." He holds up a pair of rhinestone-encrusted, white-satin slippers. "Aren't they beautiful?"

She nods.

"Just like Cinderella," he says, crouching before her and helping her slide her stockinged feet into the shoes. The heels are impossibly high. "A perfect fit. Just like

Cinderella," he repeats, standing again and looking at her, "and I'm your prince."

"Yes, you are."

Just keep talking to him, she tells herself, trying to ward off the panic that threatens to overtake her. *Just act as though this is normal.*

As though you aren't the least bit alarmed at having been kidnapped by a psycho from your past.

As though you didn't mind undressing while he stood there leering at you.

As though you don't think he's out of his mind, forcing you to put on this wedding gown and veil.

As though you aren't terrified of what he's going to do next.

"This," Stephen says gallantly, presenting a bouquet with a sweep of his arm, "is for you. I know how you love roses. Red roses . . . the color of blood," he adds in a faraway voice.

"Th-thank you," she whispers raggedly, taking the flowers in her trembling hands.

"Now it's time, Sandy," he says, taking her arm firmly and leading her to the end of the white runner on wobbling ankles, her skirt rustling along the floor as she moves.

"I'm going to walk to the front of the room and wait, and I want you to come down the aisle when your music starts."

Bile rises in her throat, gagging her, and she forces it back, unable to speak.

"You know which music I mean, Sandy, don't you?"

She shakes her head, her mind whirling.

I have to get away. I have to get out of here before he . . .

Before he hurts me.

Or worse.

"The wedding march, of course. You know . . . *Here comes the bride . . . dum dum da dum,*" he sings cheerfully. "You'll recognize it. It's coming up next. Now," he adds, letting go of her arm and giving it a pat, "don't start walking until your music starts."

"I won't," she promises, and braces herself.

It's now or never, she thinks as he turns his back and starts walking up the aisle, careful to step on the floor at the edge of the runner.

When Stephen is almost at the first row of seats, Sandy tosses the bouquet aside, kicks off the satin pumps, grabs her skirt, and runs.

Back through the French doors and into the parlor, then the foyer, and then, because she knows the front door is locked, up the stairs.

Up the stairs? What are you doing? she screams at herself frantically as she reaches the second-floor hall. *How are you supposed to escape now? There's no way out!*

She hears him cursing and chasing after her, approaching the bottom of the stairs. After a split-second pause, she turns and runs down the long hall. She has to hide someplace . . .

In one of the bedrooms.

And then what?

He'll find you! her mind shrieks. *It's only a matter of time before he'll find you!*

Blindly, she throws a door open at the end of the hall and finds herself in a study. She closes the door behind her, then flattens her back against it and tries to catch her breath without making a sound.

His running footsteps have come to an abrupt halt, and she hears him coming down the hall. "Lorraine? Where are you?"

Lorraine? Whom is he talking to?

"Come on out, sweetheart. I won't hurt you," he says plaintively. "I'll never hurt you

again. Why did you run away? You were going to be my bride, Lorraine. We were going
to get married and live happily ever after.
Come out, Lorraine. Please."

He's sobbing now, and Sandy holds her
breath, praying that he'll just go away.

But Sandy hears him opening doors
along the hallway, looking into the rooms,
trying to find her.

He thinks I'm someone else . . .

"Please don't leave me, Lorraine. I'll give
you anything. . . . I'll give you everything.
Everything you want. Please stay. Don't
leave like the others . . ."

He's insane.

Sandy closes her eyes briefly, then opens
them again. Though the room is shadowy,
she can make out the silhouettes of familiar
objects. A chair . . . a desk . . .

Her gaze falls on something that's sitting
on top of the desk. Swiftly and silently, she
moves across the room to it.

Picking up the telephone receiver, she
prays for a dial tone.

Yes!

She forces her fingers to stop shaking as
she punches out 9-1-1 and waits for the
emergency operator to answer.

But there's nothing but a tone, and then a recording that begins, "We're sorry. There is no 9-1-1 emergency service in this location. To reach your local police or fire officials, dial—"

Sandy depresses the button on the phone. Her mind races.

Outside the door, she hears the footsteps stop. The doorknob jiggles.

"Lorraine, I know you're in there. But I'm going to get you out."

Panicking, Sandy clutches the receiver and stares, wide-eyed, at the door. She hears a dull thump, as though Stephen has thrown his shoulder against it.

"Lorraine, open this door. Right now. I mean it. If you open it, everything will be fine. If you don't . . . I'll get it open myself. And trust me, Lorraine, you'll wish you had done as I asked."

There's another thump, and a grunt.

And then another thump.

Sobbing now, Sandy starts dialing the phone again, automatically punching in the first number that comes to mind, knowing there's nothing anyone can do to help her . . .

But praying for a miracle anyway.

* * *

"Oh, terrific." Danny Cavelli groans and looks down at his wife, who's lying beneath him on the bed. "Why does that damn thing always have to ring when we're right in the middle of something?"

"Better get it," Cheryl says, untangling her fingers from his hair. "It could be important."

"It's probably Tony, telling me another branch fell into his gutter. Or Pop, wanting me to come over and jump start his truck for the fiftieth time this week. We never should have bought a house this close to my family."

The phone rings shrilly again.

"Danny . . ." Cheryl lifts her head from the pillow to look at it on the nightstand. Her eyes are wide, fearful. "It might be my mother. What if Daddy's . . ."

She trails off, and Danny nods. Cheryl's father has been in the hospital for over a month now, suffering terribly from the last stages of lung cancer.

"Okay, I'll get it, babe," Danny says, rolling off her and reaching for the receiver. "Hello?"

For a moment, he doesn't hear anything, just heavy breathing.

Scowling, he turns to Cheryl and is about to tell her it's just an obscene phone call when he hears a voice.

"Danny . . ."

It's nothing more than a faint whisper, but he recognizes it, and his blood runs cold.

"Sandy?" He clutches the receiver. "Where are you? What's going on?"

"Danny, help . . ."

"Sandy, I can barely hear you. Speak up."

"I can't . . . oh my God, Danny . . ." Her voice trails off.

"Jesus . . . Sandy? Sandy, where are you?"

Behind him on the bed, Cheryl sits up and leans toward him, brushing his wrist with her fingers. "Danny, what's wrong?"

There's a sudden crashing sound on the other end of the line, the sound of a male voice, ranting something that sounds like "Open the door!"

Sandy lets out a blood-curdling scream.

"Sandy?" Danny shouts. "Sandy!"

But the line has already gone dead.

Eight

"How dare you?" Holding the butcher knife high above his head in his left hand, he throws the phone against the wall with his right. It crashes to the floor with a jangling thud. "Did you try to make a *phone call*?"

"I tried, but I couldn't—"

"Speak up when you talk to me!" he thunders.

"Please . . ." she whimpers, shrinking back, then trying to scurry across the floor like a cockroach.

"You're pathetic." He reaches down and closes his fingers over her ankle, then pulls her toward him. Her heavy body slides across the polished wooden floor with a rustle of silk even as she claws the air with her arms, trying to take hold of something.

He grabs her arm and turns her toward him, then leans down and lifts her chin roughly, forcing her to look up at him.

"I told you, Lorraine . . ." He trails off, gaping. "You're not Lorraine."

"No . . . please, Stephen, don't hurt me."

Befuddled, he stares into her round face. "Where is she?"

"I-I don't know."

"Lorraine . . ." Confused, he closes his eyes and tries to remember. What happened to Lorraine?

Images flash in his memory—a red-and-white blur.

Roses and baby's breath . . .

Full lips and ivory skin . . .

Blood on silk . . .

Lorraine's blood, spilling over the wedding dress she wears as she lies crumpled on the floor of her suite.

Now it's coming back to him. Leaving the brownstone through the back door in a frenzy while two hundred guests and the minister mill around wondering what happened to his bride and speculating on where he's going.

When he reached the door of her suite, she had opened it quickly, saying, "You can take the bags that are—"

Then she'd seen that it was he.

"Stephen," she'd said, growing pale. "I thought you were the bellman. . . ."

"Where the hell are you going?" he'd asked, taking in her jeans and jacket, the luggage stacked by the door, including the trunk he'd bought her for their honeymoon. It was empty, he knew. She was planning to fill it with the lovely things he would buy for her as they traveled around the world.

You'll have the finest Scottish wool, Lorraine, and silks from the Orient and the latest dresses from Paris . . .

He remembered, as he faced her in the hotel suite, how his promises had made her clap her hands together in glee, like a child getting excited about the prospect of an ice-cream cone on a sweltering August day.

"Lorraine," he'd said, softening, "you're not going anywhere without me, are you? We're going together, remember? Just as soon as we're married, we're leaving for Europe. Tonight, Lorraine. Just a few more hours. Now come on, let's go back home. The minister is waiting, and all of our guests, and—"

"No, Stephen, I can't. I just can't marry you. I changed my—"

"Stop it! Don't say it, Lorraine! You love

me. You told me that you love me. You said you want to marry me. Now do it!"

"I can't. . . . I-I have to go, Stephen," she'd told him, sounding as though she were on the verge of tears. "Please . . ."

"Please . . ." sobs the woman who cowers at his feet now. "Let me go."

"Shut up!" he barks, squeezing his eyes closed, seeing only Lorraine.

Lorraine had backed away from him as he stood there in the doorway, as though she couldn't stand to be near him. She'd averted her eyes, as though she couldn't stand looking at him.

And he'd snapped.

Stepped into the hotel room and slammed the door closed behind him, sliding the bolt and fastening the chain. The first thing he saw was the white-silk confection of a dress that hung in the corner of the room, perfectly pressed and hooded in clear plastic. A wedding dress, waiting for the bride to step into it.

"Why aren't you wearing that?" he had demanded.

"Because I'm not going to marry you," Lorraine had replied, lifting her chin, suddenly defiant.

"Yes, you are."

"No, I'm not, Stephen. I'm leaving town. Going back home to Chicago for a while, until I figure out—"

He'd slapped her then, hard, across the face, leaving a harsh red handprint on her white cheek.

"You're not going anywhere," he'd told her. "You're going to put that gown on, and you're going to marry me."

"No . . ." She looked less certain now, taking another step backward and watching him with frightened green eyes.

"Yes, dammit! Today is our wedding day. And we're going to get married. Now put . . . on . . . the . . . dress." He'd said it in a deadly quiet tone, locking his eyes on hers.

When she didn't respond, he reached into his jacket and removed the thing he had brought with him for some reason . . . the ice pick he'd swiped from the caterer's cart that had been set up in his kitchen. He held it up at her and raised his eyebrows, as if to ask whether she wanted him to do something he'd regret.

She had come to her senses then and, with trembling hands, reached for the dress. As she fumbled to release it from its plastic shroud, he had leaned back against the wall to watch her, his arms folded and his jaw set resolutely, his hand still clutching the ice pick.

She tossed the jacket, sweatshirt, and jeans aside and stood there for a moment wearing only her white-lace bra and matching panties and a look of dread.

"Put it on," he'd urged her, his eyes fastened on the swell of her breasts in the delicate lace cups, on her flat belly and her long, firm legs. Even in February, her body was tan, thanks to Christmas in Hawaii and their January trip to St. Bart's.

Lorraine had pulled the dress over her head, and it settled around her with a soft *swoosh.* She hesitated for a moment, glancing up at him, and then began to fumble with the row of buttons at her back.

There was a knock at the door then, and she froze, her eyes widening as she glanced in that direction. She opened her mouth; but before she could speak, he was beside her, covering her lips with his hand and muffling the sound of her voice.

Another knock and then he heard the bellman's voice calling, "Miss LaCroix?"

After a few moments of silent waiting, the

footsteps faded down the hall outside the suite.

"Now, Lorraine," he had said in a reasonable tone, his hand still clamped over her mouth, "I'm going to let go of you and you're not going to make a peep. If you do, you'll be sorry. Do you understand?"

She'd nodded, her eyes big and round above his fingers.

"Good." He'd let go, and she'd instantly opened her mouth to scream.

"Damn you!" he'd hollered, grabbing her and throwing her onto the floor. "I told you to be quiet!"

"I'm sorry. . . . Please, Stephen, I'm sorry. I'll be quiet. Please, no," she'd begged as he advanced on her, brandishing the ice pick. "Please, don't hurt me. Oh, God . . ."

"Don't hurt me," the woman at his feet is whimpering now as he stands over her, holding the butcher knife. "Please, don't hurt me."

"Shut your mouth!"

She obliges, staring up at him with frightened eyes, just as Lorraine had.

"Sandy," he says softly, suddenly remembering.

She only stares at him, waiting.

"You don't love me. You don't want to marry me, either. You ran away, just like Lorraine did."

"No . . ."

"Yes! I bought you this dress, and I made everything beautiful for you downstairs. I got roses . . ." He drifts off, wondering if she likes roses, as Lorraine did.

"Stephen, I'm not Lorraine," she says, looking somewhat calm though her voice bears a telltale high pitch. "I never said I would marry you."

"Why not?" he asks abruptly, his eyes snapping back to her.

"Don't get upset again, Stephen. I didn't say I would marry you because I was just a kid when I knew you."

"But you're not a kid now."

"No . . ."

"And you're going to marry me now!"

"Okay, okay, I'll marry you now." Her voice is shaky. "I will. Whatever you want."

"Before we get married, though . . ." He leans over her and, in one swift movement, shoves her so that she goes sprawling onto her back.

"No, please . . ." she says, clearly realizing exactly what his intentions are.

"No?" he asks, hesitating, watching her. His fingers clench around the knife-handle.

She's shaking. "I just meant . . . not . . . not like this, Stephen."

"Yes, just like this." Still holding the knife, he fumbles with the fly on his black tuxedo pants.

"Oh, God, no . . ."

He looks down at her and sees that she's squeezing her eyes closed.

"Look at me!" he commands her.

She doesn't move, just lets out a little sob.

"I said . . ." He bends over her so that his face is only inches from hers. "Look at me!"

She opens her eyes. They're rimmed with smudged mascara and eyeliner, and tears are streaming down her cheeks.

Disgusted, Stephen yanks her dress up around her hips and rips off her panties and stockings, exposing her abundant, ripply white thighs and hips and droopy lower belly.

"Look at you," he says, shaking his head. "You're fat."

She looks up at him hopefully, as though he might have changed his mind now that he sees her.

But he steps calmly out of his pants, then his boxer shorts, and, still holding the knife, sinks to his knees, his mighty erection throbbing as he imagines sinking into all that quivering flesh.

"Stephen, please . . . no!" Her voice explodes into a shrill scream as he forces her legs apart and rips into her.

He pounds away, trying desperately to sate himself. But he can't . . . not even with his powerful climax, not even as he imagines that he's pumping her full of himself, possessing her completely.

He collapses on top of her, panting and shuddering all over, but still filled with pent-up urges that have nothing to do with sex.

As soon as he catches his breath, he rolls off her and sees that she's lying still, eyes closed. The only thing that's moving is her mouth, and it takes a moment before he realizes what she's doing.

She's praying, her voice a mere whisper.

"Stop it," he orders her, and slaps her face.

She does. Still her eyes are closed.

As he pulls his underwear back on, he calmly says, "Open your eyes."

She does. Her expression is one of panic. And hate.

She hates me, he thinks, stepping into his trousers again, and the knowledge doesn't bother him. Not anymore.

Lorraine hated him, and he took care of her.

Now he'll take care of Sandy.

He zips his pants, then says, "Get up," raising the knife in warning.

When she doesn't move fast enough, he grabs her arm and pulls her to her feet, the white wedding dress falling around her again to hide the blood that's streaked between her chubby thighs.

She sways as though she's going to faint, then seems to get hold of herself. She even meets his gaze and lifts her chin.

"I wouldn't look so defiant if I were you, Sandy," he says softly, "because I'm the one who's in control here. And I have a sneaking suspicion that you're not going to like what I have planned for you next."

With that, he starts to laugh, a wild, frenzied sound that releases more of his pent-up frustration. . . .

But not nearly enough.

There's only one way to rid himself of it,

only one way to satisfy the intense craving that fills him to the very core.

Clutching the butcher knife, he leads Sandy out of the room and down the dark hall.

"Hello, Laura, are you there? Laura? Okay, this is Keegan again. Please call me as soon as you get in. 555-4107, just in case you didn't get the number when I left it before. I'll be home all night. . . . Make sure you call, Laura. Thanks. Bye."

Frustrated at having reached the answering machine yet again, he hangs up the phone and taps his fingertips against the arm of the couch in a jittery staccato beat. For all he knows, Laura isn't planning on coming home at all tonight.

In fact, he'd almost bet that she won't be back until tomorrow. After all, she's been known to spend the night with guys on first dates, and this Shawn is someone she's been seeing since before Keegan and Jennie broke up.

Correction—before Jennie dumped you. No warning, no excuses. She just dumped you, buddy, like a beat-up piece of trash.

Keegan sighs and gets up, moving restlessly into the small kitchen of his one-bedroom apartment. He grabs a Molson from the refrigerator and pops the cap off, tossing it in the general direction of the trash container in the corner. He misses. The cap skitters across the linoleum and disappears into the gap between the refrigerator and the stove.

Normally Keegan, who hates disorder of any kind, would grab a yardstick and fish it out, but tonight he merely shrugs. He's too distracted to care about anything but Jennie.

Jennie . . .

Forget about her, he tells himself yet again as he takes a gulp of beer, then stifles a burp.

She doesn't care about you—why should you worry about her?

But he is worried. So worried that he can't seem to focus on anything else. For over an hour now, he's been pacing around the apartment, wondering if Jennie's okay. There's no reason, really, to think that she wouldn't be . . .

Except that the damn sweepstakes was a scam.

Still, that doesn't necessarily mean Jennie's in danger.

But Keegan can't shake the feeling that she is. He's been a cop for too long, seen too much not to listen to his instinct, especially when it's this strong.

Listen to it, yeah. Make a fool out of yourself over it, no.

He takes another gulp of beer and walks back into the living room, imagining what Laura will think when she gets home and finds that he's left three messages. And the last one sounded almost frantic.

And over what?

Nothing at all.

He sighs and stares blankly at the television screen, where an episode of "America's Most Wanted" is drawing to a close with a recap parade of mugshots.

Maybe, he tells himself, *your anxiety over Jennie is coming from the break-up, and not from anything that has to do with that bogus sweepstakes or her trip to Tide Island.*

For a month now, he's been trying to get to her, but she hasn't returned his calls. All he wants is an explanation—for her to tell him why she left him like she did.

He'll never forget the way she did it. They'd been taking a walk on the frozen, deserted beach at Scituate, just the two of them. He had been thinking about how lucky he was to have her, toying with the notion that next year at this time, they might be married, or at least engaged. After all, he'd known from the start that Jennie was the woman for him. It was only a matter of time, as far as he was concerned, before they made a formal commitment.

So there he was, daydreaming about what Jennie would look like in a wedding gown—antique, no doubt, with rich ivory lace and a train—when she'd suddenly pulled her gloved hand from his and stopped walking.

Startled, he'd turned to ask her if something was wrong. And the moment he saw the look on her face, he knew. He hadn't been expecting it. In fact, if anyone had asked him mere seconds before whether Jennie would ever break up with him, he would have laughed and said, "Don't be ridiculous."

But there it was. A somber, distant look in her lilac eyes that said it all even before she did.

Not that she said much.

Just that she had done some thinking and she couldn't see him anymore.

He'd asked questions, but she'd refused to answer them, only repeating what she'd already said, as though the lines were from a script she'd over-rehearsed. So he'd protested, then argued—or at least, tried to. Jennie hadn't argued back, had only closed her mouth resolutely and stared straight ahead.

So that was it. They were through.

And it had happened on New Year's Day, no less, as though she'd re-evaluated her life and made a resolution to get him out of it.

Why, Jennie? he'd asked her countless times that day, has asked himself countless times since.

Why did you leave? he wonders again now, peeling the label off the beer bottle and discarding the shreds of sticky paper on the hardwood floor without thinking.

All I want is an explanation.

But that's not true, he realizes a moment later. He wants much more than that.

He wants Jennie back.

And I'm not going to give up, he vows,

finishing his beer in one long swallow, *until she's mine again.*

More than anything, Danny Cavelli wants Theresa Benedetti to be home tonight. As he dials her phone number, conscious of Cheryl's frightened eyes on him, he prays for Theresa to be there. But it's not likely. Not on a Saturday night. She usually hangs out at the Knights of Columbus on weekends. And tonight they're having their annual pre-Ash Wednesday Mardi Gras Night.

"It's ringing," Danny informs Cheryl, who nods and pats his shoulder. He's perched on the edge of their bed again, just where he was when Sandy called.

It's been over a half hour since then. He kept waiting for her to call back, not wanting to tie up the line in case she tried. But the phone has been silent, and he finally decided he can't wait anymore. He has to try and find her.

Please God, let Theresa be home. Please God, let Theresa be home. Please God, let—

"Hello?"

"Theresa?"

"Yeah," she says in a scratchy voice that doesn't even sound like her. "Who's this?"

"It's Danny, and I've got to—"

"Danny who?"

"Cavelli. Sandy's brother. I've—"

"Oh, hi, Danny. What's up? She's not sick, is she? Because I just found out I've got strep—"

"Theresa," he interrupts, "listen to me. Do you know the name of the inn where my sister's staying on Tide Island?"

There's a pause. "Sandy told you she went to Tide Island?"

"Yeah," he says impatiently. "And I need—"

"I thought she wasn't going to tell anyone. She said your father would freak out."

"He did. Theresa, I mean it, you've got to listen to me. I need the name of the place where she's staying. You've got to tell me."

"Why?" she asks suspiciously. Theresa and Sandy have been best friends since they were toddlers, and Danny realizes that she knows Tony Cavelli too well. Well enough to instinctively want to protect Sandy.

"It's a long story. Just tell me, please."

"I don't want to get Sandy into trouble. She—"

"Theresa, she's already *in* trouble!" Danny explodes. "For God's sake, tell me where she is!"

"Why? What happened?"

Danny shakes his head, and his eyes meet Cheryl's. Then he glances at the clock on the nightstand behind her. Too much time has passed since Sandy called. He has to find her, before it's too late . . .

"Theresa, she called me, and she sounded terrified. Like some guy was doing something to her," he says desperately. "She didn't say what."

"Some guy was *doing* something to her?"

"And then she screamed, and I heard someone yelling at her."

"What?"

"Tell me where she is, Theresa. You've got to." His voice breaks, and he runs a hand raggedly through his hair. Every muscle in his body is tensed, and his fingers ache from being coiled into tight fists.

"It's the ivy . . . no, the rose," Theresa says, "the Rose-something Inn. No, I think it's the Something-rose Inn. It's something that makes me think of a fairy tale. . . ."

"Oh, Jesus Christ," Danny mutters, then automatically clamps his hand over his mouth. Angie Cavelli would faint if she heard that.

"The Thorn-rose!" Theresa shouts triumphantly, despite her hoarse throat.

"Is that it?"

"I don't know." She sounds hesitant. "Something like that . . . The Bramble Rose?"

"The Bramble Rose?"

"That's it. I'm positive. Danny, you really think she's in trouble? Because there's something else you should know."

"What is it?"

"She was placing personal ads in a magazine. You know, to meet guys."

"*Sandy* did a sleazy thing like that?"

"And that's why she went to Tide Island," Theresa continues. "To meet someone."

"Who?"

"Some guy. I can't remember his name, but he's rich, and he's a lawyer—no, a doctor. She got this great letter from him, inviting her to the island."

Danny is too stunned to reply to that. How could his sister be so stupid? How could she go away for a weekend with a total stranger?

Beside him on the bed, Cheryl watches him, asking, "What? What is it?"

He looks at her and shakes his head, fresh worry coursing through him. He's going to find out who lured his sister out to Tide Island; and if the guy so much as laid a hand on her, Danny's going to beat the crap out of him.

"He'd better not hurt her," he tells Cheryl, and Theresa, clenching his hands into fists.

"But if she called you, Danny, she was probably afraid of him," Theresa points out.

"Yeah, well, a lot of times when Sandy calls me to bail her out of something, it turns out to be a false alarm," Danny says, even though he knows in his heart that this time, his sister is really in serious trouble. The memory of her terrified voice, and the way the call was abruptly cut off, makes his blood run cold.

"You're right," Theresa says optimistically. "She was probably just over-reacting to something when she called you."

"Yeah. Thanks for helping me out, though," Danny says.

"Let me know what happens, okay, Danny?"

He hesitates, then says, "Sure. I'll have Sandy call you. Bye." He hangs up the phone and turns to Cheryl, struggling to ignore the fist of fear that's clenching his gut. "I'm going to call the inn on Tide Island and find out what's up."

"Everything's probably fine, Danny. Don't worry until you have to," Cheryl says, patting his arm reassuringly.

But Danny can hear the anxiety in her voice. And as he dials the number for directory information, he can't help bleakly wondering if there's anything he can do even if everything *isn't* fine.

After all Tide Island is miles away, out in the ocean, and there's a wicked storm brewing. If Sandy really is in some kind of trouble, she's on her own.

The satin pumps are scuffed from her struggle with Stephen, Sandy notices vaguely as she stands with the toes exactly lined up at the edge of the white runner. She clutches the bouquet of roses he forced into her hands and tries to convince herself that everything will be fine if she just keeps doing what he tells her to.

"Okay, ready?" he calls from the front of the room where he's fiddling with the tape player.

She nods; and when he looks up sharply, as though to make sure she's acknowledging him, she calls weakly, "Ready."

"Good." He presses the *play* button, then takes his place at the head of the runner. "Now, wait for my cue," he says, as if he's a high school drama teacher directing a musical revue.

Sandy knows better than to try to run this time, even if she had the strength. She's weak and her legs feel bruised, particularly between her thighs. The thought of what he did to her upstairs fills her with revulsion, and she forces the memory out of her mind.

She takes a deep breath as she stands there waiting, telling herself to calm down. If she panics, she's dead.

Maybe literally.

The thought immediately overwhelms her with a renewed sense of alarm that chokes her throat with bile and makes her want to pass out. She forces it back, clutching the bouquet in trembling hands and watching

Stephen from behind the layer of illusion veil he arranged over her face.

Just pretend you're playing bride, the way you and Theresa used to do when you were little. Just pretend it's a game. . . . Pretend he doesn't have that knife tucked into his tuxedo pocket.

He's insane—that much is clear. But Sandy has no idea why he's making her go through this grotesque charade.

Why me? she wonders desperately again. *Why after all these years?*

She'd almost forgotten Stephen Gilbrooke, having resigned him to some distant corner of her mind reserved for storing the memories of particularly unpleasant adolescent experiences. It had been a shock to recognize him here, to realize that he hadn't forgotten her . . .

Far from it.

Apparently, her rejection had a major impact on him. Major enough to make him want revenge.

Sandy feels sick again, and it's all she can do to remain standing as the first strains of music waft from the portable stereo across the room.

"All right," Stephen says, holding up his index finger, then pointing it at her, "Now."

Sandy gingerly takes the first slow step forward with her right foot, then glides to meet it with her left and pauses. It's the walk she first learned when she was a junior bridesmaid at her brother Tony's wedding, the walk Stephen showed her just before he went to start the music. He had been fairly bouncing along the white runner when he demonstrated it, saying, "This is how you're going to come to me, okay, Lorraine?"

She hadn't corrected him. He kept mistaking her for someone else, someone who had obviously rejected him, just as she had.

Sandy wonders now, as she makes her way fearfully down the aisle, who Lorraine is, where she is now, and whether Stephen freaked out on her, too.

Did he force himself on her?

Is he going to rape me again when I get to the end of the runner?

She watches him fearfully from behind her veil and she keeps walking because if she doesn't, he'll hurt her. She knows that he will. Even though he's acted relatively calm, even gleeful, ever since he brought her back downstairs, she's glimpsed the deranged expression in his eyes, and it terrifies her.

"Come on, Sandy," he calls above the rhythmic strains of the wedding march. "Pick up the pace."

She does, although everything inside her is screaming for her to back away, to run away. If there were any possible way to escape, she would try it.

But there's not.

And the thought of Stephen chasing her again, and catching her and violating her, makes her physically ill. Anything would be better than that.

She's almost reached him now. She is close enough to see that his mouth is set grimly, that his eyes look glazed as he stares at her, as though he's seeing someone else.

Lorraine—who is she? Sandy wonders again, taking another deep breath, trying desperately to stay calm as she forces herself to draw nearer.

The moment she's within arm's length, Stephen reaches out and hooks his elbow around hers.

Startled, Sandy bites her lip to keep from crying out. He walks a few more steps alongside her until they reach the edge of the runner. Then, as the music ends, he lets go of her arm, turning her to face him.

"Lorraine," he says softly, reaching for the wisp of veil covering her face. "I've been waiting for this moment for so long."

Sandy stays absolutely still and silent despite the violent thudding of her heart in her ears.

"I love you," he says and lifts the veil, leaning toward her as though he's going to kiss her. His eyelids start to drift closed, then open again abruptly as he zeroes in on Sandy's face.

"You're not Lorraine!"

Sandy numbly shakes her head.

"Where is she?"

"I . . . I don't know, Stephen," she says in a small voice, wanting to beg him not to hurt her again, but knowing, from the crazed look in his eyes, that he wants to.

"Where's Lorraine?" he asks again, dropping the veil back over her eyes.

"I don't know," Sandy repeats, hearing the hysteria creep into her voice.

Stephen's right hand is moving toward his pocket . . . the pocket that has the knife.

Sandy's head is filled with a buzzing

sound and she sways as though she's going to faint. Struggling to stay alert, she watches him reaching into the pocket, sees him produce the deadly blade.

He runs his fingertips over the handle almost lovingly, then looks up at her again.

"Lorraine, I don't want to do this," he says in a near-whisper. "But you've left me with no choice."

"Stephen, no!" Sandy protests, reaching for the veil so that she can show him, again, that she's not Lorraine.

But it's too late. Horrified, she sees the silver blade slashing at her, feels the sudden stinging pain as it slashes her on the forearm.

She screams when she looks down and sees her own red blood spilling over the sleeve of the dress, dripping down onto the skirt.

"Shut up!" Stephen hollers and raises the knife again.

"No!" Sandy howls, reaching blindly forward to stop him.

But the blade descends rapidly again, and again, even after she's collapsed in a heap on the floor, vaguely aware of what's happening to her.

He's killing me, she thinks incredulously. *I'm dying.*

The last thing she's aware of before blackness descends over her is the brilliant flash of a camera and Stephen's gleeful voice saying, "Smile for your wedding portrait, Sandy!"

Nine

The rain stings Jasper's face as he hurries toward the back door of the inn, relieved that his grim task is over. He's disposed of Sandy Cavelli's belongings just as Stephen told him to—buried her suitcase in the deep pit he'd dug earlier in the dunes behind the inn, concealed by the tangle of beach grasses.

It took longer than he thought because of the weather—his hands were numb and clumsy because of the cold, and the wind made it difficult to work efficiently.

But the weather is a blessing, too, Jasper thinks as he nears the inn. Because of it, the wave-battered beach is deserted.

No one in their right mind would venture outside tonight, Jasper thinks, then realizes he's outside himself. His lips curve into a tight smile at the irony.

But, anything for Stephen, he tells himself, quickening his pace over the rough, muddy ground.

He owes everything to Stephen Gilbrooke, his only friend in the world for as long as he can remember.

They'd met back when Jasper was still going by his real name, Arnold Wentworth—one of *the* Wentworths of Philadelphia. He'd been miserable at prep school until Stephen came along. The other boys constantly made fun of "Arnie," as they insisted on calling him—tripping him in the halls and teasing him in falsetto voices, telling him that everyone knew he was "queer," so he might as well admit it.

But Arnold refused to—wouldn't even admit it to himself, back then. Even though he'd had those strange, unacceptable feelings since childhood. It had started out as mere admiration for other boys, usually the strongest, smartest, most popular ones in his class at the private school near his parents' mansion. But it rapidly progressed into a series of crushes, and then full-fledged obsessions, where Arnold could think of nothing but what it would be like to kiss the object of his affections on the lips, to touch him in places that made Arnold blush with mingling pleasure and shame at the mere thought.

His father, Grayson Wentworth, had been a football star at Princeton in his youth, and he was horrified that his only child was not only uncoordinated and clumsy, but a "sissy," as he called Arnold. He had long since given up on trying to make a "man" out of his son, but regarded him only with disgust from the time Arnold was five years old.

Meanwhile, Arnold's mother, who spent her days at home drinking gimlets and her nights on the town drinking straight vodka, could have cared less about her husband or her son.

It was a blessing for Arnold when the Wentworths decided to send him away to school in New England, having virtually washed their hands of him.

One day, during his first semester there, Arnold found himself taking a shower in the dormitory bathroom, right next to his current obsession, Gregory Sloane. He'd struggled not to stare at Gregory's naked body so tantalizingly close to his own, but he couldn't resist stealing glances.

The next thing he knew, as he was furtively stroking his hard, soap-slicked penis while he stared at Gregory, the other boy had suddenly turned and caught him in the act.

"Oh, my God," Gregory had shouted, pointing at Arnold's pulsating erection. "He's getting off on me!"

Instantly, the steamy stall seemed to have been filled with Gregory's friends, who had first ridiculed the humiliated Arnold, then manhandled him out into the dressing room, where they forced him to lie, naked, on a hard bench. Someone produced a tube of Ben-Gay, and they started smearing it all over Arnold, coating his bare flesh with the stinging stuff as they jeered him.

He didn't know which was more excruciating—the harsh, true words the boys flung at him, or the physical pain.

They left him there, at last, sobbing and writhing on the floor where they'd shoved him.

And it was Stephen Gilbrooke who had found him. One of the new students, he was a virtual stranger to Arnold; but for some reason, he decided to become his savior.

Stephen had helped him up and wiped the Ben-Gay off with warm, wet towels, talking to Arnold in a soothing voice. Arnold had never remembered what he said, only that he was kind. Kinder than anyone had ever been to him before.

And he'd fallen in love with Stephen Gilbrooke on the spot. He didn't look like Arnold's usual crushes. Stephen was blatantly ugly, with a face that had earned him the nickname "Elephant Guy" among the other boys. But Arnold swiftly came to overlook Stephen's appearance.

All he cared about was that Stephen was nice to him. And he seemed to understand how it felt to be an outcast—and how it felt to have parents who didn't care at all.

The two boys had become inseparable by Christmas, and they were the only ones in the dormitory who didn't go home over holiday break.

One night, as they lay on Stephen's bed in the deserted dorm, playing chess, Arnold had impulsively leaned over and kissed Stephen square and hard on the lips.

It was something he'd wanted to do for months, but as soon as he pulled back, he chastised himself. How could he have been so stupid? Now he would lose his one and only friend.

But to his surprise, Stephen hadn't recoiled in horror or even surprise. He had simply said quietly, "I know how you feel about me, Arnold. And it's okay."

"It is?" Arnold had been utterly shocked.

"Sure." Stephen had laid a hand on his thigh then, sending quivers of pleasure through Arnold's whole body.

It hadn't gone any further that night, or for a long time afterward. But Arnold had thrilled to the secret knowledge that Stephen loved him back.

And he had ignored the irritating voice in his mind that sometimes told him to be careful . . . that Stephen was too good to be true. That maybe Stephen wasn't who he seemed to be.

The voice seemed to surface whenever Arnold found himself doing a favor for Stephen. Like the time he stole the answers to the math test out of the teacher's locked drawer. Stephen was failing the course and he needed a passing grade or, as he said, his father would beat the hell out of him.

And on several occasions, Arnold had agreed to meet Stephen's dealer in the city to pick up a bag of marijuana or a little vial of cocaine or whatever it was that Stephen was in the mood for.

He didn't mind doing favors for Stephen, even when there were risks involved, because he got so much back in return. Stephen let Arnold hold his hand—when no one was around, of course—and a few times, when Arnold tentatively kissed him, he opened his mouth and kissed back.

Arnold sensed that Stephen wasn't getting as much pleasure out of it as he was, but that was probably because Stephen was more reserved, more uptight about things like that. He just needed to learn to relax and enjoy himself, Arnold decided, and there was plenty of time for that. After all, they were going to be together forever. He was sure of it.

And here we are, together still, he thinks now as he reaches into his pocket and produces the key to the back door of the inn. *And I'll still do anything for Stephen. Anything at all. That's the way it should be when you're in love. . . .*

He pauses just inside the door, listening. Oh, Lord, that's the phone ringing. If it's Stephen, he'll be so upset that Jasper didn't answer on the first ring.

Tossing the keys on the counter, he scurries toward the front of the house. He's rushing down the hall toward the foyer when the phone abruptly stops ringing.

"Hello?" he hears a female voice saying. "Yes, it is . . ."

Panicked, Jasper dashes around the corner and sees Liza Danning standing in a slinky black-lace nightgown behind the desk, speaking into the receiver.

"I'll take that," he says, grabbing the phone out of her hand and glaring at her. Stephen's going to be furious.

"I was coming out of the bathroom, and I heard it ringing," she says, yawning. "So I thought I'd better get it."

"Thank you," he tells her curtly, clearing his throat. Into the phone, he says pleasantly, "Hello?"

"Uh, I need to speak to one of your guests," says an unfamiliar male voice. "Sandy Cavelli."

A chill runs through Jasper's veins. He's conscious of Liza watching him, though, and forces himself to seem unruffled. He's gotten very good at that these past few days.

"Can you excuse me for a moment?" he says into the phone, then covers the receiver and turns to Liza. "Thank you for your assistance," he says shortly. "I'll take care of this."

She narrows her eyes suspiciously at him. "It's not D.M. Yates, is it?"

"Of course it isn't."

"I didn't think so," she says, wearing an odd, calculating expression in her otherwise sleepy green eyes as she stares back at him.

But Jasper's too preoccupied to worry about Liza right now. He waits until she starts up the stairs, then turns his back and quietly says into the phone, "Sandy Cavelli? I'm afraid she's already checked out."

"She checked *out*? When?"

"Who is this, please?" he asks crisply.

"It's her brother, and I need to know where she went."

"I'm afraid I have no idea. She said she was leaving the island on the late afternoon ferry."

"But she called me just a little while ago . . ."

Jasper's ears prick up. Sandy had called her brother? From where? How had she gotten to a phone? Where was Stephen?

"What did she say when she called?" he asks carefully.

"She sounded like she was—nothing. Never mind," the man says abruptly, as though he has changed his mind about offering any information.

Jasper frowns and wonders if Stephen knows Sandy made the call. He should tell him.

"Thank you for your time," the man is saying into the phone.

"Of course. I'm sorry I couldn't offer more information." He replaces the receiver in its cradle and rubs his chin, wondering if Stephen—

"Who was that?" a voice asks, and Jasper gasps, then turns to see Liza standing on the landing.

"Who was that?" Jasper echoes awkwardly, grasping for something to tell her. He impulsively opts for the truth. "It was Sandy's brother, wanting to speak with her."

"Why?"

"Because of the storm . . . he heard there was a terrible storm and he was worried about her," Jasper says smoothly, looking Liza in the eye.

"Oh." She shrugs, still wearing the same shrewd expression as she watches him.

Frantic inside, Jasper tries to recall what

he said on his end of the conversation. Was there anything that might have made her suspicious? No. No, he doesn't think so.

He dismisses Liza with a wave of his hand. "Good night, Miss Danning. Have pleasant dreams."

"Yeah, right," she says bluntly and turns to climb the stairs.

He watches until she reaches the top, then listens until he hears her shut and lock the door to her room.

"Good riddance," he whispers in her direction before turning to the matter at hand.

He hurries down the hall toward the back of the house again, stopping in front of a closed door just beyond the parlor. With a key from his pocket, he unlocks it and slips inside.

It was once a storage room, he knows, and it's too small, really, for a bedroom. Yet this is where Stephen wants him to sleep, on an old, narrow bed with a lumpy mattress.

Jasper knows it's only temporary, though.

Soon, he'll be sharing Stephen's king-sized bed, for good.

Stephen promised.

Urgently, he reaches for the cellular

phone Stephen gave him and dials the number he's supposed to use only in an emergency.

The fact that Sandy Cavelli called her brother qualifies. It means that everything isn't going exactly according to Stephen's plan.

If anything goes wrong with the plan, Stephen might decide that Jasper is somehow to blame. Then, Jasper's dreams of a glorious future alone with Stephen will be ruined.

And Jasper can't let that happen. No matter what. He's so close, so tantalizingly close, to winning Stephen forever . . .

Nothing is going to stand in his way.
Nothing.

Sherm Crandall has been the chief of police on Tide Island since the early seventies. Back then, his biggest problem was keeping a rein on the flocks of hippie artists who tended to smoke a lot of marijuana and skinny dip on public beaches, which wasn't exactly good for tourism—at least, not the family trade that frequented other New England coastal islands.

These days, while hippies and grass and nudity aren't unheard of on the island, Sherm doesn't get so uptight about them. He's gotten older, yes, but a lot less conservative than he was in his youth. The horror stories he hears about crime in big cities and even suburbs on the mainland make him a lot more tolerant of Tide Island's few problems.

At least here, there are no car-jackings—few people even bother to have vehicles on the island—and no teenage gangs, unless you count the four boys who formed a rock band and pierced their noses, to the horror of some of the island's old-timers.

In fact, during the off-season, Sherm's the *only* cop on duty for Tide Island. About the most pressing issue he ever has to deal with is a storm.

And the way things look tonight, they're in for a doozy.

Sitting at his desk in the small, gray-shingled cottage that serves as Tide Island's municipal building, Sherm looks up as the door opens and someone blows into the room on a gust of wind.

"Pat, is that you?" he asks, recognizing

the shock of red hair that's sticking out from under the hood of the big storm coat.

"Sure is," he says, his voice muffled until he unwinds the scarf from around his face. "It's nasty out there, Sherm."

"The kind of night your father would have called 'fit for the devil,' huh, Pat?" Sherm asks, with a fond grin. Robert Gerkin was one of his boyhood buddies here on the island. In fact, they'd been best man at each other's weddings, and Sherm is Patrick's godfather.

It's hard to believe that Robert's been gone almost a year now. Damn cancer moved so fast no one had a chance to say a proper goodbye.

"Dad loved a good nor'easter," Patrick says, sitting in the chair by Sherm's desk. "As long as there wasn't serious damage."

"Well, I hope that's the case this time, son. But it looks like this one's pretty powerful. I just talked to Joe Dominski at the weather station on the mainland and he says it hasn't diminished any. If anything, it's getting stronger and the rain is becoming snow as the temperature drops."

"We haven't had snow all winter."

"Nope." Sherm shrugs. "And it's a little

late for 'Jingle Bells' and chestnuts roasting over an open fire and all that stuff, huh? But who knows? Maybe it won't be that bad."

"Well, I made the rounds of the evacuation route, anyway," Pat says.

"Anyone give you any trouble?"

"Just Old Man Mooney."

Sherm chuckles, thinking of the eccentric octogenarian who lives in one of the old houses on the north shore. "As usual. Did he threaten you with that toy shotgun of his?"

"Yeah, and the thing looks real, Sherm. If I didn't know better, I'd think he really was going to blow me away with it. Anyway, he says he's not going to budge, no matter what the weather does. Says he's been here on Tide Island too many years to worry about some little storm."

Sherm shakes his head. "Someday that old fool's gonna find himself floating in the Atlantic in his rocking chair. But there's nothing you can do. Everybody else knows to go to the church, right? Including the weekenders staying at the Seawind Hotel and Millers' Guest House? Those are the only two places open for tourists during the off-season."

"And don't forget the Bramble Rose," Pat adds.

"Oh, right. Almost didn't remember that place is open for business now, huh?"

"I guess. There were two women staying there, and I don't know who else. I didn't get to talk to the owner, but I told them to let him know that they might be evacuated."

"Good." Sherm pauses, then remembers something else. "What about the old Gilbrooke place?"

Pat frowns. "What about it?"

"I saw a light on inside when I drove by on patrol earlier. Looks like someone might be there."

"I thought the Gilbrookes haven't used the place in years. Didn't they used to spend their summers at that fancy estate in Connecticut instead?"

"They sure did." Sherm shakes his head, thinking of the beautiful old oceanfront mansion that's gone to waste ever since Andrew Gilbrooke married that Greenwich snob who decided Tide Island's summer crowd wasn't high-society enough for her.

"So you think they sold the place or something?"

"Not that I know of. Someone might be back—probably the son."

"Well, it can't be the old man. He's in a loony bin, isn't he?"

Sherm thinks of pathetic old Andrew Gilbrooke, who had been a summer playmate of his when they were kids. He'd been rich as hell, but the most spineless son of a gun Sherm had ever known, ruled first by his overbearing mother, then by his tyrannical wife, Aurelia.

He looks at Pat, nodding sadly. "Yup, I heard Andrew went off the deep end after his wife killed herself. But the kid's still floating around someplace. He was a real mess, too—mentally and physically. I had only met him a few times, when he came out here with his father to check on the property. Poor kid had the ugliest face you ever saw. Last I heard, he had taken over the family import-export business a few years back. Maybe he's back here on the island for a while, though, to get away from the rat race or something."

"Maybe." Pat puts his hood up again. "You want me to go out there and check?"

"Would you?"

"No problem, Sherm. Then I'll come back and help you board up those windows."

"I'd appreciate it. After that, I'm going to head on home and take care of things there."

Pat hesitates in the doorway. "Any word from Carly?"

"Nope." Sherm shrugs, as though it doesn't matter that his wife of thirty years hasn't called or written in months.

"Any idea where she is?"

"Nope. But I can tell you one thing. She sure as hell isn't on an island," he says on a bitter laugh.

She never liked it out here in the first place, even though she'd grown up a Tide Islander just as he had. She hated the island as much as he loved it and had married him despite knowing he never wanted to leave. Then she'd complained and pestered him about it for the next three decades.

Finally, last fall, she'd left with the last of the tourists, telling Sherm she wanted out for a while. "I'll be back," she'd promised as he'd stood with her on the ferry dock that rainy September morning.

"For good?" he'd asked hopefully. "Or just to pick up the rest of your stuff?"

"I'm not sure."

Carly is nothing if not honest. Brutally so, sometimes. He still vividly remembers the day she told him that the doctor had called with results of the tests they had both undergone after trying unsuccessfully to have a baby.

"I'm fine. It's you. You're sterile," she'd said flatly, as though informing him that he had ketchup on his chin. No beating around the bush, ever—not with Carly.

"So Sherm, I'll see you in a little while, okay?" Pat asks from the doorway now.

"No problem." He watches Pat head out into the storm again. The room seems quieter than ever when the door closes behind him, shutting out the howling wind.

Sherm leans back in his seat, stretches, and reaches for the paperback detective novel that's opened face-down on the desk. He tries to get back into the story, but he can't seem to concentrate.

He's read the same sentence five times without comprehending it when the sudden shrill ringing of the telephone shatters the silence.

Sherm grabs for it immediately. "Tide Island Police."

Maybe it's Carly, he tells himself, feeling a flutter of excitement in the vicinity of his heart.

He thinks that every time a phone rings anywhere. And it's never her.

"Uh, yes. I, uh, have a missing person to report."

"Excuse me?" Sherm puts down his novel and sits up straighter in his chair.

"At least, I *think* she's missing."

"Who is she?"

"My sister. She's spending the weekend on the island, and she supposedly left on the late afternoon ferry; but I just called the ferry office in Crosswind Bay, and according to the schedule on the recording I heard, there's no late ferry on Saturdays."

"No, there isn't." Sherm picks up a pen and grabs the pad he uses to take notes in situations like this—which, on Tide Island, occur once in a blue moon. Usually, when someone calls the police department out here, it's to report a missing dog or cat.

"She's in trouble," says the man on the phone. "She called me a little while ago, and someone was doing something to her—some guy. She screamed, and—"

"Whoa, hang on," Sherm cuts in. "I need you to backtrack and start at the beginning. What's your name?"

The caller sighs. "Danny Cavelli. And my sister's name is Sandy. She was staying at the Bramble Rose Inn."

There's a coincidence, Sherm thinks, writing it down. *That's the second time in five minutes that someone's mentioned the place.*

"And you don't know where she is now?"

"Missing!" Danny Cavelli practically shouts into the phone. "Aren't you listening to what I'm saying? I can't find my sister. Do you know what it's like to have no idea where to find someone you care about?"

Sherm's eyes fall on the framed photograph of Carly that sits on his desk.

You bet I do, he thinks grimly.

Aloud, he says only, "Please go on with your story, Mr. Cavelli."

Stephen is methodically washing his hands with strong, anti-bacterial soap, watching Sandy's blood mix with water in the kitchen drain, when a sudden, shrill, ringing sound shatters the silence.

His eyebrows shoot up and he turns to look at the old-fashioned black telephone on the desk by the window. Only one person has the number here: Jasper. Well, that's not entirely true. Father has it, of course— but considering where Andrew Gilbrooke is, he's not likely to be making phone calls.

Frowning, Stephen hurriedly turns off the faucet and dries his hands on a paper towel instead of the dish towel, just in case there are still telltale remnants of blood on his fingers. Then he picks up the phone.

"Yes?" he asks cautiously.

"Stephen, it's me."

"Jasper, what the hell are you doing, calling me out here? I told you only in an emergency—"

"I know, and I'm sorry—" Stephen curls his lip in distaste at the near sob in the fool's voice. "—but this *is* an emergency."

"What do you mean?" Stephen's stomach churns slightly, and he looks back in the direction of the drawing room, where Sandy Cavelli's bloodied body lies in a heap on the floor.

"She called her brother," Jasper says in a near-whisper.

"Who called her brother? What are you talking about?"

"That Cavelli girl. She got to a phone and called her brother, Stephen, and now he's worried about her."

Stephen frowns, thinking back to when he cornered Sandy in the upstairs study. Everything was a blur. . . . But she *had* been holding the telephone, he realizes now, his heart dropping with a sickening thud. At the time, he'd been too frenzied to realize that she might have actually made a call.

"How do you know this?" he asks Jasper urgently.

"Her brother called here looking for her a few minutes ago."

"What did you tell him?"

"Just what I've been telling the other two guests . . . that she left the island on the late ferry."

"You idiot! There *is* no late ferry today."

"I know, Stephen, but I got so confused and I didn't know what else to say . . ."

"You were supposed to say that she checked out early and you saw her leaving with her date!" Stephen rakes his fingers through his hair, trying to think straight.

"I know, I . . . I forgot." Please don't be mad at me, Stephen. I'm sorry. I just got nervous, and—"

"Shut up so I can figure this out!" he barks into the phone and is met by instant silence.

After a moment, he asks, "Did you get rid of her stuff, like I told you?"

"Yes, I buried it out in the dunes, just where you said," Jasper replies quickly.

"And what about the other two? Where are they?"

"Upstairs. When I went out to get rid of Sandy's bags, they were having dessert and tea in the parlor; and when I came back, they were already up in their rooms."

"Thanks to the sleeping pills you tucked into their dessert . . . right?"

Is it his imagination or does Jasper hesitate slightly before answering, "Of course, Stephen."

"Are you sure?"

"Yes, I'm sure. Everything is under control. Don't worry about anything."

"Then don't give me any reason to."

Stephen hangs up and examines his

short fingernails for traces of blood. Nothing. Good.

Reaching into a kitchen drawer, he pulls out a pair of gardening gloves and slips them on. Then he returns to the drawing room and stands over Sandy's body, clad in the red-stained white wedding gown.

Just like Lorraine, he thinks, pleased, remembering that day in the suite at the Waldorf-Astoria.

Getting rid of her had been surprisingly simple, though, thanks to that fancy brass-trimmed steamer trunk he'd bought her for their honeymoon.

A smile curls his lips as he remembers how he'd tipped the eager-to-please bellhop fifty dollars to bring the pile of luggage to the lobby for him.

At first, the guy had looked perplexed when Stephen had opened the door of the suite. "I was just up here a little while ago," he'd said. "Miss LaCroix called the concierge and asked for someone to bring her bags down. But no one answered the door when I knocked."

Stephen had thought rapidly and pasted a sly smile on his face. "Oh, well, we, uh . . .

you know, we're about to be married, and we, uh . . ."

"Gotcha," the bellhop had said with a wink. "Say no more, sir."

With that, he had carted the bags, including the trunk and its macabre cargo, down to the lobby. Stephen had met him there and stood by as the luggage was loaded into the trunk of a yellow cab. He'd instructed the driver to take him to the Connecticut estate that had been deserted ever since his father had been committed to a mental hospital a few years before.

That night, by the light of a full February moon, Stephen had buried his unfortunate bride deep in the barren, sandy soil of what had once been his mother's herb garden . . . a few feet from the decaying corpse that had once been his mother.

Now, he sighs and eyes Sandy. Too bad he can't just bury her on the cliff behind the house and have it over with. But what with the erosion that plagues the coast of the island, he can't take any chances. Especially since this time, he's going to have three bodies to worry about.

No, he'll have to go along with his original plan. That means stowing her body on board his yacht, which is moored in the water behind the house. Then, when he's left Tide Island for good, he'll simply toss Sandy Cavelli—and Liza Danning, and Laura Towne—overboard and let the shark-infested waters of the Atlantic destroy the evidence.

A gust of wind slams into the house as Stephen bends over Sandy's body, and he remembers the storm that's raging outside. No, he can't bring her out to the boat now. He'll have to find someplace inside to keep her until the weather dies down.

He's dragging her across the floor when a sudden ringing sound makes him stop short.

He mentally curses Jasper again.

Then he realizes, with a chill, that it isn't the phone after all.

It's the doorbell.

Ten

Sherm Crandall waits until nearly midnight for Pat to return to the police station.

Finally, yawning and closing the still-unfinished detective novel, he stands and goes over to look out the window. From here, across the wide main street, he can see the waves slamming fiercely into the deserted ferry dock. The storm is gaining momentum, and if he doesn't start boarding up windows now, it might be too late.

Reluctantly, he reaches for his coat on the hook behind his desk.

He wonders idly whether Danny Cavelli's sister Sandy is out somewhere in this weather, maybe lost or disoriented . . . or worse.

But there's not much he can do at this point. He's already called the Bramble Rose and spoken to Jasper Hammel, the manager. The man confirmed what Cavelli said—that the sister had checked out earlier.

"Do you know where she was going?" Sherm had asked, his pen poised over the pad on his desk.

"She said she was leaving on the late ferry, but of course, there is no late ferry on Saturdays," Hammel had told him. "I didn't let on that I knew that, though, because I assumed there was a reason she was lying to me. I seem to remember that she had earlier said something about meeting a date here on the island . . . a blind date. Maybe—and this is indelicate, I know—but I got the impression that she didn't want me to suspect she might plan on spending the, er, *evening* with the man."

"I see. Is there anything else you think might be helpful?"

"No. There was no reason for me to think anything unusual was going on, so I didn't pay much attention to Miss Cavelli while she was here. Do you . . . you don't think something happened to her, do you?"

"I hope not," Sherm had said, thinking not just of her worried brother but of the negative publicity it would bring to Tide Island—and its police department.

"It would be a shame . . . such a nice,

cheerful girl. If I think of anything else, Lieutenant Crandall, should I call you?"

"Please."

After Sherm hung up, he'd made a mental note to stop by the Bramble Rose as soon as he got a chance, to check it out. It was probably less expensive than the other island hotels that were open during the off-season. His sister Michelle and her husband had wanted to come out and visit him over Easter, and Sherm didn't have room to put them up at his place.

No, it's not that you don't have room. . . . It's that you've let the place go to hell every since Carly left. Cleaning, cooking, laundry . . . that was all her department. Now it's barely fit for you, let alone company.

With a sigh, Sherm glances again at the pad where he jotted down the notes about the Cavelli girl. Since she hasn't been missing for twenty-four hours yet, his hands are tied—something her brother failed to understand.

"But what about that phone call?" he kept asking Sherm, a note of desperation in his voice. "She sounded so scared . . ."

"It could have been a joke," Sherm had told him, hating himself for the cold efficiency in his own voice. But it was his job to handle this by the book. It wouldn't be the first time that some young girl had taken off with a guy and made her family crazy with worry.

"And even if it weren't a joke," he'd added, "I have no way of finding your sister without a trail to follow."

"Can't you just go out and *look* for her?"

"Where do you suggest I start?"

"I don't know. . . . Isn't it a small island?"

"Everything's relative, Mr. Cavelli. We're in the middle of a nasty storm out here; and anyway, I can't just go driving around aimlessly, looking for your sister. At least, not at this stage." With exaggerated patience, he repeated, "She's not officially a missing person until she's been gone—"

"Yeah, yeah, I know. Twenty-four hours." Danny Cavelli's voice had an edge, and he said curtly, "I'll be in touch again before that, believe me."

And with that, he had hung up with a sharp click.

Now, zipping his coat up to his throat and pulling the hood snugly over what's left of his graying hair, Sherm puts Cavelli and his sister out of his head.

As he heads for the door, his thoughts return to Pat. It isn't like him to say he'll do something and then not do it. But then again, the poor kid's not even supposed to be on duty in the off-season, and here he is, going out of his way to make sure everyone on the island knows where to go if they need to evacuate.

Pat lives in a small, weathered cape on the north coast of the island, not far from the old Gilbrooke place. Sherm decides that he probably headed home for a while to change out of his wet clothes or grab something to eat.

After pulling on his thick, insulated gloves, Sherm starts to gather the hammer and other supplies he'd gotten ready earlier, then pauses.

Something's making him uneasy, and it isn't just the fury of the storm, or the run-in with Cavelli.

After a moment, he goes back to his desk and takes off his right glove. He checks the number in his Rolodex, then punches out the buttons on the phone and waits for Pat to pick up.

After four rings, the answering machine clicks on.

"Hey, you've reached Pat Gerkin. You know what to do. Later."

At the tone, Sherm says, "Pat, this is Sherm. . . . I waited for you at the station, but it's almost midnight and I'm heading out now. I'll be home if you need me, and I'll call you if we have to start evacuating. If not, have a good night, and thanks for helping out."

He hangs up the phone, frowning.

If Pat isn't home, where is he?

Don't drive yourself crazy. . . . The kid has a lot of friends on the island. Probably stopped off for a beer or a hand of cards somewhere, Sherm tells himself, and pulls his glove on again.

But as he heads out into the roaring wind to board up the station windows, he can't shake the feeling that something isn't quite right on the island tonight.

And after so many years of police work, Sherm's instincts are usually on target.

Danny Cavelli paces the bedroom, as he's been doing ever since he hung up with the Tide Island police station over an hour ago.

"If she would just call again," he tells Cheryl, glancing at the silent phone on the nightstand. "I mean, I just want to know that she's okay."

"I know you do. I still think you should call the local police. And your parents."

"Oh, jeez Cheryl, we've been through this. What are the Greenbury cops gonna do if the Tide Island police don't even give a shit about Sandy and she disappeared out there? And I'm not dragging my parents into this unless I have to. Maybe nothing's wrong . . ."

"Maybe not."

Danny stops pacing and looks at his wife. "No. No, she's in trouble. I know she's in trouble. The way she sounded . . . she would never play a joke like that on me."

"I know."

"Some guy was doing something to her, dammit!"

"Even if he were, Danny . . ." Cheryl gets off the bed and walks over to where he's standing by the dresser. She puts a hand on his wrist. "Even if some guy *date-raped* her . . ."

He winces at the words.

". . . *if* that's what was going on—she's going to be okay, Danny," Cheryl finishes. "She'll have a hard time getting over it, but she'll be okay."

"And if that's what happened, I'm going to kill the son of a bitch with my bare hands," Danny says, shaking his head and narrowing his eyes. "I swear to God, Cheryl. I'll find him and kill him."

"Okay, Danny, calm down. It's not helping Sandy if you get carried away . . ."

"And it's not helping Sandy if I just hang around here waiting for something to happen, either," Danny announces suddenly, slapping his palm on the dresser-top so hard that the framed wedding photograph of him and Cheryl topples onto the floor.

"What are you going to do?" she asks, bending to retrieve it.

"Go out to Tide Island."

"Danny, don't be—"

"Cheryl, I can't just sit here. I've got to find my sister; and if the cops don't want to help, that's fine. I'll do it on my own."

"No, you won't," she says quietly, and he spins angrily to face her. But as he opens his mouth to lash out, Cheryl adds, "You won't do it on your own, because we'll do it together."

His jaw closes; and wordlessly, he gathers her into his arms and gives her a grateful squeeze.

In the attic of the Bramble Rose, Stephen carefully removes his blood-soaked tuxedo from the plastic bag he used to transport it back from the house by the water. He had so wanted to wear the same suit again for Liza, and for Laura, but he had forgotten about the blood.

It splattered him from head to toe as he stabbed Sandy, something he hadn't taken into consideration earlier.

And that bothers him. He'd trusted himself to think of everything—how could he have overlooked such an important detail?

It's not a good sign.

That—coupled with Jasper's phone call about Sandy Cavelli's brother, not to mention the unexpected visit from that redheaded kid—is making him nervous.

Somehow, his careful plan suddenly seems in danger of derailing.

No, it won't, he tells himself as he feels

along the sloping wall for the familiar loose board. *Everything is fine. There's no problem, not really. Just a few complications.*

He finds the loose board, pulls it away from the wall, and shoves the tux into the space behind it. He'll deal with it later. Then he removes the wedding album he'd stashed there and replaces the board.

Sitting in his rocker with the album on his lap, he closes his eyes momentarily and takes a deep, cleansing breath, then exhales.

Better . . . much better.

He begins to rock, gently so as not to creak the floorboards and wake anyone below . . . not that Liza and Laura are likely to stir, considering the strong doses of Seconal Jasper was supposed to give them in their dessert.

Flipping the album open to Sandy's page, he replaces the old name card with the new one . . . the one written in her blood. Squatting beside her body in the drawing room, he'd taken the time to painstakingly letter her name in calligraphy, dipping an old-fashioned pen again and again into the pool of red on the floor as he worked.

Now he holds the wedding album away

from his face a bit to admire his handiwork, then glances over at the camera he put on the table by the door. Such a pity he can't go ahead and develop the photographs he'd taken of her as she lay dying at his feet.

Now, thanks to an unexpected interruption, he might as well wait for the others. He'll do them all at once, in the makeshift darkroom back at the waterfront house.

Again, he thinks of how messy things got.

Why did that damn kid have to come along and ruin everything?

He hadn't opened the door, not even when the kid rang the bell persistently and kept calling, "Anybody home?"

Then, just when he'd thought the intruder had left, two things had happened simultaneously.

He'd remembered that he'd left the car parked in front of the door and the porch light on so that Sandy wouldn't get suspicious when he'd brought her here earlier. . . .

And he'd glanced up to see the kid's face pressed against the window of the drawing room as he stood on the porch, peering in.

The horror in those eyes as they took in

Stephen and the bloodied body of Sandy Cavelli was clear even through the rain-spattered glass.

He'd leapt into action, dashing for the door and collaring the kid as he tried to get away. If the intruder hadn't been so shaken by what he'd just seen, Stephen had no doubt that he would have escaped. After all, he had an athletic build and he was strong. But as it was, his shock and fear had undoubtedly slowed him down and it took little effort for Stephen to restrain him long enough to pull out the knife he'd used to kill Sandy.

As soon as the kid saw the blade, he'd started begging for his life.

Stephen had only debated for a brief moment before realizing what he had to do. The kid had seen too much. There was no way he was going to let him go now.

So he'd done it swiftly and effortlessly, slashing the jugular in the kid's strong young neck and feeling warm, sticky blood gush over his just-washed hands.

He'd wondered, as he dragged the kid's body into the first-floor closet under the stairs, who he was and why he was here. Not that it mattered, really.

He'd gone back to the drawing room for Sandy, hurriedly dragging her, too, into the closet, dumping her heavy body on top of the other one. He had a lot of cleaning up to do after that, and it had taken him well over an hour to wash the blood carefully away from the front porch and hardwood foyer and drawing room floors. He'd congratulated himself for not getting any blood on the white satin runner, at least. That, he would need again . . . for Liza, and then for Laura.

With a contented sigh, he closes the wedding album and stands. The night isn't getting any younger, and he's been looking forward to paying Liza a visit.

Stealthily, he moves across the attic floor to the steps. Then, pocketing the ring containing the special keys to the doors of the guest rooms, he slips down the stairs.

Jennie is running through the deserted shopping mall again, desperately trying to get away, when all of a sudden a freight train slams into the side of the building.

She cries out as everything shudders around her, flinching and waiting for the inevitable. . . .

Then, suddenly, she's awake, staring into her pitch-black room at the Bramble Rose Inn.

It was just the same old nightmare, she realizes, sitting up and turning on the light on the bedside table.

But the noise of the freight train was real—apparently caused by a sudden blast of wind off the ocean. It continues to batter the old house now, rattling the windows and howling like a mournful ghost.

Still trembling and breathless from her dream, Jennie swings her feet over the edge of the bed and gets up to go to the bathroom for a drink of water. After pulling on her robe, she pads across the chilly floor in her bare feet and reaches for the doorknob.

It's stuck again, she realizes as she tugs on it.

She remembers what Jasper said about the old wood swelling in damp weather and pulls more forcefully. It refuses to budge.

Then, feeling an edge of panic rising within her, Jennie puts both hands on the knob and tries, with all her might, to open the door.

It's not stuck, she realizes with a stab of fear. *It's locked . . . from the other side!*

"Help!" she screams spontaneously, hoping to wake Liza, whose room is just down the hall. She bangs on the door. "Help! Someone get me out of here!"

Then she realizes that whoever locked the door is possibly nearby and the last thing she should be doing is attracting attention.

She clamps her mouth shut and backs away from the door, her heart pounding furiously as she hears footsteps pounding up the stairs and down the hall toward her room.

There's a long pause, and then Jasper Hammel's voice reaches her ears above the incessant sound of the wind. "Laura . . . Miss Towne, it's me. Are you all right?"

"I'm locked in," she says in a small voice, shrinking into the shadows at the far end of the room and staring at the door.

"I know, I'm sorry, I . . ." There's a jangling noise, and then the sound of the locks clicking. The door swings open, and Jasper is standing there, wearing a pair of striped blue-cotton pajamas.

"I must have locked it by accident," he

says, stepping into Jennie's room, wearing an apologetic expression. In his hand is an oversized key ring. "I was, uh, cleaning in the empty guest rooms earlier, and I somehow must have locked yours instead of one of those."

Jennie only stares uneasily at him for a moment, then nods. "Don't worry about it. It's all right."

"I'm so sorry," Jasper says again, sliding the ring over his wrist and rubbing his hands nervously. "You must have been so startled . . ."

"It's all right," she says again. "Really."

With a final apology, he steps back out into the hall and shuts the door behind him.

Jennie waits until she's heard his footsteps retreat back down the stairs to the first floor. Then she goes over and locks the inside bolt again . . . unsettled by the thought that it doesn't matter—not really.

Jasper, of course, can unlock it any time he feels like it. He just did.

And as for what he said about mistaking her room for one of the empty guest rooms . . .

She's well aware that the doors to the

empty rooms are kept open and unlocked. Isn't that what Liza told her earlier?

Liza.

Strange that she didn't hear Jennie screaming.

Biting her lip, Jennie unlocks her door again and slips quietly out into the dark hallway. It's deserted, and she knows Jasper is back downstairs because she heard him go, but she still can't get past the strange but distinct feeling that someone is lurking nearby.

Don't be paranoid, she commands herself. *Who on earth would be doing a thing like that? And why?*

But as much as she knows it doesn't make sense, she can't seem to shake her anxiety.

Wrapping her robe more tightly around herself, she hurries to Liza's door and knocks quietly. When there's no response, she knocks again, calling, "Liza?" in a hushed voice.

No reply.

She hesitates there, considering knocking or speaking more loudly. But that might bring Jasper Hammel up the stairs again.

Shaking her head, she tells herself that

Liza is probably just a deep sleeper, like Laura. Her twin sleeps through blasting alarm clocks, ringing telephones and doorbells, everything.

And anyway, there's the noise of the storm, Jennie remembers, as she becomes aware, once again, of the pounding rain and ceaseless wind howling outside the old inn. It probably drowned out the sound of her screams earlier, and the knocking now.

Slowly, Jennie retreats down the hall to her room and locks her door again. Then, feeling slightly ridiculous, she quietly pulls a straight-backed chair from the desk across the floor and wedges it under the doorknob.

Trembling, Jennie stares at it for a moment, wondering what she's trying to protect herself from. The only person who might ever want to hurt her is dead.

But you're not supposed to be Jennie right now. . . . You're supposed to be Laura.

And who knows how many enemies flighty, irresponsible Laura has made?

Trying not to think about the most obvious one—her sister's ex-husband, Brian—Jennie goes back over to the bed. She slips beneath the blankets again, leaning her back against the headboard. Bringing her knees up to her chest, she wraps her arms tightly around them and stares at the lilac-patterned wallpaper, vowing not to let herself fall asleep again tonight.

Stephen is trapped in Liza's room, afraid to move, afraid to breathe.

He stands with his back flat against the closed door, listening for another sound from the hallway. A few moments before, he heard Laura Towne go back to her room and close the door, but he can't help thinking it was a close call.

What if her knocking had woken Liza?

Not likely, thanks to the Seconal, but there's always a chance. . . .

Stephen presses his fingertips against his throbbing temples and tries to calm himself, glancing toward the bed for reassurance that his sleeping beauty is still sleeping.

Even in the darkness, he can see the blond hair on the pillow, the pale, creamy skin of her bare arms against the eyelet bedspread.

He had barely been in her room for a few minutes when that Towne woman had started screaming for help. Stricken, he'd realized that she'd found herself locked in.

Thank heaven for Jasper, who had come rushing up the stairs just as Stephen opened Liza's door and peered out into the hall. He'd wordlessly handed the key ring to Jasper, who had nodded his understanding and hurried toward Laura's room, which had grown curiously silent.

There was nothing for Stephen to do but close Liza's door again and wait as Jasper went to Laura's aid. He'd listened with relief as he'd heard Jasper's spur-of-the-moment explanation, followed by his retreat back to the first floor.

Then, just as Stephen was about to give up on Liza for tonight and slip out of her room, he'd heard Laura's door open, and then her knocking and whispering.

Clearly, the woman is suspicious . . . or, at the very least, concerned enough to want to discuss it with the other guest.

You should just get it over with, Stephen tells himself, clenching his fists and setting his jaw grimly. *It's getting too dangerous.*

But then he turns to look again at Liza on the bed. And he exhales raggedly, struck by how innocent and unsuspecting she looks as she sleeps just a few feet from her worst enemy.

He makes up his mind. This isn't something to be done in a rush. It's something that needs to be savored.

He'll stick with the plan.

Sighing softly in pleasure, Stephen stealthily moves across the floor to stand beside Liza's bed, reaching with one hand for the edge of the eyelet bedspread, and with the other for the already taut fly of his trousers.

Keegan wakes from a nightmare in a cold sweat and looks around, disoriented.

He realizes that he's on the living room couch, sprawled in an uncomfortable position, still holding the television remote control in his hand. The last thing he remembers is thinking about Jennie and wishing Laura would call him back, but knowing that if she hadn't yet, she probably wouldn't until tomorrow.

Keegan sits up and rubs his eyes, then glances at the television, where a real estate infomercial is blaring away at ear-shattering volume. He points the remote control at it, hits the power button, and zaps the screen into dark silence.

There.

Now, at least, he can think.

Jennie . . .

In his dream, he had been struggling to reach her as she screamed for help, balancing precariously on a narrow raft in the middle of the storm-tossed ocean.

Hold on, Jennie, he kept calling to her. *I'm coming. I'll get you. Just hold on!*

The dream was so incredibly real that Keegan can still hear the roar of the waves—and Jennie's piercing screams.

"Dammit, Jen," he says aloud into the empty room. "Where the hell are you? Why do I have this feeling that you're not okay?"

Keegan checks his watch. Just past three A.M. He debates for a moment, then reaches for the phone. If Laura's pissed that he's calling her at this hour, he'll be pissed right back at her for not calling him the moment she got home.

And if she's still not home . . .

Well, he'll have to figure out what to do next. Because he definitely has to do *something.*

After dialing the familiar number, Keegan

listens to the phone ringing and then, just as he'd anticipated, the answering machine picking up again.

"Damn," he says, and slams down the receiver.

For a few minutes, he sits there, staring off into space and trying to figure out what to do.

Then, his mind made up, he stands abruptly and heads for the bathroom to take a quick shower before setting out.

In his first-floor bedroom, Jasper rolls over noisily on the narrow, lumpy mattress and punches the pillow beneath his head.

He wonders what Stephen is doing upstairs in Liza's room.

No, you don't wonder. You know. He's looking at her, probably touching her . . .

Jealousy bubbles up inside of Jasper as he squeezes his eyes shut against the image of Stephen with a woman . . . Stephen with someone else.

Oh, Jasper's no fool. He knows Stephen has been with women since he came along. And even though he believes Stephen when he promises that they mean nothing . . .

He's still troubled by the knowledge and haunted by unbidden images that fill his thoughts, especially at night.

At least now, Jasper tells himself, Stephen is taking steps to rid himself of those women for good.

He still remembers his own excitement when Stephen had first revealed his plan nearly a year ago. It seemed too good to be true . . . just like what had happened to Lorraine.

Jasper thinks back to that horrible February day—Valentine's Day, wasn't it?—when Stephen was all set to marry Lorraine. He'd actually asked Jasper to be his best man, promising him, secretly, that things between them wouldn't change.

I just need a wife to keep up appearances, he'd told Jasper. *You know, for the sake of the business. You understand how it is.*

Jasper had acted like he did, because he didn't want to disappoint Stephen. He didn't see any point in reminding Stephen that *he,* Jasper, hadn't bothered to keep up appearances in his own life. No, he'd gone straight to his parents as soon as he realized he was in love with Stephen and he'd told them the truth.

Of course, his parents had disowned him on the spot. His father had told him to get his "pansy ass" out of the house and never come back.

Jasper hadn't.

Had never wanted to, or needed to.

His home, from that day on, had been with Stephen. Stephen, who'd been generous enough to put Jasper on his payroll as an assistant. Jasper had been only too happy to be at Stephen's beck and call.

He was the one who had made the funeral arrangements for Stephen's mother, handling all the messy details since there was no body to bury.

Aurelia Gilbrooke had unexpectedly jumped off the Tappan Zee Bridge in the wee hours of the morning, leaving her Mercedes idling in the breakdown lane and a suicide note tucked under the floor mat.

Or so everyone thought.

Only Stephen and Jasper knew the truth. It was Jasper who, roused out of bed after midnight by a distraught Stephen, had helped him dispose of his mother's bloodied body in the garden. And Jasper who had come up with the suicide story. And Jasper who had donned Aurelia Gilbrooke's favorite blond wig and fur coat with the hood—just in case anyone happened to glance into the Mercedes as he drove it from the Connecticut estate to the bridge, with Stephen trailing along behind in his own car.

Luck had been with them that night, and no one had seen Jasper abandon the car on the bridge, then hop into Stephen's Cadillac for the trip back to Connecticut. And since Aurelia had been such an unstable, miserable woman, no one had ever suspected what had really happened, either.

No one except Stephen's father.

But Andrew Gilbrooke had gone completely off the deep end when he'd figured it out, first flying into hysteria and then slipping into a catatonic state from which he had never recovered. Now he spent his days in a mental institution, staring off into space with a trickle of drool spilling from his slack lips.

Everyone thought poor Andrew, who had always been emotionally frail, couldn't handle the loss of his wife. No one ever realized that what he couldn't handle was the knowledge that his only child had killed his own mother.

Jasper, of course, understood why Stephen had done what he had, although they'd never discussed it, not before Aurelia's death and not after. But he had always speculated that the mother-son relationship was twisted. Apparently, Stephen had finally just snapped.

And, luckily for Jasper, the same thing had happened with Lorraine.

As he waited in Stephen's rose-laden brownstone that February day, he'd outwardly wondered, along with the minister and wedding guests, where the groom had gone and why the bride hadn't shown.

But inside, Jasper had been hoping, praying, that Stephen would do to Lorraine what he had done to his mother.

And that was exactly what had happened.

Again, Jasper had helped Stephen come up with a story. Lorraine, they had told people, had simply gotten cold feet. That much, of course, was the truth.

She had taken Stephen's car, they said, and all her luggage and left the city for an unknown destination. They didn't report her disappearance to the authorities, of course. And by the time the car was located, months later, in long-term parking at La-Guardia, most everyone had forgotten about the curtailed Gilbrooke-LaCroix nup-tials.

Everyone, except Jasper.

He has long since forgiven Stephen for feeling like he needed a woman to keep up appearances, for not wanting the world to know that he, Jasper, was his one true love.

But he has never forgotten.

In the back of his mind, he occasionally wonders, with a sharp little pang, whether Stephen really meant it when he promised that the two of them will sail away together for good, just as long as Jasper helps him with his plan.

Of course he means it, he tells himself now, flipping restlessly again on his bed.

But he can't help wondering why, if he's the only one Stephen really cares about, he's going to so much painstaking trouble with these three women. And why Stephen insisted that Jasper drug them with their dessert so that he would be able to creep into their rooms unnoticed after they've gone to bed.

After the way Stephen had hollered at him when he'd called the mansion earlier, Jasper hadn't dared to tell Stephen that Laura Towne had barely touched her dessert. Which meant that she wasn't drugged.

Which was obviously why she had unexpectedly awakened to find herself locked into her room.

Stephen is going to be so angry when I tell him that she didn't eat her dessert and that I kept it from him earlier, Jasper thinks, staring into the darkness.

So then don't tell him, a voice says reasonably inside his mind.

But I don't like to have secrets from Stephen. I've always told him everything.

And do you think, the voice scoffs, *that he tells you everything in return?*

Not wanting to answer that, Jasper flips over and pulls the pillow over his head tightly to drown out the annoying voices in his head.

Eleven

Sunday morning dawns raw and stormy in Boston.

Laura opens her eyes to find herself entangled in the twin sheet on Shawn's bed as he slumbers peacefully beside her. It amazes her how he can sleep that way—naked and uncovered. For all her own brazen sexuality, Laura always makes sure to slip her own nude body under the covers when she falls asleep.

Jennie, she thinks idly, *probably doesn't even sleep naked when she's with someone.*

She can easily imagine her prudish sister climbing out of bed after Keegan's asleep and pulling one of her warm flannel nightgowns over her head.

Then again, it's surprising that Jennie is sleeping with Keegan in the first place . . .

Was, Laura corrects, remembering that Keegan is history.

Then she remembers something else.

Last night, she'd been worried about her sister for some reason . . .

For no reason, she tells herself, recalling her inexplicable uneasiness over Jennie's trip to the island.

She'd managed to put it out of her head last night, thanks to Shawn's expert hands and lips and—well, everything. But now the memory of her worry comes back to Laura full force and she sits up and frowns.

"Laura?" Shawn asks groggily, stirring beside her on the mattress.

"Yeah. I have to go home."

"Huh?"

"I have to leave," she says, already on her feet and reaching for his robe to wear for a quick trip to the bathroom down the hall.

"But it's lousy outside," he says, sitting up and looking toward the window. "And you don't have to work today. Stay here with me . . ."

"I can't," she says, feeling a distinct sense of urgency taking over. "I have to get home and check on my sister."

"I thought she's away for the weekend."

"She is, but I have this feeling that she

might have tried to call. I'm worried that something's wrong with her."

Shawn frowns, apparently about to say something but thinking better of it. Instead, he asks, "Can't you access your answering machine from here?"

"Uh-uh. I've never been able to figure out how to do that. Jennie's the one who knows how, but . . ." She shrugs. "Anyway, I have to go."

"I'll go with you," Shawn says, getting out of bed and stretching, his naked body magnificent in the gray morning light.

Surprised, Laura asks, "How come?"

"Because I want to be with you," he says simply.

A small smile plays over her lips. "Good" is all she says.

But she's thinking that she's found Mr. Right at last.

Jennie wakes with a start.

Oh, God, you've been sleeping. . . . How could you fall asleep? she scolds herself, looking around the room. She's still sitting up with her knees up against her chest, and the bedside lamp is still on. She looks toward the window and sees dim light filtering through. It's morning, and the storm is still ranting outside.

Harry, Jennie remembers suddenly.

She'd been dreaming of him. The details are fuzzy, but she recalls his face and the fact that he was telling her something, over and over.

"What was it?" she whispers to the silent room. She closes her eyes, trying to bring the dream back.

It's the strangest thing. She can see Harry's familiar face wearing an uncharacteristically serious expression as he speaks to her, and she can hear the urgent tone of his voice. . . .

But she can't seem to grasp the words themselves.

Jennie gives up, for now, and checks her watch. It's nearly nine o'clock.

She grabs the small nylon bag containing her bathroom stuff, then pulls on her robe and heads for the door. She moves the chair she'd wedged under the knob and reaches out to open the door, wondering, with a sudden stab of trepidation, whether she'll find it locked again.

No. Though it sticks slightly, it opens, and

Jennie steps out into the hall, relieved. She glances toward Liza's door, wondering if she should check in with her.

Later, she tells herself and continues across the hall.

The bathroom pipes groan loudly in protest as she turns on the faucets, and the water that comes out of the ancient overhead spout is a mere lukewarm trickle.

I'll be glad to take a real shower when I get home, she thinks as she steps into the ancient tub and pulls the curtain closed around her.

Home . . .

That's it.

In her dream, Harry was telling her to go home. To leave the island . . .

"You're in danger, Jennie," he kept saying. "Trust me. You have to leave. Get out of the inn and off the island. Hurry, Jennie, before it's too late . . ."

Keegan pulls his red Toyota into the ferry parking lot at Crosswinds Bay, turns off the motor, and gives a sigh of relief.

You made it, he tells himself. *Barely.*

I-95 from Boston to Rhode Island is never

a pleasant road to travel, but today it was more treacherous than ever. Visibility was terrible because of the storm, which grew steadily worse as daybreak fell and he drew closer to the coast. The rain had turned to sleet, then to heavy, wet snow that coated the already-slick surface of the highway and made it impossible to go faster than thirty miles an hour. Just outside of Providence, there had been a three-car pile-up that slowed traffic to a standstill for over an hour.

Seeing the red flashing lights of rescue vehicles and police cars, Keegan had debated stopping to see if he could help, then guiltily decided against it. He had to get to Jennie, and there was no time to waste.

In the few seconds since he turned off the car, the windshield has been covered over with sloppy snow, making it impossible for Keegan to clearly see the ferry terminal building just ahead of his parking space. He turns on the wipers again and sees that there's a sign on the door.

"Uh-oh," he says quietly and zips up his jacket. He opens the door and is met by a gust of wet, blowing snow. Slamming the door behind him, he hurries across the narrow stretch of parking lot to the door and tries the knob without reading the sign.

It's locked.

"Damn," Keegan says over the wind and glances at the bold black magic-marker scrawl.

All Tide Island Ferries Canceled Until Further Notice Due to Storm.

"Damn!" he says again and turns to go back to the car just as a battered dark-green Buick with Connecticut plates pulls up next to him.

"Hey, what does that sign say?" the driver, a handsome, dark-haired man who appears to be in his late twenties, calls to Keegan after rolling down his window and poking his head out.

"It says the ferry's canceled," Keegan shouts over the wind.

"What?"

"It's canceled!"

The driver shrugs, motioning that he can't hear him, and Keegan goes over to the car. "Are you looking for the Tide Island ferry?" he asks the guy, noticing that he has deep purplish circles under brown eyes that look distinctly troubled.

"Yeah . . . we have to get out there."

For the first time, Keegan notices that there's a passenger in the car—a pretty, petite woman with long, dark-blond hair poking out from beneath the hood of a bright-pink ski jacket.

"Sorry," Keegan tells them, "but the ferries to the island are canceled because of the storm."

"Shit!" The guy bangs the steering wheel and looks at the woman. "We've got to get to her."

Keegan frowns. "What was that?" he asks, knowing it's none of his business.

"It's my sister," the guy says, turning back to him. "She's out there on the island, and she's in trouble. We have to get out there and find her."

Keegan hesitates only a moment before saying, "My girlfriend's out there, too. I feel the same way."

"Yeah?" The guy reaches over his shoulder and unlocks the back door. "Why don't you get in out of the snow for a few minutes? Maybe we can figure something out. I'm Danny Cavelli, and this is my wife, Cheryl."

* * *

It's past ten o'clock when Liza finally hurries down to the first floor of the inn. She doesn't know what's wrong with her—she never sleeps in on weekends at home. But this morning, she woke late, feeling groggy and unable to keep her eyes open, even after a shower.

The tub was already wet when she got in, and she figured Laura must already be up and about. When Liza knocked on her door on her way out of the bathroom, there was no answer.

Now, as she arrives in the quiet foyer, she smells coffee and wonders if Laura's in the dining room having breakfast.

"Good morning, Miss Danning," Jasper Hammel's voice says as she heads in that direction, and she turns to see him standing behind the front desk.

"Oh . . . good morning. I didn't see you there." She rubs her temples, still feeling out of it.

"Sleep well?" he asks, his mustache twitching.

"I guess. Have you seen Laura?"

"No, I haven't," he says, frowning slightly. "In fact, I was just going to ask you the same thing."

"Oh. Well, I haven't seen her. And I don't suppose D.M. Yates has called looking for me, hmmm?"

"No, I'm afraid not."

"I didn't think so." Liza shoots him a level gaze through her bleary eyes, wondering if he knows that there *is* no D.M. Yates on the island . . . and whether he's in on this nasty little practical joke someone's obviously playing on her.

"Listen, Jasper," she says pointedly, trying to stifle an uncontrollable urge to yawn, "I was wondering if you happen to have a ferry schedule handy there."

His eyebrows shoot up beneath his neatly trimmed auburn hair. "A ferry schedule?" he echoes. "I . . . I'm not sure. Why?"

"Because I'm going to leave on the first ferry this morning, that's why," she says firmly. "And if you don't have a schedule, I'll borrow your phone and call the dock."

"No, don't do that. . . . I'll look for it. I'm sure I have one here someplace," he says, rummaging through some papers on top of the desk. "It'll take me a moment to find it, though. Why don't you go into the dining room and help yourself to some breakfast and coffee?"

Liza is about to say she's just fine and she'll wait right here, when she feels yet another yawn stealing over her.

On second thought, coffee *would* be a good idea. She can't seem to shake her drowsiness this morning. Must be the weather.

She mumbles a thanks to Jasper and goes down the hall to the dining room where she helps herself to a mug of steaming hot coffee. She sits at the table to drink it and is halfway through when she hears the unmistakable sound of footsteps going up the stairs.

It has to be Jasper.

Annoyed, Liza debates following him up and demanding to know why he hasn't produced the ferry schedule yet.

But for some reason, the thought of going all the way back to the foyer and up the stairs seems daunting. She's so numb with exhaustion this morning that her limbs feel weak and useless.

Hopefully, the coffee will help, she thinks again and reaches for the carafe on the table to refill her mug.

* * *

Sherm Crandall wakes, as he has every morning for the past thirty years, in the master bedroom of the gray-shingled cape on the west side of Tide Island. The house sits on a little rise more than half-a-mile from the beach; but even from here, the first sound that reaches Sherm's ears is that of waves crashing over the rocky shore.

Sherm stretches and sits up to look out the window, which is on his side of the bed.

My side . . . as if Carly still has a side, he thinks, glancing at the empty pillow beside him.

Even after all these months, he still sleeps on the right, never crossing the imaginary line into the territory that had always belonged to his wife. And it's funny, because he'd always felt that their double bed was too small for both of them. He'd wanted to buy a queen-sized mattress and box spring for the longest time so they'd have more room, but Carly always said they couldn't afford it. Since she was the one who kept the checkbook and paid all the bills, Sherm had always let her decide what they needed and what was a luxury.

Now, he wonders what she's living on— and where she's living. She might be waitressing somewhere—she'd spent a few summers working part-time in island restaurants when they were first married—or maybe she's doing secretarial work. She always was a good typist . . .

Stop thinking about her, Sherm commands himself, looking away from the empty pillow, back to the window. It's one of the few he left uncovered last night, figuring he had to be able to see out.

The bedroom's on the west side of the house, so the morning light is never good in here. But even from the bed, without his glasses, Sherm can see that the storm hasn't let up at all. Looks like it's snowing out now, and the sky is ominously dark.

With a sigh, Sherm swings his legs over the edge of the bed, wincing as his bare feet hit the cold wooden floor. Damn place is so drafty. Most of the old houses on the island are. The bedroom doesn't even have a radiator, and Sherm hasn't bothered with the portable electric heater since Carly left. She's the one who was always cold . . .

"Warm me up, Sherm," she used to say on cold winter mornings, snuggling up to him beneath the worn blue-and-red patchwork quilt her grandmother had made them for a wedding present.

And he would, gladly.

Sighing again, he pulls on his robe and pads quietly through the silent, lonely house to the kitchen, where he stands at the sink and fills the glass coffee carafe.

And as he does, he remembers Pat.

He'd never stopped by or called last night, and Sherm had been up into the wee hours, nailing plywood over most of the windows of his house.

Frowning, Sherm dumps the water into the old Mr. Coffee machine on the counter, measures some grounds into the filter, and presses the button. Then he goes over to the wall phone and dials Pat's number.

After one ring, the answering machine picks up.

The beep is pretty long, suggesting that Pat never played the message Sherm left for him last night.

He leaves another one, then hangs up and rubs the razor stubble on his chin.

Maybe Pat is seeing someone and spent the night at her place. But whom? The number of eligible females who live year-round on the island is practically zero. . . . And besides, Sherm would have heard if Pat were seeing someone, even if Pat didn't tell him himself. Tide Island is a gossipy kind of place.

Okay, so if Pat never made it home, why hadn't he?

What if that clunker Chevy of his broke down somewhere and he was stranded out in the storm all night?

I should have gone out looking for him last night, Sherm tells himself, shaking his head. *He was going to the old Gilbrooke place. That's way the hell at the end of the north peninsula, and most of the other houses out there are closed for the winter.*

He pictures Pat, shivering, in a broken-down car in the middle of nowhere.

Some godfather you are, Sherm scolds himself.

When Pat's father, Robert, had found out he was dying, what had he asked Sherm to do?

"Look out for the kid, okay, Sherm? Make sure he's all right, will you?"

"Sure, I will," he'd promised.

And that's just what he's going to do now.

Turning abruptly, Sherm heads for the bedroom. He'll get dressed, then grab a quick cup of coffee and head out toward the Gilbrooke place to see if he can't find Pat.

Her head still bent against the biting wind and driving snow, Jennie sets down her bag and reaches out to open the door of the ferry terminal.

It's locked, she realizes with a stab of panic. She walked all the way here, rushing so she wouldn't miss the eleven o'clock boat, and the door is locked. The ramshackle wooden building looks deserted, too.

That can only mean one thing . . .

Sure enough, Jennie sees a sign taped to the glass window beside the door.

Sunday Ferry Canceled.

"No," she cries out softly, shaking her head.

She has to get off the island.

She *has* to . . .

But how?

There's no way. You have to go back to the inn, she tells herself, trying to be reasonable. But returning to the Bramble Rose is the last thing she wants to do.

She had felt so relieved as she slipped out the door earlier, her hair still damp from the shower. It had taken her all of ten minutes to pack and get dressed once she'd made up her mind to leave. And she hadn't even had to deal with Jasper, who had been nowhere in sight when she'd come down the stairs.

She supposed it wasn't very responsible of her to simply leave, but since her room was paid for, there was no reason to go through the formality of checking out and providing the innkeeper with an explanation.

She *had* felt guilty just leaving Liza. But she hadn't wanted to take the time to stop and say goodbye to her.

With Harry's dream-warning still echoing in her ears, she'd left in a rush.

And now, for all her urgency to get away, she's stranded on the island.

It'll be all right, she tells herself as she stands on the dock, buffeted by wind and snow, the fine, grainy kind that stings like blowing sand.

But I'm afraid. . . . I have to get off this island, she whimpers mentally, desperately looking back at the window and hoping that the cancellation sign will have miraculously vanished.

But it's still there, of course, and there's nothing for Jennie to do but start trudging back through the storm toward the inn.

Jasper finds Liza sitting in the dining room, staring moodily into space. She looks up when he pokes his head in the doorway, and says, "Well?"

"There's an eleven o'clock ferry," he says smoothly, "and I've called to arrange for a car service to bring you to the dock."

She frowns and sets her mug down on the table. "You did? Why?"

"Surely you don't think I'm going to let you walk all the way to the ferry, with your luggage, in this weather." He gestures toward the window behind her, where the snow is falling steadily.

"Well, I appreciate it," she says after a pause, during which she had seemed to be trying to decide whether to accept his offer. She pushes back her chair and gets up. "I'll go up and get my bags. When is this car service supposed to show?"

"In about twenty minutes," Jasper tells

her and moves over to the sideboard to flick a speck of dust from the gleaming wooden surface.

"Okay. I'll be ready. You didn't see Laura while you were upstairs, did you?"

She heard him go upstairs? He keeps his expression carefully neutral as he says, "No, I merely went up to find the schedule, which I correctly thought I had left in one of the guest rooms."

"Mmm." The blonde is staring at him with a calculating look, and Jasper nervously wonders what she's thinking.

Well, it doesn't matter now, does it? In twenty minutes, she'll be leaving the inn for good. And he'll never have to worry about her again.

Two down, one to go, he thinks, humming softly to himself as he leaves the room.

"Come on, Keegan, pick up," Laura says, listening to the phone ring for the tenth time.

"He's not there?" Shawn, standing at her side, asks. "Doesn't he have an answering machine?"

"No, and it used to drive Jen crazy when they were dating."

Her sister was going to get him one for Christmas, Laura remembers, but then she had decided it was too impersonal. She'd bought him a pair of antique cufflinks instead . . . then dumped him a week later. Go figure.

"You might as well give up, Laura," Shawn says, as she continues to let Keegan's line ring.

"I guess you're right." She plunks the receiver into its cradle and looks at him. "Where do you think he went?"

Shawn shrugs. "He was pretty anxious to talk to you. Maybe he's on his way over here."

She contemplates that, then shakes her head. "He left the last message in the middle of the night. It's—" She checks the stove clock. "—past ten-thirty now. He would have called back this morning before coming all the way over, don't you think?"

"I guess." Shawn shoves his hands into the front pockets of his faded jeans and leans against the counter. "Now what?"

"I have no—oh, yes, I do. I'm going to call

the inn where my sister's staying and make sure she's all right."

"Good idea."

"But first," she says, looking around with a puzzled expression, "I have to figure out where she is."

"You don't know?"

"I can't remember. But I got a letter when the sweepstakes people told me that I'd won, and I'm pretty sure it mentioned the name of the inn."

"Did you keep the letter?"

"I think so," she tells Shawn, jerking open a drawer and starting to shuffle through the papers inside. "I'm just not sure where. But it shouldn't take me long to find it . . ."

Liar, she scolds herself, closing the drawer and opening another one. *It's going to take forever. And Shawn—Mr. Right—is going to find out that you're a pack rat and a slob.*

The sign on the diner near the ferry parking lot at Crosswinds Bay says *We Never Close.*

"Isn't *that* the truth," Danny mutters as he and Cheryl follow Keegan McCullough inside.

After all, the weather can't get much worse than it is on this dismal Sunday morning, but the place is lit up and there are even a few people inside.

They take one of the empty booths along the wall, and a waitress instantly appears to pour steaming coffee into the cups that are already on the table.

"You want menus?" she asks, tossing a handful of sugar and creamer packets onto the chipped formica surface.

"No thanks," Cheryl says, and Danny and Keegan shake their heads.

As soon as the waitress leaves, Danny takes a sip of the hot coffee, not bothering to add anything, though he usually takes it light and sweet. Then he says, "Now what?"

For a moment, Keegan says nothing. He's the quiet type, Danny has noticed in the brief times since they met. Hasn't said much, except to tell him and Cheryl that he's worried about his girlfriend, who's out on the island.

When Cheryl had asked him why he was worried, he'd just said, "Because of the weather."

Danny suspects it's more than that, but

he wasn't about to push it. He had told Keegan, briefly, that his sister had gone out to the island to meet some blind date, then made the phone call that had alarmed him and Cheryl. The guy had asked a few questions, acting concerned, which Danny thought was pretty nice, considering that he seemed to have problems of his own.

Now, Keegan shrugs and tells Danny and Cheryl, "We obviously need a boat. I thought we might find some fisherman types in here."

Danny glances at the counter where two men, one elderly, the other barely out of his teens, sit on adjoining stools, having a cheerful, loud argument about something.

"What about them?" Danny asks, pointing. Keegan nods. "I'll go talk to them." He gets up and ambles over to the counter.

Cheryl looks at Danny. "You okay?"

"Fine," he lies.

"You look beat."

"Yeah, well, it wasn't exactly a pleasant drive down here," he reminds her, and gulps more of the bitter, hot coffee. Then he turns to look at Keegan, who's having a conversation with the two men.

From here, it's impossible to hear what's

being said, but the fact that the men are shaking their heads doesn't seem to be a good sign.

As Danny watches, Keegan reaches into his pocket and pulls something out, showing it to them.

Whatever it is seems to have a big impact, because now the men are nodding reluctantly and getting to their feet.

Cheryl and Danny exchange a puzzled look.

"What do you think he's up to?" she asks.

"Beats the hell outa me." Grimly, Danny swallows more coffee, burning his throat and not caring.

Keegan comes back over to the table and says, "We're all set."

"What do you mean?"

"The older guy's retired, but the younger one's still a lobster man. Has a boat. He doesn't want to take it out on the water in this weather, but he'll let us borrow it."

"Yeah?" Danny raises his eyebrows. "How'd you talk him into that?"

"Showed him my badge."

"You're a *cop*?"

"Yeah."

Relief courses over Danny. "Thank God. I

know you need to find your girlfriend, but maybe you can help me with my sister . . ."

"I'll try." Keegan tosses a couple of dollar bills onto the table. "You guys ready?"

"You bet," Danny says and takes Cheryl's hand as they get to their feet.

"So you know how to drive the kind of boat this guy has, right?" she asks Keegan as the three of them approach the two men at the counter again.

From the look on his face, Danny knows what's coming.

"Actually, I don't," Keegan tells her slowly. "I've never driven a boat in my life. How about you two?"

"I know how to row," Danny says feebly as Cheryl turns white and shakes her head.

"What about the weather?" she asks, glancing toward the plate-glass window of the diner. Outside, the churning Atlantic is clearly visible several yards away, the same brackish color as the sky.

"You two can stay here if you want," Keegan says, following her gaze. "But I have to go. I have to get to Jennie."

"I'll go," Danny tells him resolutely, thinking of his sister, hearing her panicked voice again. He turns to his wife and squeezes her clammy fingers. "But, Cheryl, you stay here."

"No way," she says, shaking her head. "If you go, I go."

Danny is about to protest, but knows, from the gleam in her blue eyes, that she's not going to waver now that she's made up her mind.

He turns to Keegan. "We're with you. Let's go."

Twelve

Liza is standing in the foyer of the inn, looking out the window, when a big black car glides to a stop at the foot of the driveway.

"That must be the car service," she says, turning to Jasper Hammel, who's at the desk behind her.

He looks up from the paperwork he's been doing and comes over to look through the window. "That's it," he says.

"Do I need a voucher or anything to give the driver?"

"A voucher? Oh, no. It's all taken care of. The inn has a contract with the driver."

"Okay." She picks up her bag and reaches for the doorknob.

He gets to it first. "Allow me, Miss Danning." He opens the door with a sweeping gesture. "It's been a pleasure having you as our guest. Please come back to stay with us again."

Not on your life, she thinks, but merely nods as she steps out into the icy wind.

Then, remembering something, she turns and looks back at him. "Do me a favor. . . . Tell Laura Towne to look me up if she's ever in New York." She reaches into her purse and pulls out one of her business cards.

Jasper Hammel takes it and smiles. "I certainly will."

Liza hurries through the wet snow toward the car, thinking, *Good riddance, you little creep.*

The driver steps out and opens the trunk so that she can put her bag in, holding an umbrella over her head. He's a tall man; and though Liza keeps her head bent against the stinging snow, she notices, in surprise, that he's wearing a long dark coat and a cap with a visor.

Who would expect a formal car service on such a podunk island? *This is more like it,* Liza thinks to herself.

Pleased, she smiles and thanks him as he holds the back door open so that she can get into the car.

He nods, and she sees that he's wearing tinted aviator glasses—the kind that went out of style years ago.

Oh, well, she thinks, *I guess upscale service and high fashion would be too much to ask out here. And it could be worse. He could be wearing a leisure suit or something . . .*

Amused with her thoughts, she settles back against the upholstery—real leather, at least, she notes, running her fingers over the seat.

The driver gets behind the wheel again and shifts the car into Drive. Its engine purring, the car pulls away from the shoulder of the road.

Liza is so busy thinking about how thrilled she is to be leaving that, for a few seconds, she isn't paying attention to where they're going.

Then, with a start, she glances out the window and says, "I'm supposed to be taken to the ferry dock."

The driver merely nods.

Uneasy, Liza looks out the window again, then back over her shoulder at the winding road.

"Isn't the dock back that way?" she asks.

The driver doesn't reply, just keeps looking straight ahead through the windshield, his black-gloved hands expertly maneuvering the steering wheel as the car speeds along the winding seaside road.

Liza frowns and tries to ignore the edge of panic that's working its way through her. "Excuse me," she says frostily, trying to keep the shakiness out of her voice. "I asked you a question. Isn't the ferry dock back in town?"

He nods.

"And aren't we heading *away* from town?" Her voice sounds shrill to her own ears as she stares out the window at the remote landscape, then looks at him again.

His only response is to step on the gas so that the car picks up speed, barreling in the wrong direction.

She sees him watching her in the rearview mirror; and though she can't see his eyes behind the tinted lenses, there's no mistaking the cunning smile that plays over his lips.

Liza looks wildly about, terrified. For a moment, all she can do is wonder who this man is, why he's doing this to her—and *what* he's doing to her. Abducting her? For what? Money? Revenge?

Revenge.

Her mind fills with rapid-fire images of her

past, of the things she's done, the men she's used. . . .

Somewhere along the way, she realizes, she crossed the wrong person.

Now someone wants to make her pay for her sins.

She can't bear to consider what he has in mind, and she has no intention of finding out.

So she does the only thing she can think of to do.

Her heart beating a frenzied staccato, Liza waits until he slows the car slightly to go around the curb.

Then, in one swift motion, she reaches for the door handle, opens it, and—silently offering the first prayer she's said in years—hurls herself out of the moving car.

Jennie finds Jasper Hammel in the foyer, behind the desk, when she comes in.

He glances up and says pleasantly, "Good morning, Laura."

Then a tiny frown darts over his face as he catches sight of the traveling bag over her shoulder.

"I, uh, was planning to take the ferry

home this morning," she says, because she feels that she should.

"Oh?" He raises his eyebrows and seems to be waiting for more of an explanation.

"I wasn't feeling well, so I thought . . ." She shrugs.

"But you changed your mind?"

She wants to say yes, but decides against lying. "No. Actually, the ferry was canceled."

"I see. Because of the storm, no doubt."

She nods and starts for the stairs, then remembers something. "Is Liza around?" she asks Jasper over her shoulder.

"Liza?" He looks blankly at her.

"The other guest? Liza Danning?"

"Oh, of course," he says, nodding. "She . . . I haven't seen her yet today, no."

"I saw a car pulling away from the inn as I was coming around the curve in the road, and I thought maybe she was leaving for that meeting she was planning to have with that author." Jennie watches him carefully.

But he only says, "I don't think she left. I've been right here for the last half hour."

Jennie nods. She wants to ask him who was in the car, but decides it's really none of her business. Instead, she nods toward the stairs and comments, "I guess Liza must still be in her room."

He looks as though he's about to say something, then apparently changes his mind. "She must be," he agrees.

Jennie heads up to the second floor with her bag, conscious of Jasper Hammel watching her until she rounds the landing.

He's definitely an odd man.

But is he dangerous? she wonders, going toward her room. *Is all of this my imagination or am I really in trouble here?*

Not wanting to dwell on her fear again, she unlocks her door, deposits her bag on the floor just inside, and then goes back down the hall to Liza's room.

The door is closed, and there's no answer to her knock.

Puzzled, Jennie calls, "Liza?" and jiggles the knob.

No reply.

Maybe she's still sleeping, she thinks. *Or she might be listening to a walkman or something and can't hear me.*

But as she stands there in the hallway, staring at the closed door, Jennie senses that there's no one behind it.

If Liza really is gone, she thinks, suddenly

feeling a case of the jitters descend over her again, *then where can she be?*

Even if Liza had decided to take the ferry, not realizing it was canceled, Jennie would have seen her down at the dock or on the road between here and there.

Maybe she did leave to have her meeting with that author, Jennie thinks hopefully before she remembers what Pat Gerkin told them about D.M. Yates last night.

I guarantee you that he doesn't live here.

But the fact that the man doesn't live on the island doesn't mean he wouldn't come out here to meet with Liza. On the other hand, why would he? And Liza herself had seemed to have doubts about it.

Her mind jumbled with disconcerting thoughts, Jennie turns away from Liza's locked door and slowly makes her way back to her room.

Sherm drives slowly up the narrow lane leading to the old Gilbrooke place at the northern tip of the crescent-shaped stretch of coast. There's been no sign of Pat's Chevy so far, but maybe he got stuck at the house itself.

In winter, when the trees are bare, the Victorian mansion is visible from the road that winds by it and then away from the coast. In summer, when the Gilbrookes used to use the place, it's shrouded from view by dense trees and shrubbery that border the edge of the property. The Gilbrookes liked it that way, Sherm recalls. They were an odd bunch, even before Aurelia came along.

Andrew's father, Andrew Senior, had made a fortune in his Manhattan-based import-export business in the early part of the century. He and his wife, Helena, used to throw lavish parties on the island when they spent summers here.

Of course, back then, Tide Island had been a fashionable resort for the social elite of Boston and New York. It was even dubbed "Little Newport" in the roaring twenties, when the enormous homes on the northern coast of the island were filled with wealthy urbanites every June, July, and August.

But then, with the depression years and then the war, the summer crowd had gradually dwindled. Many of the rich had sold their lavish oceanfront homes.

The Gilbrookes never did, though. In fact, they seemed to like the island better when it became less populated. They had always been big on privacy, keeping themselves carefully apart from the rest of the island's inhabitants.

Andrew Senior and Helena had spent their summers here well into the fifties, usually with their son Andrew, who had been Sherm's playmate when they were both children. His parents probably hadn't been crazy about their son's mingling with the locals; but then, they might have been grateful he had any friends at all.

These days, Sherm thinks, *kids would call old Andrew a wimp. Back then, he was a sissy.*

But a sissy who has money, Sherm had learned, is more attractive to women than a virile kid who doesn't. When they were in their teens and met vacationing girls on the island, it was Andrew they were always drawn to, once they found out who he was.

And you didn't care when they bypassed you, Sherm reminds himself. *You always had Carly.*

His mouth set grimly at the thought of his wife, Sherm steers around a huge pothole in the lane, then turns his thoughts back to the Gilbrookes.

As Andrew Junior grew older and was being groomed to take over his father's business, he had spent less time on the island. Then his parents died within months of each other and he met Aurelia, and that was it.

The big old house has been virtually abandoned ever since.

But maybe the son is back, Sherm thinks, maneuvering the last sharp bend in the lane. Stephen, his name was. Rumor had it that Andrew hadn't named his son after himself and his father because of what he referred to as the boy's "hideous facial deformity."

Supposedly, he'd wanted his wife to bear him another son, one worthy of being a namesake. But Aurelia, according to the island gossips, had wanted no part of pregnancy and childbirth, having already experienced the "torture" once.

Sherm had only met Andrew Junior's wife once or twice. Though she was an attractive woman, her disposition made her unpleasant to look at. Her mouth was permanently turned down at the corners, as if in distaste, and her black eyes had perennially bore a sharp, beady gleam.

She had undoubtedly married poor Andrew for his money as she clearly had no patience for him, or anyone else. And as for Andrew—Sherm supposed he had married Aurelia because she told him to. He was that kind of man.

He pulls up in front of the Gilbrookes' sprawling old Victorian and sees fairly recent tire tracks in the snow. Is Stephen Gilbrooke back on the island?

Or did the tracks come from Pat's car . . .

And if so, where is it now?

Sherm had driven by Pat's small house on the way out here, but there was no sign of anyone there. The few inches of wet snow on the driveway and walk had been undisturbed.

Sherm had considered stopping by Rosalee Gerkin's place to see if she'd heard from her son, but had decided against it. Ever since she lost her husband, Rosalee has been a nervous wreck. No need to worry her if Sherm doesn't have to.

Frowning, Sherm puts the police car into Park and leaves it running as he gets out and picks his way across the messy drive to the front steps. They're snow-covered, but he can make out indentations where some-one walked up and down at some point re-cently. Probably Pat, checking on things.

Clinging to the icy railing and wincing against the stinging wind and snow that are whirling off the ocean, Sherm climbs the steps and knocks on the door.

He waits, then knocks again, and calls, "Anyone home?"

He doesn't expect an answer. The wind would probably have drowned out his voice, and anyway, there doesn't seem to be anyone here.

With a sigh, Sherm goes back to his car and gratefully slips into the heated interior.

"Where the heck are you, Pat?" he says aloud as he shifts into reverse and backs carefully away from the house.

"You okay?" Keegan calls, looking over his shoulder at Danny Cavelli and his wife Cheryl. They're huddled on the bench be-hind him, clinging to the sides of the boat as it rocks violently in the foaming water.

"Fine," Danny shouts above the roar of the engine and the wind.

Cheryl doesn't reply. She looks green.

Keegan sees Danny glance at her in concern, saying something in her ear.

She nods and offers him a valiant smile, clinging to his hand.

She must really love the guy, Keegan thinks, turning to look ahead again at the surging gray-black water. *She's doing this for him—risking her life on this damn boat in a storm, with an inexperienced idiot at the helm.*

And Keegan, the inexperienced idiot, is risking his life for Jennie.

And why? he wonders bleakly.

She doesn't even care about you. And you don't even know that she's definitely in trouble. . . . You just think she might be.

What's wrong with you? Are you crazy?

No, he tells himself, he's not crazy. He's doing it for Jennie because he really loves her. And he can't make himself stop, no matter what she's done to him.

And she loves you, too, he thinks, then narrows his brows in surprise.

She does. If you didn't believe that, you wouldn't be hanging on after almost two months.

Keegan ponders the notion that Jennie

loves him and feels hope surging within him at the realization that it's true. Somehow, he just knows that it is.

She loves you, but she can't be with you for some reason. There's definitely something she's not telling you.

But, Keegan promises himself, when he reaches the island and finds her, he'll make her see that no matter what her reason is, it isn't good enough to justify leaving him.

He pictures her lilac eyes and wonders why he never asked her about the haunted expression that sometimes filled them. He'd always sensed that she was keeping something from him, but he'd figured that she'd tell him when she was ready.

Never had he imagined that there wouldn't be plenty of time for that.

And even after she'd unceremoniously broken up with him, he hadn't quite grasped that she meant it. Reeling from shock, he kept thinking that she would come to her senses eventually . . . that if he could just talk to her, she'd realize that they belonged together.

Never had he expected her to refuse to answer his calls or see him.

But this time, Jennie Towne, he tells her

silently, *I'm not going to let you get away with it.*

As soon as I get to you—

A monstrous wave breaks over the front of the boat then, and Keegan grips the steering wheel with all his might to keep control, remembering the few pointers the fisherman had given him back at the dock.

If I get to you, Keegan amends, wiping the stinging saltwater from his eyes with his shoulder as he clings to the wheel, *I'm going to grab you and hold you and I'm never going to let go again.*

Stephen drives as fast as he dares along the slippery coastal road, still jittery from the shock of seeing Liza jump out of the car.

He hears a thump and a muffled groan from the trunk and grits his teeth. His knuckles are white as he grips the wheel, clenching it as much out of necessity as out of fury.

What the hell did she think she was doing? he asks himself, his eyes narrowed into angry slits behind the tinted aviator lenses.

Then again, it shouldn't surprise him that Liza would figure out what he was up to and try to escape. She'd always been the perceptive type, he remembers, even when he first met her.

He remembers the way her green eyes had sized him up that first day . . .

He'd been browsing through a stack of imported woolen socks in the large Brooks Brothers store on Madison when he'd felt someone watching him. Glancing up, he'd seen a gorgeous, slender blonde standing a few feet away. She had a scarf in her hands, and she was running her fingers lovingly, absently, over the fine cashmere as she looked directly at him.

He'd found himself mesmerized, first by the sensuous way her fingertips stroked the scarf, then by how she slowly and oh-so-tantalizingly slipped her tongue from her mouth and ran it over her full lips.

Then she'd smiled and raised her eyebrows slightly at him, as if in silent invitation.

Stephen had glanced over his shoulder to be sure it was he she wanted, and not someone else. But he was the only one in the vicinity, and Liza had tilted her head coyly at him, appearing amused at his uncertainty.

He'd moved to stand beside her in a matter of seconds.

"Hello, there," she'd said in that wonderfully throaty voice of hers. "I'm Liza Danning."

"Stephen Gilbrooke," he'd responded, holding out his hand and taking the manicured fingers she offered. Her grip was warm and confident, and she'd let her fingertips play over his knuckles before he released them.

Then she'd let her green eyes wander down the length of him, and Stephen had felt as though he were standing there stark naked and absolutely alone with her.

When she raised her gaze to meet his again, she had grinned suggestively.

"Married?" was all she said.

Stephen blinked and shook his head.

"Good."

With that, Liza had slipped her arm through his and leaned up to whisper in his ear, her cloying perfume swirling around him in an enticing, heady cloud. "Take me to dinner tonight."

Of course, he had. It wasn't every day that a beautiful woman threw herself at him. Oh, Stephen was used to gold diggers, of course—he'd always encountered his share. They were easy to pinpoint, because they wanted nothing to do with someone who looked like him . . . until they found out who he was.

"You're one of *the* Gilbrookes?" they would ask, their eyes growing suddenly interested.

But Liza was different, at first. She seemed interested in him right from the start, before she even knew his name. It wasn't until later that night, over dinner at Le Cirque, when he'd caught the calculating way she looked at his Rolex, that Stephen realized she was a gold digger like the rest of them.

But by then he didn't care, because her hand was doing astonishing things in his lap beneath the tablecloth and he thought he would die from sheer pleasure.

He had taken her back to his brownstone that night and watched her absorb the authentic antique French furnishings, the Impressionist collection started by his grandfather, the Persian carpets, and the rest of the trappings that trumpeted his vast wealth. He told himself it didn't matter that she was obviously fascinated by his money, that all that mattered was the fact that she was there, that she was going to let him make love to her.

But she hadn't . . .

Not that first night.

No, *she* had made passionate love to *him,* pleasuring him repeatedly, beyond his wildest dreams, leaving him sated and exhausted and mad with the need to see her again and again and again.

He had showered her with gifts over the next several weeks, not caring that she hinted for the lavishly expensive things she wanted or that she barely bothered to hide her greed as she accepted them from him. All that mattered to Stephen was that she did incredible things to his body with hers.

And then one night, out of the blue, Liza had seemed moody and cold over dinner at Lutèce. Stephen had tried to draw her out, plying her with fine French food and champagne and outrageous compliments in his flawlessly accented French.

But he had sensed, when she turned those bored green eyes on him as he'd helped her into the mink he'd bought her, that she was about to bring their affair to a close. She had gotten everything she needed from him.

Simmering with rage, Stephen had driven her back to his place, not bothering to ask whether she wanted to be there. She'd gone along with it, probably planning to play him for a fool one last time and see what he would give her in return for her sexual services.

But the moment Stephen had closed and locked his bedroom door behind them, he had been the one in control for a change.

Instead of letting Liza tease him by undressing bit by bit, he had ripped her clothes off her. Instead of lying back, naked, and letting her hands and mouth and hair trail over his body, he had thrown her onto the bed, face down. And instead of turning her over, he had entered her, roughly and swiftly, from behind, eliciting a scream of fury and pain from those pouty lips of hers.

When he was finished, he had roughly flipped her over onto her back, expecting to see her sobbing, or at least weakened and ashamed.

Yet to his utter astonishment and dismay, those hard green eyes of hers had betrayed nothing but disgust for him.

"Are you finished?" she'd asked coldly, sitting up, then standing. "Because I'm going home now. I'm through prostituting myself to a cretin like you, although it was definitely worth it. Even this last little tantrum of yours."

Stunned into silence, he had merely watched as she pulled her dress over her head.

"And Stephen? If it weren't for your money, I never would have given you the time of day in the first place. I was hanging around Brooks Brothers that afternoon just waiting for a rich sucker like you to come along."

Laughing, she had grabbed her coat and purse and left the room, leaving him lying on the bed, reeling from her cruel words . . . even though he had known the truth all along.

Now, as Stephen slows the car to make the turn into the lane leading to his family's old summer house, he thinks, *We'll see who gets the last laugh now, Liza.*

He's chuckling to himself when he stops short, spotting a car coming toward him down the lane . . .

A police car.

Stephen's blood runs cold as he slows and pulls over to the side. What else can he do? There's no room on the narrow lane for the cars to pass each other, and anyway, it would seem suspicious for him to try to keep going.

Panic screams through his mind as the other car stops alongside him. The uniformed man behind the wheel is rolling down the window and leaning out, despite the nasty weather.

Stay calm, Stephen commands himself, pasting an artificial grin on his mouth and raising his right hand in greeting after rolling the window down with his left. *The wind will muffle any sounds coming from the trunk. And no one can possibly recognize you or the car.*

After all, he hasn't been to the island in years, and the last time was before he had the plastic surgery. And there's nothing flashy about the American-made black sedan he's driving. He left his own silver Mercedes and cherry-colored Porsche back in Manhattan. He won't need them where he's going after this.

"Hello there," the man in the cop car

calls, waving back. "I'm Sherm Crandall, chief of police on the island."

Stephen nods, still grinning, and says over the roar of the wind, "Nice to meet you. My name's . . ." He hesitates for the merest second before uttering the first thing that pops into his head. "LaCroix. John LaCroix."

"Oh, yeah? I was half-expecting one of the Gilbrookes."

"You were?" Stephen wonders if the cop can tell that he's barely managing to keep himself together. Hopefully the blowing wet snow is obscuring his face somewhat. "Who are the Gilbrookes?"

"The family that owns this place."

Play dumb, and he won't get suspicious.

"What place?" he asks, making his eyebrows furl as though he's confused.

The officer gestures with his head at the house behind him, just out of sight, Stephen knows, around the bend.

"There's a big old mansion back here," Crandall tells him, his breath coming out in white puffs in the frigid wind. "Thought that was where you were headed."

"If I am, it's not on purpose." Does he sound too edgy? He shrugs, trying desperately to appear casual. "Just wanted to turn around . . . looks like I'm lost."

"You a tourist?"

"You bet."

"Where are you trying to go?"

"Back to the inn where I'm staying," Stephen says, thinking quickly.

"Which one is that?"

Is the cop just making conversation or is he suspicious? It's impossible to tell. It *feels* like an interrogation, but it might just be Stephen's own guilt.

"Where are you staying?" the cop asks again.

"The Bramble Rose," Stephen says quickly.

"Oh, yeah? How is that place?"

"Very nice. I like it."

"Good. I might have relatives coming to visit soon, and I thought they might like to stay there. The place is new, so I haven't heard much about it."

"Uh huh." Why won't the guy just move on? Stephen wonders, agitated. He realizes that he's jiggling his leg impatiently on the brake pedal and stops abruptly. He makes a big show of shivering, as though it's the cold that's making him antsy.

Sherm Crandall doesn't seem to have noticed. But he's not moving on, either.

"Say," he says, as though he's just thought of something, "you wouldn't have happened to run across a young girl named Cindy staying at the Bramble Rose this weekend, would you? No, wait—not Cindy. Sandy. Italian last name . . . Cavelli. That's it."

Fighting to maintain his composure, Stephen shakes his head and blandly responds, "Nope. Didn't see her."

"Huh." The cop rubs his chin thoughtfully, then shrugs. "Well, if you do, you let me know, okay? You can call me down at the police station."

"I sure will." He hesitates, wanting badly to ask, knowing he should just leave it be, but ultimately unable to stop himself. "What's up with this girl, Officer? Is she in some kind of trouble?"

Is it Stephen's imagination or is Sherm Crandall suddenly eyeing him more closely?

You shouldn't have asked, Stephen scolds himself. *Now look what you've done.*

"No, she's not in any trouble that I know

of," the cop says. "I just want to talk to her, is all."

"Okay. Well, I'll let you know if I see her." Stephen gives a cheerful wave and shifts in his seat to let the cop know their conversation is over.

"You have a good day now," Sherm says with a wave and rolls up his window.

Stephen does the same, pulling the car ahead, then turning it around on the narrow road, because he knows the cop is probably watching him through his rear-view mirror as he drives away.

Stephen slowly drives away from the house, following the police car back out onto the highway. It turns left, toward town, and Stephen watches until it disappears around a bend in the road.

He waits a long time after that, parked at the edge of the lane, hoping the cop won't decide to get nosy again and turn around and come back to check on him.

Finally, after a good ten minutes, Stephen turns the car around once again and heads back toward the house.

And as he drives, he wonders if Liza Danning is unconscious in the trunk. He hasn't heard a sound from her in awhile, for which he *was* grateful. . . . But now he dearly wants her to be awake. He can't wait around for her to regain consciousness now that that cop is snooping around, asking questions about Sandy Cavelli.

No, he'll have to get Liza over with quickly, and then it will be Laura's turn.

Filled with regret that he won't have the luxury of savoring their reactions, making them suffer for a while before he kills them, Stephen sighs and pulls the black sedan around to the back of the house.

He drives into the ancient carriage house and parks beside the clunker of a Chevy that nosy kid had been driving.

By the time anyone finds it, Stephen will be long gone.

Thirteen

"I've got it!" Laura exclaims, backing out of her closet and waving the letter at Shawn, who's sitting on her bed.

"Where was it?"

"In this plastic milk crate where I toss things I need to put somewhere but I'm not sure where . . . never mind," she finishes hastily, not wanting to make herself come across as any more sloppy and disorganized than she already must seem to him.

He nods and asks, "So, where is this place?"

Laura sits back on her heels and skims the letter. "The Bramble Rose Inn—I've got to call there right away. The number's right here."

She starts for the kitchen with Shawn right behind her.

"You still feel that Jennie's in trouble?" he asks as she hurries toward the phone.

"More than ever. I know it sounds

strange, but it's just this . . . this *twin* thing, I guess." She pauses to dial the inn's number, then adds to Shawn, "The last time I felt this way about my sister, she was in real trouble. It was—hello?" She interrupts herself as someone picks up the line on the first ring.

"Yes, may I help you?" It's a polite, male voice, and Laura can barely make it out because of static.

"I'd like to speak to my sister—she's staying at the inn. Her name is Jennie Towne."

There's a pause, and for a moment, Laura thinks the connection has been broken.

Then the voice slowly repeats, "*Jennie* Towne? Are you sure that's—"

"Oops, I'm sorry, wrong sister," Laura interrupts him quickly, chastising herself for being a total idiot. "Her name is *Laura.* Laura Towne."

"Oh, Laura . . . yes, she's . . . I don't believe she's—Oh, Miss Towne," he says suddenly, to someone on the other end. "I didn't realize you were right there. Someone wishes to speak to you. It's your sister."

Laura hears Jennie's voice murmuring something, then she's on the line saying a cautious "Hello?"

"J—Laura, it's me," Laura says, realizing that whoever answered might still be within earshot.

"Oh, hi," her sister says, sounding glad to hear from her. "How's it going?"

"Fine, here, but are you okay?"

Jennie hesitates just long enough to tell Laura two things—one, that the man who answered is hovering nearby and she doesn't want to say anything in front of him; and two, that she's not all right.

Laura's heart does an anxious flip-flop and she frowns as her sister's hollow voice says, "Sure, I'm great. This place is beautiful."

"Jen," Laura lowers her voice to a whisper, "you're not okay, are you?"

The line dissolves into static then, and Laura turns to Shawn. "I don't know what— hello?"

"Can you hear me?" Jennie's voice is saying as the static dissipates.

"Now I can. What's going on out there? Are you having bad weather?"

"Yes, there's a storm."

"Jennie, I'm worried about you. Are you okay? Tell me the truth."

"I . . . I'm not sure."

Laura glances at Shawn, who's watching her. He raises his brows, and she shakes her head.

"Listen, Jen," she says hastily, keeping her voice down, "something's up with that sweepstakes I entered. I talked to Keegan, and he said it's not—"

Suddenly, the line explodes into static again. Laura jerks the phone away from her ear at the loud noise, then puts it back and calls, "Jen? Jen?"

"What happened?" Shawn asks.

"I don't know. . . . I think the line went dead."

"I think the line went dead," Jennie tells Jasper, who's looking curiously at her.

"It's the storm." He glances toward the window.

Jennie knows he's right. She saw an enormous bolt of lightning moments before she lost contact with her sister.

But if Jasper hadn't been standing here the whole time she was talking to Laura, she would almost think he somehow . . .

No. It was the storm.

Despite that knowledge, Jennie is suddenly looking at the man through different eyes. Suddenly, he seems almost sinister.

If she hadn't happened to come downstairs just as the phone was ringing, would he have let her speak to Laura?

She'd heard him starting to tell her sister that she wasn't available—at least, that's what it had sounded like.

Was he just being lazy about tracking her down?

Or was there another reason?

"Are you all right?" he asks now, watching her carefully from where he's standing behind the desk.

"I'm fine." She hands him the receiver and he replaces it in the cradle.

What was Laura about to tell her? Something about the sweepstakes . . . and Keegan? What does Keegan have to do with anything?

"Miss Towne?" Jasper says it loudly, as though he's repeating it.

She blinks. "Yes?"

"I asked if you'd like me to fix you something for lunch? I realize that with the weather so horrid, you won't be able to leave the inn."

You won't be able to leave the inn.

The words send a shudder through her.

"I'm . . . it's okay; I'm not hungry," Jennie tells him. "Thank you anyway."

"Are you sure? There's no telling how long this weather will last, and it's going to get worse before it gets better."

"I'm sure, thanks. I had just come downstairs to see if you had heard anything from Liza yet. I just knocked on her door again, and there's no reply."

"Oh?" He looks surprised . . . or does he? "That's strange. I haven't seen her all morning."

"Maybe she's having that meeting with D.M. Yates, the author she was supposed to meet," Jennie suggests, and waits for his reaction, just to see . . .

"Yates?" He shrugs. "As I told you earlier, I really have no idea where she is."

"Mmm. Well, if you do see her, will you have her come and find me?"

"Of course."

Jennie turns back toward the stairs, hoping he doesn't sense how nervous she is. She can feel his eyes on her as she walks back up toward the landing.

* * *

Sherm Crandall sits at his desk in the police station, still trying to get through his detective novel and nibbling on half a ham hero that's left over from yesterday afternoon.

It isn't very good, but he's so hungry he'll eat anything at this point. He'd stored the sandwich in the tiny dorm-sized refrigerator behind his desk, and the bread has, unfortunately, absorbed the strong food-smells from two weeks' worth of leftovers.

Sherm isn't exactly vigilant about getting rid of things, either here or at home. In fact, he wouldn't be surprised if the fridge at home still contains stuff from before Carly left.

He takes another bite of the sandwich and wrinkles his nose, then washes it down with a swig of Pepsi from the can on his desk.

The door opens just as he's swallowing, and he glances up expectantly, hoping to see Pat.

But it's Ned Hartigan who steps into the room and pulls the door closed behind him. His normally ruddy complexion is redder than ever from the biting wind and snow, and he shakes white flakes out of his whiter hair before saying, "Hi, Sherm."

"Hey there, Ned." He sets the sandwich down and stands, brushing the crumbs off his uniform pants. "What's going on?"

"Not much. Just wondering if we're going to evacuate. Pat Gerkin was by last night and told Shirley he'd let us know."

"So far, we're okay. I'm keeping a close eye on things, though."

"Well, I figured I'd better check in with you in person since the phones are down."

Sherm looks at him in surprise, echoing, "The phones are down?"

"Yep, went out a little while ago. Shirley was on with Myra Tallman when the line went dead on her."

"Great." Sherm reaches for the phone on his desk and picks it up. No dial tone. "I've been waiting for Pat to check in with me. . . . Maybe that's why I haven't heard from him. You haven't seen him today, have you?"

"Not since early last night, around supper time. Why?"

"I'm just a little worried, is all," Sherm tells Ned, rubbing his chin. "I sent him out to the old Gilbrooke place to make sure there was no one staying there, and he was supposed to come back here right afterward. Never showed, and I don't think he was home all night, either."

Ned's normally twinkly eyes look concerned. "You don't think something's happened to him?"

"Naw." Sherm tries to sound upbeat. "He's probably just over visiting one of his friends or something."

"Probably. So, you don't know if there was anyone out at the Gilbrooke place?"

"Didn't look that way. At least, no one answered my knock. I did see some footprints that were blown over by the time I got there. They were probably Pat's."

Ned nods.

"You know, I bumped into someone as I was pulling out of the lane onto Salt Marsh Road," Sherm goes on. "A tourist. The guy was lost, trying to find his way back to the Bramble Rose Inn. There was something familiar about him, but I'm pretty sure I never met him before. I never forget a name, and he said his was LaCroix."

"LaCroix?" Ned repeats thoughtfully. "Wasn't that the name of the woman that young Gilbrooke kid was supposed to marry a few years back?"

"Was it?"

"I'm pretty sure. The reason I remember is that we get the *New York Times* in on Sundays; and in the winter when business is slow, Shirley likes to read it. She always looks at the wedding announcements—you know, women like that kind of thing. Reads every darn word, and I can't understand why she cares. 'Shirley,' I tell her, 'why do you care? These people are strangers.' And she says, 'But they're so interesting.' And then one day, she runs across a familiar name—Gilbrooke. What a coincidence, huh? And I remember her saying something about the kid being engaged to someone named LaCroix."

Sherm is frowning. "Are you sure about that name?"

"I'm positive. Shirley commented on it, because she has a cousin who married a woman named LaCrosse right around the same time, and I remember her saying, 'Isn't that funny, Ned? LaCroix and La-Crosse—they're almost just the same.' "

"And you're sure it was the Gilbrooke kid who was marrying this woman?"

"Positive. That's what caught Shirley's eye. She dated poor old Andrew Gilbrooke back when he used to spend summers here on the island, you know. Told me the guy was so afraid of women that he could barely work up the nerve to kiss her. That was when I was serving overseas, you know? I'll tell you, it seems like only yesterday . . ."

Sherm nods, tuning Ned out and thinking back to his encounter with the man in the black sedan. There was something odd about him—something that's been bothering Sherm, though he hasn't been able to put his finger on it. It isn't just that the guy seems familiar. . . .

No, more than that, he seemed edgy. He didn't look Sherm in the eye when they spoke. And the way he'd given his name—it was almost as though he were making it up on the spot.

Abruptly, Sherm says, "If you'll excuse me, Ned, I have to go out and check on something."

He realizes, from the expression on Ned's face, that he must have interrupted him, and he quickly says, "Sorry. But something just occurred to me and I need to check it out."

"What's that, Sherm?"

"I just want to go over to the inn where that LaCroix fella was staying. We had a missing person's report about a young woman who's a guest there over the weekend, and he did seem a little nervous when I talked to him, now that I think of it."

"A missing person's report? Not that sweet young girl from Boston?"

"No, she's from Connecticut. You didn't meet her, did you? Name's Sandy Cavelli?"

"Tall, thin, blond hair?"

"No. The description her brother gave me says she's on the short side and overweight, with brown hair."

"Didn't see anyone who looks like that."

"Who's the tall, thin blonde? You say she's from Boston?"

"No, the one from Boston has dark hair, too, and the prettiest eyes you ever saw. Light purple, like Liz Taylor's."

Trying to mask his impatience, Sherm asks again, "So who's the blonde?"

"I don't know, but she's staying at the Bramble Rose, too. She was rude to Shirley when she came in for coffee, and she gave me hell because I don't carry black silk stockings. Wanted *real* stockings, the kind you wear with a garter belt. I said, 'What do you think this is, Filene's?' And she was real snippy with me. If you ask me, she—"

Sherm cuts him off because if you let Ned get started, he'll talk all day. "I really have to get on over to that inn now, Ned. But you tell Shirley I said hello, will you?"

"I sure will. Say, you haven't heard anything from Carly, have you?"

"Nope," he says shortly, grabbing his key ring from the desk and shoving it into his pocket.

"Too bad."

"Yep."

The trouble with living on an island as small as this one is that everyone knows everyone else's business. Which really helps when Sherm is conducting an investigation, but irks him when it comes to his own private life.

"Listen, Ned," he says, grabbing his storm coat and walking with the other man toward the door, "do me a favor. If you see Pat around anywhere, let me know."

"Will do."

"You opening the store today?"

"In this weather?" Ned shakes his head. "I'm going home and build a fire in the old woodstove. Put my feet up, listen to some Benny Goodman. If you want to swing by later, Shirley's making her chowder for Sunday dinner. I know it's probably been awhile since you had some good home-cooking."

"Yeah, it has," Sherm says, glancing down at the discarded sandwich and trying not to let the wistful note creep into his voice.

Carly used to make chowder on Sundays, too, creamy and rich, with succulent bits of shellfish and potato. Chowder or a big pot of beef stew or spaghetti sauce . . .

Together, he and Ned step out into the blustery world of swirling snow.

"See you, Sherm," Ned calls, lifting a hand. "You swing by later if you're hungry."

"Maybe I will," Sherm calls back, watching Ned with envy as he goes trudging off toward the cozy old captain's house he shares with Shirley.

Feeling lonelier than ever, he gets into his car to drive over to the Bramble Rose Inn.

* * *

Someone has glued Liza's eyelids shut. At least, that's what it feels like. She can't seem to lift them.

Dazed, she wonders where she is, why her body feels battered and raw . . .

Then, as consciousness overtakes her again, she remembers, with a start, what happened.

She was in the back seat of the car . . .

And the driver was watching her in the mirror with that sinister smile . . .

And she'd thrown herself out onto the road.

That was the last thing she knew before now.

Please, God, let me be in the hospital, she prays fervently and, concentrating with all her might, forces her eyes to open.

For a moment, everything is blurry . . . and white.

Am I in heaven?

No, because there can't be pain in heaven, and I'm in agony.

She blinks and tries to focus again, but still, all she can see is filmy white.

Biting down on her inner lip to keep from crying out, she lifts her head slightly . . . and realizes that something is draped over her face. Some kind of white netting . . .

And she seems to be wearing white, too—a hospital gown?

No . . .

Numb with horror, Liza stares down at herself through the mask of illusion veiling that covers her eyes.

It's not a hospital gown; it's a wedding gown.

Someone has dressed her in a wedding gown!

Liza opens her mouth to scream, then clamps it shut again as a face appears, hovering a few feet above her.

"Hello, sleeping beauty," a masculine voice says, and chuckles. "I'm so glad you're back among the living . . . although, it's a pity it won't be a permanent stay."

It's the chauffeur from the car, Liza realizes, only he's changed his clothes, too. His face is rimmed by a white collar and a black bow tie. . . . Good Lord, is the man really wearing a tuxedo?

Nothing makes sense. It's like some grotesque dream—

Liza groans as she feels him lifting her shoulders, then forcing her to sit up. She squeezes her eyes closed for a moment to fight the anguish that wracks her body, then opens them to see that she's in a vast, empty room.

Empty, that is, of people, except for the nut case in the tux.

But there appear to be rows and rows of chairs . . .

And flowers everywhere, red roses . . .

And—oh, God—there's a white-satin runner stretching ahead in front of Liza.

"Get up," barks the chauffeur's voice from somewhere above. "We're already late getting started."

"Started with what?" she murmurs, feeling her body sway. It's so tempting to let herself sink back down to the floor again, to give in to the gauzy darkness that keeps trying to edge its way back to her.

"Started with what? The wedding, of course! What did you think?" His voice floats above her somewhere.

"Do you like the dress?" he goes on. "I had it made especially for you—remembered that you're a perfect size five. I should remember. . . . I bought you so many lovely clothes. Do you remember?"

She's vaguely aware of being lifted further. "Stand, damn it. Stand up. I can't just hang around here and hold you, you know."

It's as if some other part of Liza takes over, and her aching legs automatically lock into place so that she finds herself standing on her own.

Still, she can't grasp what's going on.

Suddenly, she hears the sound of music playing. It fills her ears, some old love song that seems faintly familiar . . .

What the hell is going on, here?

She turns her head and sees him beside her, his face only inches from hers.

"What are you doing? And—who *are* you?" she whispers, searching her memory for his face and coming up with a blank.

He looks pleased. "You don't recognize me, do you?"

"No, I . . ." Her voice trails off as she feels herself swaying, about to go down. But somehow, she manages to fight the impulse, wins another few moments—she hopes—of consciousness.

"It's me," he announces gleefully, his face twisted into a distorted grin. "Stephen!"

"Stephen?" she repeats fuzzily, trying to remember.

"Stephen Gilbrooke," he elaborates.

"Stephen Gilbrooke . . ."

He waits.

She searches her memory desperately.

Stephen Gilbrooke?

There have been so many men. No way she can remember all of them, the ones she used and then casually discarded like used Kleenex . . .

Oh, why hadn't she been more careful? Why hadn't she realized that it would catch up to her someday?

"Stephen Gilbrooke," he says again, this time more harshly. "You do remember me, Liza . . ."

She shakes her head faintly, still trying to recall the name, the face . . .

Suddenly, he's grabbing her shoulders roughly, shaking her so that her body screams in pain.

"Stephen Gilbrooke," he keeps repeating.

"I remember you," she blurts finally, trying desperately to remain alert, though she's fading fast.

"You do?"

"Of course . . ."

It's a lie. She has no idea who he is. She's never been good with names, and the face is totally unfamiliar. . . .

So many men, she thinks vaguely again. *Too many men. . . . Which one is he?*

"Who am I, then?"

A shred of panic rises in her weary, tormented body, a fearful response to something ominous in his sharp command.

"You're . . . Stephen."

"Where did we meet?"

"New York," she guesses weakly, watching him through heavy-lidded eyes.

For a split-second, he seems appeased. Then his gaze narrows and he says, "Where?"

"Manhattan . . ."

"But *where?* Tell me, Liza. Right now. If you really know who I am, tell me where we met!"

"I—I don't know!" Her voice is a whimper.

He slaps her, hard, across the face, and she starts to crumple; but he's grabbing her, forcing her to keep standing.

"You don't know me! After everything I gave you, everything we did together, you don't know me?"

She can only shake her head mutely, too frightened to lie to him again.

The stranger's face is contorted by rage

now, his grip on her shoulders a deadly vise from which she can't escape.

"You never cared for me at all, did you? You never loved me, after all I did for you. I gave you everything your heart desired, but you never loved me, Lorraine."

Lorraine? Who's Lorraine?

Oh, Christ, who is this lunatic? What is he going to do?

"I'm not Lorraine," she protests weakly as he releases his right hand from her shoulder.

For a moment, she believes he's going to let her go.

But then, paralyzed with terror, Liza watches as he reaches inside his coat, his movements slow and almost mechanical. His blue eyes are still focused on her veiled face, but they suddenly seem void of recognition.

"You don't want to marry me, do you?" he says in a faraway voice, and it isn't really a question.

"Yes," Liza says anyway, hoping desperately to divert him. "Yes, I want to marry you . . . Stephen."

"Why?" He's removing something from his jacket.

She sees that it's a butcher knife.

He looks at it intently, strokes the handle almost lovingly.

Trembling all over, she battles to keep the sob out of her voice as she answers, "Because I love you, Stephen. I've always loved you. I always will. Marry me, Stephen."

For a moment, he looks soothed by her words.

But when he raises his gaze to her again, he frowns and looks startled.

"No!" he barks abruptly, brandishing the knife. "You're not Lorraine, and you don't want to marry me. You don't even remember me, Liza."

"Yes I do," she cries plaintively. "I remember you, Stephen. And I love you. Please don't—"

Even though she sees the knife slashing through the air toward her, she's stunned to hear her own voice suddenly dissolve into a bloody gurgle as the unmercifully sharp blade slices into her throat.

"Don't lie to me," he shouts as he brings the knife up, then jabs it into her again, this time catching her across her wrist as she brings her hand up to shield her face. Blood spurts like a fountain as her vein is severed; and she falls, bewildered, to the floor.

As the frenzied stranger continues to stab her, Liza's mind screams *Why? Why? Why?* in a chilling refrain until black silence swoops over her like a shroud.

Fourteen

Jasper paces the tiny first-floor bedroom, wishing Stephen would hurry up and get back here so that he can tell him what happened.

He can't risk calling the emergency phone number again.

Not after what happened last time.

Not when Stephen is right in the middle of . . .

Well, taking care of Liza Danning.

And the blond bitch deserves everything she gets, Jasper tells himself, remembering how she had spoken to him, how she had looked at him as though he were a mere speck of dirt.

It was all he could do, the entire time Liza Danning was staying here, to treat her as a guest . . .

To keep from informing her that *he,* Arnold—no, Jasper Hammel—is the person

Stephen Gilbrooke has chosen to spend the rest of his life with. *Not* Liza . . .

Or Sandy.

Or Laura.

Or Lorraine.

Frowning, Jasper runs his hands over his neatly trimmed hair and tells himself that everything will work out fine.

Despite the fact that the plan isn't going as smoothly as he and Stephen had expected.

He thinks again about the phone call for Laura Towne. He isn't sure what, exactly, her sister had started to tell her, but it doesn't matter, not really.

A bolt of lightning had miraculously intercepted the call.

And if that isn't a sign that everything will be all right, Jasper tells himself reassuringly, *I don't know what is.*

All he has to do now is keep an eye on Laura to make sure she doesn't get any ideas about leaving again . . .

And wait.

Wait for Stephen to come back to the inn.

Then wait for him to leave again, with Laura.

Then wait for him to come back a final time, for Jasper . . .

And then we'll sail away together, Jasper tells himself contentedly. *Just as Stephen promised—just the two of us, forever and ever.*

But somehow, his image of bliss is marred by an elusive, but nonetheless disconcerting sensation that keeps flitting through his mind . . .

The nebulous notion that maybe everything isn't as it should be.

That maybe things are about to go horribly irrevocably, wrong.

And when the doorbell rings suddenly and shrilly a moment later, the thought lands with a dull thud.

His fury spent once again, Stephen stoops down and slowly pulls the knife out of the heap of red-stained, white-covered flesh at his feet.

Liza Danning will never look at me again with that superior smile and smug green gaze of hers.

The knowledge should leave him with some degree of satisfaction, but Stephen feels oddly unsettled.

She didn't remember you, he thinks incredulously and gives the bloodied corpse a frustrated kick with the toe of his black wing-tip shoe.

How could she have forgotten?

Had he meant that little to her?

Of course he had. He had known all along that she'd never cared about him, only about his money and the things that it could buy for her.

But never had he imagined that she would forget he had ever existed. That to her, he wasn't even worthy of a tiny, distant corner of her memory. He had been invisible to her even when they were together; and after their affair had ended, she had simply wiped her mind clean of any remnants of Stephen Gilbrooke.

"Bitch," he mutters, and kicks her again, noticing the pool of blood that's seeping at his feet.

He ought to get Jasper over here and make him clean up the mess, he thinks, distastefully eyeing the gore he's created. After all, he might as well put the simpering pain in the ass to some good use, instead of letting him sit back at the inn, twiddling his thumbs.

But no, that would be impossible. There

isn't time. Not when there's a chance that that dolt of a police officer might get suspicious and come back snooping around here.

Stephen would rather not have to raise the body count even higher. It would be so . . . messy.

And besides, when he's made a plan, he likes to stick to it.

It's bad enough that he can't wait until tomorrow to take care of Laura Towne, as he had originally intended.

Oh, well.

Reaching into his pocket again, he thoughtfully takes out the blank rectangular place card and black-handled pen he'd brought along with him. He crouches beside Liza's lifeless body and dips the tip carefully into the thick pool of blood, then begins to letter her name in swirling calligraphy.

He's almost free . . . almost to the point where he can banish, forever, the demons that have been tormenting him for so long.

Just a few more things to take care of, and he'll be home free . . .

Sailing off into the proverbial sunset toward a glorious future . . . alone.

* * *

Sherm rings the doorbell again, thinking that it seems strange that the door of an inn would be locked, when suddenly, a face appears in the glass, startling him.

Even through the ice-encrusted window, he recognizes the man, having seen him around the island lately. Must be Jasper Hammel, he thinks as the door swings open.

Sherm doffs his hat and pastes an affable smile on his face. "Good afternoon," he says pleasantly above the roar of the wind. "You the fellow who runs the place?"

"I'm Jasper Hammel, yes," the man says, offering his hand, but making no move to gesture him inside.

"Sherm Crandall—I'm chief of police here on the island. We spoke earlier." Sherm grasps the man's fingers in a firm handshake and notes that they're clammy.

Well, it's a raw, chilly day. That could be all it is.

On the other hand . . .

"Just thought I'd drop by," Sherm goes on, stepping past the innkeeper into the foyer of the inn, "to check things out."

He turns and glimpses a startled expression in Hammel's eyes; but it vanishes quickly, and the man seems composed as he smiles and says, "Of course. Please come in."

"I'm already in," Sherm notes.

"Yes, you are, aren't you?" Hammel closes the door, shutting out the blasting storm, and turns to Sherm expectantly.

"Nice," he comments, looking around the foyer, his sharp eyes taking in the fussy antique furniture and globed lamps. On the check-in desk is a basket of magazines, a telephone, a tall vase filled with dried flowers, and a bowl of pink shredded things that look and smell like potpourri. Carly always loved that stuff.

"Is there anything in particular that I can help you with?" Hammel asks in a clipped tone, watching Sherm cautiously sniff the cinnamony contents of the bowl. "As I said earlier, I'm afraid I've told you everything I know about that woman . . . Sandy, isn't it?"

"Yep, it is." Sherm wonders if it's his imagination or if Hammel seems edgy as he moves across the small room and takes up a post behind the desk.

"I wish I could tell you something more . . ."

"That's all right. I'm actually not here on business," Sherm lies. "Thought I'd check the place out, see what it's like. I've got some relatives coming to the island soon, and I need to find someplace for them to stay."

"Oh, we'd love to have them."

Is that relief spreading over the man's face above his neatly trimmed mustache, or merely a cordial response to a business deal?

"Are you pretty booked for the upcoming months?" Sherm asks.

"Oh, no, we have plenty of availability."

"How about this weekend?"

"*This* weekend? I thought they weren't coming until—"

"No, I mean how booked are you this weekend?"

"Why do you ask?" This time, there's no mistaking the look in Hammel's eyes. He's definitely on guard.

"Just curious," Sherm says casually, yet focusing intently on the man's face. "How many guests do you have staying here?"

"This weekend? Well, I don't know off the top of my head . . ."

Sherm raises an eyebrow.

The place isn't *that* enormous. He doesn't say it, but the pointed look on his face gets the message across to Hammel, who smiles nervously back.

"I guess . . . Let's see, there's Sandy Cavelli, but she left, as you know. And . . . oh, yes, there's Miss Laura Towne . . ."

The Boston brunette with the Liz Taylor eyes, Sherm wonders, or the blond bitch?

"And," Jasper finishes, "that's about it."

"That's it?" Sherm keeps his expression carefully neutral, though his mind is racing.

That can't be it.

Even if Ned Hartigan was mistaken about the blonde staying here, what about that LaCroix fellow Sherm had spoken to out at the old Gilbrooke place?

Jasper Hammel is thrumming his fingertips on the desk-top.

Somebody's lying, Sherm thinks, *but who?*

Judging by the innkeeper's actions, he's hiding something. *But why?*

Sandy Cavelli's disappearance is looking more suspicious by the second.

"Officer . . ." Hammel says after another moment of silence.

"Oh, sorry—I wonder if I could look at a few of the rooms? Just to see if it's what I have in mind for my sister. She's pretty fussy. You know women," he throws in, adopting a good-old-boy attitude.

Hammel does his best to rise to it, nodding and agreeing, "Certainly. I know women."

I'll just bet you do.

"So how about it?"

"The rooms?"

Sherm nods, thinking that the guy can't possibly worm out of this one. He just finished saying that there are only two guests at the inn this weekend, and one of them has already checked out.

"I . . . of course. I'd be happy to show you," the man says abruptly, as though he's just reached a decision. "Just let me find the keys . . ."

"No problem."

Just as Hammel starts digging through a drawer, there's a distinct creaking noise above. Footsteps.

Sherm turns to look toward the stairs,

wondering if the woman from Boston is about to make an appearance.

He'd like to ask her—

The thought is cut short by a swift and sudden blow to the back of his head.

Stunned, Sherm sinks to his knees and looks up to see a blurry image of Jasper Hammel holding the heavy crystal vase of dried flowers.

As the police chief opens his mouth weakly in futile protest, Hammel brings it down again, obliterating Sherm's senses with the brutal impact.

Jennie pauses with her hand on the doorknob, frowning.

She just heard a thud from the foyer downstairs, as though something heavy has toppled onto the floor.

She stays absolutely still, listening for the voices to resume their conversation, but there's only silence.

Oh, God . . . something happened to the police officer. What did Hammel do to him?

She had been napping on her bed when she'd awakened to hear muffled voices floating up from below. She couldn't hear what they were saying. Though one voice was a deep, unfamiliar rumble, she easily recognized that the other belonged to Jasper Hammel.

After trying to make out the conversation, she had gotten up and looked out the window that faced the front of the inn. A police car was parked there.

Jennie had been both elated and frightened.

If the cops were here, did it mean Jasper really was up to something? And if so, had something terrible happened to Sandy and Liza?

She was about to go downstairs and see what was going on when the thud had stopped her cold.

Now, she wonders, with a sinking feeling, what's going on down there. She hears a faint groan—Jasper again—and then the sound of something being dragged across the floor toward the back of the house.

He's killed the cop, and now he's taking the body away.

What should I do?

Run for it?

Jennie considers that option, and discards it.

The inn is virtually in the middle of nowhere, and there's a storm raging outside. Even if Hammel didn't hear her leaving, where would she go?

She could take the chance that she'd find someone in one of the few houses between here and the boardwalk, but what would she tell them?

She has no proof of anything. She's not even sure what's going on here. If she goes running to a total stranger and starts raving about something strange happening at the inn and there turns out to be nothing wrong, it'll mean she really is crazy.

She'll have to start seeing Dr. Bonner again, with his unforgiving dark gaze, and he'll make her talk about Harry and relive the terror of what happened to him again and again and again . . .

And she can't do that.

You're not crazy, she tells herself fiercely. *You didn't hear anything downstairs. And nothing strange is happening here.*

But then where are Sandy and Liza?

And what was Laura trying to tell you when she called?

And what about Harry, in the dream?

Stop it! Everything is fine. It's just your

imagination again, and you have to stop letting it take over. You have to prove you're not crazy!

You're not crazy!

Shaken, Jennie slowly removes her hand from the doorknob and returns to her bed.

She curls up into a ball on her side, hugging her knees against her chest. She closes her eyes tightly and rocks back and forth, trying desperately to shut out the memories that are trying to force their way into her consciousness.

"There it is!" Danny shouts, pointing off to the port side of the boat.

"What?" Keegan shouts back over the roaring wind and water, his hands wrestling with the wheel.

"I just saw a speck of land over there. . . . It has to be the island!" Clenching his teeth to keep them from chattering, Danny squints against the driving mist of seawater and snow, trying to find it again.

But the boat is rocking violently on the enormous waves; and every time he thinks he might just be able to see it, they tilt crazily away in the opposite direction.

He glances back to make sure Cheryl's okay. She's still sitting on the bench behind him, clinging to the rail and looking frightfully pale with fear and nausea. She's already thrown up twice, miserably choking and gagging as Danny held her head and tried to keep her steady despite the wildly pitching boat.

"We're almost there, babe," he calls to her now, and she looks up and offers a weak, trembling smile.

At least, I hope we're almost there, Danny thinks, grabbing the rail and pulling himself cautiously forward along the deck until he reaches Keegan's side.

"What do you think?" the man asks, turning to Danny. He, like Danny and Cheryl, is drenched and shivering violently.

"I saw it. . . . I'm almost positive. Out there." He points to the left.

"That's where it should be," Keegan hollers back. "And I'm trying to steer toward it, but it's impossible to fight this wind. We might be way off course."

Danny's stomach turns over. "You mean we could be lost on the open sea?"

"What?" Keegan yells, shaking his head to indicate that he can't hear.

Danny doesn't repeat it. He doesn't want to risk letting Cheryl hear that. She'll be terrified.

Grimly, he wipes at his eyes, which are stinging from the salt spray and grainy snow, and peels them on the distant horizon again.

Nothing.

Oh, Jesus . . . we're going to die trying to reach you, Sandy.

The thought of his sister in trouble eats away at him, and he tries to put it out of his mind. Tries not to think of how upset and scared she had sounded when she called him.

Tries not to wonder where she is now . . .

Whether she's all right.

The deck lurches suddenly as they ride over an enormous breaker, and Danny grips the rail with all his might.

He turns again to make sure Cheryl is all right, and for a moment, panic seizes him when he can't find her.

But no, there she is, crumpled on the floor of the boat as a gush of water pours over the tilting rail directly onto her face.

Danny bellows, "Babe, are you all right?"

She doesn't reply.

"Babe?"

"Is she all right?" Keegan shouts.

"I don't know . . ." Petrified, Danny makes his way along the rail and crouches at Cheryl's side.

She opens her eyes, looking dazed, as soon as he cups her face in his icy hands.

"Cheryl?"

"That wave knocked me off the bench. . . . I guess I hit my head and passed out for a second . . ." She draws her brows together in a confused furrow.

Danny pulls her into his arms, cradling her. "This is insane. . . . We've got to go back. . . . I can't put you through this . . ."

He turns toward Keegan and raises his voice. "Hey, McCullough! McCullough, we've got to go back!"

"There it is!" Keegan hollers simultaneously, pointing off to the horizon on the port side. "I see the island! It's right there! We made it!"

Jasper can't seem to stop shaking.

What have you done? he asks himself over and over as he stares at the unconscious Sherm Crandall, whom he's managed to drag into the small storage room off the kitchen.

You need to kill him, Jasper thinks, *before he comes to.*

He fingers the meat cleaver he'd taken from a drawer in the kitchen and imagines plunging it into the man's soft belly.

What would it feel like? Would there be sinewy resistance or would the tip of the blade sink into flesh like a sharpened stick into a marshmallow? Would blood spurt out or would it ooze slowly from the wound?

Jasper doesn't want to know.

It was difficult enough to hit the police officer over the head with the lead-crystal vase. He'd done it impulsively when the man turned his back, realizing he'd heard Laura Towne's footsteps. In another few moments, Jasper had thought desperately, Crandall would be questioning her. She would tell him about Liza, and he'd find out that Jasper had lied.

And he'd done such a clumsy job of it, too, he thinks, wincing at the memory of his lame cover-up.

Stephen would be furious if he knew.

But you couldn't help it! The damn cop caught you off guard! He made you flus-

tered, made you so nervous you couldn't think straight!

Jasper shakes his head, thinking none of that would make a difference to Stephen. He never gets nervous under pressure. Even when he'd snapped and bludgeoned his own mother to death, he hadn't seemed all that flustered.

Jasper still recalls the matter-of-fact way in which Stephen had revealed what he'd done—"I killed Mother."

As if he were informing Jasper of something as mundane as "I had tuna for lunch."

Back then, and again with Lorraine, Jasper had come through for Stephen, helping him to hide the evidence of his gory crime.

He's counting on you again, Jasper reminds himself. *And you've let him down.*

No, you haven't. Not yet. Everything is still under control. No one knows what happened.

He'd been half-expecting Laura Towne to come bounding down the stairs after Crandall hit the floor, but there had been only silence from above.

Maybe that isn't such a good sign, Jasper thinks reluctantly.

He can't risk making her suspicious. She's the only thing standing between Jasper and his future with Stephen. If she somehow figures out that she's in danger, if she somehow escapes, he's in big trouble.

No, he has to make sure she's here and unaware when Stephen comes back for her.

And he has to get rid of Crandall, too.

Again, he fingers the handle of the cleaver in his hand.

It would be so easy . . .

All he has to do is lower the blade until it sinks into Crandall's heart.

Jasper swallows hard and closes his eyes for a moment.

I'm not capable of murder.

That fact makes itself known as suddenly and as plainly as another, long-ago revelation had—when he had realized, with sudden clarity, that he was a homosexual.

He acknowledges this new self-discovery with the same, frank acceptance as he had the old. He can't change it, can't force himself to be something other than what he is.

No, he's not going to kill Sherm Crandall.

If Stephen wants to do that when he returns, he can.

For now, Jasper will simply lock the door

to the storage room and then do something about the police car parked in front of the inn. Thanks to the storm, there's not much chance that anyone would be out and about and have noticed the car there, but he can't let it stay indefinitely.

Gingerly, he bends and rolls Sherm Crandall over, retrieving a key ring from his coat pocket.

"First, I'll move the car," he says softly to the unconscious man, "and then, I'll take care of Miss Towne."

"Well?" Shawn asks expectantly as Laura comes back into the living room, where he's sprawled on the couch.

"No luck," she says, shaking her head. "The phones are still out of service there. I keep getting a recording."

"Did you try the police station again?"

"On Tide Island? Yes. Same recording." She plops heavily into a chair and looks at the gray, blustery world outside the window.

"She's probably fine, Laura."

"Probably," she agrees hollowly.

"After all, you were just going on a hunch when you decided something was wrong."

"What about the bogus sweepstakes?" she points out. "And Keegan? He was obviously worried when he kept calling me and leaving messages."

"Did you try him again?"

"No answer. I don't know where he could be. I tried the precinct, too, and they said he called in sick this morning. I know he's not sick because I saw him yesterday. And Keegan's not the type who would play hooky without a good reason."

"Well, there's nothing you can do but wait, Laura."

"I know." She looks at him bleakly. "And maybe everything really is fine. But I keep thinking about . . ."

"What?" Shawn prods her.

"It's Brian. My ex. He's a nut case, Shawn. *I* was the one who was supposed to be out there this weekend, not Jennie. What if Brian—" She cuts herself off abruptly, shaking her head.

"Did you try calling him?"

"I have no idea where he's even living now. And his parents moved to Florida months ago, and I have no idea where."

"How about finding him through one of his friends?"

"Those creeps?" She makes a face. "They'd never tell me where he is. They all think I'm a cold bitch. That's what he told them. And you know what? I *can* be a cold bitch, when someone treats me the way Brian did."

She stares off into space, remembering her ex-husband's cruel mind games and violent temper. She can still feel the sting of his hand smacking her face, the agonizing pain of his cigarette butt searing into her skin.

"Do you honestly think Brian is up to something?" Shawn asks her, and she shrugs.

"I don't know. There *was* something familiar about the man who sold me the ticket. . . . I told you that. But I can't seem to place him. Every time I feel like I'm about to remember who he is, it flits right out of my mind. It's driving me crazy, Shawn."

"Well, do you think he has something to do with Brian?"

"No." She frowns. "That's the strange part. I don't think he does. But for the life of me, I can't figure out who else it can be."

"Was there anyone else you dated . . . or

knew . . . who might have something against you?"

Laura hesitates, not wanting to get into her past with Shawn. He's the first normal guy who's come along—she doesn't want to scare him away by telling him anything that might make her seem promiscuous . . . or hard up.

Then again, it's helping to think aloud and she has to do whatever she can to jog her memory. For Jennie's sake.

"Let me see," she says slowly, looking off into space. "I went out with this real asshole for a while after I dropped out of college. But he's definitely not the one who sold me the ticket."

"How do you know?"

"The guy I dated was Hispanic. The one who sold me the ticket was definitely white, and he had these bright blue eyes—you know, the kind you wouldn't forget. Like yours."

"Mine are contacts."

"I know, but . . ."

"Maybe his are, too."

"Maybe, but even so, I'd recognize the face. And it wasn't Orlando."

"Okay, so who else did you know who was a real jerk?"

"There *was* someone," she goes on thoughtfully, remembering, "about a year ago. A real S.O.B., it turned out, but he seemed totally normal—had a lot of money. I met him when I was working at the Four Seasons last spring to make extra cash to pay off my Visa bill . . ." She catches herself before she spills the rest of it—that the Visa account had been delinquent and a collection agency had come after her. No reason to tell him *that.*

"And . . ." he prompts.

She shrugs. "He was in Boston on business for the month, staying at the hotel. We went out a few times. He wined and dined me. Then he turned into a creep."

"What happened?"

She hesitates, not wanting to tell him that, either. How the guy had been pissed off because she wouldn't sleep with him one night. She just wasn't in the mood.

But things had gotten ugly. Who would have guessed that such a supposedly mild-mannered businessman would have a nasty temper? Well, with everything you heard about date-rape these days, maybe she should have been more careful.

But she had been truly shocked when he had turned into a ranting lunatic, ripping off her clothes and forcing her to have sex with him.

And not just the regular way.

No, he'd gotten out the handcuffs, the leather S&M gear, the vibrator—all the little toys she'd introduced him to, which he kept stashed in the drawer next to his bed in his hotel suite.

Suddenly, that awful night, the props that Laura had used as innocent, pleasure-enhancing gadgets were transformed into terrifying instruments of torture. She still remembers how helpless she had felt when he'd cuffed her to the bed and had his way with her body, poking and prodding her endlessly, laughing when she sobbed and begged him to stop.

If the guest in the next room hadn't called the management to complain about the noise, who knew what would have happened?

"Laura . . ." Shawn asks, still waiting.

What would he say if he knew what she

had done? Would he feel that she had gotten what she'd deserved?

Of course he'd think that. Laura thought it herself. How many times, since that dreadful night, had she chastised herself for being habitually promiscuous? She was lucky she hadn't run into trouble before the Four Seasons guy and that she'd gotten away from him relatively unharmed.

The experience had made her vow never to sleep with a virtual stranger again, never to use toys or play kinky sex games again.

She'd kept that promise, too. Oh, she and Shawn *were* sleeping together and she still had a healthy appetite for lovemaking. But when she'd met him, she'd played hard to get for the first time in her life. She hadn't slept with him until their fourth date. And he'd been pleasantly surprised, he told her, to discover that she wasn't a prude after all. She'd gotten a private kick out of *that*— imagine, someone thinking *she* might be a prude!

"What about this guy?" Shawn asks again.

Laura snaps out of her reverie. "Oh, right. Well, he was a major creep. But he definitely wasn't the guy who sold me the ticket that day in the parking lot."

"Are you sure?"

"Positive. And anyway, he comes from big bucks, like I said. His family's pretty famous."

"For what?"

She shrugs. "Just being rich, I guess. The other clerk at the hotel recognized his name right away the first time he checked in."

"Really? What is it?"

Laura frowns, trying to remember.

Then she nods and says, "Oh, yeah, that's right. It was Gilbrooke. Stephen Gilbrooke."

Jennie is still huddled on her bed in a fetal position when the noise of the storm ebbs momentarily and she hears footsteps approaching her door.

Her entire body grows tense as she listens and waits.

It has to be Jasper Hammel.

A short time ago, she had heard the front door slam, and then a car engine starting up.

By the time she had reached the window to see what was going on, the police car that had been parked out front was no longer there.

Either the cop had left . . .

Or Hammel had moved the car.

Jennie wanted desperately to believe the latter was just another example of her imagination carrying her away. But minutes after the car had vanished, she had heard the front door open and close again.

Which meant Hammel could have parked the car someplace nearby, but out of the way, and now he was back.

In the half hour or so that had passed since then, all had been still downstairs.

Not that Jennie could have heard much of anything, anyway. The storm had grown steadily more powerful, and now the wind was fairly screeching around the house and the wild sea was leaping at the rocky coast like a rabid dog straining on its leash.

Now she waits, wondering if she really did just hear footsteps or if it were—

No, there they are again.

Frightened, Jennie turns to look expectantly at the door, as though any moment,

Jasper Hammel is going to splinter it and burst into her room, a raving madman.

The thought should seem ludicrous, but it isn't. Not entirely.

There's a knock at the door, a brief, staccato rapping that causes Jennie to shrink back into the pillows in wide-eyed fear.

"Miss Towne?"

It's Jasper Hammel, all right. But he sounds like his usual self—formal and pleasant.

Still, Jennie can't seem to find her voice.

"Miss Towne?" he calls again with another knock. "Are you in there?"

"Yes," she finally manages, realizing that he would have the key so there's no point in trying to hide.

"Oh, good. There's a call for you."

For a moment, she's too startled to reply.

"Do you want to take it?" Hammel asks through the door.

"I . . . I thought the phones were knocked out," she says thinly.

"They were, but they've made repairs."

She doesn't say anything, wondering whether to believe him.

"In fact," Hammel goes on, "when one of

the island police officers stopped by awhile ago to see that we were all right, he promised me that the local phone company was working on the lines. And a short time later . . . *voilà!* The phone rang."

She ponders that, still hugging her knees tightly to her chest. She didn't hear the phone ringing. But then, the noise of the storm would probably have drowned it out anyway.

"Who is it?" she asks Hammel after another moment's hesitation. "On the phone for me, I mean."

"It's your sister. She says it's important or I wouldn't have disturbed you."

It's Laura again.

Jennie debates only another split-second before getting off the bed and going over to the door.

"I'll take it," she says, opening it.

Too late, she realizes that she's made a big mistake.

Jasper Hammel instantly reaches out, grabs her, and clamps a damp handkerchief that reeks of something acrid over her mouth and nose.

"Breathe deeply now, Laura," he says in his proper, clipped way. "That's the girl.

You're going to take a nice nap, and when you wake up—"

The rest of his words are lost on her as she collapses in his arms.

Fifteen

The big black sedan skids on the icy gravel drive as Stephen pulls around to the back of the inn. He steers into the skid, regains control, and parks beside the gardening shed, thinking that if it keeps snowing like this, he won't be able to get back out to the house. And what about leaving the island on the boat? It's going to be terribly treacherous in this weather.

He sits with his hand poised on the door handle, wondering whether he should go back to the original plan and wait until tomorrow to deal with Laura Towne.

If he does, there's a greater risk of being caught—especially if that cop he met earlier actually is suspicious.

But if he goes ahead and takes care of everything today and leaves by nightfall, what about the nor'easter? He's an accomplished yachtsman, thanks to all those years at prep school; but skill, he knows, can become moot when Mother Nature is venting her fury.

No, he probably shouldn't chance it. The thought of drowning in the Atlantic isn't exactly a pleasant one. And besides, if the cop comes snooping around again, he can be easily taken care of . . . just like the red-haired kid.

Stephen makes up his mind to wait. He'll stay here, in his attic room, for the night, he decides, and then he'll be able to sneak down and sneak a peek at Laura once she's safely asleep later.

Just the way he did with Sandy. And Liza.

It's like a tantalizing little appetizer before the main course, he thinks, his lips curving into a smile as he thinks of those stolen moments in the wee hours of the morning, when he'd fondled the unsuspecting women as they slept.

And Laura . . .

Well, when he had dated her last year, she had been a regular tigress. Stephen writhes slightly on the leather car seat just thinking about the things she had done to him in that suite at the Four Seasons.

He's in for a real treat once again, he thinks, feeling slightly breathless.

In fact, too bad he can't keep her around—let her come with him when he leaves the island.

But then he remembers how she had turned on him, just as the others had.

He thinks back to that night in the hotel suite, when she had tried to resist his advances. At first, he'd thought she secretly wanted him—that her cold fish routine was just an act, to tease him, get him all worked up. He'd gone along with it, forcing her—cuffing her to the bed, using those devices of hers, working himself into a frenzy.

Then she'd started crying and calling for help, and the hotel management had come knocking on the door, wanting to know if everything was all right. What a mess. He'd played the role of a sheepish guest, apologizing to the night manager if he and his "girlfriend" had gotten a little out of hand.

When he'd closed the door and gone back over to the bed, Laura had looked at him darkly through her mascara-smudged lilac-colored eyes and ordered him to unlock the handcuffs. "If you don't," she'd threatened, "I'll scream so loudly that the management will be back here in two seconds flat."

For a wild moment, he'd considered killing her right then and there, as he had Lorraine. But then he realized that there had already been a complaint, that the manager knew who he was, and that he would never get away with it.

So he'd let her go.

The next afternoon, he'd come back from his meeting to find her working at the desk, dressed in her deceptively prim, high-collared, navy-plaid dress with her hair coiled at the back of her neck in a schoolmarm's bun.

He'd gone over to her and whispered suggestively that if she came upstairs to his suite when her shift ended, he'd pretend to be a naughty schoolboy and let her spank him.

"You pig," she'd said in a low voice that barely contained her palpable wrath. "If you don't get out of here right this second and leave me alone, I'll go to the police and tell them what you did to me last night."

Shocked, he'd protested, "What did I do?"

"You raped me."

"I did not! You wanted it. You loved it. You know you did."

"You actually think I *wanted* to sleep with an ugly son of a bitch like you? What are you, nuts? I never wanted you, not from the start. The only way I could get off with you was to use those toys . . . and close my eyes and pretend you were someone else. Someone who looked *human*."

Stung, Stephen had simply closed his mouth and walked away. By the next day, when he had decided he had to do to her what he had done to Lorraine, it was too late. The girl behind the desk told him that Laura had quit abruptly after her shift ended the day before. And no, she wasn't at liberty to give out Laura's home address or number.

At first, he had planned to track her down immediately and make her pay for what she had said.

Then he had thought again of Lorraine . . .

Of how incredibly satisfying it had been to see her vivid red blood spill over the white-silk wedding gown.

And he had thought of Liza Danning . . .

And Sandy Cavelli . . .

And how they, too, had hurt him.

That was when he came up with the plan. It had taken awhile to put it into motion.

First, he'd had to arrange a leave of absence from his father's company. He'd been running it—and better than meek Andrew ever had—ever since his father had gone off the deep end. When Stephen had made arrangements for a year off, he'd explained that he was simply burnt out from all the international travel the business required. No one questioned him—or suspected that he had no intention of ever coming back.

Then there had been the plastic surgery, which he'd always intended to do. He'd gone to Europe, where he had plenty of connections—and where privacy was ensured. And now, thanks to one of the world's most prominent surgeons, he bore no resemblance to the "Elephant Guy" who had been taunted all through school, scorned even by his own parents.

Finally, of course, he'd had to buy the inn and get it ready. He'd chosen Tide Island because his mother had always complained about how remote and sparsely populated it was. She'd said repeatedly over the years that she didn't know why Andrew insisted on keeping that Victorian albatross, which was so far off the beaten path that it made the rest of the island seem positively urban.

What better place, Stephen had decided, to carry out his plan?

And now, his long hours of meticulous preparation have paid off.

Sandy Cavelli is dead.

Liza Danning is dead.

Only Laura Towne remains.

The pain she caused him is the freshest. Torturing her will be sweeter, even, than it had been to torture Sandy and Liza.

He imagines Laura in the white wedding gown he'd bought for her.

It's more daring than the others were. Sexier. It has a plunging neckline and skin-tight skirt. When he'd bought it, he'd pictured her in that daring lingerie she was always wearing.

Now, he frowns slightly, thinking of the plain white-cotton underwear he'd found in her suitcase yesterday. It isn't at all like her to be so modest and . . . boring. Obviously her tastes have changed over the past year.

Oh, well.

Stephen opens the car door and steps

out into the storm, hurrying across the frozen drive to the back door of the inn.

He's no sooner closed it behind him and shaken the snow out of his hair than Jasper is standing in front of him, looking agitated.

"I've been waiting for you, Stephen . . ."

Irritated, he rolls his eyes. "Why?"

"I . . . here, come in and I'll show you."

Stephen steps into the kitchen, then follows Jasper through the dining room and into the parlor, saying, "I hope this doesn't take long. I have to change out of this tuxedo. It's covered with—"

He stops short when he sees her.

Laura Towne.

She's lying flat on her back on the old rose-colored sofa beneath the window, her hands folded over her stomach. She appears to be sleeping peacefully.

Stephen looks at Jasper, who blurts, "I had to do it, Stephen! She tried to get away."

"What the hell did you do?" he asks hoarsely. "You didn't—"

"No, I only knocked her out with chloroform. She'll come to in a little while," Jasper says nervously. "And that's not the only thing . . ."

Stephen scowls, bracing himself.

"An Officer Crandall came here, wanting to know about the inn, asking all kinds of questions . . ."

That nosy cop I met on the road. I should have guessed.

"You didn't tell him anything, did you?" Stephen asks Jasper. "You didn't—"

"Of course not. But you'd be proud of me, Stephen. I knocked him out with that vase from the desk, and then I locked him into the storage room off the kitchen. And his car is parked out back, near the dunes. I left the keys in it so that—"

"I want you to finish him off," Stephen interrupts tersely, jabbing a finger at Jasper, "and then I want you to meet me out at the summer house."

The little twerp gulps visibly. "But how will I get there?"

"Take my car," Stephen says, tossing him the keys to the sedan.

Jasper misses, of course, and they go clattering onto the carpet.

"But then how will you get—"

"I'll take the cop car, you idiot," Stephen bites out in disgust. "What else can I do?

Who knows how long it'll be before someone else comes snooping around here?"

"But I took care of the cop, and—"

"And now he's missing, too. Who knows
how many people he told about Sandy
Cavelli? He was looking for her. I bumped
into him on the road earlier. He seemed
suspicious. But never mind, it doesn't matter now. Just take care of him. Can I trust
you to do it, or are you going to screw up on
this, too?"

"I'll do it," Jasper says firmly, raising his
chin. "You know I'd do anything for you,
Stephen."

He lays a tentative hand on Stephen's
arm, and he fights the urge to recoil. He
can't risk putting Hammel off now. He still
needs him.

He forces himself to soften his gaze as he
looks at Jasper, to say soothingly, "I know
you'll do anything for me. And I appreciate
it."

"You do?"

"Of course I do."

Jasper smiles happily. "Thank God. I was
a little worried that you might not want me
to come with you, the way you promised. I

thought maybe you'd change your mind . . ."

"Why would I do that?"

Jasper hesitates, then says, "You wouldn't. I know you wouldn't. You promised. It's going to be you and me forever, just like you said."

Though his words are decisive, there's a note of uncertainty in his voice, and Stephen wonders if little old Arnie is more perceptive than he gives him credit for being.

"Sure. You and me forever, Arnie," he says to reassure him.

The man's mouth quivers beneath his mustache. "You haven't called me that in years."

"And I didn't mean to now. It was a slip of the tongue. You're Jasper. . . . Don't forget that."

"I won't."

"Good."

"I love you, Stephen."

"I love you, too."

Stephen sighs inwardly. There are times when he thinks he's lucky to have this eager-to-please flunky on his side. But other times, he worries that he's making a big

mistake trusting someone who's one sandwich short of a picnic.

Still, it won't matter after a few more
hours, he reminds himself.

Like Laura Towne, Jasper Hammel—
a.k.a. Arnold Wentworth—will be history.

Keegan looks back over his shoulder at
the boat that bobs furiously in the water
where he docked it.

"You think it's going to hold?" Danny asks
him.

"I don't know. The rope's pretty strong,
but with this storm . . ." Keegan trails off
and shakes his head.

"Should we go back and see if we can
make it sturdier?" Cheryl asks, clinging to
her husband's arm and ducking her head
against the driving wind and snow.

"We can't worry about it now," Keegan
replies, looking toward the cluster of weathered buildings near the boardwalk straight
ahead. "We've got to find out about your
sister, and my—and Jennie."

Walking as swiftly as they can despite the
powerful wind and icy pavement, they make
their way toward the nearest building.

"It's the police station!" Danny calls as they draw closer to it, pointing to a sign above the door.

"Yeah, but it looks deserted," Keegan points out, shaking his head.

"The windows are probably just boarded up because of the storm," Danny argues.

"Probably, but it doesn't look like anyone's there," Keegan tells him.

They approach it anyway and find the door locked.

The three of them huddle in the doorway beneath the shingled overhang that barely offers protection from the nasty weather.

"Now what?" Cheryl asks, shivering and stamping her feet on the concrete step, a note of despair in her voice.

"We go to the Bramble Rose Inn," Danny says decisively, turning to Keegan. "Right?"

"Right. First we have to find someone who knows where it is, though." Keegan looks around and spots a big white house with a widow's walk at the top right on the water near the boardwalk.

"There's a light on in the window of that old house," he tells the Cavellis, pointing. "Let's go see if someone there can help."

The three of them set out again, and it

feels like hours before they finally reach the house, though it's probably only a matter of minutes. Keegan can no longer feel his feet, and his face is so stiff from the cold that it feels as though it's going to crack open every time he speaks.

Please let someone answer the door, he begs silently as he, Danny, and Cheryl stomp up onto the porch of the old house. *If I don't get out of the wind and cold for a few minutes, I'm going to collapse.*

He glances at Cheryl and instantly feels ashamed of himself. If he's overcome, she must be barely hanging on. Her face looks wan and she seems weak and shaky, as if she'd wilt and drop to the ground if she weren't hanging onto Danny for dear life.

Keegan reaches out and, with numb fingers, pushes the old-fashioned buzzer beside the door.

Moments later, it's thrown open and a ruddy-faced man is there wearing a welcoming smile.

"Oh," he says, and the pure-white brows that match his hair furrow at the sight of three bedraggled strangers standing on his porch. "Thought you were going to be Sherm Crandall."

"Crandall? The police chief?" Danny asks.

"That's right. You know him?"

"I talked to him last night, about my sister. She's missing."

The man looks taken aback. "Did you say your sister is missing?"

"Yeah, why? You know something about it?"

"Sherm mentioned something about it—a girl from Connecticut, right?"

"Right. You don't know if he found her, do you?" Danny asks excitedly.

"He hadn't—least not when I saw him around lunchtime. He was on his way over to the inn where she was staying—wanted to have a look-see, I suppose."

"Ned?" calls a female voice from the back of the house. "What are you doing with that door open? You're letting all the heat out!"

"That's the missus—Shirley. And I'm Ned Hartigan," he explains, and steps back, gesturing for the three of them to step inside.

They do, and Keegan gratefully unzips the top of his jacket, lifting his chin away from the soaked fabric at last. The house is like an oven, and a savory aroma fills the warm air. The white walls of the hall they're standing in are covered in wood-framed photographs, and two bright rag rugs are scattered on the honey-colored plank floor.

Ned closes the door firmly behind them just as a lanky gray-haired woman comes into the hall, wiping her hands on a dish towel. Her thin eyebrows shoot up at the sight of three strangers dripping on the doormat.

"Thought Sherm might be here for dinner," is all she says, glancing at her husband and then back at the visitors.

"So did I, but this is the fella whose sister is missing from the inn—remember I told you what Sherm—Say," he interrupts himself, "how did you folks get here, anyway? There's no ferry service today."

"We borrowed a boat," Keegan says simply.

"Pretty brave of you to come across the water in this storm, I'd say."

"Would you like some hot coffee?" Shirley asks, looking with concern at Cheryl, who's still trembling from head to toe.

"My Shirley brews the best coffee on the

island. Ask anyone, and they'll tell you," Ned says proudly.

Danny and Keegan exchange a glance. "We really don't have time," Keegan says reluctantly, thinking about how heavenly it would be to stay in the warm house and sip something hot.

But there's no time to waste.

Not when Jennie might be in trouble.

"But if you wouldn't mind, why don't you let my wife stay here for a little while and warm up," Danny puts in.

Cheryl starts to protest, but Shirley swoops right in like a mother bird and puts her arm around Cheryl's shoulders. "Don't you be silly," she says. "You look like you're about to faint. Now you come right back into the kitchen and sit by the fire and have some chowder."

"Go ahead, babe," Danny urges his wife, who looks at him questioningly.

"But what about Sandy?"

"We'll go see what we can find out," he assures her, and she nods.

"Can you tell us where the Bramble Rose Inn is?" Keegan asks, turning to Ned. "Is it within walking distance?"

"It would be if it weren't snowing and

blowing like the dickens. But come on. We'll take my pickup . . . if it starts."

It does . . . after several tries.

As Ned Hartigan pulls out onto the ice-covered road that leads back toward town, Keegan peels off his wet wool gloves and blows on his numb fingers.

"Frostbite?" Hartigan asks, glancing at him.

"Hope not."

"My feet are starting to sting like crazy," Danny says.

"That's a good sign. Circulation's coming back."

Keegan tries not to think about his own feet. He can't feel them at all.

"So did you see my sister at all this weekend?" Danny asks. "She's a little chubby, but pretty, and the sweetest girl you'd ever want to meet."

"Well, the gal I saw who was staying at the inn was anything but sweet," Ned says with disdain as the truck creeps along the road. "Blond, and acted like she was the Queen of England."

Definitely not Jennie, Keegan thinks. Glancing out the window at the slowly passing buildings along the boardwalk, he asks, "I don't suppose you came across the woman I'm trying to find. She was staying at the inn, too."

"From Boston?"

"Yeah!" Keegan turns excitedly to Ned. "Jennie Towne. You met her?"

"Does she have the prettiest light-purple eyes—like Liz Taylor's?"

"That's her! Where'd you see her?"

"Came into my store—that's it over there, by the way," Ned says, pointing to a building on the boardwalk that's fronted by a painted Victorian-style sign that reads "Hartigan's." "Anyway, she came in yesterday and was nice as can be. Then she sat down and had coffee with the nasty blonde, which surprised me because I didn't think the two of them could be friends. Although my wife, Shirley, is a good woman and she has some friends who are downright obnoxious, I'll tell you. This one gal, Myra's her name, Myra Tallman, well she—"

Keegan, sensing that Ned Hartigan is the kind of man who can easily lose track of a conversation, interrupts. "Excuse me, Mr. Hartigan, but how did the woman from Boston seem?"

"How did she *seem*?" he repeats, not

missing a beat, which tells Keegan that he must be used to being interrupted. "What do you mean?"

"Was she . . . I don't know. Nervous?"

"Not really. Just a little stand-offish, maybe. But real nice. You could tell. She was probably just shy. Didn't want to open up much about herself, not like some of the tourists who stop by."

That's Jennie, all right, Keegan thinks as Danny says, "My sister doesn't have a shy bone in her body. You'd know if you met her. She's a real chatterbox."

"Wish I could say I'd seen her, son," Ned replies.

They all fall silent as the pickup truck plods along the road that has started curving away from the boardwalk. Keegan stares vacantly out the window at the boarded-up shops and hotels, some bearing signs that read, "See you in June!"

Dusk is falling rapidly and the snow is coming down harder than ever. The truck's windshield wipers beat a bleak rhythm that seems to be echoing the refrain in Keegan's head—*Find Jennie. Find Jennie. Find Jennie . . .*

"There's the inn, up ahead," Ned Hartigan

says suddenly, pointing. "On that little rise, to the right."

Danny and Keegan lean forward, peering through the stormy twilight outside the truck.

Keegan's shoulder and arm are against Danny's, and he can feel the guy's apprehension as Hartigan slows the truck even more and starts to pull off the road.

"Say," Ned Hartigan leans forward over the wheel, "isn't that . . ."

Keegan catches sight of what he's looking at. A car is just pulling out onto the road from the other side of the inn, its headlights cutting an arc through the blustery shadows.

"Is it a cop car?" Danny asks just as Keegan catches a glimpse of the official insignia on the door and the round dome on the roof.

"Sure is . . . only one on the island. That's Sherm Crandall," Ned says. "Must be headed back to his house. Lives up toward the center of the island."

"Shouldn't we follow him and see if he knows anything about Sandy?" Danny asks urgently.

Keegan's heart sinks. He knows Danny's

desperate to find his sister; but now that they've arrived at the inn, he can't bear the thought of not getting to Jennie right away.

"Can we just—Look, I just want to stop here," he says, "to see if Jennie's inside. You two can go on and catch up to the police officer."

"Yeah, but look at Sherm go," Ned comments with a low whistle. "Looks like he's on someone's trail."

"I'll come in with you," Danny says, turning to Keegan. "Just to see if the innkeeper knows what's going on."

As Ned pulls up in front of the inn, Keegan watches the police car driving rapidly away in the opposite direction, the red taillights visible for only a few seconds before disappearing around a curve.

Jennie stirs, then opens her eyes, wondering why her bed is shaking violently. Can it be an earthquake?

Not in Boston, she thinks groggily.

But you're not in Boston, she remembers, trying to think straight. Why is it so cold? She must have kicked the covers off . . .

Boston?

No! You're on the island . . .

And you're not in your bed, she realizes as she gradually regains her senses. *It's pitch black, and you're lying on some kind of rough carpet, and . . . and . . . you're moving.*

That's it . . .

It's not your bed that's shaking . . .

You're going over bumps in a road . . .

Thoroughly confused, she squints into the darkness and tries to remember what happened.

Then it comes rushing back to her.

Jasper Hammel standing in her doorway and the cloth he'd clamped over her nostrils and that overpowering smell . . .

He knocked you out!

The knowledge fills Jennie with a chill more intense than the one caused by the frigid temperature.

He knocked you out, and now you're . . . you must be in the trunk of a car, and he's driving you somewhere . . .

Oh, God.

Oh, God!

Panicking, Jennie squirms, then kicks her legs, only to find that they're bound together at the ankles of her jeans.

And her wrists, too, are bound, behind her back so that she can't move, can only lie helplessly on her side as the car whisks her closer to . . .

Where?

Where is he taking me?

Calm down! She orders herself fiercely, taking a deep breath, and then another. At least there's no gag in her mouth . . .

She can scream for help as soon as—

No. She can't. If Jasper Hammel—or whoever's driving this car—thought there was a chance of anyone hearing her, he would have made sure she couldn't make a sound. Wherever he's taking her, it must be someplace where no one will ever hear her. Where no one will ever find her.

Squeezing her eyes tightly shut again, Jennie whimpers softly to herself, feeling tears slipping down her cheeks.

Why? she keeps asking herself.

Is Jasper Hammel some psycho who abducts unsuspecting women?

And who then . . .

What?

Rapes them?

Tortures them?

Murders them?

She pictures the odd little man with his formal, clipped way of speaking and shudders. Is he a psychopath in disguise?

You knew something was wrong all along, she tells herself. *Why didn't you listen to your instincts?*

Because you thought it was just your imagination acting up again, she responds flatly to the plaintive inner voice.

Ironic, isn't it, she thinks, that after all the times when she's panicked for no reason, she really is in danger again?

Just like the time with Harry—

And Harry, she recalls, had come to her in a dream to warn her.

Tears trickle down her cheeks as she thinks of the man she had loved, of how he had given his life for her.

That day three years ago had started out as one of the happiest Jennie had ever known.

She had woken in Harry's arms in his small apartment and glanced out the window beside the bed to see that it was snowing. Big, downy flakes, the kind that would turn Boston into a winter wonderland.

And it was a Saturday, which meant that

she and Harry would be together every minute for another forty-eight hours; and Christmas was right around the corner; and Harry's engagement ring was sparkling on the fourth finger of Jennie's left hand. . . .

She had actually shivered with joy.

"Wake up, you big lug," she'd said playfully. "It's going to be a wonderful day."

"Why?" he'd asked groggily.

"Because it's snowing and I love you and we're going to go shopping."

He'd raised one eyelid. "What was that last thing?"

"Come on, Harry, we have to go to the mall. I haven't gotten any of my shopping done, and Christmas is this week."

"That place will be insane on a Saturday."

"So? It'll be fun. Get you into the spirit."

"It'll get me *out* of the spirit, Jen. You know I hate to shop."

But she'd gotten her way, of course. Harry always gave in when she wanted something. And besides, he had shopping of his own to do. He wasn't going home to Portland for the first time ever, having decided to spend the holidays with Jennie, and that meant he had a lot of gifts to ship to his family.

After a leisurely breakfast of waffles and freshly-ground hazelnut coffee, they had taken the T over to the Colonial Mall so they wouldn't have to fight for a parking space. The fake-cobblestone corridors had been jammed with people, just as Harry had predicted.

For several hours, they had traipsed from store to store, buying gifts for their families, and even a few for each other. Harry kept trying to peek into the sporting goods store bag Jennie was carrying, knowing she'd stashed something for him inside, along with the in-line skates she'd bought for Laura.

Finally, they had everything they needed. Harry wanted to beat a hasty exit, but Jennie had persuaded him to stop at the food court for hot cocoa. "My feet are killing me," she'd said when he protested, "and you know we're going to have to stand on the T all the way home."

He'd given in, of course.

Jennie has wondered, so many times a day, every day of the past three years, what her life would be like now if Harry had said no to that cocoa. Or if they'd driven to the mall instead of taking the T. Or even if they'd arrived at the food court a few minutes earlier, or a few minutes later.

And even though she knew it was useless to torture herself with idle speculation, she couldn't seem to help it.

If things had been just slightly different that day, Harry would still be alive.

It was while Jennie and Harry were seated at one of the small wrought-iron tables in the skylighted food court, sipping their hot whipped-cream-laced cocoa, that the first shots had rung out.

"What was that?" Jennie had asked, frowning and looking over her shoulder.

"Sounded like—Oh, Jesus."

"What?"

Baffled, Jennie had seen a throng of people pushing frantically toward them.

Someone screamed, "He's got a gun! He's got a gun!"

There were more shouts and shrieks, more staccato blasts—sounds that would later haunt Jennie's nightmares.

She had seen the man with the gun coming at them, firing haphazardly to the left and right. He was so nondescript, she would tell the police later, still dazed. He looked like a balding, middle-aged English teacher or salesman, wearing glasses and jeans and a down jacket like so many other people at the mall that day.

Her eyes had locked with his as he happened to turn his head toward the table where she was sitting with Harry. She had seen him swing the gun again and point it in their direction, right at her.

"Oh, Christ, Jennie, duck!"

Harry had stood and leaned over the table, plastering his gigantic palm over the top of her head and shoving her down, throwing his big body over hers just as another shot rang out.

Jennie heard someone holler "Grab him" and turned her head to look up, bewildered, past Harry's arm that was thrown across her face, toward the commotion above.

That was when she had seen the man with the gun, with swift efficiency, placing the barrel into his own mouth. He pulled the trigger without hesitation, and blood and bone and brains had exploded from his head instantly.

Repulsed and panic-stricken, Jennie had screamed, "Oh, God, Harry, he just—"

And then she had seen him.

Harry.

The man she loved, the man whose engagement ring sparkled on her hand, the man who only moments before had been smiling at her across the table . . .

The left side of his face was oddly intact, the eye open and fixed vacantly on Jennie . . .

But the right side . . .

The entire right side of Harry's face was gone.

Later, much later, she would find out that the man who had done this—who had killed seven innocent people in a matter of moments—was married and had five children and had been laid off from his factory job the week before. He was despondent over mounting bills, his wife said, and wondering how they were going to heat their rented house this winter and get food on the table, let alone provide Christmas presents for their kids.

"I guess he just snapped," the grief-stricken woman was quoted as saying in an article in the *Globe.*

He just snapped. . . .

The words had stayed with Jennie.

A stranger had snapped, and her entire world had instantly fallen apart.

It wasn't fair.

For a long time after that, she hadn't cared whether she lived or died.

Then she'd met Keegan and fallen in love before she'd realized what was happening.

It wasn't until Christmas approached, bringing with it memories of what had happened to Harry—memories she had fought so hard to shut out—that Jennie had realized what she had to do.

She could never live with loving a cop—a man whose entire job was about danger and violence, a man who laid his life on the line every day.

She could never live with the constant fear of losing Keegan the way she had lost Harry, in the split second it takes for someone to pull the trigger of a gun.

And now, Jennie thinks in despair, futilely kicking her bound legs against the side of the car trunk, *I'm the one who's going to die.*

Sixteen

Jasper Hammel has just stepped into the storage room where officer Sherm Crandall's big body lies unconscious on the floor, when the sound of the doorbell pierces the air.

He freezes, his heart erupting into a rapid pounding as he waits and listens, wondering frantically what to do.

It rings again, more insistently this time.

It can't be Stephen. He wouldn't come to the front door, and besides, he has a key.

Jasper hesitates only another moment before tossing the meat cleaver onto the floor. It clatters across the scarred wood and stops just short of the cop's big belly.

Turning, Jasper flees the storeroom, stopping only long enough to lock the door so that the man can't get out if he comes to.

I'll be back to take care of you later, Jasper promises him, even though he knows it's a lie.

He wouldn't have been able to do it. He knew that even as he had stood over the man, clutching the knife, seconds earlier.

He's half-grateful to whoever rang the doorbell and saved him from having to attempt murder and half-furious that the unwelcome visitor is forcing him to take flight like a frightened gull.

He scoops the keys to Stephen's car off the kitchen counter, then slips out the back door as the bell rings again.

Racing across the frozen yard through the driving snow, Jasper wonders who can be at the door. He knows Crandall is the only cop on the island in winter. Who else would be stopping by in the middle of a storm?

Does it matter? he asks himself as he reaches the car and jerks open the door. *All that matters is that you get out of here.*

He gets behind the wheel, jabs the key into the ignition, and starts the engine. As he drives around to the front of the big old inn, he thinks wistfully of his packed suitcase waiting in the little room on the first floor.

He would have to leave it behind now. All the mementos he had collected through the years—a lock of Stephen's hair, a photograph of the two of them at prep school graduation—not to mention the new wardrobe he had bought to take with him.

Stephen had said they would be living on a tiny island in the West Indies—an island he had bought with cash. He had paid off a lot of people to erase the trail of paperwork that might lead the authorities to connect him to the island.

"No one will ever find me, Jasper," he'd said gleefully.

"You mean *us*," Jasper had said. "Don't you?"

"Of course I do. No one will ever find *us*."

Jasper remembers how much fun he'd had shopping for the clothes he'll need on the island—splashy tropical-print shirts and Bermuda shorts and sandals. Now he'll never get to wear them. . . .

But you'll get new things, he promises himself. *Stephen will buy you anything you want, when you get to the island.*

He pulls carefully out onto the highway heading north, looking back at the inn through the rear-view mirror. Before the snow obliterates the view, he makes out a battered-looking pickup truck parked in front of the Bramble Rose.

"Farewell forever, whoever you are," he calls softly as he heads up the coast toward the old Gilbrooke mansion.

"Did you see that?" Danny asks Keegan and Ned, watching the big black sedan disappear up the highway in the same direction the police car had taken.

"Something's up," Keegan says, nodding and pounding on the door of the inn. "Anyone here?" he calls.

"No way anyone could hear you from inside," Ned advises. "Not with this wind."

"Who do you think just left in that car?" Danny asks.

Ned shrugs. "Never saw it before. Not many cars on the island, either, in the off-season. I'd know most of 'em. Must be a tourist."

"We've got to follow them," Danny tells him and Keegan, stepping away from the door. "This is useless. There's no one here."

"Might be," Ned says thoughtfully, "that the evacuation is in effect."

"What evacuation?" Keegan asks as Danny pauses impatiently at the top of the steps.

"Because of the storm, Sherm said we might have to evacuate along the shore. Bet that's it. That'll mean Shirley and me have to clear out of our place, too. I best be getting back—"

"No!" Danny cuts him off abruptly, unable to contain himself any longer. "Look, my sister is out here somewhere and I've got to find her. Please, can't we just drive up that road a little ways to see if something's happening?"

"It's not a bad idea," Keegan agrees, looking from Danny to Ned. "That police officer was going like a bat out of hell. It seemed like he was rushing to get someplace."

"Well, I suppose we can check it out," Ned says after a long moment, with a sigh. "Sherm *did* mention something about the old Gilbrooke mansion, and it's up in that direction."

"The Gilbrooke mansion?" Danny and Keegan echo, practically in unison.

"What's that?" Danny asks. "Does it have something to do with my sister?"

"Probably not, but something might be going on out there. I'll tell you what I know in the truck," Ned says, starting down the steps toward the pickup. "Come on, let's head out there."

Stephen opens the trunk and peers inside, expecting to see Laura still slumped and unconscious.

Instead, she's looking directly up at him, her startled gaze visible even in the shadows of dusk.

"Who . . . who *are* you?" she asks as he bends and gathers her into his arms.

"I'll tell you when we get inside," he promises, inhaling the scent of her silky hair as it brushes against his face. It's not the musky fragrance he remembers her wearing, he thinks, frowning slightly. No, it simply smells . . . clean.

He reaches down to close the trunk, then trudges up the steps and balances her carefully over his shoulder as he unlocks the door.

"Home, sweet home," he says lightly, carrying her over the threshold. Just like a bride, he thinks, and smiles to himself.

He deposits her on the sofa in the parlor, then steps back to look at her. "Well?" he asks. "Do you remember?"

"Remember what?" She looks frightened, but oddly under control—as though she's resigned herself to the fact that she's help-less here.

"Oh, come on, Laura," he croons, starting to take off his coat, then thinking better of it. There hadn't been time for him to change out of the blood-stained tuxedo. No need to have her start panicking so soon.

He smiles and says, "You can't have for-gotten me so quickly." He reaches down and trails a finger lightly down her cheek.

She opens her mouth as if to say some-thing, then clamps it closed again.

"What is it?" he prods. "Do I seem famil-iar?"

She shakes her head, watching him, and he can feel her trembling as he moves his finger under her chin and tilts her face up toward him.

Strange, he thinks as he studies her, *she seems . . . different, somehow. Softer, even though she's trying to be defiant. And not quite as . . . overtly alluring. Her beauty seems more subtle now.*

"Here," he says, stepping away, opening a closet door and taking out the plastic-wrapped wedding dress he had made for her. "I had to guess the size because I didn't have time to find out exactly, but . . . are you a seven?"

She nods, looking bewildered.

"Then put it on. Oh," he remembers, reaching for the rope that binds her wrists. "Guess I'll have to untie you first. Don't you dare try anything funny, though. If you do, I'll have to do to you what I did to Sandy."

"Sandy?" she echoes in a whisper, and her eyes take on a sudden look of stark fear.

"Don't worry," he says, moving down to untie her feet. "If you're a good girl, you'll be fine."

She's visibly shaking as he hands her the dress.

"Go ahead," he orders, sitting on the edge of the sofa and folding his arms across his chest. "I want to watch. You always did like to strip for me, remember? You wore those lacy black underpants . . ." He moans slightly at the memory of her teasing him as she removed them, slowly and tantalizingly, in his hotel suite.

Now she studies him for a moment, then fumbles awkwardly with her sweater. She raises it over her head, and he sees that she's wearing a plain white bra underneath. He considers asking her to remove it, too, so that he can see her wonderfully firm breasts bare one last time, but realizes that it might cause him to get carried away and there probably isn't time for that.

So he simply watches, and squirms on the uncomfortable sofa, as she lowers her jeans to reveal white-cotton panties, the high-waisted kind that hide even her belly button.

He can't help feeling another prickle of disappointment. What happened to daring, provocative Laura and her seductive lingerie?

She steps shakily into the dress and pulls it up over her shoulders. It hugs her curves just as he'd thought it would, but he can't help feeling that maybe it wasn't the right choice. Suddenly, it seems as though a traditional, lacy gown might have suited her better after all.

Oh, well. At least the dress fits perfectly. He stands and says, "I'll do the zipper for you."

She nods mutely, and he rises and moves behind her.

He can feel her shaking as he tugs the

zipper pull up along her bare back, can sense her acute fear.

But for some reason, it isn't making him feel quite as satisfied as it had when he'd seen Sandy and Liza shaking in terror. Something's different . . . but he can't put his finger on what it is.

He moves around to stand in front of her again.

"Well?" he asks, watching her watch him. "Do you recognize me?"

"No," she says simply, "I don't."

"I don't look the same," he tells her. "I've changed in the *four seasons* since we were together. That's a hint," he adds, delighted with his own clever pun.

"Laura worked at the . . ."

She trails off abruptly. "You worked there, yes," he says, thinking vaguely that it's peculiar that she'd refer to herself in the third person. "And we met there . . . and made love there."

He waits.

Nothing.

She's fastened those lilac eyes blankly on him, as though she has no idea what he's talking about.

"Oh, come on, Laura," he says, feeling

anger surging up inside of him. "Did you sleep with *every* businessman who came through that hotel?"

Maybe she had, he realizes. Maybe he was only one of many.

And maybe, like Liza, she has completely forgotten that he ever existed.

Furious at the prospect, he grabs her arm and jerks her to her feet, holding her steady.

"I'm not," she begins, then stops.

"You're not what?" he bites out, glaring at her. "You're not a slut who can't even remember someone who took such good care of her?"

He slaps her, hard, across the face.

"I'm not Laura."

He stops short, poised with his hand raised to slap her again. "What are you talking about?"

"I'm not Laura Towne."

He brings his flattened palm down on her face again, sees her bite her lip against the pain. "What do you think I am, a fool?" he lashes at her. "I know you're Laura Towne."

"No, I'm her twin sister. Jennie."

"She doesn't have a twin," he says, frowning. *Or does she?* He would have no way of knowing.

But Laura always was the cunning type. He wouldn't put it past her to come up with a story like this, anything to save her skin.

"She does have a twin," the woman in front of him protests. "I swear, I'm her sister. Look at—my face."

"What about it?"

"Look at my cheek. Laura has a scar under her eye. If you really know her, you've seen it. And I don't have one."

He peers at her, remembering the scar, remembering the way he had kissed it tenderly the first night they were together in his hotel suite. She'd winced when he touched it and refused to tell him how it got there. He remembered suspecting that it wasn't the result of some innocent childhood accident, that someone had hurt her.

Now, all he can see on her cheek is an angry red smear where he slapped her.

The scar is gone.

Bewildered, he meets her eyes again, not wanting to believe that his plan is actually about to fall apart—that he's abducted the wrong girl.

"I'm Jennie," she says again, the only hint of her fear a slightly high-pitched tone in her voice.

"You're Jennie," he repeats, stunned. "You're not Laura?" Just to make sure . . .

"I'm not Laura."

She's telling the truth. He knows it, without a doubt. It would explain why she's wearing different underwear, why she smells different, why he feels different this time. . . .

He shakes his head, closes his eyes, tries to figure out what to do next.

"You'll have to be punished," he concludes after a few moments thought. "As long as you're here in your sister's place, you'll have to die in her place. It's that simple."

"You really should eat something," Shawn says with a full mouth, looking up at Laura over the sandwich he's just bitten into. "You haven't had anything all day."

"I'm not hungry." She stands across the table from him, both hands resting on the back of a chair, and shakes her head. "I feel sick."

"What's the matter?"

"I can't explain it . . . I just—my stomach. It's messed up. And my head is killing me, too. I feel awful."

"Do you think you're coming down with something?" he asks, putting the sandwich down and coming to stand beside her. He puts a hand on her forehead.

"No, not that kind of sick," she says, pushing him away. "It's Jen. I just know she's in trouble. I feel it so strongly that it's like . . . taking over my body. And there's nothing I can do to help."

"You really do think it has something to do with that guy, Stephen What's-his-name?"

"Gilbrooke. I don't know. It doesn't make sense. The man who sold me the ticket looked nothing like him, but there was something about him, I guess, that *could* remind me of him. . . . But what does it matter? It's not helping Jennie for me to sit here and think about some creep I used to date."

"Laura," Shawn says quietly, "right now, there *is* no way for you to help Jennie."

"I know," she says, and buries her face in his shoulder, sobbing.

You'll have to die.

The stranger's words ring through Jennie's brain, and she simply stands there and stares at him.

Then something snaps inside her. Something that causes her to stiffen her spine, narrow her gaze, and say resolutely, "You don't want to kill me."

He looks taken aback.

"What do you mean?" he asks suspiciously. "Of course I want to kill you."

"Why?" She forces herself to take a step closer to him, to run her finger along his cheek, just as he had done to her moments before. "Why would you want to kill me when you haven't even gotten to know me yet?"

"I—" He shuts his mouth, looks puzzled.

She moves her finger down, trailing it along his neck to his chest. He's wearing a thick wool overcoat, and she glimpses a bow tie and white shirt beneath it. The shirt is smeared with something . . .

Oh, Lord, Jennie realizes in horror, *it's blood.*

She swallows hard and bites her lower lip to keep from screaming. She doesn't speak for a moment, waiting until she's certain her voice won't dissolve into a frightened sob.

Then, she says seductively, "Laura may have slept with everyone she met, but I haven't. And I don't want . . . anyone but you."

His eyebrows shoot up beneath his dark hair, and his cornflower-blue eyes widen. "You want me?" he says hoarsely, then shakes his head abruptly. "You do not. You're just saying it. Like the rest of them."

"I am not." She knows what she has to do, and the thought of it sends repulsion coursing through her, threatening to gag her.

She fights back the bile and stands on her tiptoes, clamping her mouth firmly over his. She moves her lips over his cold, rubbery lips, hears him groan in surprise and passion deep in his throat, feels his lips opening against hers, his wet, invasive tongue slipping through to probe hers.

It's all she can do not to retch as she pulls back and exhales shakily—as though she's carried away by passion, not overcome with revulsion.

"I want you," she whispers again, watching him, praying fervently that it will work.

"You want me," he repeats, and sighs. A slow smile slips over his features, and he nods. "You do. You're not like the others."

"I'm not," she agrees, her mind screaming, *What about them? Sandy? And Liza?*

She keeps her eyes focused on his face, not letting them wander lower, where the blood-stained shirt is still visible inside his coat.

"I'll take you with me," he says just as the front door opens.

Jennie spins and looks through the archway leading to the hall, half-expecting to see that someone's come to save her.

But the man stepping into the hall and stomping the snow off his feet is distressingly familiar.

"Miss Towne . . . fancy meeting you here," Jasper Hammel says with a wave.

"Can't you go any faster?" Keegan asks, finding himself jabbing at the floor of the pickup truck with his unfeeling right foot as though he's stepping on an imaginary gas pedal.

Ned shakes his head and frowns. "Not unless you want me to get us all killed. The tires are really bad on this truck, and the roads are a mess. We're lucky we haven't skidded into a ditch yet. In fact, we should just—"

"No!" Danny says forcefully. "We can't go back. Not yet. We have to get to that place."

Keegan nods.

Ned Hartigan sighs and keeps driving, inching the truck along the perilous stretch of highway that follows the coast.

Keegan thinks of what Hartigan told them. How Sherm had run into a suspicious character out here, a man who seemed to be using an alias—and claimed to be staying at the Bramble Rose. How Sandy Cavelli isn't the only person who's missing on the island this weekend. One of the part-time cops is gone as well, and the last place he was known to have headed was the old Gilbrooke mansion.

Oh, Jennie, Keegan asks silently, *are you somehow involved in this? Where are you?*

Beside him, Danny Cavelli beats a staccato rhythm on the dashboard with nervous fingertips. "How much farther to the house?" he presses as Ned slows the truck to creep around a sharp curve.

"Another mile or so, I'd say."

Keegan groans inwardly. At the rate they're going, and with the storm showing no sign of letting up, it's going to take ages for them to get there.

And by then . . .

What if it's too late?

* * *

"What are you doing here?" Stephen asks, frowning.

Jasper crosses the floor to the parlor, saying, "I know you told me to wait, but I had to come right away, Stephen. Someone showed up at the house just after you left."

"Who was it?"

"I have no idea," Jasper tells him, moving to sit on the edge of the sofa. "I didn't answer the door. I just left as fast as I could."

"And what about that fat cop?"

Jasper hesitates only a mere second before deciding to lie. Stephen will never know. Not after they've left this island for good. "I took care of him first, just the way you said to," he tells Stephen, sinking with relief onto the sofa cushion.

Everything's going to be all right now.

He made it here, having driven dangerously fast over that treacherous highway. There were a few times when the sedan started to skid and he thought . . .

"What do you think you're doing?"

"Excuse me?" Jasper looks up at Stephen, puzzled.

"Get up!" he barks and grabs Jasper's

arm, pulling him to his feet. "Can't you see that I'm not finished here?"

"Oh, of course. I'm sorry." Jasper looks from Stephen to Laura, who stands, looking pale, in a white, ridiculously low-cut wedding gown. He smiles at the thought of what Stephen's going to do to her and can't resist taunting her a little.

"It's too bad you're going to ruin that lovely dress with all that blood," he says, grinning.

"Shut up, you idiot!" Stephen shouts and takes a menacing step toward Jasper. "Shut up!"

"But Stephen, I—"

"She's not going to die like the rest. She's coming with me."

"What do you mean?" Feeling a tide of paranoia rising in his gut, Jasper looks at Stephen's arm, which actually seems protective of the woman whose shoulder it rests upon. "You hate her, Stephen," Jasper babbles, "remember?"

"I hate her *sister,* Laura. This is Jennie, her identical twin."

In a flash, Jasper thinks back to the phone call—the woman who'd asked to speak to *Jennie* Towne. He should have realized then that the woman at the inn was an impostor, he thinks frantically. If he had, he might have been able to prevent this from happening . . .

He turns his troubled gaze back on Stephen. "But—" he begins.

Stephen cuts him off. "Let's go out to the boat," he says. "I need you to help me drag the others along."

"The others?" The woman in the wedding dress speaks for the first time since Jasper arrived. "What others?"

"Nothing for you to worry your pretty little head about, darling," Stephen says, looping his elbow around hers. "Come along. Jasper will get them."

"Where are they?" Jasper asks, fighting back the urge to burst into frustrated tears.

"In the closet under the stairs. Now, make it quick," Stephen says, and leads Jennie Towne toward the back of the house.

Jasper stands there, watching them go.

This isn't how it was supposed to happen!

It was supposed to be just the two of them, he fumes, shaking his head. Not he and Stephen and some *woman.*

Clenching his jaw, Jasper moves toward the closet and opens the door.

Inside, lying in a heap on the floor, are the three gory corpses, one belonging to the nosy kid Stephen had told him about, and the other two—Sandy Cavelli and Liza Danning—clad in blood-stained wedding gowns.

With a sigh, Jasper starts lugging the first corpse out of the closet and down the hall toward the back door.

Stephen glances again at Jennie, who's sitting on the narrow bed in the hold of his yacht, the *Aurelia.* The sea is churning from the storm, which causes the boat to rock wildly.

That, Stephen tells himself, is why Jennie looks pale. She must be getting seasick. He feels a little queasy himself.

"Don't worry. . . . We'll sail right out of this atrocious weather," he promises, admiring the way she looks wrapped in his overcoat, which he'd insisted on giving her. After all, she can't go around in this weather wearing only that skimpy dress.

He had seen the way she'd looked at his

clothes when he'd taken off the coat. "It's a shame I ruined my tuxedo with so much blood," he had said. "But I won't need it where we're going."

She had nodded and offered him a smile, and his heart had swelled with love for her.

She isn't like the rest. She really does care about me.

In all his life, no woman had ever looked at him with anything other than repulsion in her eyes.

Laura.

Liza.

Sandy.

Lorraine.

And, worst of all, his own mother, Aurelia.

All of them had used him to get what they wanted—even his mother. But for her, the attraction hadn't been money.

It had been far more unsettling than that.

Stephen still shudders every time he thinks of the first time she'd ever called down the hall to him from her bedroom. "Stevie?" she had said as he passed by on his way to his room. "Can you come in here for a moment?"

He must have been all of ten years old at the time; but even then, he had somehow sensed, by the tone of her voice, the un-speakable thing that was about to happen.

Aurelia had been propped against her goose-down pillows, wearing a filmy pink negligee that plainly revealed her round, pointed nipples and the dark triangle at the base of her flat torso.

"Sit down," she had said in a soft voice she had never used on him before.

Stephen sat, and tried to keep his eyes averted. "Where's Father?" he had asked in a small voice.

"Who cares?" Aurelia dismissed Andrew with a wave of her hand. "I have no use for a man like that. He doesn't give me the time of day—always has his head buried in that stupid paperwork. And he certainly doesn't have the first idea how to satisfy a woman. Stevie . . ." she had added. "Do you want to touch me?"

"No, Mother."

"You can admit it," she said, sounding breathless. "Go on. You can touch me here . . ." And she had slid her fingers over his, bringing his hand up and resting it against her left breast. "You can touch me everywhere."

"You'd better do it, Stevie," she'd added

when he'd sat there, frozen, his heart pounding so hard he thought it would burst through his rib cage. "This is your only chance to touch a woman. No one else is going to let someone who looks like you near her."

There's a thumping sound on the boat deck overhead, and Stephen snaps out of his reverie.

"That's Jasper again," he tells Jennie, standing and glancing toward the steps that lead out of the hold. "I'll be right back. I just want to go see where he's . . . never mind." He decides it's probably best not to say the rest—*Where he's putting the bodies.* Just in case Jennie Towne is the squeamish type.

He bends and plants a light kiss on her dark hair. "I'll be right back, my darling. I love you."

"I love you, too," she says.

Her voice is trembling slightly, and he decides that she must be as overwhelmed with emotion as he is. Dear, sweet Jennie . . . he'll make her his bride just as soon as they reach their destination.

Humming the wedding march to himself, Stephen climbs up to the deck and sees that Jasper is just depositing the third body—Sandy Cavelli's—on the rocking deck.

He looks up at Stephen. "That's it," he calls with a grunt, straightening and wiping the mix of snow and sweat from his brow. "They're all out."

"Good." Stephen is about to order him to go back to the house and clean up any telltale spots of blood when he catches sight of the distressed look on the man's face. "What's wrong, Jasper?"

"It's just . . ." The little man pauses, then takes a deep breath and says, over the howling wind, "I must admit, Stephen, that I'm somewhat upset at this most recent turn of events."

"What are you talking about?"

"Her," is the shouted one-word reply, accompanied with a gesture toward the hold, where Jennie waits.

"Do you mean Jennie?"

"Yes. I thought it was going to be just you and me, Stephen."

"You didn't really," Stephen calls, amused at the disillusionment on the man's face.

Jasper hesitates, knits his brows. "I didn't really . . . what?"

"You didn't really think I was going to take

you with me?" Stephen reaches inside his jacket and pulls out the pistol he'd tucked into his pocket earlier. He had been going to save it for later, when they were safely at sea, but . . .

Suddenly wild-eyed, Jasper looks in disbelief from the gun to Stephen's face. "What are you going to do with that?" he asks, his voice reduced to a pitiful high-pitched whimper.

"Sorry, old boy," Stephen shouts, cocking it and aiming squarely at Jasper's head. "But I've run out of uses for you."

With that, he pulls the trigger.

The shot pierces the violent roar of the storm, and Stephen's lips curl into a satisfied smile as Jasper Hammel topples backward over the rail into the foaming water.

Seventeen

"The house is right around this next bend
... there!" Ned says, pointing triumphantly.

Keegan leans forward, peering at the
gothic monster rising in front of them. There
are two vehicles parked in front, he realizes—both the police car and the black
sedan they'd seen leaving the inn.

Danny Cavelli is out of the truck like a
shot the moment Ned stops at the foot of
the porch steps.

"Wait!" Keegan calls, hurrying after him
and grabbing his shoulder to pull him back.

"Let go of me! My sister—"

"I know, but you can't go rushing in
there!" Keegan says as Ned comes slipping
and sliding around the truck on the icy
gravel. "You don't know what's going on inside. It could be dangerous. I'll go first, and
if it's all right, I'll wave you ahead."

Danny starts to protest, but Ned interrupts. "Better listen to him, son. He's right

about not rushing in there. But maybe," he adds, turning to Keegan, "it's too dangerous for us to fool around here at all. Maybe we should just leave and—"

"I'm a cop," Keegan says resolutely. "I'm trained in this kind of thing. But you two need to step back."

"Fine," Ned says, shrugging. "In fact, I'll wait in the truck."

"Good idea." Keegan looks at Danny. "And you should—"

"Forget it. I'll be right behind you."

Realizing it's not worth it to waste time arguing, Keegan gives a curt nod and says, "Fine."

With Danny Cavelli right at his heels, he steps carefully up onto the porch and peers through the windows. His instincts tell him that the place is deserted, but the cars parked out front mean that at least two people are around here . . . someplace.

Reaching for the knob, Keegan is surprised to see that the door isn't locked. He slowly pushes it open and steps inside just as Ned hollers something from the pickup truck.

Startled, Keegan turns to see what's going on.

Danny is already hurrying down the steps.

"What is it?" Keegan calls above the roaring wind.

"He says there's someone out in back of the house by the boat dock!" Danny is already running awkwardly across the icy gravel toward the lawn that sweeps down to the water.

"Wait!" Keegan hurries after him, hearing Ned's bellowed, "Be careful!" coming from the direction of the truck.

Running on the snowy grass is far easier than it was to make his way across the driveway, and Keegan quickly overtakes Danny, grabbing his shoulder and forcing him to the snow-covered ground in front of a low shrub.

"Get your hands off of me!" he says, jerking under Keegan's sturdy grasp.

"Just wait," Keegan says, lying on his stomach beside Danny and pointing in the direction of the water. "We're sitting ducks up here if anyone sees us. I just want to see what's going on. Stay still and stay down, dammit."

The younger man suddenly obeys, and Keegan can hear Danny's heavy panting mingling with his own and with the roaring wind as he cautiously raises himself to peer over the top of the bush.

The lawn descends to a short dock that juts out into the water, and moored at the piling is a large luxury yacht. From here, despite the snow and darkness, he can make out the figure of a man standing on the deck. As he watches, whoever it is descends into the hold.

This whole thing could be entirely innocent, Keegan tells himself.

But his sharply honed police officer's instincts tell him that something sinister is going on.

And he can only pray that, somehow, Jennie is still safe.

"Is everything all right?" Jennie asks, looking up to see Stephen framed in the doorway of the hold again.

"Everything's fine," he says with a beatific smile. "I just had to take care of something."

"What?"

"Nothing for you to worry about."

She nods, struggling to remain calm. He

just killed Jasper Hammel. She's certain of it. The sound of gunfire was as vivid as it had been that long-ago day at the Colonial Shopping Mall; and the moment she had heard it, Jennie had found herself on the verge of hysteria.

Only the thought of Keegan had allowed her to regain control.

I can't lose it, because if I do, he'll kill me. And I'm not ready to die. I have to get back to Keegan. I have to tell him that I really do love him. I have to explain why I left him.

And if she manages to get out of this and get back to him, she vows, she will never, ever, let him go again.

Desperation threatens to edge into her voice as she asks Stephen, "Are we going to leave now?"

"Do you want to?"

"I don't know. . . . Maybe we should stay here," she tells him, trying to sound casual, despite the terror building within her. "Just for tonight. Because of the storm."

"Well . . ."

He appears to be considering that, then shakes his head. "Too risky," he tells her.

"Oh, Stephen, come on. You're such a

strong, brave man. Don't tell me you're afraid to take a risk."

Please! she screams at him inside her brain. *Please don't try to take the boat out now.*

He has to be insane to even consider it.

She doesn't know which prospect is more chilling—meeting her death at his hands or in the violent storm-tossed sea.

"All right," he says after a moment, with a nod. "We can wait—if not until morning, at least until the weather lets up. It can't stay like this forever. Come on."

He reaches out and offers her a hand, pulling her to her feet.

It's nearly impossible for her to walk in the skintight gown with the boat beneath her feet rocking and rolling over the waves.

"I'll carry you," he says, turning and seeing her moving awkwardly across the floor.

Before she can protest, he's lifting her into his arms, holding her in a powerful grip against his blood-spattered clothing. "There . . . isn't that better?"

Feeling trapped, Jennie can only nod as he starts up the steep steps. The rancid smell of drying blood, mingled with the overpowering scent of dying roses that had filled the house, assaults her nostrils, and it's all she can do to keep from vomiting. A blast of wind and snow hits her as soon as they step out onto the deck, mercifully eradicating the scent of blood and roses.

Jennie squints against the driving snow, turning her head down toward the deck to see if there's any sign of Jasper.

The sight that greets her there causes her to gasp in utter shock and horror.

"What is it?" Stephen asks, stopping and looking down at her.

Speechless, she can only stare at the heap of corpses on the deck.

Oh, Sandy . . . She shakes her head, gazing at the unmistakable chubby figure encased in white satin that's streaked with rust-colored blotches.

And Liza . . . She sees the matted, blood-soaked blond hair and shakes her head in despair.

And . . .

The third body is face up, unlike the others, the face coated with snow, the eyes open and staring at the stormy night sky. It takes a moment for Jennie to realize where she's seen him before . . .

Patrick Gerkin.

"Jennie?"

It's Stephen, his blue eyes probing her face.

"You . . . you killed them! Oh, God! You're a murderer!" The words spill out of her before she can stop them, a harsh, unforgiving accusation.

For a moment, he merely looks surprised, and Jennie tells herself that it's okay . . . she can take it back, convince him that she didn't mean to react that way . . .

But then, before she can open her mouth again, his eyes harden into icy daggers and his grip on her tightens so that she can barely breathe.

He says nothing, only stalks across the deck toward the ladder leading to the dock.

Jennie's heart sinks as she realizes what he's going to do.

Take her into the house . . . and kill her there.

Like the others.

"Please," she says on a sob. "Please don't hurt me. I love—"

"Shut up!" he hollers at her. "You don't love me. You never did. It was a lie. You're like the others, just as I thought. But I almost believed you! How could I believe you? How could I think you were different?"

He's talking more to himself than to her, shaking her, ranting, and squeezing her tighter with every sentence so that she feels as though her ribs are going to shatter. She can no longer speak, can't inhale . . .

She's going to die like this, she realizes in horror, gasping for air . . .

He's going to squeeze the life right out of her.

Oh, God, Keegan . . . I'll never—

"Let her go!"

The words reach her ears on a gale, and Jennie thinks that it's only the wind. It can't be . . .

But that voice . . .

No, it can't be. It's just your imagination again. It's because he's on your mind, because you're so terrified, because you know that you're about to . . .

"I mean it. . . . Put her down!"

This time, Jennie realizes that the voice is real—and familiar.

It's coming from the dock above the boat, and Jennie looks up just in time to see a dark figure leaping through the air, landing on the deck a few feet away.

Stephen is so startled that he drops her as Keegan McCullough scrambles to his feet and faces him.

"You son of a bitch!" he bellows above the roaring wind and sea, as Jennie stares in disbelief.

Keegan . . .

But how . . .

Why . . .

"You son of a bitch!" Keegan repeats, advancing on Stephen.

But Stephen has regained his control and is standing his ground before Keegan, a bemused smile on his face.

"And who are you?" he asks, his hand slipping into his jacket pocket.

"Keegan, no!" Jennie finds her voice and screams as he makes a move to tackle Stephen. "He's got a gun! No!"

But Keegan is already upon Stephen, hurtling at him with a guttural cry of fury. The two men topple onto the pitching deck.

Horrified, Jennie struggles to get up. Her right leg is seared by an agonizing pain. It had twisted beneath her when she landed, and now she can only claw at the deck helplessly with her hands, unable to put any weight on her leg.

She hears another shout from the dock above. In despair, she looks up to see a second man, a stranger, standing there. He's poised as though he's about to jump onto the boat and help Keegan when, suddenly, his gaze drops to the battered corpses on the deck.

"Oh, Sweet Jesus, no!" His strangled cry pierces the noise of the storm. "Oh, God, not Sandy. No . . . please, not Sandy!"

Her brother? The one who called . . .

In numb horror, Jennie looks from the grief-crazed man on the dock back at the tumbling blur of arms and legs on the wildly pitching boat deck.

Then she sees a flash of the gun in Stephen's hand.

She opens her mouth to warn Keegan when, with a sudden, swift movement, he knocks the weapon out of Stephen's grasp, sending it skittering across the icy boat deck.

Sobbing in desperation, Jennie strains to pull herself toward the spot where it lies near the railing as the two men scuffle in the opposite direction. She's about to close her fingers over the barrel when a hand moves in and grabs it away.

Stunned, Jennie looks up to see Jasper Hammel standing over her, clutching the gun against his chest and looking dazed.

Water streams from his hair and over his body, and there's blood trickling from his temple. The bullet Stephen fired only grazed it, Jennie realizes, knocking him overboard and he must have pulled himself back on board the boat somehow without Stephen's realizing it.

"You bastard!" The voice belongs to Keegan, yet it sounds far off and muffled.

Jennie jerks her head around to see that only Keegan's lower legs are visible as Stephen dangles the rest of him backward over the rail of the boat, holding onto his ankles.

"Are you ready to die, Mr. Hero?" Stephen shouts, wearing a deranged grin.

"No!" Jennie screams, looking desperately toward the man on the dock to do something, to help Keegan somehow.

But he's gone—running across the snow-covered lawn toward the house, shaking his head blindly as if to shut out the sight of Sandy's body.

Jennie turns her head back to look at the two men by the rail just as a shot rings out.

She hears a blood-chilling shriek, not realizing for a moment that it's coming from her.

It becomes a high-pitched wail as she squeezes her eyes shut to block out the horror, knowing that when she opens them, Keegan will be gone, just as Harry was . . .

But then she hears his voice saying, "Drop the gun."

Astounded, Jennie opens her eyes and sees Keegan scrambling back up over the rail and onto the deck . . . where Stephen lies writhing from a bullet wound in his side.

Relief courses through her and she gasps his name on a nearly hysterical half-sob, half-laugh.

"Drop the gun," Keegan repeats.

Jennie turns to see that Jasper Hammel is still holding the pistol straight in front of him in both hands, arms rigid, trembling all over.

"What are you doing, Arnie?" Stephen gasps, clutching his side and looking up at Hammel in bewilderment. "What are you doing? Don't do anything foolish, Arnie. It's me, Stephen . . ."

"I know it's you." Hammel's voice is a bitter sob. "You lying bastard. You lying . . .

You never planned to bring me with you when you left. You . . . I loved you. . . . I was the only one who stood by you. And you . . . you tried to kill me."

"No, Arnie . . ."

Stephen starts to say something more, but Hammel closes his eyes tightly and fires again, this time hitting Stephen square in the throat. His words die instantly in a gurgle of blood.

"Drop it," Keegan says again, taking a step closer to Hammel.

For a brief, terrifying instant, Jennie believes that Jasper Hammel is going to fire again, this time at Keegan. But then, with a shudder, he drops the weapon at his feet and opens his eyes.

At the sight of Stephen's bloody body, he sobs. "Oh, look at you. . . . Look at what I've done to you. . . . I loved you, you lying bastard."

Keegan moves forward and grabs him, pulling his arms behind his back. Hammel doesn't resist, but, as if in a stupor, allows his wrists and ankles be tied with two lengths of rope Keegan finds in the compartment where the life jackets are stored.

Only when Jasper Hammel is restrained

and lying on his stomach on the deck, weeping bitterly about Stephen, does Keegan turn to Jennie.

"Are you all right?" he asks gently, bending over her and touching her cheek.

"My leg hurts, but . . . I'm going to be fine," she assures him, meeting his gaze. "Now that you're here."

"Oh, Jennie . . ." He gathers her into his arms. "Thank God you're all right. Don't you even think of leaving me, not ever again."

"I won't," she promises. "I'll never leave you again, Keegan."

Epilogue

The sun shines brightly on New Year's Day, glistening on the drifts of snow that blanketed Boston overnight.

"Be careful now, Jen," Laura, wearing her black-velvet matron-of-honor dress, warns as her sister's white-satin pumps hover over the sidewalk in front of the church. "It's probably icy."

"I'm all right." Jennie gathers the voluminous ivory skirt of her antique wedding gown over her arm and steps down from the horse-drawn carriage.

Laura is right behind her, carrying her bouquet and Jennie's.

They're not roses—Jennie had told her sister she'd carry anything but roses.

She has no idea how Laura got her hands on lilacs in January, but her sister had come through for her.

"Are you ready?" Shawn is waiting on the sidewalk, handsome in a dark suit and tie.

Jennie nods at her brother-in-law. He'd been so happy when she'd asked him to give her away. "I'd be honored," he'd said, and Laura had positively beamed at his side.

It is hard to believe that six months have passed since their June wedding—that it has been almost a year since Jennie's ordeal on Tide Island.

But she pushes the thought of that out of her mind. This is the happiest day of her life. There's no room today to let unpleasant memories haunt her. . . . There never will be again.

Jennie takes Shawn's arm and they walk toward the church with Laura right behind them, fussing with the back of her sister's antique-lace veil.

The church is hushed and filled with waiting friends and family.

Jennie stops at the edge of the satin runner and takes a deep breath.

"Nervous?" Shawn whispers.

She smiles serenely and shakes her head.

The organist begins playing Pachelbel's "Canon in D."

It's time.

Laura leans toward her sister and plants a kiss on her cheek. "I love you, Jennie."

"I love you, too," she says, and watches as her sister starts down the aisle, each step a saucy little sashay typical of Laura.

Then it's Jennie's turn. She and Shawn step onto the white-satin runner, and she looks up. The congregation has stood, blocking her view of the groom.

It's all right. . . . I'll see him soon enough, she thinks, and begins to move forward.

Familiar faces beam at her from the pews.

Midway toward the front, she sees Danny and Cheryl Cavelli. In Danny's arms is their three-month-old baby girl, Sandra. Cheryl had been pregnant on that icy February day on Tide Island. She had been keeping it a secret, planning to tell her husband on Valentine's Day.

Jennie nods slightly at them as she passes and is rewarded with two slightly wistful, but happy smiles—and one drooly one from the baby.

Then she's nearing the altar . . .

And there he is, waiting for her, tall and dashing in his charcoal morning coat and striped ascot.

Keegan, the man she's going to spend the rest of her life with.

He steps forward as she arrives in front of him, taking her arm from Shawn, looking down at her face with teary eyes so full of love that a lump rises in Jennie's throat.

Together, they take the final few steps to stand in front of the priest.

Looking down on the bride and groom with a benevolent smile, he begins. "Dearly beloved . . ."

M. T.
F. T.
Susan
Nancy Martin
Nancy.